KEEP THE WAGONS MOVING!

Hardship and danger lurked at every turn of the long trail to Oregon in 1846. The journey itself was difficult enough for young Jason Coit. But he had another worry as well. His small brother, Sammy, had been captured by a ruthless French trapper who was taking his own mysterious route West.

How the two brothers match wits with this audacious outlaw and meet the challenges of the Oregon Trail, makes for a spirited story of pioneer days.

KEEP THE WAGONS
MOVING !

WEST LATHROP

illustrated by

DOUGLAS DUER

RANDOM HOUSE
New York

Fic
Lat
4,796

To My Sister
Harriet

CONTENTS

ILLUSTRATIONS

I wish gratefully to acknowledge that certain historical data concerning the Oregon Trail are taken from Irene Paden's authentic and inspiring book, THE WAKE OF THE PRAIRIE SCHOONER.

West Lathrop

1

AN UNEXPECTED VISITOR

May, 1846. . . .

All through the night from a meadow on Blue Ridge, Jason Coit watched the lights and heard the constant hammering from the blacksmith sheds below in the little town of Independence, Missouri. Wagons topped with new sailcloth were being mended; horses, mules and oxen shod at the last moment. The days of waiting in a trial camp for the prairie grass to grow were over. At dawn, a wagon train would move slowly in a long white line toward the west—into the unknown. "Oregon!" would be the cry from many throats— "On to Oregon!"

With a gentle hand, Jason bent forward and smoothed the side of a large ox before him in the grass. Old Mat had been ailing ever since he left his own meadows in Illinois. He had not wished to come west, and the boy now leaning over him could still feel on Mat's red hide the welts made by Asa Strong's blacksnake whip, mercilessly urging him on. Tired as Jason was, he found it impossible to sleep in his small tent near-by, knowing that Mat lay alone in the darkness. So he kept a few embers glowing and sat beside him.

The night was full of sounds . . . the hammering over in Independence, the peeping of frogs in a creek close by, the distant whistle of a steamboat and, above all, the heavy, labored breathing of the old ox. Poor Mat. . . .

Dawn was only an hour or so away. And now that the two-thousand-mile journey was about to commence, Jason's thoughts were constantly turning homeward towards Terry-ville, Illinois. The familiar ginghamed figure of his mother in the doorway of their farm, the last sorrowing wave of her hand, continued to haunt him. It had been difficult to pry apart his small sister's hot, tight fingers as they clung about his neck. Sammy, his younger brother, had shed no tears but followed the Strongs' wagon for a long way, run-ning in the brown dust and watching Jason until he was out of sight. From inside the wagon as it lurched and creaked over the rough road, Mrs. Strong had watched, pity in her pale blue eyes discreetly shielded by her sun-bonnet. Asa Strong, who had hired Jason as assistant throughout the trip, grunted, spat over the wheels, and gave the lagging Mat an unnecessary lash from his seat in the front. Sentiment and tears were no part of Asa Strong.

Jason twisted restlessly and lowered his head in his arms as if to shut out the month-old memories which per-sisted in distressing him. A slight noise behind him, how-ever, made him turn and look about. With his mind so filled with thoughts of home, he was not surprised to imagine he saw his younger brother Sammy standing just beyond the light of the fire, leaning against a water cask. The figure

Jason continued to stare at Sammy

did not fade away as Jason continued to stare and then he knew his eyes were not deceiving him. It was his brother Samuel Coit in flesh and blood . . . small of stature, dressed in a red flannel shirt, heavy brown-homespun trousers, and topped with a wide-brimmed hat, such as the mountain men wore and altogether too large for him. As the fire emitted a sudden burst of flames, Jason could even distinguish the freckles on Sammy's short nose. The eyes, widely spaced, were staring back at him stubbornly, defiantly. Jason stumbled to his feet.

"Sammy!"

Sammy made no reply but hitched a step closer. Jason could now see that his brother showed signs of travel. His face was streaked with grime and the knee of his homespun trousers was torn.

"What are you doin' here, Sammy?" The joy which he first felt upon seeing Sammy had now given way to anger. The sick ox, roused by the sharp sound in Jason's voice, raised his head slowly, looked around with heavy eyes and then lowered his head again. A few quick steps and Jason leaned menacingly over his small brother, who remained undaunted, holding his ground.

"Answer me, or I'll give you the worst thrashin' you ever had! Did you follow me here?"

"I told you I was goin' to Oregon," Sammy's lips managed at last. "I've been tellin' you all winter I was goin' with you."

Anger mounted in Jason. Weary, disillusioned by all he had seen and heard the past month, the sight of his brother was almost more than he could bear. Here in a trial camp on the eve of departure was Sammy, small, undersized, a

runaway from the Illinois farm where he was supposed to
be the comfort and mainstay of their widowed mother.
Yes, Sammy had often talked of going to Oregon but no one
had taken him seriously. . . .

Jason's voice, when he spoke, was high-pitched and rasping, even strange to himself. "Well, you're not goin', do
you hear? Why, you doggone little runt, you! Followin'
me way out here—leavin' Ma an' Tacy——" Jason's voice
had now deepened into a roar and the younger boy, never
having seen his brother in such a rage, stepped back a pace.
As he did so, the curtains at the rear end of a prairie
schooner standing close by were pushed aside and the unkempt head of Asa Strong appeared.

"What's the noise?" Asa Strong sounded hoarse, ugly.

There was a pause and Jason answered, his voice now
calm, "Nothin' much, Mister Strong. It's Sammy here, just
sayin' goodby again. We'll go further away an' talk."

Another face had now appeared in the opening of the
curtains and was looking out over Asa Strong's shoulder.
It was Mrs. Strong, her hair hanging in two thin plaits
on either side. Without its usual sunbonnet her face seemed
unfamiliar in the gray light.

"Why, it's Sammy!" There was surprise and joy in Mrs.
Strong's gentle voice. "It's Sammy Coit from home! How'd
you leave your mother, Sammy? Is everyone in Terryville all right?" It was not difficult to read homesickness
in the soft voice and observe the eagerness with which she
leaned forward.

"You get in there an' mind yer own business, Lizzie!"
and her husband's thick-set shoulder crowded the woman
back. "Ayuh, it's Sammy all right, an' if he thinks for one

minute he's goin' to join up with this wagon, he's got another guess. There ain't another inch for anybody, and if
I *was* to take someone extry I wouldn't add on a little
no-account, sawed-off handle like him! You boys get away
from this wagon and don't go near the Adamses an' start
that brat cryin' again. An' mind that ox, Jason, or you'll
be out of a job come mornin'.'"

Asa's head disappeared, and there were sounds of surly
growling as his hand fastened the curtains together. Jason
gave a swift glance at Mat, whose breathing had not
changed, and then walked towards some cottonwood trees.
Sammy followed.

"Now you see, don't you?" Jason was trying to keep his
voice steady as he turned to the smaller boy. "Asa Strong's
a hard 'un, an' don't you forget it. No one would guess it.
You never know how folks'll turn out to be, even if you
think you know them, livin' next door! But you're not to
tell Ma or anyone, see? Soon's I get to Oregon, I'll be free
and go my own way. An' mark my words, Asa Strong'll
never be our neighbor again! Now, Sammy, there's no room
for you in that wagon. You heard what he said . . . he
meant every word of it."

"But I could be a big help, Jason. Just gimme a chance
to show you." For the first time Sammy's tongue had become loosened, and words poured out in a hoarse whisper
while one of his grimy hands pulled at his brother's sleeve.
"Ma don't need me. She's goin' to cook at the tavern an'
I'm in the way 'cause there's only one room to sleep in
. . . off the attic. Tacy an' her need it. She's comfortable
an' nice as can be. I left a letter explainin' everythin'. We
sold Fremont an' Angel ﹣ . ."

AN UNEXPECTED VISITOR

"You sold the horse . . . an' the sow . . ."

" 'Course. An' we rented the farm to a Swede named Anderson just come to town. Ma's letter'll tell you all about it. Don't you ever get any mail? Honest, Jasie, I'm sorry to make you so mad . . . but I've got to get to Oregon. . . ."

"Don't call me 'Jasie'!" With a quick motion the older boy pulled himself free of the grimy hand and stood glaring down at Sammy. "If you weren't such a little squirt I'd give you the worst beatin' you ever got in your life. I'd knock your head over into Oregon! As it is, I think I'll—I'll——" and Jason suddenly doubled his fists. Ducking quickly, the smaller boy dodged and stood a few feet away, wary, tense, and ready to run. The broad-brimmed hat was now on the back of his head, showing his hair to be light-colored and standing upright in a bristling fashion. Already Sammy had cut his hair in preparation for a long journey and a siege of growing.

For a moment Jason steeled himself and deliberated. There was nothing to be gained by fighting with Sammy. More than once he had managed to soften his brother's stubbornness with a certain gentleness and pleading in his voice. Molasses could catch more flies than vinegar, his mother had often said. Now was the time to apply molasses. Already a faint glow in the eastern sky warned him that dawn was close. The smaller boy must not be around to see the big wagons depart . . . the fever and excitement of their getaway would only add to Sammy's desire to go along. Words chosen with care and discretion, a persuasive note in his voice . . .

"Come on and sit down, Sammy. I won't lick you. I promise. Let's talk." Jason lowered his fists and sauntered to a fallen tree where he perched himself on its rough-barked trunk. The younger boy followed and seated himself with care, warily measuring the distance between his brother and himself. For the first time Jason noticed that Sammy wore a bowie knife at his belt, and he leaned forward to observe it more closely. By the light of the fire, he could see a familiar twist to the worn elk-horn handle. In another moment Jason knew he was looking at his old bowie knife. Discarded for the newer one now at his own belt, he had lost sight of his former treasure. How he had dreamed and planned of making the long journey to Oregon when he wore that same knife . . . just as Sammy was doing now! The sight of the elk-horn handle struck a soft chord somewhere within him, and Jason's tone was quiet and gentle when he spoke.

"How'd you get here, Sammy?" It would be better perhaps to let Sammy do most of the talking at first.

"On a boat." The smaller boy was still suspicious, guarded.

"A boat? Which boat?"

"The *Radnor*."

The *Radnor*! Jason stared down in amazement at the small figure beside him. The *Radnor* was an overloaded steamboat sailing the waters of the Missouri upwards for five hundred miles from St. Louis, her decks crowded with traders, gamblers, Indians, and adventurers of all kinds. Worst of them all were the "mountain men," lawless cutthroats returning from the east after disposing of their beaver skins. Anyone daring the muddy waters of the Missouri, enduring the company of such people, would be of a determined nature and in desperate need to reach some point west.

AN UNEXPECTED VISITOR

And now Jason's eyes caught sight of Sammy's feet. His brother was wearing his cast-off, knee-high boots, stubbed at the toes, run down at the heels. For a moment he could not speak. A wave of homesickness swept over him.

"How'd they let you on . . . let you ride on the *Radnor*?" Jason's voice was muffled but Sammy did not seem to notice.

"I earned my keep," Sammy answered cheerfully. "I peeled 'taters an' minded the mules."

Peeled 'taters and minded the mules! And on the *Radnor*! Sammy, his tow-headed brother, who had never traveled farther abroad than Browning, twenty miles distant from their Illinois homestead! What was he to say . . . what could he do? Perhaps . . . and Jason's mind, like a drowning man clutching at a straw, grasped at the thought of silver money. Sammy was known for his scrimping and hoarding tendencies.

"See here, Sammy, I'm going to give you some silver . . . bright, new dollars . . ."

"Huh. I don't need your money. I've got my own."

"You little shoat! Where'd you get it? If you took it from Ma . . ."

This last insinuation by Jason was like a spark put to gunpowder. There was an angry glint in the gray-green eyes of Samuel Coit as, rigid with indignation, he turned towards his brother Jason.

"I ain't no thief! I earned every penny. Picked beans for the Johnsons, helped dig Gran' Peterson's well an' tended the Blackwell twins . . . an' that's more'n you've ever done! You don't have to take care of me. I got here, didn't I? An' I ain't no thief, either. I've got every cent I earned an' can buy my own flour an' pemmican."

The sun, just below the slope of a hill, now gave enough light to show the grime and weariness in Sammy's face. There was also a bruise on his chin and a red lump over one eye. Had a mule lashed out with a hind foot or the mountain men been bullies? Jason felt his blood rising. . . . After all, stubborn, close-mouthed, close-fisted little Sammy was his brother. Blood was thicker than water. He cleared his throat to gain time.

"I didn't use the word 'steal,' Sammy. I said *if* you took that money from Ma, *teased* her into it is what I meant. . . . Now keep your voice low or we'll have ol' man Strong over here. He's pretty free with the whip when he doesn't like things. . . . Wait till I take another look at Mat. He's sick," and Jason tiptoed towards the ox. Mat was still in the same position, his eyes closed. As he turned about, Jason found Sammy just behind him, staring down at the huge animal struggling for breath.

"Huh . . . Mat's awful sick, ain't he?" There was surprise and pity in the younger boy's whisper.

"Mat never did want to leave home. Kept tryin' to turn 'round. An' Asa seemed to take his spite out on him. Mis' Strong an' I tried to stop him, but it wasn't any use. He's a devil with the whip."

"Asa warn't like that back home in Terryville."

"That's what I've been tryin' to tell you, Sammy. Maybe he's worried or excited . . . I don't know. He's changed a lot. Mis' Strong's grown kind of sickly an' I'm thinkin' she's just plumb scared. It's been awful just waitin' here for the prairie grass to come up. We got word last night it's safe to start. This camp's goin' to join another farther on. . . . Asa Strong'll beat you to a pulp if you hang 'round, Sammy."

"Huh, he don't skeer me none. You oughter see some of the folks I've traveled with."

Jason made no reply. Already his small brother had seen and done things that were only hearsay to him. As they retraced their steps to the fallen tree, Jason could see where a bullet had passed through the crown of the large hat which Sammy wore. He was gazing at it when Sammy looked up.

"Think I've growed any, Jason?" The old familiar question! It seemed to Jason that Sammy had asked this question at least once a week ever since he could talk.

"It's hard to tell in this light. . . . Where did you get your hat?"

"Got it off'n a mountain man," Sammy explained with some pride. "He said if I'd put it on an' stand still, so he could take a shot, I could have the hat . . . to wear to Oregon. You didn't leave no hat behind for me, so I let him shoot," and the boy's grimy hand reached upward while his face took on a rapt expression as he felt of the two bullet holes.

There was a long pause as Jason thought over this episode. Then he took a deep breath and plunged.

"You'll have to go now, Sammy. I've got to stay here an' tend to Mat. It's almost day. Please go home, Sammy. It's wrong for you to leave Ma an' Tacy. I'd help you if it was right for you to be goin', honest I would. But I've got all I can handle myself right now. . . . If you're smart you'll go home and thank your stars to be out of this mess.

4,796

G'wan home, kid." Tears were shining in Jason's eyes. "Tell Ma I'm fine an' I'll see her in another year. I . . . I . . . Goodby, Sammy," Jason added hastily. He turned away and then looked back.

Sammy's hat was still pushed to the back of his head and there was a grim set to the bruised jaw. In another moment he had walked away with his usual little swagger, taking steps too long for his short body. There was no backward glance as he disappeared towards the trail which wound down the ridge in the direction of Independence.

2

THE TAKE-OFF

Old Mat never rose again. With a sigh, his big body relaxed, his head sank forward and Jason knew the procession of wagons would go on without him. . . . It did not seem wise to butcher him for jerky, as he had been ailing for some time. Neither did Asa Strong, bitter with loss and shadowed with superstition, wish to be delayed and lose his place in the wagon train. So Mat's body was left undisturbed by the ashes of the fire—a prey to coyotes, who would not be long in finding him. His death left the boy cold and desolate. The ox had been a familiar sight in the meadows from his mother's kitchen window and he seemed to be part of a background which was rapidly fading away. A younger ox named King, purchased from a trader, was to bear Mat's yoke.

After a breakfast of coffee and cold sowbelly handed out by Mrs. Strong, whose eyes were red with weeping, Asa Strong and Jason prepared for their departure. Six oxen, picketed in a meadow, were hitched to the wagon and Blossom, the cow, fastened at the rear. The tent was taken down and the water casks put aboard. The entire group was about to leave when a second wagon train came clattering out of Independence to join it. The people were a jolly, rollicking crowd, fresh from their home towns, unjaded by tedious days of waiting for prairie grass to grow. Their enthusiasm and laughter were contagious. Sober, pale-faced women of the first group began to smile as they exchanged pleasantries and gossip with the newcomers.

After a short and somewhat fierce dispute, a Missourian named Mark Morgan was elected temporary captain. The train was now doubled in size. Sharp whip-cracks filled the air and, with mules braying and hoarse voices shouting, wagons lumbered forward, the line broken by groups of reserve stock. Young people, sunburned and hilarious, commenced singing and finally the whole line joined in, ending with the usual cries of "On to Oregon!"

Greatly to the disappointment of the emigrants, however, the wagon train was forced that afternoon to halt on the eastern bank of the Big Blue, a tributary of the Missouri River. From wagon to wagon was relayed the message, "The Big Blue is up!" even before the river was sighted. Recent rains had caused the tributary to rise to alarming heights, its swollen muddy waters impassable for man or beast. Mark Morgan shook his head dolefully as he gazed down into the swirling current.

"We'll wait here," he announced to the group of men clustered about him on the riverbank.

The decision was accepted by all except Asa Strong, who made a slight scoffing noise in his throat. Several heads turned to look at him inquiringly.

"Where I come from, this is a brook," spoke up Asa after

a strained pause. "What you 'feered of, Morgan? The wagons on the Westport road will get ahead an' the animals will eat up all the grass we've been waitin' for. We don't have to stay here. . . . My oxen can swim an' like it!"

Asa, plainly anxious to be captain in the final elections which would take place near the Kaw River Crossing, smirked and winked at a small ferret-eyed man at his side for approval. But Jason, standing close by and conscious of general disfavor, felt the blood mount to his face and stain his cheeks. Already there were whispers abroad of how Asa had mistreated old Mat and undoubtedly Asa was seeking to cover the prejudice against him with some act of bravado. Without answering, Captain Morgan took a long pole and attempted to test the depth of the ford which slanted upstream.

"The ford's washed out—there's a big hole there," he remarked quietly as the pole almost disappeared from sight.

"Then make a fresh start further down," advised Asa glibly.

"No animal could stand that current broadside," and for the first time Mark Morgan turned and directed his conversation to Asa. "Whoever mapped out this ford must have tried it and found it safe. I'll do no experimenting with other men's wagons and lives. By the time the stream is down again, the hole will be filled in. No, this wagon train is going to stop here." The captain's jaw squared as he spoke and his gray eyes held a steely glint. "Don't forget the Westport folks have got to cross this same river farther up. And there are plenty of hard crossings ahead without wearing down the animals on this one."

"Lor', yes," breathed a tall man at the captain's right. "Thar be the Lower California Crossin', for one."

"An' the Snake," added someone else.

Dreading to hear any more of Asa's senseless retorts, Jason turned away and walked to where the Strongs' wagon was stationed. Mrs. Strong sat in the front seat quietly knitting, her sunbonneted head bent low over her work. Upon hearing footsteps, she looked up quickly.

"What did they decide, Jason?" she called.

It had been some time since Jason had had an opportunity to speak to Mrs. Strong alone and now, in the bright afternoon light, the woman's appearance startled him. It was evident she had lost weight. Fine lines of worry had begun to etch themselves at the corners of her dark-blue eyes, and the pink bloom of her cheeks had given way to pallor. Slightly younger than his mother, Mrs. Strong now looked older. The hard fare of road travel apparently had not agreed with her, though it was more likely she was suffering with worry over Asa.

"I guess we're goin' to wait 'til the river goes down," answered Jason, hoping the woman did not see the surprise and pity he felt. "It may take two, three days."

"Asa won't like that," sighed Elizabeth Strong. "He never likes to wait for anything when he makes up his mind to go. He says he's crossin' in the mornin' anyway, an' it's 'cause he don't like Mark Morgan. Mark an' he used to go to school together years ago, an' they always fought each other. Asa don't talk about it, but I know. Oh, Jason, I wish we'd never come!" And to her own amazement, as well as Jason's, Mrs. Strong suddenly gave way to tears, her slender body racked with sobs as she leaned forward, her sunbonnet bent low. Jason picked up the knitting which had slid from her hands to the ground and took a few steps nearer, feeling helpless to comfort her.

"He might change his mind, Mis' Strong . . . Cap'n Morgan's talkin' to him now. Don't cry. . . . I . . . I . . ."

"I'm sorry, I'm sorry, Jason," and Elizabeth Strong dried her tears on the hem of her checked cotton dress and then reached out her hands for the knitting. "I didn't know I was goin' to cry. It came sudden-like. . . . I guess I'm tired. I didn't want to leave old Mat back there all alone. Asa scolded dreadfully . . . says I'm silly, an' I s'pose I am. But somehow Mat seemed part of home to me," and her voice choked again. After a moment she spoke, her eyes filled with concern as she gazed down at the boy before her.

"The trip's been hard on you, too, hasn't it, Jason? You look kinder peaked."

"Oh, I'm fine . . . though it hasn't been easy sittin' round for grass to grow!" and Jason smiled up at her. "When we see the prairie, just miles an' miles of prairie, we'll feel as though we really had started for Oregon. Everybody's a little nervous from waitin'. First it's the grass an' now it's the river!"

"I know. It's a strange new life for us all. Asa's awfully keyed up. . . . You mustn't mind much what he says or does. . . . All our money is tied up in this wagon and oxen. Asa's ambitious, he is. He wants to get ahead too fast, I'm 'feered. You mustn't mind too much," and her voice faded into nothingness, as though she might be considered disloyal for speaking so frankly.

"I understand," and Jason nodded. "He's not himself. Things'll be better farther on. Maybe I'd better get some wood for supper after I stake the animals . . ."

"Yes, yes, get some wood," agreed Mrs. Strong quickly, as if glad to change the subject, "an' I'll cook a nice supper. Maybe we'll have peaches. Asa's very fond of stewed peaches. Tell me, Jason," and Mrs. Strong rose to her feet, a forced note of cheerfulness in her voice, "what became of Sammy? I haven't had a chance to ask you before . . ."

"I don't see him around," answered Jason, "an' I'm hopin' he went home. This is no place for him."

"No, I s'pose not," and Mrs. Strong shook her head. But a faint smile curved the corners of her mouth. "I can't help wishin' he was comin', though," she confessed. "I always liked Sammy . . . he's so cheerful! If I had my way, I'd leave some of this heavy furniture behind an' make a place for him. An' as long as he's found you, your ma wouldn't worry too much. . . . I used to hear him practicin' on the jew's-harp in your ma's woodshed. He could make slow, sad songs into jigs like nobody else I ever heard."

"Sammy's got an ear for music, all right," agreed Jason. "But he's too young to leave home. He talked like he was possessed to go to Oregon. Now that I think back on't, he was mighty quiet when I left an' didn't cry like Ma and Tacy. He was probably hatchin' his own plans all the time."

"If he got here safe enough, chances are he'll get home again," comforted Mrs. Strong. She had descended to the ground and now stood beside Jason. "Sammy's the kind who'll grow up all of a sudden an' become a fine smart man. It's strange how you two boys ain't a bit alike. Sammy's light an' you're dark. I never saw your father but your ma's a mighty fine woman. . . . You're a good boy, Jason. I count on you a heap."

Jason's face brightened and flushed. He was touched and felt a little shy at her praise.

"Ma's wonderful," he added after a pause. "My father died just before you came to live next door to us. He had lung trouble . . . you'd have liked him, too. They say the sage on the plains is good for sick people an' he always wanted to take this trip west. I s'pose Sammy has heard us talk about goin' west ever since he could understand what we were sayin'."

"Sammy'll take care of himself." Mrs. Strong spoke with conviction and then stopped suddenly to stare as two figures in brown homespun appeared on the top of a hill in the distance.

"Asa's comin'. He's comin' with that . . . that Collins man. You go an' get some wood, Jason." Mrs. Strong spoke in a half-whisper and moved swiftly away. The familiar tense look had returned to her face and the light in her eyes faded as she stooped to remove the milk bucket from its hook.

Jason, with a hatchet at his belt and a basket on his arm, crossed a meadow and turned towards a growth of trees in a ravine. Elizabeth Strong's white face persistently haunted him as he walked along and his anger at Asa Strong continued to mount. The man's ruthless selfishness was taking its toll. First old Mat and now his wife . . . whip lashings and tongue lashings . . . If conditions grew any worse, he wondered if he would be able to endure them without any outward show of resentment. For Mrs. Strong's sake he determined to remain as quiet as possible. She was counting on him, depending on him! And her fondness for Sammy warmed and heartened him. She had even been willing to sacrifice some of her furniture to make room for Sammy!

To be sure, the Strongs' hickory-wheeled wagon, though well made, was loaded to the last inch with heavy chests, trunks and farming implements far beyond the twenty-five hundred pounds allotted three pairs of plodding oxen, which were supposed to cover fifteen miles a day. One could not blame a family for wishing to take its worldly goods into new lands, but Asa had gone beyond his limit. Because of its load, therefore, the Strongs' wagon, of all the wagons in the train, was least fit to lead the way across a swollen stream. Moreover, Asa could not swim and had frankly said so one evening before they left Illinois.

Already Jason had acquired great respect for Mark Morgan, a tall, gray-eyed farmer from Missouri who spoke quietly at all times. His frank, open countenance and ways had drawn people to him immediately and he was elected temporary captain of the train with no effort on his part. His family consisted of Aaron, his young son, a stocky redcheeked boy somewhat younger than Jason, and a sister known as Aunt Liddy, a buxom, outspoken woman famed for her cooking. One could tell at a glance that the three were related, for all had the same gray eyes and general bearing. More than once Jason had felt the captain's gaze upon him, as if speculating as to his connection with the Strongs. And although Jason often wished to make some advance towards Aaron, he did not feel free to do so because of Asa's open antagonism. The latter's words and actions branded him, even though he was but hired help, a neighboring boy earning his way to the west, and no kin whatsoever.

It was Aaron's work to keep his aunt supplied with wood for fuel. Glancing back in the direction of the encampment, Jason soon spied Aaron as he crossed the meadow, dressed in a gray homespun shirt and carrying a basket. Here was an opportunity to meet and know Aaron! Lonely, hoping to make a friend of the captain's son, Jason turned and walked towards him.

"Your name Strong?" asked Aaron, measuring Jason with his eyes as the latter approached. "My name's Morgan . . . Aaron Morgan."

"I'm Jason Coit," replied Jason quickly and there was a little flash in his dark eyes. "Asa Strong is no relation of mine."

"I guessed as much," replied young Aaron, and his voice sounded a little more friendly as the two boys looked squarely at each other.

Aaron appeared even younger close at hand. He had not yet attained his full height but promised to be as tall as his father. Full-faced, of stocky build, sun-tanned and red-cheeked, he was a fine healthy specimen, ready with a laugh at the slightest provocation. Undoubtedly he was the product of his Aunt Liddy's good cooking.

Jason, somewhat taller, was thin. Work and worry had slimmed him down the past month. Although Mrs. Strong had tried to give him double portions of the scant fare she had to offer, Asa had discouraged her and Jason had often gone to bed hungry.

"Well, whatever the set-up is," continued Aaron, "I hope you an' Asa Strong won't try to cross the river in the mornin'. They're arguin' over there," and he nodded in the direction of the Big Blue. "After all, they elected my father captain to lead the wagons as far as the Kaw Crossin', an' it ain't fair not to abide by his decisions."

"I'm abidin' by 'em," answered Jason heatedly, "an' don't you think I'm not. What Asa Strong thinks an' does is nothin' to me. I'm his hired boy an' carin' for the stock the best I'm able, but I don't like him any better'n you do," and now Jason's eyes were blazing with anger. It was a relief to spit out the words and clear himself of any connection with the man he had come to despise. "An' when I reach Oregon, I plan to stake my land as far away from him as I can get. I'll never want to see him again!"

A smile now lighted Aaron's face. "I know now you're on our side. . . . Let's walk up the ravine. I can see you're after wood, too. You know, Asa can stir up more trouble than a double-headed hornet. Pa uster know him a long time ago. I guess they had some trouble, but Pa never talks about it except to say Asa's full of spite an' holds his grudges. Asa's stirrin' up folks right now, tellin' 'em there'll be no grass left if they don't cross the river today. Why, Bill Brewster says the prairie's full of grass . . ."

"Who's Bill Brewster?"

"He's an old friend of Pa's . . . a scout. He'll join us pretty soon an' guide us through the worst places. Bill Brewster won't stand for Asa Strong's talk . . . his an' that man, Cal Collins'. Why, those two are talkin' now of crossin' on a raft they found further down the river. Asa hopes he can show himself smarter than Pa. The Strongs' wagon is carryin' a big load, ain't it?"

"Yes, it's jam full. That's one reason the ol' ox died. Mat couldn't step fast enough ahead of that load. An' Asa beat him . . . beat him plenty. So they found a raft?" There was worry and distress in Jason's voice. "You know what Asa's tryin' to do, don't you?" he asked Aaron suddenly. "He wants to be captain. If he can get across first, other folks will follow. Some fools will count him a good leader an' vote for him at the Kaw Crossin'. That's the trick he's pullin'."

"Looks that way."

Both boys walked a little distance without speaking, each busy with his own thoughts. Finally Aaron spoke, looking over his basket curiously at Jason.

"The Land Law says you have to be eighteen years old. Are you stakin' land for yourself?"

"I'll be eighteen come October."

"Are you alone? Ain't you got any family? How far do the Strongs go?"

"I've got a mother an' sister in Illinois. Asa an' Mis' Strong will go as far as The Dalles. Mis' Strong's got a cousin there. I'd like to settle in the Willamette Valley, but I hate to think of my mother an' sister takin' the boat down the Columbia River. Quite a few folks have been drowned. . . . A younger brother followed me out here. I sent 'im back last night. He's too young to come along."

"Does your brother wear a big hat an' is he kinder small?"

"Yes . . . why?" and Jason stared at Aaron in surprise. "Did you see him?"

"A little feller stopped at our wagon last night, askin'
the way to Asa's wagon. Pa steered him right. He said he
was huntin' for his brother. An' as Pa was on his way to
Independence for medicine for Ezra Fields early this mornin', he saw the same little feller ridin' behind someone
on a pony. They were goin' east, headed for Independence,
too. They was a long way off, but Pa said the man looked
like a trapper. Was the boy your brother?"

"Sounds like Sammy. You don't suppose he'll pick up
with those trappers, do you? They're a rough lot . . ."

"Maybe he was goin' just as far as Independence," sug-
gested Aaron.

"Maybe," agreed Jason without conviction.

"No use worryin'," advised Aaron. "If I see him around
I'll let you know. Here," and Aaron stopped beside a fallen
tree, "here's somethin' we both can work on. They say
there won't be any wood when we reach Platte Valley.
We'll be burnin' buffalo chips for fuel. It'll seem queer,
won't it? We've always had plenty of wood in our woodshed back home. Aunt Liddy kept a roarin' fire."

"I know . . . it'll be different. How do you know such
a lot about the trail?"

"I've listened to Pa an' Bill Brewster talkin'. We're
lucky to have Bill along, an' I'll be glad when he ketches up
with us. He knows the Indians pretty well. Do you happen
to know the Fields from Iowa?"

"I've seen the two little girls. They have red hair?"

"That's right. Well, there's an ol' squaw trailin' 'em.
She's crazy over their red hair an' the Fields are skeered.
Last night Ezra Fields—that's the father—shot himself in
the hand . . . he ain't used to pistols. Pa's been tryin' to

help 'em. Yes, Pa's got plenty of trouble lookin' after folks. 'Tween watchin' ol' squaws tryin' to steal kids, bindin' up sore hands, runnin' for medicine an' arguin' with Asa . . . well, it ain't no lark to be captain of a train, I'm tellin' you!" and Aaron proceeded to trim some branches from the fallen tree while Jason worked on the other side. In half an hour both baskets were full and the boys turned towards the encampment.

"I've been wonderin'," said Aaron as they stopped at the foot of the meadow before they separated, "if Asa Strong will try to make you help 'im across that river in the mornin'. If you want to cut loose from him an' stay with us a while, it would be all right with Pa an' Aunt Liddy. You could have part of my bed . . . an' then maybe Pa'd find a place for you with some other wagon."

Jason, surprised at this unexpected kindness, found himself stammering in his pleasure.

"It's fine of you . . . fine . . . but I . . . I guess I can't . . ." and his voice stopped suddenly. To be part of the Morgan family for a little while, to eat Aunt Liddy's cooking, and share Aaron's bed would be heaven itself! But in the back of his mind had flashed an image of Elizabeth Strong as he last saw her, white, tense and frightened, moving to the rear of the wagon. There was pleading in Jason's eyes as he turned to the captain's son, who stood waiting.

"You see . . . it's Mis' Strong," he explained. "She's fine . . . she's different, Mis' Strong is. Almost like my mother. She's skeered of Asa an' there's nobody for her to count on but me. I can't leave her. You understand, don't you? An' if I help Asa in the mornin', it's because of her."

3

SAMUEL COIT MEETS AN
OLD ACQUAINTANCE

Samuel Coit, following a strange path back to Independence through a growth of cottonwood trees, did not feel his usual happy-go-lucky self. Not only was he cold and wet, but his pride smarted and his hopes felt a bit dashed. Jason had not greeted him with cordial cries of welcome upon his arrival. Moreover, Jason's surroundings were not as happy as he had imagined them to be . . . old Mat on the ground sick and only half alive, and Asa's voice, rough, cruel, and full of hate . . . What had happened to change Asa so?

As a neighbor, back in Illinois, Asa had appeared kind enough. Sammy remembered, however, coming upon him once unexpectedly in a cornfield. Asa was practicing with his bullwhacker whip, gripping the short staff with both hands as he whirled the lash twice about his head. The end had spit out with a loud snap like a viper's tongue towards some dry cornstalks, severing a single dry leaf from the very top. It was an excellent piece of marksmanship but Sammy's enthusiasm faded when he caught the expression on Asa's face. The lips were snarling and the eyes savage . . . not Asa at all. Quick as a flash the expression changed. Sammy had forgotten the incident, but now the memory of Asa's voice recalled the scene.

Both Asa and Elizabeth Strong had been kind to his mother. . . . Ah, those were pleasant days to think about as one stumbled in a dim light among wet trees. Already he missed the family . . . their evenings together, seated around the red-clothed kitchen table, the map of the Oregon Trail just above their heads on the wall. His mother and sister Tacy were always shelling beans or peas or sewing, while someone read aloud by the light of the kerosene lamp. More often than not, before the evening was over, his mother would ask him to play one of her favorite songs on his jew's-harp. Jason, quiet, dark-eyed, would speak of the Trail, rising from his chair in the meantime to locate some place on the map as he talked, his mother and sister asking questions, proud of Jason's learning and bookish ways. . . . And little did they dream of the plans which he, Samuel Coit, was making as he sat silently by, drinking in every word! He had confided in no one. It was better so, and whenever his conscience pricked him at such secrecy, he comforted himself that he was departing for Oregon for the entire family's good. Six hundred and forty acres of rough timbered land were far too much for Jason to cultivate alone. Later, his mother and Tacy would approve of his great courage and wisdom in following his older brother.

There would be other trains leaving for Oregon from Independence. He would make himself useful to some kind-faced farmer and perhaps arrive in Oregon even sooner than Jason! And some day he would tell Asa Strong exactly what he thought of him. "A little sawed-off handle" . . . A handle indeed! Anger flamed anew in Sammy as he heard in imagination once more Asa's voice telling him to be off. Rounding a sharp curve in the path, he stopped suddenly, however. In the uncertain light among the trees was the dark figure of a man on his knees, thrusting something into a saddlebag with one hand while he held a burning match in the other. At the snap of a twig beneath Sammy's foot, the man blew out the match and turned swiftly about. In another moment, Sammy gazed down the round steel barrel of a pistol pointed directly at him.

"Raise de hands!" came a guttural voice from the depths of thick black whiskers.

Anger towards Asa Strong fled with the four winds. A sharp knifelike fear started from the end of Sammy's spine and shot the length of his back. And then suddenly the darkness parted and Sammy saw a row of white teeth. The stranger was smiling . . . yes, smiling . . . and his eyes were like two small stars as his hand lowered the pistol. Across Sammy's numbed consciousness drifted the images of his steamboat companions as he last saw them. The mountain men, dark, long-bearded . . . why, this was Henri . . . Henri Jules! And what was Henri doing here alone at this hour, packing his saddlebags on a path in the woods . . . Henri, who constantly hummed gay French songs beneath his breath and had asked him to play the jew's-harp more than once!

Slowly, haltingly, Sammy lowered his hands, his eyes still in a fixed stare, hardly able to realize his good fortune in finding an old friend. Here was Henri Jules, of all peo-

ple! It had been Henri who had shot holes through the crown
of his hat, never disturbing a single spear of his short yellow hair, rewarding him with the hat itself afterwards. Now
he could see the familiar blue beads Henri sometimes wore
about his hairy neck and the loose collar of his hide shirt.
On one side of his head tilted a bright red cap of wool.

"Sam-mee, de leetle museeck-maker!" exclaimed Henri,
rising to his feet with the lithe grace of a big cat. "Ah, it is
a grand surprise! You find Henri packing de bags, ready
for de long travel!"

With a swift movement, Henri stooped and folded down
the cover of the saddlebag. With another smile, he balanced
the bags over the back of a small shaggy pony waiting beside the path.

"Now you will travel wit Henri, yass? Marie says she
will be happee to take you . . . so happee to take you,"
and Henri, with a flourish, waved at the small disinterested
pony, who stood with head lowered.

"How . . . how fur you goin'?" asked Sammy, catching his breath and gulping. It would never do to let Henri
know how much he had been frightened. Plainsmen never
betrayed their feelings.

"A leetle way," and Henri waved in the direction of Independence. "Marie . . . she will be so happee to take
you," and now Henri bowed low with a sweeping gesture
as if speaking for Marie. There was a subtle insistence in
Henri's manner, however, a compelling note in his voice, and
with a little shock of surprise Sammy began to realize that
Henri was demanding that he mount and ride. This was no
polite invitation. Deciding it to be the better part of wisdom
to keep Henri blithe and smiling, Sammy obediently climbed

aboard Marie's back, his two legs protruding at right angles over the heavy saddlebags. Henri joined him, sitting in front, and recommended the back of his belt as a safe hold for Sammy to cling to in case Marie decided to sprint. However, there was little danger of Marie's bursting into speed. She was laden to her utmost capacity and the one look she gave her master through her snarled forelock clearly conveyed her indignant feelings, as she moved slowly down the winding path.

There was the odor of onions, tobacco, grease and perspiration when one sat close to Henri, and Sammy leaned back as far as possible from his traveling companion. Soon they would reach the main road to Independence and there would be other passersby. Then he could dismount and go his way, preferring to walk than ride under such conditions. Perhaps, after all, he had imagined Henri's voice and manner to be commanding. But the questions persisted: What was Henri doing alone in the woods at that hour? . . . Where had he come from and where was he going? What was in the saddlebags which Henri guarded so carefully? Did Henri suspect him of spying through the trees and knowing too much, and now was he traveling to a more secluded spot to do away with him? Mountain men were a wild lot. To take a person's life meant no more than drawing one's breath. He had seen the mountain men perform on the *Radnor*. . . . No, Henri was not a man with whom one dealt lightly. . . .

At the crossroads, where the path joined the main road to Independence, Sammy strained his eyes in quest of wagon trains heading for the camps centered about the Big Blue. But no wagon train had left Independence for the

West that morning. An empty brown road wound over meadowed hills. The sun rose hot and clear. Larks caroled from the fields and, frequently, a rabbit crossed the road and leaped into a near-by thicket. Sammy now felt he would be content to meet a single horseman, let alone a procession of wagons! The whole world seemed empty of all living creatures save himself, Henri, Marie, a few larks and leaping rabbits. With both hands he crushed his hat as flat as possible and poked it under the back of his belt. Should he finally decide to slip quietly off Marie's back and run for his freedom down the road towards Independence, there would be no danger of losing his hat. Would Henri keep on the main road to Independence or swing into some hidden bypath?

Henri turned north, definitely north at the crossroads. With an extra chirp to the lagging Marie, he headed her up a short banking onto a narrow path partially concealed by brush from the main road. He was singing softly now, a song trilled frequently with *la, la, la,* but stopped abruptly upon hearing his small passenger's voice.

"I'm gettin' off here," called Sammy.

There was a moment's pause and Henri resumed his singing. Marie continued her slow trudge.

"I'm gettin' off here," repeated Sammy in a louder voice.

This time Henri gave a grunt and turned his head. His black beard blew halfway over one shoulder and the scent of onions and tobacco was stronger.

"Sam-mee go wit' Henri today."

The trapper's tone was final. Mixed qualms of fear and anger now struggled within Sammy. Why was Henri so determined to have Sammy travel with him? Because of the

mysterious contents of the saddlebags? Now, more than
ever, Sammy felt certain Henri suspected him of spying
upon him. If only he had come upon Henri in the cotton-
woods with his bags fully packed a few moments later, all
might have been different. They would have met as old
acquaintances and parted, each going his own way.

Anger was overcoming fear . . . Sammy decided to let
go of Henri's belt and push himself backwards, regardless
of the fall on the hard earth below. At the first release of
his fingers, however, a brown hairy hand reached around
and grasped his left wrist and pulled his arm forward. This
forced him to sit even closer to Henri, crushing his nose
against the trapper's broad hide-coated back. With his free
right hand he began to pound Henri with all his might, but
his hardest blows only made the trapper chuckle and laugh
gleefully. Meanwhile Marie had been forced into a trot and
Sammy's nose against Henri's back received steady, tortur-
ing thumps.

There was nothing left for Sammy now but to use his
bowie knife. A sharp prick through the heavy shirt into
Henri's back might make the trapper let go his hold for a
moment. . . . Here again Henri was too quick for him,
seeming to divine his every move. A second brown hairy
hand grasped his right wrist and twisted it just as the boy
drew the bowie knife from its sheath. Sammy loosened his
grip upon the handle and the knife fell to the path below.
A moment later, both of Sammy's arms were wound around
the trapper's waist and his two hands locked in front by one
of Henri's. He was as helpless as a papoose strapped to its
mother's back but far less comfortable, as he could hardly
see or breathe. Henri's singing commenced again, sounding

with a deep rumble through his back. Meanwhile the knife
lay on the ground. . . .

"My knife . . . I've lost my knife!" shouted Sammy.

The music did not cease but rumbled on with its endless
la, la, las. It was useless for Sammy to kick with his feet,
as it only served to make Marie run faster. So he quieted,
biding his time. On his return he would find the knife. . . .
Perhaps Henri was only taking him a little way and then
leaving him. But why should Henri take all this trouble?
Marie, straining with her load, mounted a hill and a little
later, from the corner of one eye, Sammy could see from
the top of a bluff a great mud-colored river as it flowed
below. The Kaw River! They were following the Kaw River
northwestward, far from the beaten trail of emigrants in
their white-topped wagons. This was not the way to Oregon!

The sun's hot rays beat down without respite upon the
French trapper and his small captive as Marie plodded
through steep-walled coulees, over dried river bottoms and
across wide treeless stretches.

After a long hour Marie suddenly stopped in the shade
of some cottonwood trees by a small stream. Here Henri
let go his tight grasp of Sammy's numbed hands and slid
down from Marie's back. With another elaborate *la, la, la,*
he stretched himself to his full height and then looked at
Sammy, a smile parting his heavy beard.

"*Voilà*! Now we eet. Sam-mee have hungaire?"

"I don't want yer greasy ol' food," Sammy shouted at
the smiling trapper in a sudden burst of temper as he slid
stiffly down from Marie's back. "I'm leavin' right now to
find my knife. Some day you'll smart for all this," and
Sammy's jaw jutted out in its most truculent manner.

Henri did not seem particularly impressed or alarmed. He smiled even more broadly and finally gave way to a delighted roar as he lifted the saddlebags from Marie's back and placed them upon a rock.

"Ho! ho! De leetle museeck-maker is a leetle firebran'! Ho! ho!" and Henri slapped his thighs with both hands. "We will have good times togedder. Sing an' fight an' eet. *Sacré bleu!* What good times we shall have!"

Still talking, Henri began to unwind a long length of braided rawhide from his waist. "What a peety I should have to tie you to a tree when we could be so happee togedder."

Watching Sammy's face closely, he flung the rawhide in coils over the saddlebags on the rock. "I have some leever, nice fresh leever to eat. Den we shall rest a leetle. Marie say she is *fatiguée.*"

With no more conversation Henri set to work building a small brushwood fire, looking up from time to time at Sammy, the rawhide length and saddlebags always within reach. Some cow's liver, pork and wild onions produced from the saddlebags were soon frizzling in a fry pan, the sputtering fat filling the air with a fragrance which did not lessen Sammy's appetite as he stood watching. "The greasy ol' food" was becoming dangerously inviting and a little later Sammy accepted his portion with no further words. If he was to run away later, he told himself, he might as well run on a full stomach. Henri cooked and flavored his food with the air of one who knew his business. The meal finished, the trapper took out his pipe, filled and lighted it, and then leaned back against a tree and gazed upon his small captive with considerable satisfaction.

"You have de leetle harp with you, yass?" he queried lazily, blowing white clouds of smoke into the air. "Den you will make a leetle museeck for Henri?"

The tone, although light and casual, held a note of command. But the warm food had appeased Sammy's temper as well as his appetite. There was nothing to be lost by playing for the trapper and, should Henri appear drowsy, lulled to sleep by his playing, it would be that much easier to make his escape. With a short nod of his head, he pulled out the jew's-harp from his pocket and struck up the tune of "The Campbells Are Coming." Upon hearing the familiar strains, he felt better himself and then he swung into a favorite song of his mother's, "Oft in the Stilly Night." Pangs of homesickness swept over him and he wondered what his mother would say if she could see his present traveling companion. And Jason . . . what would Jason think?

"Turkey in the Straw" was more to Henri's liking. Far from being overcome by sleep, the trapper was roused into playfulness. He beat his moccasined toes in perfect time and ended by brandishing his arms about, one hand holding his pipe, his dark eyes sparkling with pleasure.

"It is mag-neef-i-cent! Such museeck from *un garçon!* Ev'ry day we will have de museeck. Ah, my squaw, she like museeck, too. An' she will give you good tings to eet for your museeck. I shall make de trapper of you an' *toujours* there will be museeck at night. You will grow beeg an' strong an' grow whiskers lak mese'f. Ah, you will lak de mountains . . ."

The mountains? Henri was taking him to some mountains? This was more than Sammy could bear.

"Oh, no, I won't," he shouted and jumped to his feet.

With fumbling fingers he slid the jew's-harp back into his pocket. "My name's Samuel Coit an' I belong to folks back in Terryville, Illinois. I ain't goin' to be a trapper. I'm goin' to be a farmer, in Oregon! My brother's somewhere near here an' he'll give you an awful lickin' if I don't show up . . ."

"Den you will see heem at de Crossin'," interrupted Henri smoothly, as his hand reached out and gently caressed the loose circle of braided rawhide. "It ees not far from here an' you can see de wagon sweem de reever. Now you must travel wit' Henri an' Marie. Marie is so pleased to have you," and Henri bowed cordially for Marie, who leaned wearily against a tree with her eyes closed. "Ah, we will wait an' see . . ."

"Huh! Wait an' see nothing'! I'm goin' now."

Despite his short legs, Sammy could run faster than many of the boys in Terryville. A few swift leaps and he would be beyond the trapper's reach. He turned quickly, but not quickly enough. The long length of rawhide came singing through the air over his shoulders, pinning both arms to his sides, and then jerked him backwards. He landed heavily and rolled on one side. In another moment Henri leaned over him, smiling as usual, and removed the rawhide after helping Sammy to his feet.

"Sam-mee, Sam-mee . . . eet is a nice name," he taunted. "Sam-mee, Henri an' Marie . . . we will have happy times, wait an' see. De mountains . . ."

"I tell you I'm goin' to Oregon!" There was a tawny light in Samuel Coit's eyes. Henri Jules had seen the same light in the eyes of animals he had trapped, and he bellowed with delight the next moment when he felt the small boy's fists pummel him.

"Bravo! Bravo! Ho! Ho! I like you, my leetle firebran'! You wish to fight, *oui*? Marie, our Sam-mee can fight wit' de fists! Ho! Ho! My leetle firebran'!"

An hour later Henri Jules, seated upon a small pony, followed the banks of the Kaw River, singing happily. Behind him rode a small passenger who did not join in the singing but sat silent, his gray-green eyes smoldering with anger in his freckled face and a large broad-brimmed hat tied to the back of his belt for safekeeping. Truly, Samuel Coit of Terryville, Illinois, was on his way to Oregon, but not at all in the manner he had planned.

4

CROSSING THE BIG BLUE

Leaving Aaron Morgan at the edge of the ravine, Jason recrossed the meadow, walking towards the encampment. Despite his heavy basket of wood, his step was buoyant as his feet swished through the tall grass, and for the first time since leaving home he whistled softly under his breath. He had found a new friend!

Before him, tents were springing up like white mushrooms on the green grass of the encampment. Men had picketed their horses and mules, leaving the oxen to roam where they pleased. Women's voices called, dogs barked, and a rooster, confined in a coop lashed with ropes to the back of a wagon, crowed lustily as Jason passed by. But an undertone of discontent prevailed. The entire train seemed to be suffering with impatience over the delay in not crossing the Big Blue that afternoon. Little groups of men were still arguing in lowered voices and once Jason caught a snatch of conversation between two women.

"I was hoping to see Lodisa," complained a young girl to her mother as they took turns at some churning, "but I guess they'll be ahead of us now. She an' Ed were awful smart to join up with the Westport train. I wish we had. They'll be campin' 'neath the Old Elm tomorrer night and I reckon we'll be right here. I wanted to see Lodisa."

"Well, they might not reach the Old Elm so soon, Mary," argued the mother wearily, pushing back her hair from her forehead. "Remember they've got to cross this river, too. No one seems to think of that. Anyway, I'm learning not to worry over little things any more. If we get to Oregon skin-whole, I'll be thankful. You'll see Lodisa there. Your father says Cap'n Morgan has good sense . . ." and the remainder of the conversation was lost.

No one spoke to Jason as he hurried on to the outskirts of the field where the Strongs' wagon was stationed. Each person seemed to be soberly engrossed in his own affairs. Only a small group of children on a hillside evidenced any happiness, their voices shrill with delight at the discovery of some wild roses.

"Anna! Anna!" called one of them and Jason, looking up, recognized one of the Fields girls calling to her younger sister. The last rays of sunlight burnished their red hair to a flaming glow.

"Anna!" persisted the voice, "come over here. I've found some more . . . a big, big patch of them!"

Remembering Aaron's story of the Fields family's difficulties, Jason's eyes instinctively searched about for the lurking squaw. Only a tall man with a bandaged hand could be seen hovering at the foot of the hill. Ezra Fields, the father, was on guard. There was a discouraged droop to the tall man's shoulders and suddenly Jason ceased his whistling. Once more the grim realities of the trail ahead, its dangers and its failures, swept over the boy. Of what worth would land in Oregon be to a man who had his choicest possessions, his children, taken from him? And would the frail young man wrapped in a blanket, whom he could see sitting at the back of a wagon on a chair, recover his health as they journeyed westward? Or would he be left behind beside the trail, a cartwheel showing where he lay? Sammy . . . ah, where was Sammy now? Jason's breath caught in his throat. Had Sammy left his trapper friend and was he now journeying eastward, home to their mother and Tacy? If only some word might come that all was well with Sammy!

Cal Collins was still visiting with Asa, the two seated on the broad front seat of the Strongs' wagon when Jason arrived with his basket of wood. Cal was a lazy, shiftless man, traveling at the end of the line in a cheaply constructed wagon overflowing with noisy children and a sharp-voiced wife. His only assets in life appeared to be two horses: Dandy, a dappled gray, and Kit, a chestnut, named after Kit Carson; both horses outstanding in their intelligence and beauty. Whenever possible, Cal slipped away to escape his many responsibilities, only to be recalled by some dirty-faced child saying that "Ma needed him." As the same child never appeared twice, the Collins brood seemed to be limitless. Dressed in a buckskin, his jacket polished by long wear and grease, Cal now seemed more objectionable than ever. His small eyes, red and watery from staring into the sun, were set amazingly close to the bridge of his nose and his high, wheedling voice seemed to run on endlessly. As Jason built the fire, he could not fail to observe and hear the two men as they visited.

"Sure, we kin do it," Cal was saying. "Two fresh crossbeams an' that raft'll be good as new. I seed two logs over in the grass a bit beyond. With spikes an' rope, we kin mend 'er up. Then jest roll yer wagon aboard, chain the wheels so she won't roll, an' yer boy an' my Bill will pole the whole caboodle acrost. We'll go over on the hosses with the stock between us. My horse Dandy ain't afeerd of nothin' an' Kit, his brother, follers Dandy like a shadder. They ain't never been separated. Your missus can stay in the wagon high an' dry, prim an' proper. I'll be pleased to help. That is," and Cal twisted his hands together, "if my time is worth anythin'."

Asa made no reply and Cal rambled on.

"What's Morgan know 'bout rivers, anyway? Why, he comes from a little dirt farm in northern Missouri with creeks only ankle-high. He's skeered of water, Morgan is. Nothin's wrong wi' that ford! We kin cross it! Morgan sticks a pole down a little way an' says it's deep, awful deep! Well, mebbe that hole is deep but the river ain't that deep all the way over. We'll ride them hosses sittin' pretty, once we git past that hole. Ten or fifteen feet of swimmin' 'll clear it. You'll git a good duckin' at the start but we kin dry off with a fire on t'other side. In case there's a lot of swimmin' further on, an' I'm wastin' my breath jest mentionin' it, I'm countin' on you to git off'n the horse an' swim with him, holdin' to the saddle or the tail, I don't care which. Surest way to drown a horse is to try to ride him swimmin' any distance. Any fool knows that," and Cal shot a mouthful of brown tobacco juice at a hind wheel.

Asa nodded in silent agreement.

"Folks won't be risin' early, now there's no need," Cal's voice went on after a pause. "The mornin's are misty . . .

jest like milk over the meaders. Now, who's gonna see us cross them meaders to the river? Who's gonna stop us? I'll be here before dawn wi' the horses an' Bill. An' Morgan's gonna wake up an' see you cookin' breakfast on t'other side. Say! Morgan's not goin' to believe his eyes!" and Cal burst into a shrill hoot of mirth and pounded his knees.

"An' you think lots more folks'll try to join me?" asked Asa, his set face relaxing into a pleased grin.

"I don't think . . . I know!" shrilled Cal. "Why, you've said yourself how crazy most of 'em was to join that Westport crowd. Settin' here, waitin' fer a brook to dwindle ain't goin' to make Morgan pop'lar next election, either. Mark my words," and Cal poked Asa slyly in the ribs, "there'll be a new cap'n an' his last name won't be Morgan! Chances be," and here Cal lowered his voice, as if he had just thought of what he was about to say, "I might make a pretty penny helpin' those other folks over, if I could keep the raft an' two hosses workin' most the day. Smart, eh?"

"How much you askin' me?" demanded Asa abruptly.

"You? How much am I askin' you? Oh, I'm makin' it cheap fer you, cheap. Four dollars, mebbe. No, call it five an' it's a trade." Cal's hands were almost red from their constant twisting motion.

"You said four first," growled Asa. "I'll agree on four, no more."

"Well, well, call it four," answered Cal agreeably enough. "I wouldn't ask a cent 'cept I've got a big fambly an' it's gittin' bigger next month. It's gittin' bigger every year," and now Cal's voice held an anxious note. "Seems like I'm surrounded with mouths wide open an' always hankerin' to be fed . . ."

Cal was interrupted at this point by a small gamin-like girl in a soiled cotton dress, her feet bare, who appeared suddenly at the side of the wagon.

"Ma wants yer," she called up to him. "The baby's squallin'."

"You see how 'tis?" said Cal, heaving a long sigh and looking down at the child as if trying to recollect where he had seen her before. "It's always somethin'. But after I git to Oregon, these kids'll be a big help on the land," he added, as if comforting himself. "I plan ter take it easy then. Well, I'll see you soon," and, with a knowing wink, Cal Collins descended from the front seat of the Strongs' wagon and meekly followed his daughter home.

Supper was a wordless affair except for instructions from Asa to be ready early in the morning to cross the Big Blue. There were no peaches served as a special dessert. Either Elizabeth Strong forgot the stewed fruit in her worry or she did not dare risk her husband's displeasure by indulging in the small luxury in that hour. Slam-jams and coffee, with a pickle added as a prevention against scurvy, made up the evening meal. After lugging some water from a spring and filling the empty casks, Jason put up his tent. Soon within, rolled in a blanket, he tried to shut out the sounds about him . . . voices calling, mules braying and later the scrape of a fiddle bow in the distance as some young people danced jigs, waltzes, rigadoons, and pigeon-wings in the light of glowing campfires.

Unable to sleep, Jason wondered if Aaron was there, dancing with the rest. . . . In a short while Asa Strong could be heard fastening the rear curtains of the wagon for the night and then came the sound of heavy boots falling to the floor. Silence followed and Jason turned restlessly in his blanket, trying to forget that a river, mercilessly deep and swift, was to be crossed in a few short hours . . . when the morning mists were as white as milk and there was no one to see. . . .

True to his promise, Cal Collins arrived before dawn leading two horses, Dandy and Kit, accompanied by an overgrown, stoop-shouldered boy, his son Bill. Moving carefully, for fear of rousing the other wagons some hundred yards away, the men worked quickly. Jason's tent was taken down, Asa's oxen were quietly yoked, Blossom tied to the rear, and then the big white-topped schooner left the slumbering encampment, crossing silently over the mist-shrouded meadows in the direction of the river. Mrs. Strong, white-faced and shivering in spite of the heavy red knit shawl she had wrapped around her, obediently complied with all of Asa's demands. Watching her mute suffering, Jason approached her once when Asa was out of hearing.

"Maybe the hole in the river is filled up by now," he whispered. "Maybe we're goin' to get over all right."

"Maybe," her lips answered and she tried to smile.

The Big Blue, however, still high, could be heard even before it was seen, its swift flow holding an ominous note of warning in the pale morning light. But Asa Strong seemed to be past all seeing or hearing, his mind obsessed with crossing to the opposite shore. Cal, gazing down into the swirling water, seemed to lack some of his old assurance.

"I dunno . . . seems like it's risen a bit. . . . I dunno's

I want to risk my hosses for less'n five dollars. I've put most of my money in them hosses."

"I've been expectin' this," snapped Asa. "Course if you're feered . . ."

"I ain't feered. But the water's higher than I jedged yesterday. If I lose my hosses . . ."

"Remember, you'll be a rich man by tonight, leadin' the other folks across today. I'll pay four dollars an' a half, no more, d'ye hear?"

Cal nodded, somewhat appeased.

"Jason . . . Bill!" and Asa began to pour forth a stream of orders. "You two boys pull out them logs from the grass. Here's some spikes an' ropes. Make that raft safe while I find a flat place to launch 'er. Lizzie, you keep out of the way till we get the wagon on the raft. Then you go in an' set down. I don't wanter hear a squeak outer you."

Mrs. Strong made a faint sound in her throat and seated herself upon a rock.

"An' before I forget, Lizzie, take keer of my best black suit an' don't let it get wet. An' pack the beddin' high. I don't want to sleep in a damp bed tonight. . . . No sniffin' now . . . Cal an' I will get the stock over an' wait for you on the other side. The boys'll pole the raft over. Everything's all fixed now," and Asa with feverish energy disappeared into the mist, searching for a place to launch the raft.

It was some time before the raft, safely reinforced, was launched on the waters of a small quiet inlet nearby. Upon its swaying surface the big Conestoga was backed, the wheels blocked and chained to the log floor to prevent its rolling. After the oxen had been unyoked and led back to the main ford, Elizabeth Strong climbed the steps of the wagon and walked timidly inside. Of his own volition, Jason came to her and helped her locate the trunk which contained Asa's best black suit; then he hoisted it to a safer height. With the bedding folded and stacked on the opposite side of the wagon, Mrs. Strong seated herself in a chair by the rear door to watch. Once Asa looked up as he passed by to make certain for the last time that the wheels were properly chained.

"Be gentle with Blossom," Mrs. Strong pleaded, looking down at him. "She ain't used to cold water."

"Sure, sure," consented Asa irritably, "but Blossom's got to learn like other cows. Did you put my suit up high an' dry?"

"Everything's done," replied Elizabeth Strong. "Asa, Asa . . . be keerful," she half whispered, as Asa hurried away to mount Kit, his long bullwhacker's whip in one hand.

Kit, standing at the edge of the water, reared a little, his white forefeet sawing the air as Asa threw one leg over the saddle.

"I wouldn't take that whip along," advised Cal as he mounted Dandy. "Kit's a mite skeery of them long whips. He'll foller Dandy without it."

"But the oxen won't start 'less I use a whip," objected Asa.

"Here, you two boys, cut some willers, some good strong uns. Give Asa one. They don't sound sharp like a whip," instructed Cal and turned towards the river.

Jason and Bill, returning with the willows, gave one to

CROSSING THE BIG BLUE

Asa and then waited on either side of the oxen. All watched Dandy as he pranced up and down the bank with mincing steps, as if trying to escape Cal's spurs as well as the cold water of the Big Blue. With a final neigh of protest, the gray horse plunged in and, after swimming a little way, appeared to be walking. The ford, thus far, was as Cal had predicted.

"What'd I tell yer!" jeered Cal over his shoulder.

"Hurry up, get the oxen movin'!" yelled Asa at the two boys.

The oxen, loath to enter the water, stood at the very edge. Smarting from the willow switches, each ox finally took a first step forward only to find himself sliding down the muddy embankment. Bellowing, snorting, splashing, the leader began to follow Dandy and the others fell in line. But not so Blossom, the cow. Frightened and mooing mournfully, Blossom tried to escape into some tall willows.

"Pull 'er out, beat 'er, make 'er swim," shouted Asa, his voice thick with excitement and anger. From inside the wagon, Mrs. Strong looked out anxiously through the tail curtains.

Stoop-shouldered Bill ran forward to obey Asa when he felt his arm clutched tightly. Jason had removed his heavy hide jacket and stood close behind him.

"Leave her be!" he ordered the astonished Bill. "I'll take care of her myself!"

Clinging to some brush with one hand, Jason lowered himself down the steep banking with Blossom's rope clutched in the other. As he sank in to his waist the cold muddy water numbed his whole body and his breath came in quick gasps.

"The idiot!" exclaimed Asa, but he made no attempt to interfere.

"Come, Blossom. Come, Blossom," called Jason, gently pulling at her rope. The cow, hearing the kindness in the boy's voice and bewildered by the raucous shouts behind her, came forward slowly, her eyes rolling less wildly.

"Come, Blossom . . . over here."

Another few steps and Jason could reach the cow and smooth her cream-colored neck. Gently he continued to pull her closer. And then, like the oxen, Blossom unexpectedly lost her footing in the mud and lunged into the water. Unable to turn back, the cow began to swim for the first time in her life, following the oxen some distance ahead.

Asa came next, bringing up the rear on Kit, who seemed torn between following Dandy and the dread of the cold water. But long association with Dandy won and, as the horse entered the river, Jason glimpsed the coiled lash of the blacksnake whip beneath Asa's arm. Stubborn, relentless as usual, Asa Strong had been unable to take another's advice.

Even though all the oxen had regained their feet and were now walking shoulder-deep in the water, the strong current gradually swayed them from their direct course. Jason, returned to the covered wagon chained to the raft, stood beside Bill and watched the dark figures become lost in the mist. One ox, however, lighter in weight and the last in line, seemed to be having more difficulty than the others and bellowed noisily. It was then that Asa made his big mistake. Confident that Kit had carried him past the deeper part of the river, Asa hastened past Blossom, lifted his right arm, circled the length of blacksnake whip twice above his head, and lashed out in the direction of the struggling ox. Above the noise of the river, the crack of the whip was like an explosion. Instantly Kit, with a great splash, whirled about panic-stricken and started back to the wagon and the raft.

"Turn 'im roun'! Turn 'im roun'! You pie-eyed fool!" came Cal's voice from out of the mist. "Throw 'way that whip, like I tole you . . ."

If Asa heard, he gave no heed. Excited and impatient, he jerked at the reins as he attempted to turn Kit about. Failing, he began to beat the flanks of the horse with the staff of his whip. With his white forefeet clear of the water, Kit reared and whirled again. And then, to the horror of those watching, horse and rider disappeared from sight . . . water closed over their heads.

"He's in a hole!" screamed Bill hoarsely, teetering on the very edge of the raft.

"Git off'n the hoss! Hold to his tail!" came Cal's voice from somewhere ahead on the opposite shore.

In another moment, Kit and Asa reappeared. Asa was still in the saddle, coughing and choking, his hat gone. The horse was headed downstream, fighting desperately to keep his head above water.

"Git off'n the hoss! Git off'n the hoss! You're driftin' too far down," wailed Cal's voice. "Give the beast a chance!"

But Asa, now terror-stricken, remained helplessly clinging to the horn of his saddle. Down went Kit once more in a second hole, carrying Asa with him. The spent horse, weary of his load, was making little effort to help himself and was drifting with the current, his white nose showing at times.

"Throw 'im a rope, Bill! Throw 'im a rope!" There was anger as well as desperation in Cal's voice.

For a brief moment, Jason looked about him. Blossom, frightened by the excitement, was returning safely to the shore which she had left only a few moments earlier. Elizabeth Strong, who had been watching from the rear of the wagon, could not be seen. Bill had lapsed into a state of coma. His arms dangled loosely at his sides and his mouth was open. There could be no help from Bill. . . . Seizing a rope from the end of the raft, Jason ran along the edge of the bank in an effort to keep opposite the struggling horse and rider. If possible, he intended to toss one end of the rope to Asa and pull him ashore. This would free the horse . . . that was what Cal wanted . . .

However, no human being could compete with the savage undercurrent of the Big Blue that morning. Kit and Asa were washed downstream faster than Jason could run. Moreover, a tall patch of willows and alders, growing close to the river's edge, forced him to leave the shore and circle into a bog deep with mud, which sucked and dragged at his feet. Twice he fell and it took all his strength to rise and stagger on. In the distance loomed a high knoll at the bend of the river. If only he could reach the knoll and toss the rope down to Asa . . . if only he could reach the knoll in time . . . Whatever resentment Jason felt towards Asa was now swept away by the helplessness of the man's drenched and dejected figure and the realization of how Elizabeth Strong must be suffering. With his breath coming in labored gasps, his legs sodden with mud, he reached the top and fell upon his knees.

Below sang eddies of brown water . . . Where were Asa

Excited and impatient, Asa jerked at the reins

and Kit? To the right and left, Jason's eyes searched the river and shores, but there were no horse and rider in sight. In the distance he could hear Cal still shouting. As he knelt, shading his eyes against the sun which had broken through the mist, for the first time Jason's ears caught a new sound below, the rustle of leaves, heavy breathing and a faint splash of water. Before he could rise to his feet, the low, distressed whinny of a horse reached him. Kit . . . Kit was somewhere below! And possibly Asa!

"Kit!" he shouted. "Kit! Asa, I'm comin', I'm comin'!"

Still clutching the rope, Jason stumbled down the slope, beat his way through a thicket at one side and approached the river. The water along the shore of the bend appeared shallow, the full force of the current swinging along the opposite side. The earth beneath the knoll had worn away and, crowded into a hollow roofed with ancient tree roots and vines, was the dark figure of Kit, wet, exhausted, his empty saddle twisted, his head low and reins dragging. There was no sign of Asa. Upon hearing footsteps, the horse lifted his head wearily and whinnied once more.

"Kit, you poor fella . . . you poor fella!"

A little later Kit, safe on the shore above, tried to hide his wet head beneath the boy's arm as if to shut out the river and its sounds.

Before leaving, Jason returned to the knoll, hoping to catch some sign of Asa. The sun shone clearly now and the river flashed gold and amber lights against his straining eyes. Up and down he scanned the shores carefully, but the search was useless. Even the meadows, the woods, and the skies were empty. . . . Not a living thing stirred.

5

JASON MAKES
NEW PLANS

Voices, angry and excited, shouted from the river. Jason,
leading Kit along the edge of the bog, now knew that Cal's
frantic calls had roused the sleeping encampment. In a few
moments he would be surrounded by men who would question and criticize, perhaps openly condemn him for trying
to assist Asa Strong in crossing the Big Blue that morning.
With his mind still numb, stupefied, he wondered vaguely
how he would answer those questions, finally arriving at
the conclusion that nothing mattered much now he was no
longer bound for Oregon. For him, the long journey was
finished.

Asa was dead. . . . There was no doubt of this in Jason's mind. Yes, Asa was dead, the river's muddy waters
had claimed him. Hatred for Asa had disappeared; there
remained only pity and a sense of awe. He had never before seen death claim its victim so quickly and he wondered
dully what Elizabeth Strong would do. Perhaps she would
return to her people in southern Illinois, a woman broken
in body and spirit, and it would be his duty to take her

there. It would be too late to return to Missouri and join another out-going train. May was the month for the take-off . . . May, and no later.

The weary journey around the marsh was nearly finished when a stocky figure in a red shirt suddenly appeared from out of the willows. It was Aaron, who, regardless of the black muck, plunged knee deep into the bog and came forward to meet him.

"Golly! I'm glad you're all right!" he shouted. "And you've got the horse! They've just found Asa . . . he's dead!" Lack of breath did not permit Aaron to continue as he struggled for a few moments to lift one foot high before the other. "I couldn't see much," he resumed finally, having reached an old tree stump where he balanced precariously. "The whip was wound all around Asa's legs . . . he's covered with a blanket now. Golly! You must have started early. We tried to get here in time . . ." Words, muffled and incoherent, followed as Aaron again struggled with the mud.

Jason, unable to answer, stood motionless beside Kit, who had come to a stop. Poor Asa . . . the whip used so mercilessly on old Mat was now the cause of his own death. And what of Elizabeth Strong? Where was she? Where were the oxen? Suddenly Jason was roused to the realization that the weight of responsibility had shifted from Asa's shoulders to his own.

"Where's Mis' Strong?" he called out hoarsely.

"She's gone back to the wagon. The women'll look after her."

"Blossom and the oxen are safe?"

Aaron, splashed with mud, had reached Jason and stood

staring, his round, usually smiling face sober. "They're safe. Golly, it was pretty bad, wasn't it?" he asked, still gazing first at Jason and then at the horse.

"Pretty bad. Where's Cal?"

"He's come over to this side again an' the men are asking him questions. Some of 'em wanted to flog him. They were awful mad an' excited. There's some superstition that drownin' brings bad luck. Where'd you find the horse? He sure is all tuckered out."

"He's got to be rubbed down. I found him below the bend. So Asa's dead. . . ."

There was a note of finality and despair in Jason's voice. Aaron continued to look at him, as if wondering why Jason should feel Asa's passing so deeply.

Then understanding flashed across his face. "I see," and he nodded slowly, "I see. I didn't realize before. . . . Maybe you'll be going back to Illinois now Asa's gone?"

In the silence which followed, water could be heard dripping from Aaron's boots and a fish hawk's cry seemed to scrape the length of the sky overhead. Jason's voice was scarcely audible when he answered. "Yes . . . back to Illinois. . . . Mis' Strong won't be going to Oregon. She's homesick. She told me two days ago."

Mark Morgan, accompanied by four men, met the two boys before they reached the river. There was only concern and pity in the captain's eyes as he gazed at the spent horse and white-faced boy before him. One of the men led Kit away.

"Aaron told me last night what you were up against," Captain Morgan told Jason. "And you did well to locate

the horse. Now, you and Aaron go along home. Aunt Liddy
will give you something hot . . ."

"I want to make sure the wagon's safe, and the oxen . . ."

"Everything's taken care of. There's nothing you can do
around here. Go to my wagon and get some sleep, if you
can. We'll talk things over when I get there."

"We'll talk things over." . . . Captain Morgan's words
repeated themselves over and over in Jason's mind as he
followed Aaron through the fields to the encampment. What
was there to talk over? The trip home? He could hardly call
Terryville home now. The farm had been leased to strangers, and his mother, Tacy and Sammy were living at the
tavern. There was no home to return to! "Talk things over."
. . . Silently he followed Aaron. Soon Asa Strong would
be buried, like all other emigrants, with his head towards
the west, and he and Mrs. Strong would return eastward
over the roads on which they had come and he would spend
the winter explaining to the people of Terryville what had
happened. Asa's experience would hardly inspire others
from that locality to make the journey west. Absorbed in
his disappointment, Jason was scarcely conscious of passing
men on their way to the river, or of women in little groups
talking in hushed voices, and was surprised to turn the
corner of a wagon and come upon Aunt Liddy, red cheeked
and muffled in a shawl, bent over a fire. A pot of coffee
steamed close by and the smell of broiling bacon filled the
air. After one look at the two muddy boys Aunt Liddy
straightened up.

"Good gracious!" she exclaimed. It did not take Aunt
Liddy long to produce shirts, trousers and boots for Aaron
and Jason, and a little later she stood over them while they

drank coffee and ate the crisp bacon she had prepared. A woman of action and few words in a crisis, she did not question Jason, for which he was grateful, and, warmed by the coals of the fire, the boy felt his strength return.

"Now you look better," Aunt Liddy told him after regarding him critically. "I'm going to put your clothes to soak and you wear Aaron's today. Pull in the belt and nobody'll notice they're big for you." Then, under protest, Jason was made to enter Aaron's tent and curl up under the warm blankets of a bed far more comfortable than his own.

"Just an hour of sleep and you'll be fine," Aunt Liddy told him, tucking in the blankets about his shoulders. There was nothing to do but obey. Aunt Liddy, as determined and resourceful as her brother, Mark Morgan, was a woman with whom it was difficult to dispute. In spite of himself Jason dozed. And then a deep sleep blotted out his discouragement and the bitter haunting realization that in a few hours the wagon train would go on its way to Oregon without him.

It was Aaron who finally roused Jason.

"A boy just came with a message. Pa wants you to go over to the Barretts' wagon. Mis' Strong's over there . . . she wants to see you. You know, the wagon with the blue-and-yellow trimmings."

The Barretts' wagon was not far away. Jason walked slowly. Every step was taking him nearer to the news he did not wish to hear. Captain Morgan stood outside conversing with a short, stout, red-faced man whom he introduced as Mr. Barrett.

With a cordial smile, the latter waved Jason towards a short flight of steps at the rear of his wagon. "Go right in, son. Mother's in there with Mis' Strong. They're waitin' to see ye."

Mrs. Barrett, better known as "Mother," was a small wiry woman with dark alert eyes. As though the wagon were a nest, she leaned sparrowlike from the doorway to beckon Jason in, a bottle of smelling salts in one hand and her voice chirping the while.

"Glad to see you, son. I've two grandsons little older'n you at home. They're still in school. Here he is, Elizabeth . . . he looks just like you said he did. . . ."

A moment later Jason was gazing down at Elizabeth Strong, bolstered high with pillows and half reclining on a short-legged feather bed. At the sight of her face, startlingly white in contrast to the red knit shawl she still wore, Jason forgot his own unhappiness. Only Mrs. Strong's eyes, as they smiled at him, seemed familiar.

"Jason!" she exclaimed, putting out her hand to draw him closer. "You're all right, ain't you? I want to talk with you just a little. . . . Oh, Jason!" and tears began to stream uncontrollably down her cheeks.

"There, there, dearie," and Mrs. Barrett leaned over Mrs. Strong with the smelling salts. "She's all to pieces, poor lamb," she told Jason. "You do the talkin', Cap'n," appealing to Captain Morgan, who had quietly entered. "She's been doin' fine an' I don't want her to get all het up."

"I'll be glad to," answered Mark Morgan. "Come over here on the bench beside me, Jason. Mrs. Strong can add whatever I leave out. We will not stay long and I'll be brief. I might as well start with saying that Mrs. Barrett's an old friend of Mrs. Strong's sister. They live in the same village in southern Illinois . . ."

"I remember seeing Elizabeth visitin' her sister," chirruped Mrs. Barrett swiftly. "It was only yesterday I learned who she was and I was fixing to introduce myself today, when we heard the awful news early this mornin'. So Tom ketched up the mules and we drove down to the river and fetched her here with us. Go on, Cap'n . . . guess I broke in on you."

"So that's why she's here, Jason," finished Mark Morgan. "And pretty fine for her, too. It was part of my duty to come here and make final arrangements for Asa, and after we had finished our talk Mrs. Strong wished to discuss a little business . . . what she should do with her wagon and the stock . . ."

"I know," answered Jason. It was coming now, the news that he must return to Illinois. His body stiffened as if preparing for a physical blow, and he lowered his head with eyes blurred. If only he might receive this final verdict in some quiet place where there were no eyes to watch him!

"To my surprise," the captain's voice was continuing, "I found Mr. and Mrs. Barrett had made up their minds to turn back to their home in Illinois. They very kindly offered to take Mrs. Strong with them . . ."

"Take Mis' Strong with them?" asked Jason, slowly raising his head. The captain's voice had seemed to reach him from a long distance and he wondered if he had heard aright.

"Tom got word yesterday his brother an' wife are both sick in bed with rheumatiz," interrupted Mrs. Barrett. "The neighbors are carin' for 'em 'til we get there. Naturally we ain't got the heart to go off an' leave 'em that way. Of course we can take Elizabeth right along with us. We're sellin' the plow an' things to folks here an' there'll be plenty of room for her things. We'll take the dear lamb right to her sister's door. I've been tellin' Tom right along we're too old to go gallivantin' west . . ."

"Mother, let the cap'n talk," interrupted Mr. Barrett, now seated on the top step with a pipe in one hand. "When you get rantin' . . ."

"It's all right," answered the captain pleasantly, "she's helping a lot. So you see, Jason, Mrs. Strong is well taken care of. But she's worried over you and your plans. She knows how much store you set on reaching Oregon to make a home for your mother. She has a plan, and I'll be very frank and say I haven't encouraged her very much. But here it is: She wants you to go ahead with the wagon and stock just as you planned . . ."

"Go ahead . . . go to Oregon?" Incredulous, Jason stared from one person to another.

"Just as we planned, Jason." Mrs. Strong was speaking now, her voice faint but clear. "I'll come out next year with my sister and claim the land. I'll be in better health by then. You and Sammy go ahead with the stock to The Dalles and leave the wagon there with my cousin . . ."

"Sammy? But Sammy's gone home! I can't reach him now . . ." Jason had risen to his feet in his distress. "Didn't you say . . . Aaron said . . ." Jason, now turning to the captain, was unable to go on.

"Sit down, boy, till we finish," and Mark Morgan pulled Jason down to the bench once more. "Yes, I did see Sammy traveling east on horseback with a trapper towards Independence. But at a fork of the roads they turned directly north to follow the Kaw. How do I know? One of my scouts saw them at a distance, followed a short way up a path, and later picked this up." The captain reached beneath his belt and held up an old bowie knife with a twisted elk-horn handle.

"My knife! My old knife!" Jason reached out his hand to take it. "See! There are my initials, J C, and Sammy has tried to make an S over the J. He was wearing the knife in his belt the other night. Then Sammy's gone on . . . he isn't going home . . . he's on his way to Oregon!"

"Looks like it," agreed the captain. "He's made friends with a trapper who knows all the old back trails, and they'll probably reach the Kaw before we do. We might meet them there. If this brother would be a help to you, and Mrs. Strong thinks he would, I'll consent to let you go ahead with her wagon and oxen. Otherwise I'm not in favor. It would be too much for you to handle. You understand, don't you, that one wagon can hold up a whole line?" The Captain's gray eyes were looking directly into Jason's.

"Yes, I know," answered the boy.

" 'Keep the wagons moving' is the cry of the trail. Those who can't must drop out and let the others go ahead. It's the only way, cruel as it may seem, that we can arrive in Oregon by winter. If you manage to reach the Kaw River by yourself and meet your brother there, well and good. Possibly I would let you continue alone to Fort Laramie where most of the trappers wait over . . . Your brother might be there . . . It's the last port this side of the Rockies. It all depends on how well you keep up. How old are you?

The Land Law requires a person to be eighteen before he can stake land . . ."

"I'll be eighteen come October," interrupted Jason a little breathlessly.

Captain Morgan regarded him thoughtfully and then nodded his head. "Well, what do you think about it, Jason? Do you wish to go ahead? A lot of these folks will be going on to Santa Fe in a few days. We'll turn northwest . . . 'bout thirty wagons in all. Think carefully before you decide. . . . The Indians are restless and the British at Fort Hall are doing everything they can to discourage folks from entering Oregon. Every day we're hoping to hear that the United States and England have come to some settlement and signed the treaty. There are hard days ahead for every one of us."

"Cap'n Morgan, Mis' Strong, let me try! I know I can do it! I know I can! Sammy'd help, he'd be a big help. He's probably plannin' to meet me at the Kaw Crossin', thinkin' I won't turn him back if he gets that far west. I know there'll be hard times ahead . . . I've heard them talk. But I'll get your wagon to Oregon, Mis' Strong. I know I will!"

No one could mistake the ring of sincerity in Jason's voice. He had risen to his feet again, the words tumbling from his lips, his dark eyes lighting his pale face. Mark Morgan watched him intently while Tom Barrett's red face stretched in a broad grin behind wreaths of pipe smoke.

"That's the stuff, my boy. Makes me wish I was goin'," exclaimed Mr. Barrett. "An' how I wish I was twenty years younger! Harkee, that's the spirit of a real pioneer speakin'! Let 'im try it, Cap'n."

"Of course he can make the try," agreed the captain. "Personally, I'll be glad to have him along. But I want him to know what he's getting into. It won't be a picnic."

"You can move right into the wagon, Jason." Elizabeth Strong was smiling faintly, her voice tremulous. "There's food in the barrels, an' with my preserves you'll have plenty. Use your own judgment on everything. I know you'll take good care of the stock . . . I saw what you did for Blossom this mornin'. Asa's gun . . . take that, too. Send me word when you reach my cousin."

"Oh, Mis' Strong!" Jason was now by her side, glowing, eager, happy. "I'll watch out for everything . . . *everything*. You're mighty fine to let me try, Mis' Strong . . . you an' the cap'n. I'll be meetin' Sammy, I know I will, and please tell my mother not to worry. Maybe you'll come west together next year. Anyway, I'll be out there waitin' for you. I'm sorry . . . I'm sorry it happened this way . . ." Stammering, Jason paused for words.

"We didn't plan it this way, did we, Jason?" and there was a catch in Elizabeth Strong's voice. "You're a good boy. I've told you that before, an' you know how I feel 'bout Sammy. Come tomorrer before we leave, I'll want to see you again an' give you a message for my cousin. I'm a little tired now . . ."

"P'raps you'd best be leavin'," and Mrs. Barrett edged closer with the smelling salts. "Tomorrer she'll be stronger. Elizabeth thinks a sight of you, young man, an' somethin' tells me you're not goin' to disappoint her."

"Now you're really talkin', Mother," agreed Mr. Barrett. "I'm of the same mind an' Lor'! how I wish I was goin', too!"

6

STORM ON THE PRAIRIE

Asa Strong was buried late that afternoon on the hillside
covered with wild roses, his head towards the west. Elizabeth Strong was not able to be present and, after a brief
goodbye the following morning, she departed with the Barretts for the east. Three hours later the entire train, headed
by Captain Morgan, crossed the receding Big Blue. With
two oxen borrowed for the occasion, Jason was able to drive
his own wagon across and found Blossom and the Strongs'
oxen unharmed, in charge of an English-speaking Kanza
Indian sent there for that purpose by Mark Morgan. No
accidents occurred during the crossing save the spilling of
one of the Collins' children from an overcrowded front
seat. However, no damage was done and the child looked
cleaner for the mishap. Cal, subdued and temporarily chas-
tened, appeared to be more engrossed with Kit's welfare
than his family's. The horse, highly nervous, refused to
enter the stream and it was Jason who finally returned and
rode him across. Kit now had confidence in the boy, who
talked to him quietly and carried no whip.

STORM ON THE PRAIRIE

A few miles beyond the crossing, the emigrants looked back and saw that they had left all forest land behind them. The sky above stretched high and wide like a huge inverted bowl over endless miles of rolling hills green with grass and bright with flowers. It was the beginning of the prairie and more than one pulse quickened at the sight. How many times the word "prairie" had fallen from their lips through long months of planning, prior to leaving home!

Captain Morgan called an early halt on that first afternoon because of some distant thunder clouds in the west. And while the oxen were unyoked, horses hobbled, and tents put up, a bitter cold wind came sweeping over the green knolls and sudden darkness fell.

"It's a prairie storm!" came the cry. "Drive your tent stakes deep!"

Thunder rumbled like the low beat of drums and then grew louder with a deafening roar as streaks of lightning glared in the sky overhead. Men, women, and children hurried to safeguard the stock. Voices screamed, dogs howled and, in the midst of the excitement, five oxen broke loose. Frightened at the sight of white canvas ripped from a wagon top by the wind, the panic-stricken creatures pounded through the encampment, leaving even more excitement and devastation in their wake.

Suddenly, there was a fresh commotion near the end of the line. Between rolls of thunder a woman's voice, high and piercing, called, "Anna! Jessica! Anna! Jessica!"

With the cries came a flash of lightning so blinding that Jason turned and shielded his face in his arm against the side of the wagon. But not before he caught a glimpse of women clustered about the Fields' wagon. The old squaw

. . . was she causing trouble? The memory of Ezra Fields' weariness and dejection, as he stood guard over his children while they gathered flowers, flashed once more before Jason's eyes. Quickly he buttoned his coat about him and began to run towards the group of women and the crying mother. He had not gone far before a deluge of water descended from the sky.

"The girls . . . they're gone!" Mrs. Fields was crying to the women about her. "They were here just before the oxen went by. I told them to run . . . to go under the wagon. I had to stay and tie Buttercup . . . she was loose. The girls ran," a great sob choked the woman for a moment, "and when I tried to find them, they were gone! They were gone!" Her voice rose into a hysterical scream. "That old squaw's got them . . . I know it! The old squaw with the umbrella! She's traveling with the Mexicans. She tied a red handkerchief around her head so I wouldn't know her! Oh, please, someone go and find them! My little girls . . . my little girls . . . " and Mrs. Fields sank to her knees, with rain and hail beating down upon her upturned face and glistening in her hair.

Ezra Fields suddenly appeared with a lantern. Its feeble flickering light showed his bandaged arm in a sling, his face haggard, and his wet homespun clothes clinging tightly to his gaunt figure.

"I've been down to the wagons!" he shouted. "They ain't there! Now I'm goin' into the prairie. Mary, go inside!" He lifted his wife to her feet. "It ain't good for you to get so excited," he told her more gently.

"Come, Mis' Fields, he's right," and two women lifted the stricken mother to her feet. "He'll find them. He'll bring

them back," they comforted her, as they half carried her
into the wagon. "Soon's our men stake their oxen, they'll
help. They'll all help. . . ."

"It'll be too late . . . too late," moaned Mrs. Fields.

Ezra Fields had gone again, the small flicker of his lantern showing through the sleet as he walked out onto the
prairie. Every other emigrant was engrossed in caring for
his own family and animals and Ezra walked alone in his
search. Facing the blast of the storm, Jason ran after him.

"Mister Fields, I'm Jason Coit. Maybe I can help . . ."

"Bless you, boy, I'm nigh crazy," and the man stopped
for a moment and dried his wet face on his sleeve. "It's that
ol' squaw. I saw her myself this afternoon. . . . Cap'n
Morgan says she won't do no harm, she won't go fur with
'em . . . she just wants to pull an' snap the girls' red
curls . . . but I ain't so sure. He says not to hurt her or
we'll have a whole tribe down on us. But seein' her hang
aroun' my kids is more than a human bein' can stand! If I
ever ketch 'er . . . Anna! Jessica! Papa's callin'!" and
holding the lantern high with the light shining frostily before him, Ezra Fields began his frantic search once more.

The man's arm was now out of its sling, his bandaged
hand shading his eyes as he strained to catch some glimpse
of the missing children.

"I heered somethin'," he shouted once above the roar of
the wind.

But Jason, though he listened carefully, could hear nothing which resembled a child's cry.

"I heered it again," shouted Ezra a little later, and this
time Jason believed he had heard the same sound . . . the
wail of a child not far away.

The side of a high ridge loomed ahead and now the father ran, his breath choked and rasping, with Jason at his heels. At the top of the ridge they paused an instant for breath and then peered down into the gully below.

"Papa," called a muffled voice.

Without answering, Ezra Fields plunged down the embankment, holding out his arms to the two little girls who came running to meet him.

"Jessica, how did you get here? Anna baby! There, there . . ." and he had the smaller child in his arms.

"Papa, oh, Papa!" Crying and shivering, Jessica clung to her father's hand. "We tried to get away from the oxen, but the wind made us run! It blew us away! I held on to Anna's skirt . . . It was dark . . . the ol' squaw found us. . . . She said she'd take us back to Mama, but she didn't. . . . We went on an' on an' on . . . Oh, Papa, I'm so glad you've come!"

"I didn't wanter go . . . I didn't wanter go!" sobbed small Anna on her father's shoulder.

"Where's the squaw now?" abruptly asked Ezra Fields of his older daughter, putting the younger child down. "Where'd you leave her?"

"She heard you call, so she let us go. She's down there," and Jessica pointed to the bottom of the gully.

As suddenly as it had commenced, the storm ceased. The last roar of wind faded away and light began to seep along the edge of the western horizon; the tops of distant slopes glimmered whitely. At the foot of the gully could be seen a crouched figure wrapped in a blanket. It was the squaw, and she made no effort to escape as Ezra Fields approached. Stolidly she watched him come closer, squinting up at him out of small black eyes, water running down her wrinkled cheeks.

"So it's you, is it?" roared the father, holding the lighted lantern close to her face. "I thought I told you to leave my children alone!"

"No hurt chill'en," answered the old squaw, her lips scarcely moving. "Ox make chill'en run."

"Well, they didn't have to run way out here, did they?"

"I wanter go home . . . I wanter go home. She wouldn't put up her umbrelly . . . we're all wet," complained Anna tearfully, clinging to Jason's hand.

"So you wouldn't put up your umbrelly!" stormed Ezra Fields, working himself into a rage.

Looking down, Jason could see the wooden handle of an umbrella projecting from the folds of the woman's blanket. In another moment the father had spied it. With a quick motion he reached forward and tore it from the Indian's grasp. Holding it high, he brandished it menacingly over her head.

"So you were goin' to take my kids away, were you?" he shouted. "I'll l'arn you different. You get outer here, an' if I ever see your ugly face again I'll use my shotgun! D'ye hear?"

The old squaw remained motionless, her small black eyes staring up at him.

Regardless of his bandaged hand, Ezra Fields yanked the woman to her feet, faced her towards the prairie and roughly pushed her forward. Then, with a swing of his arm, he pitched the umbrella into the air. It fell some twenty feet away. With an agility unusual for one of her years, the squaw turned and ran, pounced upon the umbrella and held

it tightly to her. Then she stood and looked back at Ezra
Fields. For a long moment she stood there, the light from
the west showing her face drawn in an ugly scowl. Silently,
her feet making no sound in the ice-crusted grass, she disappeared over the next slope.

Ezra drew a deep breath and turned to Jason and his
astounded children. "Well, I s'pose I've done it now. Made
the ol' woman mad an' she'll get even with me if she can.
Blast her dirty hide! Stealin' my kids! . . . Blast her!
Blast her!"

The sun gave out a sudden warm glare; the prairie storm
was over. Little shallow pools reflected the sun's crimson
glow, lighted up the two bedraggled little girls, their cotton dresses streaked with mud, their wet red curls, and
their tearstained faces. With a muffled exclamation, Ezra
knelt and drew them close, kissing each one in turn. Later,
still swinging the lighted lantern, his feet splashing through
the puddles, he led the way back to the encampment.

7

A SCOUT ARRIVES
WITH NEWS

Two days later, forty-one miles from Independence, came the division of the trail. The older, battered, grimy-topped wagons bound for Santa Fe continued ahead, but the newer wagons with white unweathered tops halted hesitatingly about a small sign of simple lettering: "The Road to Oregon." Suddenly a cry rose from a hundred throats in one accord. "On to Oregon!" "On to Santa Fe!" sounded the train of wagons southward bound, and the line passed slowly from sight as it dipped and climbed over the prairie slopes. It was the parting of the ways and for the first time the pioneer homesteaders, bound for Oregon little less than two thousand miles away, faced their task alone.

"Well, I'm glad they've gone," called Joel Adams, next in line to Jason, as the wagons moved slowly past the wooden sign. "Most of us speak English. An' we're homesteaders, not traders. They say the Westport trains have been delayed an' we're goin' on without 'em. . . . I hope that kidnappin' ol' squaw went to Santa Fe, though it wouldn't surprise me none if she popped up further on. She's mad, an' I wish Ezra Fields hadn't been quite so rough. My own kid's got some red in her hair . . ." There were grim lines of worry in Joel Adams' lean young face.

"I'd say it was more gold than red," called back Jason. Poor Joel Adams was only one of many parents upset by the Fieldses' experience during the storm, and if possible Jason meant to allay Joel's fear. "Anyway, your baby's a lot better now. I don't hear her cryin' so much."

"She's gained weight since we changed to your cow's milk," spoke up Joel's bachelor brother Seth, who was accompanying Joel and his wife Sally Adams to the west. "But Joel says you don't own the cow. I wish you did. We'd like to buy her."

"No, she belongs to Mis' Strong. But the baby's welcome to the milk, so long's you help me over the creeks," returned Jason, and both Joel and Seth Adams nodded understandingly. Jason's offer of Blossom's milk to their sick child several days prior had been appreciated by the entire Adams family, and the two brothers had willingly assisted him in the crossing of Indian and Bull Creeks.

Jason alone could not possibly have managed the crossings without help and there was now no doubt in the mind of the most optimistic traveler that the journey ahead was one of toil and hazard. The creeks in themselves were warning enough. Before descending the steep banking, rear wheels were chained lest each wagon pitch downward too quickly. The ditch gained, the wheels were unlocked that they might churn through the muddy water and the animals begin their struggle up the opposite bank. Often the driver, at the first lurch, was thrown from his seat. Whenever possible, women and children walked, waded or climbed in order to relieve the load. And meanwhile the contents of the wagons, if not securely fastened, would crash forward with the downward dip, only to be hurled back again as the weight shifted on the upward climb. More than one woman wept with homesickness and dismay as she later examined her cracked lustreware. For every family carried some cherished heirloom . . . dear reminders of the past . . . which seemed to increase in value with each mile.

Misfortunes and disappointments of various sorts, however, were already serving to unite as one family this little band of people. Men and women found themselves sharing with each other, encouraging and assisting one another. A new top was fashioned for the roofless wagon the day after the storm and, though it was a patched affair of green, yellow and blue calico, it symbolized generous hearts and willing hands. The missing cattle which caused the stampede were also recovered through combined efforts. Among the women, food was shared, cooking rules exchanged and more than one lasting friendship formed over a washboard in some brook.

There were those, however, who did not respond to the tests of the trail with such loftiness of purpose. High-pitched squeals mingled with happy shouts of children had been heard coming from the Collins' wagon, and as only three of the four escaped pigs had been recovered on the eve of the storm, it was suspected by many that Cal was harboring an unlawful supply of pork. But the unfortunate owner of the pigs, Elisha Jefferson, stoutly bent upon investigation, quailed before Mrs. Collins' unkempt head and steely eyes as she emerged from the rear curtain to greet

him, a pistol swinging from her right hip and a baby balanced on her left.

"I've got a good mind to go in there an' get that pig,"
threatened Aunt Liddy, stopping by to call upon Jason one
evening. "I'm not afraid of sech folks. What if she does
carry a pistol and is high-tempered! And just imagine all
of 'em living together in one wagon with a pig . . . a dirty,
squealin' little pig! Mark says there's no proof it's stolen;
all little pigs act an' look the same, an' maybe it was in
there when they left Independence. He don't want any row
'cause he thinks the Collinses will leave the train soon anyway. Already Mis' Collins made Cal trade in that gray
horse, Dandy. She scolds a lot, sayin' Cal should have
bought oxen. They haven't enough food now an' their
wheels are loose already. . . . Mark's got his mind on
Indians. He's worryin' plenty, if you want to know."

"Has he heard anything new?" asked Jason quickly,
making room for Aunt Liddy to sit down.

"Oh, now an' then scouts come in with warnings," replied Aunt Liddy vaguely, as she looked about her. "My,
you're neat as a pin in here. Where's your feather bed?"

"Feather bed? I didn't bring one. And Mis' Strong took
hers with her, of course. I roll up in blankets . . . they're
warm enough."

"Gracious me! I wouldn't think of comin' west without
my feather bed. Why, both Mark and Aaron have theirs.
. . . Maybe I could fix up one for you, too. . . . We'll
see. Mis' Strong left you plenty of food?"

"More'n I need," replied Jason.

"You hang onto it, son," Aunt Liddy advised. "The time
may come when we'll have to share alike and not squander

a mite. An' don't you dare drink the water from these pools on the trail without strainin' it an' makin' tea or coffee. Why, I never saw sech big polliwogs in all my life as those playin' in the bottom of the pail Aaron brought in tonight. An' queer little fish with tails a-wiggling. The men call them 'wiggle-tails' and I saw a few folks, too tired an' thirsty to strain the water, swallow 'em down whole. Made me sick to watch 'em. You be careful, son. I may sound funny, but you mind what I say!" and Aunt Liddy departed as suddenly as she had come.

A little later, Jason examined the water he had drawn from a pool only a few hours before and was amazed to discover several young tadpoles and small fish swimming about in the bottom of the cask. Knowing he would be questioned later by Aunt Liddy, he obediently strained the water and made tea for his supper, remembering the while how clear and sparkling the water had always appeared when drawn from his mother's well in Illinois.

Little qualms of homesickness were apt to rise during this hour when he ate alone, his wagon dimly lighted by the glow of the campfire outside. To break this spell, on previous evenings he had industriously overhauled the contents of the wagon and established an order of which he was now proud. It was, as Aunt Liddy had said, "neat as a pin," and her approval alone had repaid him for his time and labor. From the gun swinging on leather loops from the arch over the front seat to the plow hanging at the tail gate, each article had its place. With Mrs. Strong's wooden chests, feather bed, horsehair trunk and weaving frame removed, he had ample room to arrange his boxes of food in a row and lash them securely to the side walls for support.

Coffee, tea, sugar, beans, dried fruits, herbs, flour, rice, corn, molasses, bacon, pickles . . . they were all there. Heavy chains dangled from wooden pegs. The churn, two water casks, the Dutch oven, skillets, pots and pans were solidly stacked against each other. Patch pockets made by Mrs. Strong lined the canvas roof and walls and held such articles as fish hooks, nails, spare bolts, string, cord, wire, pins and needles, thread and small carpentering tools. And strung to the top of the ceiling were the rose roots which Mrs. Strong had planned to plant in her new garden in Oregon.

Poor Elizabeth Strong! How grateful he was to her for her confidence in Sammy and himself! And how surprised Sammy would be to meet him at the Kaw Crossing, traveling alone in such an outfit . . . a wagon fully equipped, six oxen and a cow. How Sammy's eyes would bulge! Plucky little Sammy! Now he was glad of Sammy's persistence in following him. Foolhardy, yes . . . but as Tom Barrett had said, it took just such spirit to settle new country. And although Sammy was small for his age, perhaps he would gain weight and grow tall in the air that would soon be fragrant with turpentine and that was considered healthy by most people. Yes, it was best after all that Sammy had determined to come. Jason found himself counting more and more on his younger brother's company.

It was not unusual now to be visited by wandering Indians, curious and overfriendly in some instances, who suddenly appeared from behind a hillock, eager to see the wagons cross the sloughs or creeks. They were indescribably dirty, usually accompanied by squaws carrying papooses on their backs, by wolflike dogs with litters of pups, and small burros dragging travois. And though at first children were herded into their respective wagons by frantic parents, fear gradually diminished at the continued absence of the "ol' kidnapin' squaw," as she was called. Terror lessened for all except Mary Fields, who, unable to forget the horror she endured on the night of the first storm, still kept strict vigilance over her small daughters. Despite protests, at the appearance of Indians Anna and Jessica Fields were always hidden beneath their feather bed, bribed by a little horehound candy and accompanied by their dolls. Such was the penalty for being born with red hair. . . .

The Wakarusa crossed, the train plodded steadily on its way at the rate of two miles an hour. Meanwhile, Mark Morgan had been busy planning a daily routine for the welfare of his people. The long day started at four o'clock in the morning when a sentinel awakened the encampment by discharging his rifle. While breakfast was prepared, men and boys appointed as herders rounded up the livestock which was picketed and hobbled and grazing in near-by grass. There were cries of "Ketch up! Ketch up!" and "Whoa!" and "Haw!", the rattle of cooking kettles and the smell of smoke, and at seven o'clock the train was ready to move on. The thirty wagons were divided into small platoons of four, the leading platoon becoming the rear platoon on the following day. At night a corral was formed, a wagon in the rear being connected with the wagon in front by its tongue and ox chains. Tents were pitched outside this strongly entrenched circle, which formed a barricade against marauding Indians and stampeding cattle.

"Look out for the hoss thieves ahead!" came the warning
from emigrants returning homeward from the trip to Oregon because of discouragement or sickness. "The worst are
the Pawnee Indians. They're the slickest hoss thieves in the
world! A Pawnee can crawl roun' on all fours under an
antelope hide an' take the hosses away right out from under
yer nose! Yes, we're goin' home . . . that's where we belong. Don't talk Oregon to us!"

Horse thieves! The very words chilled Jason with fear
for Kit, whom he had come to love. Not wholly trusting
the guard posted throughout the night to watch the grazing
stock, Jason often rose from his bed to make sure the horse
was safe. A word with the sentinel and he would locate
Kit, who learned to expect him and greeted him with a soft
whinny of joy. Jason would remain with Kit for some time,
filling the emptiness of his own heart by smoothing the
horse's tangled mane or brushing down his chestnut-brown
coat. Cal Collins, anxious and disturbed also, sometimes
appeared to make sure of Kit's whereabouts. But Cal had
other pressing duties now, as the greater part of his family
appeared to be ill. Tadpoles and fish had not been excluded
from their drinking water and the squeals of the incar-
cerated pig were often mingled with sighs and groans
caused by diarrhea.

"They'll be droppin' off soon," was the general com-
ment. "Wait till we reach the Kaw. If the water's high,
they'll never be able to sail over. That wagon bed is full
of leaks and almost in pieces right now."

The train was thirty miles distant from the Kaw when
Jason was invited by Aaron to have supper with the Morgans one evening. He arrived to find Aunt Liddy, flushed

and triumphant, removing a large apple pie sweetened with molasses from her Dutch oven.

"I rolled the crust on the front seat," she informed Jason, "an' it's the best flour board I ever used. An' look in the kettle. Prairie peas, just like our garden peas!"

Aaron, in charge of the potatoes baking in the hot ashes, waved enthusiastically and pointed at his father, who was turning a plump wild turkey over the fire on an iron spit. "It's my birthday an' this turkey walked right into the camp as if he knew it!" he exclaimed.

"Just in time, Jason," called the captain. "I'll be cutting into this bird in another five minutes. Bill Brewster's here. Bill, this is Jason Coit, a friend of Aaron's."

Jason, entranced at the sight of food, looked up and found himself staring with undisguised curiosity at a tall lean man standing in the shadows, a gold-colored mustang tethered just behind him. So this was the scout, Bill Brewster! Tough and sinewy as old whipcord, with gray hair falling to his shoulders and wearing a flat, broad-brimmed hat, Bill appeared to be all Jason had imagined, a plainsman of the first order. At the belt of his fringed and beaded buffalo jacket he carried a tomahawk. On his back were slung a bow and quiver filled with arrows. Shrewd, bright blue eyes looked back at Jason from beneath heavy gray eyebrows.

"Bill brings us all kinds of rumors about the treaty," continued Captain Morgan. "England and the States seem to be deadlocked as usual and you can't believe anything you hear. He says a lot of folks are settling in Polk County. Bill knows every inch of land around these parts. We're paying him a little extra to take care of us from here on

. . . keep the scalps on our heads till we reach Oregon. A dollar a head isn't too much, is it? So make him your friend, 'cause he's a bad enemy."

"Now don't skeer the lad," and Bill Brewster's bright eyes smiled at Jason. "I'm as harmless as a prairie dog. Out fer land, Jason?"

"Yes, in Oregon."

"Whar?"

"I don't know yet. Willamette Valley sounds pretty fine if I can get my mother and sister down the Columbia safely."

"They talk of new roads openin' through. There'll be some short-cuts soon, I'm thinkin'. Folks want to reach the Willamette before snow flies. You single?"

"Yes. I'm expectin' to meet a young brother at Kaw Crossin'."

"Here, you two boys, get busy an' pass the plates an' cups." Aunt Liddy reached for the huge pot of coffee which steamed over the fire. "I've made lots of coffee 'cause I know Bill Brewster likes to wallow in it."

"Like the buffalo," and the old scout's thin weathered face creased into a hundred fine wrinkles as he smiled.

"Mark, that turkey's done . . . so's the 'taters," bossed Aunt Liddy. "An' watch Aaron's plate . . . he's puttin' on fat again. What's the Kaw like, Bill, since you've just come from there? Is she high?"

"She's high, Ma'am. Snows from the north have made her riz."

"Does that mean we caulk the wagon beds?" asked Aaron eagerly.

"Some folks will. There's a ferry runnin' fer folks who can pay. Seen any Injuns?"

"A few," and Captain Morgan gave a brief account of the disappearance of the Fieldses' children.

The old scout shook his head slowly as he listened. "Fields shouldn't 'a teched the ol' woman. Thar's no tellin' which tribe she comes from or what she'll do next. I'm warnin' yer, Cap'n. An' they say the Cheyennes an' Gros Ventres are thick 'roun' Red Buttes an' the Sioux are mad as hornets at folks comin' through their land. You'll have to be ready with presents an' food ter keep 'em happy." As he talked Bill Brewster's bright eyes followed the captain's knife as it slipped down the brown crust of the turkey's breast. In one hand Bill clutched his tin cup, soon to be filled with coffee.

"We're ready for 'em," promised Aunt Liddy.

"With your ways of cookin', Miss Liddy," the old scout's eyes twinkled, "I reckon you'll be pop'lar wi' the chiefs. That apple pie . . ."

"I'm makin' no apple pies fer Injun stomicks," snapped Aunt Liddy indignantly.

"Well, you may have to turn about on some of yer plans," answered Bill Brewster mildly. "Seen Henri Jules?" he asked Mark Morgan suddenly.

"Who's Henri Jules?" asked the captain, now severing the turkey's legs.

"Mountain trapper, French . . . married a squaw . . . got a black beard an' is always singin'. One of the trickiest devils this side of the Rockies."

"Guess I don't know him," replied Mark Morgan. "We had a few trappers with us after we left Independence but they all scattered different ways. Why, what's Henri . . . what'd you call him? . . . done now?"

"Jules . . . Henri Jules. He's done plenty, I'd say," and the scout began to sip his coffee with evident enjoyment. "Two months ago a Comanche Injun robbed a train coming from New Mexico, carryin' gold. Well, it 'pears Henri robbed the Comanche an' is now headin' straight for the Rockies wi' the gold, lookin' fer a good hideout. Or mebbe he's aimin' fer his squaw further west. He was last seen near Independence an' had a young kid ridin' with him . . . a boy with a big hat. Thar's a reward posted for 'em."

"You say the boy wore a big hat?" Jason, white-faced and wide-eyed, had almost dropped his plate.

"That's right. A leetle feller with a big hat. Rode with Henri on a pony. Know him?"

"I . . . I . . . guess so. It sounds like my brother, Sammy. . . ."

No one moved. The fire flared and crackled and lighted up Aunt Liddy, Captain Morgan and Aaron, all staring, listening, the food untouched on their plates, consternation and sympathy in each face.

8

THREE CAPTIVES

A week of travel in the wilderness with Henri Jules, the trapper, proved an unforgettable experience for Samuel Coit. It left its mark on his body as well as his mind. For the paths taken by Henri were of his own choosing and generally led through dense thickets of briars which yanked at Sammy's clothes, etched blood-red lines across his freckled face and tore at his hands and wrists. Frequently asked why he did not follow the regular trail, Henri always replied that his paths were "queecker."

"Quicker fer gettin' where?" Sammy would demand impatiently, as he rubbed a newly acquired and smarting wound. Invariably he received the same reply: "De mountains! De mountains!"

"But I don't wanter go to the mountains!" and Sammy would grow red with rage. "I'm goin' to Oregon an' you ain't goin' to stop me either, you big, overgrown, black-whiskered ape! I'm sick of travelin' with you an' your onion breath. I'm sick of it, I tell you! Always runnin' an' hidin' into thickets like a skeered rabbit. You're skeered . . . skeered of every little shadow, every little noise. What you got in your bags, anyway? Who you skeered of, the dragoons?"

Henri never answered Sammy but appeared inordinately amused by the boy's boldness. And it was evident Henri was finding Sammy useful as well as amusing. The care of Marie, the washing of kettles in brooks, the gathering of firewood, polishing of the horse pistol, and even some of the cooking, now fell upon Sammy's shoulders, while Henri relaxed in obvious contentment. Resisting these bonds of enslavement, Sammy in high temper upset kettles of water, wasted matches, and scorched food, but always paid in some measure for his folly by extra tasks conjured up by Henri. Gradually the boy grew wiser in his methods of annoying his big captor. A knot inconveniently tied in a rope, a burr placed in the toe of Henri's boot, the entire bag of salt overturned in the stew . . . little accidents of everyday living, quietly managed, sometimes gave Henri much discomfort and Sammy keen satisfaction.

"My squaw, she will be so pleased wit you," Henri was fond of telling Sammy over and over again. "We will make of you a fine trapper, like mese'f!" and Henri would pound his bewhiskered chest. "My squaw, she like museeck, too," and a big hand would point at Sammy's jew's-harp. "But nevaire, nevaire must you marree a squaw," he warned Sammy confidentially one day. "The squaw is *très belle*, but her familee, *sacré bleu*! Always de familee come an' eet! An' she have manee, manee peoples in de familee!" Here Henri gave a great sigh which nearly stretched his hide shirt to the bursting point.

On they had gone towards the north, skirting Kanza farms, passing through Kanza villages demolished by warring Pawnees, on through the thickest briar patches Henri could find, avoiding with great care any passer-by headed towards Independence. Upon reaching a deep river which he called the Kaw, Henri built a small raft, using large bundles of willows as floating supports, and poled Sammy to the opposite shore in the dark of night. Reluctantly Marie followed, snorting her indignation. There were no lights on either shore and Sammy wondered if this could be the regular ford used by the emigrants. Had Jason arrived and gone? If only he might leave some sign to show Jason he had passed that way, should his brother be crossing in a day or so. . . . But he had neither paper nor pencil and a tattered piece of red flannel from his shirt would mean nothing to Jason, who supposed him to be at home by now. Disconsolately, Sammy was hurried towards the high bluffs which overlooked the river.

Strangely enough, Henri now seemed willing to rest a bit, to relax before going on. But on no condition, he warned, was Sammy to stand up, make any signs, or attract attention should anyone appear at the ford.

"If you move," the big trapper threatened, an ugly look coming into his black eyes although his voice was pleasant enough, "I pull you back wit de rope," and he pointed at his long rawhide. From previous experiences, Sammy knew that Henri meant every word he spoke. The rawhide had a cruel sting and he feared it more than any other punishment.

On the second night of their stay, a faint hammering could be heard from across the river. Small pale fires of greasewood burned on the shore and later came the sweet strains of voices singing and the strum of a guitar. A wagon train was preparing to cross the Kaw the next day! Caulking their wagon beds with strips of rags and tar! Hardly able to contain himself, Sammy slept fitfully and, as soon as light broke in the east, he was in his place at the edge of the bluff, peering through the deep grass for some glimpse of Jason. For surely this must be Jason's train!

Already, to his surprise, eleven of the wagons had crossed the Kaw, whose turbid waters were bright yellow in the early morning sunlight. Four more were being launched, with stock swimming behind. Still other wagons were crossing on a ferry poled by two Indians. There were thirty wagons in all.

The eleven wagons which had arrived safely were directly below. How wonderful to see them and hear them! Oh, where was Jason? Occasionally Sammy was conscious of Henri looking over his shoulder and of a few words such as "You must be st-eel" being hissed in his ear to remind him he was being watched. But even this failed to dampen his enthusiasm and joy.

It was a stirring sight! Down below were people of his own kind, English-speaking people, and Sammy was sure Jason was somewhere among them. But though he tried to distinguish Jason from the rest, the distance between the people and himself made it impossible. Some person who resembled Jason a little was drying off a chestnut horse but most of the time the body of the horse obstructed the view of that person. Anyway, what would Jason be doing with such a horse? He would be driving Asa Strong's wagon! If only Jason had worn a red flannel shirt like his own! In vain he searched for Asa, brandishing his long whip. Could this be the wagon train Asa Strong and Jason had joined? Except for one wagon, which bore a top of many colors, all the wagons looked alike. How was he to know? The wagon with the vari-colored top perplexed him. There had been no such wagon in the camp on the Big Blue River.

Now and then Henri glanced over Sammy's shoulder, but the big trapper was not particularly interested nor alarmed at the presence of the emigrants.

Down below, some Indians had now appeared from along the river's edge. They walked in a little group, with the squaws and children trailing. One of the men carried something lashed to his pony's side and to Sammy it appeared like a huge turtle. It was difficult to tell which Indians they were . . . probably friendly Pottawatomies, who wished to exchange food for trinkets or tobacco. A tall man, evidently the captain of the train, had walked out to meet them and now they stood together as they bartered.

The unexpected arrival of the Indians did not seem to distract the sunbonneted emigrant women, who continued to unfold blankets on the meadow grass. One woman, however, upon seeing the strangers, ran towards her wagon at the edge of the meadow near the forest, tripping over blankets in her hurry. She disappeared into the wagon but returned almost immediately, raising her arms above her head as she gave a shrill, agonized scream. For a moment the sound seemed to paralyze the people below into statues. Soon they came running to her from all directions. What had happened? Even the white man bartering with the Indians turned and hurried to her, giving sharp orders the while. Then pandemonium broke loose and the meadow was full of shouting people. At least ten men mounted horses and galloped away in different directions, while others proceeded to search the bushes and shores of the river. The Indians alone remained quiet, a stiff little group huddled defensively together while the cries of the distressed woman sounded high above all.

In his excitement, Sammy had risen to his feet. But a hand upon his shoulder forced him down again into the grass and then he was dragged bodily over some hummocks down to the small campfire.

"*Allez vite!*" roared Henri in Sammy's ear. Startled, angry, Sammy's foot shot out and caught Henri on the shin, but this did not slow down the trapper as he ran to catch Marie, eating grass nearby. Dragging the unwilling Marie towards the fire, Henri put the saddlebags over her back, dashed out the tell-tale fire with water and tied his kettles to odd ends of ropes. Henri was breaking camp!

"*Allez vite!*" Henri again commanded.

A blanket was thrown over Marie's back to prevent the kettles from banging against the rocks and then her short legs were lashed with a rawhide whip. Marie began to sprint. Down the northern slope of the bluff she ran, with Henri following and pulling the rebellious Sammy after him by the wrist. Fortunately Sammy's hat was still fastened to the back of his belt. Sometimes his feet traveled the earth, but often he lost his footing and was dragged, his knees striking rocks and his heavy homespun trousers snagged by briars. Angry, humiliated, he bit at Henri's hand, but beyond a muttered exclamation this had little effect on the trapper. Up the side of another bluff they scrambled, Henri continuing to lace Marie's legs with his whip. There was a brook at the foot of the second bluff, and into the water splashed Henri, Sammy and Marie. The brook led through some prairie grass at the farther end of which stretched a broad belt of cottonwood trees. It was not until Henri reached the edge of the trees that he stopped to look back to see if they were being pursued. To Henri's relief and Sammy's disappointment, the sides of the bluff were free of horsemen.

In the center of a small clearing among the trees, Henri unloaded the exhausted Marie and removed her blanket. In another moment he sprawled against the saddlebags upon the ground to regain his breath and motioned Sammy to do the same. Sammy, winded and perspiring, sat down with an angry thud some distance away and then stared at the earth in surprise. The heel of his boot had scuffed up dead leaves and now revealed the gray ashes of an ancient fire. So! Henri had been here before . . . these trees were an old rendezvous! Yes, the trapper knew every back trail, every bluff and every brook in the region round about. Who else knew of this hiding place, Sammy wondered.

A long silence followed and Henri appeared to be listening intently, his eyes half-closed while Sammy, still raging inwardly, examined the damage done to his trousers. A great three-cornered rent extended from the right hip to the right knee. It flapped dismally about when he moved, showing scratched and reddened skin beneath. Cloth was an unknown quantity in the wilderness. A pair of soft tanned-hide trousers would do very nicely, but where was he to find them? Fort Laramie? Meanwhile should he use one of the tails of his shirt as a patch?

And now his ears caught what Henri was listening for . . . the sound of hoofs coming nearer, nearer to the edge of the trees. Henri sat up straight and watched him warily, a menacing light in his black eyes. Henri was worried, and suddenly Sammy began to enjoy the situation. Now was the time to get free and pay Henri off. One loud call of "Help!" at the proper moment would guide the horseman into the woods. So sure was Sammy of his plan succeeding that he grinned impudently at his big captor. Still nearer came the pound of hoofs, but not quite near enough as yet. No one would hear his voice quite so far away. One moment more and he would draw a deep breath, ready to give a piercing yell. . . . He was still grinning, watching Henri out of the corners of his eyes, when Henri's arm moved swiftly. Something dark sailed through the air overhead and descended upon Sammy, shutting off the long indrawn breath he had planned to take. It was the blanket Marie had worn to muffle the kettles and now it was being used to muffle him! Before he could throw it off, he felt Henri pinning him down. And though he yelled, the sound was indistinct, even to himself. Henri had fooled him again!

Even now Henri was chuckling softly just above him. Sammy twisted, wriggled and fought savagely, but Henri managed to keep him beneath the blanket. Horsehair, dust and leaves choked him. When at last Henri let him free, there was no sound of horses' hoofs and the trapper smiled down at him, his white teeth flashing. For some reason, Henri derived increasing pleasure from these little bouts of wit and brawn, ending each fracas by calling him, affectionately, his "Lil' Firebran'."

In very bad humor, Sammy sulked the rest of the day. His brief glimpse of the emigrants made him more determined than ever to escape his captor. The thought of traveling to Fort Laramie with Henri fairly made him ill. Moreover, the camp among the tall trees was not as open and sunny as on the bluff. He spent the afternoon sitting cross-legged on a blanket, trying to restore the rent in his trousers, wondering, with a lump in his throat, how his mother did such things. He had never sewed before. He had tied the two top corners of the patch to the main part of his trousers with some wool raveled from the blanket when Henri began to take an interest. A buffalo calf's hind legs, he exclaimed, were just what Sammy needed. And he, Henri, would obtain them when the Platte Valley was reached.

"I take de skin off . . . so!" Henri demonstrated with a heave of his arms, pulling at an imaginary carcass, "an' you put eet on . . . so!" making motions of drawing on trousers over his own long legs. "*Oui*, de skin is wet . . . but dey shape heemse'f. I mese'f will cut off zee tail!"

The prospect of wearing the skin from a buffalo calf's hind legs was scarcely appealing and Sammy bent to his sewing with renewed fervor. His money, nine dollars, was still safe in an inside pocket. There would be no pockets in Henri's style of trousers. He had heard rumors of trappers clothing themselves in green skins this way; also, they sprinkled gunpowder on their food for lack of salt. Now he was sorry he had disposed of Henri's salt . . . would he be forced to flavor his food with gunpowder, too? Life with Henri for the past week convinced him now that all these things were possible. It was more important than ever that he run away before Henri disappeared too far from the trail. If he failed and was thrashed, the try would be worth it. He had made several futile attempts before, which only amused Henri. This time it would be different.

At the coming of darkness, Henri stirred himself and built a very small fire. It was hardly large enough to heat water from the brook for their coffee, and the remainder of the meal consisted of cold fish, raw wild onions and hard biscuit. Sammy ate because he was ravenously hungry and because it might be his last meal for several days should he make his escape that night. Ordinarily Henri demanded music after their evening meal. Only too glad to attract a prowling horseman, Sammy drew the jew's-harp from his pocket and began softly to twang one of the trapper's favorite songs, feigning innocent surprise when Henri stopped him. The two then resumed their silence, watching the flames of the small fire.

Henri's head had tilted forward and the very first snore was blowing through the whiskers spread fanlike over his chest when Sammy heard a faint sound at the edge of the wood. It was the noise of horses' hoofs finding their way along the ground, the snap of twigs, the swish of underbrush. Someone was coming directly towards them, as if he knew the way to the little camp! In another moment Henri sat bolt upright and held his pistol in readiness. The moon was now high in the sky and, as the two sat tensely waiting, the head of a small pony appeared from around the trees. Almost instantly a shawled figure with an umbrella under one arm also appeared. And on the pony's back sat two children half asleep and propped against each other for support.

"*Sacré bleu!*" breathed Henri.

It now became clear that the shawl enfolded an old squaw who, without further ado, led the pony closer to the fire, put down her umbrella with a regal air and proceeded

On the pony's back sat two children half asleep

to remove the two sleepy children from the pony's back, giving Henri no sign of recognition.

"*Sacré bleu!*" Henri now roared, forgetful of his former silence.

But whatever Henri thought, said, or did seemed to be of no consequence to the old squaw. She had taken possession of the camp and her object now was to make the two children and herself comfortable. With careless indifference she threw some wood on the fire and, in the light of the blaze, gave Sammy a swift, searching gaze. Satisfied he was merely a white boy with a scratched face and tow-colored hair, whom she could consider harmless, she set up a small tepee. Slowly but surely there was wafted on the night air the penetrating odor of skunk.

Henri's roar had awakened the two little girls, who stood clinging to each other, staring dazedly about them. It was plain that they were sisters. Their linsey-woolsey dresses were torn, their arms and legs scratched. The hair of the smaller girl had become unplaited and hung loose, a shower of red upon her shoulders. The older of the two, also red-haired, had now spied Sammy and ran towards him, dragging the younger one with her, a look of frantic hope in her blue eyes.

"You're a white boy?" she asked in a choked voice, reaching forward to feel his sleeve.

"Sure. I'm white. Who're you?"

Before the girl could answer, the squaw and Henri burst simultaneously into a loud and bitter harangue. Frightened, the smaller girl began to cry and threw herself against Sammy, clinging to him with all her might, much to Sammy's embarrassment.

THREE CAPTIVES

"Anna, Anna, ssssh, ssssh." The older girl tried to comfort her and pull her away at the same time. "Don't, Anna. He's a white boy and he'll help us if we don't cry so. Ssssh, Anna." But her own sobs prevented her from succeeding and now she herself was clinging to one of Sammy's hands. Hardly knowing what to do, Sammy managed to squirm free of their hold and awkwardly patted their shoulders, suddenly conscious of the frailty of his patched trousers and that he had always despised girls. In all his life, he had scarcely spoken to one!

"Be st-eeel!" rasped Henri, now aware of the noise they were making. However, overcome again with rage, he joined the squaw once more in their heated argument.

It was very evident that the squaw and Henri were not friendly and that they had met before. With familiar contempt, the woman launched a swift kick at Henri's saddlebags, as if she already knew their contents, spitting out her venom in sharp strange words while the trapper pointed at the two red-haired children, bellowing the while.

"I'm Jessica . . . she's my sister Anna," the older girl whispered to Sammy, in spite of the noise. "The ol' squaw stole us from our wagon."

So this was the commotion he had witnessed from the bluffs that morning! Two little girls had been stolen from the train . . . perhaps Jason's train . . .

"You know Jason Coit?" he asked eagerly. "He's my brother. He's traveling with the Strongs . . ."

"Why, we know Jason," answered Jessica excitedly. "He helped Papa find us when the squaw took us away before. Oh, please, we don't like the Indians. Won't you take us back? We want to go back to Mama and Papa."

"Mama! Papa!" suddenly howled Anna.

"Be st-eeel!" Henri now hung over all three in a threatening attitude until there was utter silence. Apparently the trapper and the squaw had come to some agreement. She had hung her umbrella by its handle to the limb of a tree and was tying the pony to another. Henri finally moved away to inspect the tiny animal, a sturdy, shaggy little fellow with a white mane and bright eyes.

"Is Jason all right?" whispered Sammy softly.

Jessica nodded. "He's driving the wagon all alone," she whispered, "an' he keeps looking for you . . ."

"For me? Why, he thinks I've gone home!"

"Someone saw you and told him you were going towards Oregon."

"Golly!" For a moment Sammy lost his breath. "But Asa . . . Asa Strong . . . where's he? You say Jason's drivin' alone?"

"Asa was **drowned** . . . **an'** the lady went back home . . ."

"Asa drowned!"

Again Jessica nodded, her eyes on Henri lest he see them whispering. Sammy subsided into an amazed silence, his gray-green eyes round and his light hair seeming to stand on end.

"You said he was lookin' for me?" he asked again incredulously, after a safe pause.

Jessica nodded. The squaw now came forward with some cold biscuit and fish for the two girls. Later she brewed some herb tea for them to drink and placed a heavy hide mat beneath Sammy's blanket. Content with the arrangements she had made with Henri, she did not attempt to separate the girls from Sammy. The little girl Anna leaned wearily against him. From a pocket, Jessica produced a small piece of horehound candy which she offered to Sammy. Though he shook his head in firm refusal, Sammy's eyes gleamed hungrily. Upon her second offer, his grimy hand reached out in spite of himself. It had been a long time since he had tasted candy and he rolled it slowly around in his mouth four times and then reluctantly deposited it in his shirt pocket for safekeeping. Anna was now asleep, clutching him about the neck, and there seemed to be nothing he could do to release himself. Whenever he strove to loosen her fingers, she clung more tightly.

"I'm glad you're Jason's brother," whispered Jessica. "We like Jason. . . . When can we run away?"

"I've got to think about it," answered Sammy.

"I wish we didn't have red hair," continued Jessica with a catch in her voice. "It's our hair that ol' squaw likes . . ." and Jessica launched forth into a breathless recital of what had happened. "She kept followin' us 'cause our hair is red. Mama hid us under our feather bed as soon as we crossed the river because she saw some Indians way off on the hills. Ol' Squaw wasn't with the Indians Mama saw. She must have been hiding in the woods next to our wagon. Anna sneezed. A loose feather made her sneeze and then I guess Ol' Squaw knew we were there for sure. She had a knife and she cut a big hole in the canvas. Then she pulled us out. We cried, but the cattle were making so much noise nobody seemed to hear. She took us to a cave on the riverbank and tied some old cloth over our mouths 'cause Anna lost her doll with the china head and kept crying. Then we walked and came to the pony tied in some woods. I think she stole the pony, too. Sometimes we heard folks calling but we couldn't answer. It was awful!" and here Jessica struggled to keep back her sobs. "She kept sayin' . . . the ol' squaw, I mean . . . that she knew someone not far away and we would travel with him. I guess they're related somehow. She talks quite a little in English when she wants to. Why are you here? Do you want to go with these people? Oh, please help us! Did the man make you come with him?"

"Not exactly," replied Sammy, disliking to admit his helplessness and the extent of his menial labors. "I'm sorter travelin' with Henri. We met on a boat. He likes my jew's-harp. I play tunes he likes. You just keep quiet an' let me manage things." He was surprised at the brave note in his voice. "From now on, you do as I say," he added masterfully.

"We will," promised Jessica meekly. "But couldn't we start tonight?"

"No, there'll be better nights than this," objected Sammy, deciding he must hold on to his authority. "You leave it all to me. D'you s'pose you could get this kid's arm off my neck? I can't breathe."

With Jessica's help, Sammy was released. Hunched with his chin on his knees, he moved a little apart while Jessica continued to whisper.

"Do you know where they're going?" she asked, nodding in the direction of the squaw and trapper. "I don't think they like each other much, though they are related."

"Henri lives in some mountains," replied Sammy. "Say,

does the ol' lady sew?" he asked suddenly, again conscious
of his torn trousers.

"I don't know," answered Jessica absently. "She carries
lots of things in those little bags tied to her belt. There's
skunk oil in one of them. She puts it in her hair. I'm glad
she doesn't make us sleep in the tent with her."

"I thought I smelled somethin' awful around here," and
Sammy made a wry face. "Well, I've got a little job of
sewin' I'd like done. It ain't easy, either. D'you s'pose . . ."

But Jessica was not listening. She had fallen asleep,
curled on her side and breathing evenly. Sammy regarded
both girls silently. Escape from Henri would be more difficult now with the girls dragging at his heels. To Sammy's
credit, he never once thought of leaving them behind. But
Asa was drowned and Jason was alone, expecting him . . .
needing him! Just this bit of news would have made him
attempt escape that night . . . but now, with two girls
whispering, crying, asking questions and bothering . . .

If there was anybody Sammy detested, it was girls . . .
and here he was, pinned in on either side with them, both
moving closer because of the cold. Cautiously he reached
forward and folded a corner edge of the blanket over each
of them. Then, with careful deliberation, he hitched himself
backward, still in a sitting position, until he reached a tree.
Here he planned to sleep, sitting upright. Sooner or later
the two girls would find each other and keep warm but he,
Sammy Coit, did not intend to be caught in the middle! It
was chilly without a blanket and the tree was hard against
his back . . . maybe later he would crawl closer to the
fire . . .

Mad at himself, mad at the girls, and mad at the whole

world in general, Sammy finally fell asleep after a short
comforting suck on the horehound candy. An hour later,
stiff with cold, he sought the edge of the blanket once more,
his back turned defiantly upon his two red-haired companions.

9

AUNT LIDDY
ENTERTAINS

The slashed canvas, the doll dropped in the grass, and the broad imprint of moccasined toes in the damp earth soon told their story to the stricken parents, Mary and Ezra Fields.

"It's that squaw . . . I know it's that squaw," Mrs. Fields repeated over and over after her first agonized scream. "She's mad at Ezra because he threw away her umbrella an' scolded her. Oh, what will she do to my babies . . . my babies . . ." and then suddenly, with no warning, Mary Fields crumpled, fell forward and lay deathly still in the tall grass. Already heavy with another child, she was tenderly carried within the Fields' wagon where she lay motionless, with only her lips moving as she faintly called each child by name. "Anna . . . Jessica . . . Oh, my little Anna."

Ten men, headed by the old scout, Bill Brewster, rode into the hills. Those who did not own horses beat the bushes with sticks, searched the surrounding gullies and followed the banks of the river. Others held the group of Indians as prisoners. The redskins stubbornly maintained their innocence, declaring they had seen no children with hair the color of the sunset. They had only come to barter with the white man. Their leader, a tall, fierce-eyed man, sat with his hand on his tomahawk, alert and angry.

Jason and Aaron had been among those instructed to search the upper banks of the river. Meanwhile, the loss of the Fields' children gave Jason a feeling akin to terror. Little Jessica and Anna were gone . . . and where was Sammy? This was a wild strange land where children were not safe. And now, when he had come to the Kaw Crossing, the first possible place where Sammy might have met him, there was no small red-shirted brother running forward to meet him. Only the night before, Aunt Liddy had presented him with a feather bed, a welcome gift, for the nights were cold. After supper he had plumped it into two warm nests and covered the entire bed with blankets in anticipation of Sammy's arrival. The evening waned away. And though he kept his fire burning throughout the night and even walked along the shore calling Sammy's name, still, no Sammy! There would be no reunion here at the Kaw Crossing. White-faced and chilled by the early morning air, Jason continued to hunt for the Fields' children with Aaron, unaware of covering the same ground twice.

"We've been all over this once before," Aaron was saying, his round face red from climbing the sides of steep gullies. "No use in going over it again. We may as well go back to the wagons. Maybe your brother has come in by now."

"Maybe," but there was discouragement in Jason's voice.

"I was just thinking about what Bill Brewster said. He didn't believe there would be much chance of Sammy's joining me at the Kaw, did he? He thought the fort more likely."

"That's what he said. There's lots of trails to the fort an' the trappers know 'em. Some of 'em don't cross the Kaw. Henri won't dare to travel the regular road, Bill says. An' if Sammy is wise to the gold, Henri won't let Sammy get away from him too soon. But I'm bettin' on your brother. I think we'll see him any day now."

"I hope so. I don't know . . . Sammy could always pull himself out of scrapes at home, but here . . . well, it's strange an' so different. That scream of Mis' Fields still rings in my ears. All I can think of is my mother an' how she would feel if she knew about Sammy now."

"They say the Indians are good to white children," added Aaron in an attempt to encourage Jason. "They treat them just like their own. If Henri has a squaw, as Bill says, she may take a shine to Sammy an' dress an' feed him like the rest of 'em."

"Somehow I can't see Sammy made into an Indian." Jason smiled ruefully. "He's got freckles all over his face, a snub nose, hair like straw, and gray-green eyes like a barn cat we used to have. The only thing he can do like an Indian is to yell and whoop. But maybe he'll be at the fort, as Bill Brewster says. P'raps he's there now, jailed. I wouldn't mind much, so long as he's safe."

At that moment, visions of Sammy chained to a wall with an iron ball attached to one ankle in company with a black-bearded trapper did not seem so horrible to Jason. At least his brother would be housed and fed until he could be rescued. Captain Morgan did not seem to feel that a boy

Sammy's age could be seriously incriminated with a man like Henri Jules. Henri was known throughout the country for his trickery. With a few words of explanation and Sammy's identification established, the two Coit brothers could go their way westward. But if the trapper disappeared utterly into the north, taking Sammy with him, it might be years before the two brothers would see each other again. The wilderness had swallowed more than one person, only to spew them out again years later, more Indian than white.

"Indians are a queer lot," continued Aaron as they walked along. "I heard Bill tell Pa the other night that they don't reason much. If someone in the train ahead of us should make them mad, they'll wait an' take it out on us. The Pawnees are mean to handle an' we'll be seein' a lot of 'em soon. They pretend to be friendly but all the time they're sizin' up our cattle an' hosses. They call our cattle 'spotted buffalo' an' our mules 'elk dogs with long ears.'" Aaron chuckled.

"I've sort of been guardin' Kit. Cal's watchin', too . . . He misses Dandy. I guess Mis' Collins is the boss, all right. She managed Dandy's sale. I hope the little Fields girls are gettin' enough to eat. Every mouthful I take I wonder what Sammy's havin'. P'raps we'll find all three of 'em at Fort Laramie," and Jason gave a half-hearted smile as he left Aaron and walked in the direction of his wagon.

Sammy was not in sight as Jason approached the wagon. The oxen and Blossom, drying in the sun, seemed little the worse for their swim. Bill Brewster had driven Jason's wagon across the Kaw, leaving the boy free to ride Kit, who would not enter the water otherwise. Gradually scouting parties on foot returned to the meadow and there was speculation among little groups of people as to what steps Captain Morgan would now take. Mark Morgan, reelected captain only two nights before, with Elisha Jefferson as lieutenant, already faced overwhelming problems. How long should the wagon train wait at the crossing to recover the stolen children? How far into the hills could the searching parties travel in safety? Though the oxen benefited by the rest, the horses were getting fagged and food supplies were dwindling. Already the daily diet was reduced to two items, beans and bacon.

Captain Morgan and his men returned that night, weary and discouraged by their failure to find any trace of the missing children. The old scout, Bill Brewster, did not accompany them, but went on farther north, promising to meet the train along the trail. The Indians were finally released and it was determined that another group of men would continue the search the following day. Little Anna and Jessica Fields had been loved by young and old. With guards posted that night, the camp slumbered, an exhausted and sorrowing people.

The second day's search brought no results and after a lengthy conference it was decided the wagon train must move on the third day. Heartless as it seemed, the law of the trail must be obeyed. "Keep the wagons moving!" Neither flood, drought, death, nor missing children could intervene. There were other urgent reasons, also, why the westward-bound schooners should not delay. Old Grandpa Meekins was ailing and his son in Oregon was waiting for him to arrive. A young man with lung trouble was eager to reach the sage country where it was hoped the odor of sage would relieve his cough. Moreover, it was thought unwise for Mrs. Fields to linger at the scene of the tragedy in her condition, though she pleaded to remain. The Fields' wagon must go forward with the others. There was little chance that the children might escape and wander back to the deserted camp and every chance that they were being taken north. Bill Brewster's last advice had been to go ahead and report the loss at Fort Laramie.

And so the Fieldses' wagon moved forward with the others on the third morning, Mary Fields white-faced and heavy-eyed as she looked behind at the country she was leaving. The green valley gradually disappeared and the wagons began to roll over the brown prairie. "Keep the wagons moving!" Ah, yes, the wagons must be kept moving.

Now the long stretches of prairie, at first so pleasant to the eye, began to pall upon the emigrants. Some of them were homesick, longing for their hills at home; and many were terrified by the thunderstorms at night. At noon there was no shade from the broiling sun, which parched and blistered their skins. Food spoiled quickly, clothes mildewed, and wood was scarce. It was not strange to see an occasional cookstove left behind on the trail, for oxen were growing tired and all unnecessary weight must be eliminated. Women walked who hitherto had ridden. The tops of the wagons, once so glaringly white, were now a drab gray.

Bill Brewster had not returned from searching for the children and Captain Morgan missed him sorely. From a distance, small parties of Pawnees had been seen and it soon became evident they were growing bolder. It was only a question of time before they would invade the camp, demand food, and look over the stock with greedy eyes.

"Treat them well," warned Mark Morgan, as the train traveled towards the heart of the Pawnee country. "They don't want us crossing their land and we must not offend them in any way. Share with them whatever you are eating; give them beads or mirrors, anything you can spare, but watch your horses and guns; they are born thieves. Above all, though, keep the upper hand. Don't let them know we are wary or nervous. It's possible they will give us news of Jason's brother and the two little girls if we show we are friendly."

Strangely enough, it was pink-cheeked, plain-spoken Aunt Liddy, the Captain's own sister, who was his greatest worry when it came to Indians. From the very first she had fearlessly shown her dislike of them, and no amount of lecturing could change her attitude. She complained that they were filthy, smelled, and were alive with vermin. Her gray eyes would snap at the mere mention of them. Oddly enough, every redskin who came to visit the train ended by lingering about the Morgan camp, evidently attracted by Aunt Liddy. He would plant himself firmly on his haunches and feast his eyes upon the buxom, energetic white woman who could sew, make cloth upon a weaving loom, and scarcely gave him so much as a glance, despite his gifts of catfish and prairie peas.

The wagons halted earlier than usual one rainy afternoon while a party of men, with Captain Morgan among them, rode across the plains to recover some stampeding oxen. The usual circle had not been formed for the night and the Morgans' wagon stood foremost, facing the prairie. Taking advantage of the lull, Aunt Liddy persuaded Aaron to build a fire as she wished to bake bread for the evening meal in a large flat-covered kettle commonly known as a Dutch oven. Despite the rain, she believed she could bake six loaves safely by holding a large black umbrella over herself, the fire and the oven. It was a task which she decided never to repeat, for when she finished two hours later, her dress and shoes were wet and muddy and her hair in strings. But the bread was perfect! Never had she baked such light, fluffy bread! Tired and wet, but jubilant with success, she sent Aaron after Jason to join them for the supper hour.

"That boy is alone too much," she told Aaron. "He's worryin' over that little scamp Sammy. An' he's feered of losin' Kit. If I ever get the chance, I'll put that Sammy over my knee and let him know what a real spankin's like. As to the hoss, I'd like to own him myself. Now hurry, go find Jason. I wish I didn't feel I had to mother every lonely boy in sight . . . always makin' more work for myself . . ." and still sputtering, Aunt Liddy slipped into the wagon for a moment to change her shoes. When she reappeared, Aaron was gone. But she was not alone . . . A long line of highly painted Pawnees awaited her return, introducing themselves with the single word, "How!"

"How!" replied Aunt Liddy with a short jerk of her head. Startled in spite of herself, she hurried forward to protect her six loaves of bread. For the first time, her brother's lectures on deportment when dealing with Indians seemed to bear a little weight, and she struggled to recall what he had said only that morning, with his eye sternly upon her. "Keep the upper hand . . . share your food . . .

but be very polite . . . don't let them know you don't want them . . . it's possible they will give us news of Jason's brother and the two little girls." . . .

There were ten of them in all. From over her shoulder, hunched beneath the umbrella, Aunt Liddy counted . . . ten broad-chested, powerful Indians, their brown skins shining with rain, their ears and noses pierced with brass and bone rings and necklaces of wolves' and bear teeth adorning their throats. They seated themselves expectantly in a stiff row and proceeded to watch Aunt Liddy silently as she replenished the fire, outwardly calm but inwardly seething. "Share your food" . . . Must she share her fresh loaves of bread with these smelly horse-thieving heathen? And what of the pot of beans baked only the night before, and her last jar of chili sauce and her small pat of butter? The bread, still in the shallow kettle and out of sight, must be saved! At that moment Aaron and Jason appeared and Aunt Liddy got her first bit of satisfaction watching their startled faces when they discovered their dark line of fierce visitors.

"Your pa come yet?" she whispered to Aaron out of the corner of her mouth. "He ought to be here. I s'pose I've got to feed these monkeys . . ."

"Pa's still roundin' up the oxen," replied Aaron, his eyes focused upon the Pawnees. "Golly, they look pretty bad, don't they? Shall I go get someone?"

"No, we'll manage this ourselves." Aunt Liddy was still whispering. "I've just had an idea an' you two boys'll have to help. Now, first dump the coals off the lid of the kettle, but keep the cover on. I don't want them varmints to see what's inside. Take the kettle by the handle . . . here, use these old holders . . . and carry the bread into the wagon. Keerful . . . it's hot. Set it on the floor where it can't do much damage. When you come out, bring that big pot of beans settin' on the barrel . . . the pot with the blue cover. We'll warm up those beans an' I'll make coffee."

"But, Aunt Liddy, the beans in that pot . . ." But Aaron was shut off quickly by his aunt. "Hurry, Aaron, the sooner we feed these . . . these . . . an' get rid of 'em, the better. When they're done eatin', I want to ask if they've seen Sammy an' the little girls."

"But, Aunt Liddy . . ."

"Aaron!" Aunt Liddy's eyes flashed and her mouth set. Aaron and Jason, gingerly holding the hot handle of the Dutch oven, vanished into the wagon with the covered bread and came out tugging a heavy pot of beans with a blue cover. Jason was then put to work counting out ten tin plates. Meanwhile, he gave sighs of relief as he gazed at the row of Indians who stared about them. Kit was safe, out on the prairie with Captain Morgan's party. And he hoped the Indians would depart before Captain Morgan and his men returned.

"Count out ten cups, too," commanded Aunt Liddy with a purposeful glint in her eyes as she bobbed about under her umbrella.

"Aunt Liddy," said Jason, approaching her a bit hesitatingly, "I've some bacon in my wagon. Couldn't I bring it over? Aaron says . . ."

"No, they'll get beans an' coffee. You keep your bacon, Jason," she answered pleasantly. "We're doin' all right now." With the bread safely out of sight, Aunt Liddy was amiable enough and even hummed beneath her breath as she stirred the beans in the big skillet. Ten pairs of black eyes watched her. Aunt Liddy and the beans were far more interesting than stock or guns at that moment.

"Will you look at that one on the end," commented Aaron to Jason, "the one with the green scalp in his belt. He can't keep his eyes off'n Aunt Liddy. Do you s'pose he's come courtin'?" and Aaron stifled a laugh.

"Something tells me she might take him," returned Jason.

"Boys! Boys! They might understand more'n you think," scolded Aunt Liddy, laughing in spite of herself. "Some of these Indians speak English. Jason, pass the plates. Aaron, follow with the beans . . . they're warm enough now."

"Aunt Liddy," there was a desperate note now in Aaron's voice, "didn't you know . . ."

"I know everything, Aaron. Now come, like a good boy, an' dish out those beans. Heap up the plates an' give them plenty, like your father said."

With a look of helpless resignation at Jason, Aaron bent to his task, piling the tin plates to overflowing, glancing bewilderedly at Aunt Liddy now and then. The Indians devoured their beans noisily, using their fingers and smearing their faces as they ate. Aaron had no sooner finished filling the tenth plate than it was time to start down the line again. It was the same with the coffee, which had been sweetened with molasses.

"I thought I had a pretty good appetite," murmured Aaron to Jason as they passed each other, "but these folks have got me skinned a mile."

"I just hate to think of tomorrow," replied Jason. "Honest, Aaron, it might be serious. . . ."

"Brut!" suddenly demanded one of the Indians of Aunt Liddy, pointing a finger towards the wagon.

"Brut?" asked Aunt Liddy calmly, even sweetly. "You mean bread, don't you?" So here was an Indian who recognized the fragrance of freshly-baked bread!

"Brut!" demanded the Indian a little louder.

"Of course," and Aunt Liddy put down her umbrella and went inside the wagon. She returned with a loaf of bread under one arm. Cutting the loaf in ten even pieces, she passed the bread about and Jason, assisting her, knew that the bread was not freshly baked. Smart Aunt Liddy, how much longer could she keep the Indians satisfied? Did they know the difference between fresh and stale bread?

"More beans, Aaron," Aunt Liddy was prompting. "Give them plenty. No one shall ever say he left our camp hungry. This is exactly what your father says we should do, Aaron," and Aaron dutifully obeyed, filling the plates until the big pot was empty of every bean.

"We go," and the leader of the ten Indians rose to his feet. The others stood, most of them hiccoughing, but there was satisfaction on all their faces.

"Jest a minute," and Aunt Liddy planted herself squarely in front of the leader. "We've lost two," holding up two fingers, "little girls . . . papoose, you call 'em. They have hair," and she pointed at her own beneath her sunbonnet, "the color of the sunset at night. Red! Like those gewgaws you're wearin' . . . them beads. Have you seen 'em? Answer me the truth now."

Nine of the Indians stared blankly as the leader struggled to grasp her question. Finally he answered, shaking his head slowly, "No white papoose."

"Well, I kinder believe you," replied Aunt Liddy. "Your stomick's full an' there ain't no use in your lyin'. Now I'll ask about your brother, Jason. Have you seen," and Aunt Liddy again addressed the leader, "a little feller on the trail, travelin' with a trapper?"

"He wears a red shirt," added Jason, pointing to his own brown one, "an' a big hat . . . a very big hat." His right hand made circles above his head.

"No white papoose," and again the leader shook his head.

"Well, if you do see any of these children, you let us know an' I'll give you more beans," promised Aunt Liddy. "Remember now . . . more beans if you see the children."

"We go," announced the leader a second time, majestically and slowly, apparently proud of his English. Then, as noiselessly as they had come, the ten Indians departed and were soon lost to sight among the rolling hills.

Aaron watched carefully until he knew they were surely gone. Then he turned to his aunt, who was complacently gathering up the tin plates. "Aunt Liddy! You wouldn't let me tell you! Those beans . . ."

"Those beans were sour . . . sour as sin, almost ready to sprout," finished his aunt. "Those were the left-over beans which you did not bury, like I told you to three days ago. They turned during the hot spell. Of course I wouldn't let you talk! Those heathens understood more English than you thought!"

"But the beans'll make them sick! If they're sick, they may attack us . . . they'll blame us! They were all makin' queer sounds when they left . . ."

"Sick? Tush! Who ever heard of a sick Indian? Those

leather-bellies! Why, it wouldn't be possible. They might have a few pains," she added after some thought, "but horse thieves should have pains . . . lots of 'em! Now gettin' those beans et up is what I call good old New England economy. My mother came from Boston! Come, come, boys. Where's yer spirits? What you 'feerd of? Mark said 'share yer food' an' 'keep the upper hand. Be polite.' Well, I've done it. The sour beans are gone and there's fresh ones in the wagon. An' nice light bread," she added proudly, "the best I ever made. Bring'em out, Aaron, an' stop yer fussin'. I saved yer supper for you, didn't I? Sorry we didn't larn somethin' 'bout the children, though," and with no visible qualms of conscience, the captain's sister began to prepare the next meal.

Beyond the loss of a horse, which wandered away in the night, and a grass fire, which was destroyed by setting counter fires, Captain Morgan's train passed safely over a long stretch of prairie. However, the emigrants were not spared the frequent Pawnee visitors, who sometimes arrived in great numbers. As several of Aunt Liddy's former admirers reappeared at the Morgan camp, still in good health, Aaron and Jason came to the conclusion that an Indian's stomach was something of a marvel and it took courage like Aunt Liddy's to find it out.

The country changed with startling rapidity the next few days. There was no sign of the missing children. Mary Fields, when not staring up and down the trail in search of them, sat motionless in a stupor. After the Red Vermilion River had been crossed, the wagons halted at the Big Vermilion to cut hickory wood. Wagon tongues, axle trees and oxbows were replaced and mended for the sterner pull ahead. The roaring Big Blue River forded, the schooners now began to climb towards the Little Blue River, anticipation speeding their progress. To Jason, listening to the talk around the campfires, there seemed to be many Blue Rivers, actually three in all, but the Little Blue River held a special significance in the minds of many. Returning travelers spoke with affection of the Little Blue's clear cool water and green shady banks where grapevines twisted among the sycamore, oak and aspen trees and wild turkeys, elk, deer and antelope meat supplanted tiresome beans and bacon.

Three days later Jason found the Little Blue to be all he had dreamed of . . . a gentle stream of water singing through a long green valley of unusual beauty.

Standing knee-deep at the river's edge, Blossom and the six oxen drank long and contentedly while Jason scrubbed himself clean of prairie dust and mud in the deeper current. Everything washable was washed, from wagon wheels to blankets. Later, woodfires glowed, voices sang, and the fragrance of roasting meat filled the air. The Little Blue was Paradise itself and for a while the heat, the cold, the terror of the prairie were forgotten.

But Life and Death accompanied the wagons up the long green valley. Grandpa Meekins, too frail to finish his last journey, died peacefully in his sleep. And while the train halted to lay him at rest, with a cartwheel and wild flowers of every color marking the place, Mary Fields gave birth to a tiny dark-haired girl who came to be known as Bluette, daughter of the Little Blue.

10

BUFFALOES!

To the sun-scorched emigrants, toiling along the prairie ridge towards the Platte River, the cool leaf-shaded waters of the Little Blue faded· into the past. Despite the talk of buffaloes, the excitement of the hunt, and the delicious meat they would all soon enjoy, thirst persisted for man and beast as the hot swaying schooners plowed over sandy dunes and bluffs. . . .

The first indications of buffaloes were the old and deserted wallowing holes, which still contained the putrid black and fermented water once used by these animals for bathing and drinking. The stench from the holes was noticeable even at a distance and, although there were no animals in sight, the very presence of the pools revived interest in and talk of buffaloes. When would one see the first herd and how long had it been since the animals frequented the old wallow holes? Later, great circles of grass growing in the sandy soil told their story. Buffalo cows, in protecting their calves at night, had encircled them, and the calves within, carrying seeds in their heavy young manes, had unwittingly planted a large round garden of grass mixed with mushrooms and pigweed. A few miles beyond, the emigrants had their first glimpse of bleaching bones and large skulls, the remnants of a slaughtered herd, with small lizards scuttling in and out. . . .

From then on, "buffalo chips" spotted the desert. They were the deposit of the herds and could be burned like charcoal. Light as cotton, thin as cardboard, nearly white from exposure, buffalo chips took the place of wood and every able-bodied person carried a bag on his arm to collect them for his evening fire. And great was the joy of the women when the burning chips proved to be odorless.

"If they warn't," scolded Aunt Liddy, "you wouldn't ketch me bendin' over them things an' doin' the cookin'. The Morgans would eat cold victuals from here to Fort Laramie!"

The Platte River, called the Nebraska by many, was first seen from the top of a high ridge. The river lay below, flat and gray, its wide stream dotted with green islands. Beyond, on either side, stretched miles of barren desert, the wastes inhabited only by roving buffaloes, antelope and wolves.

"Glad we're not settlin' here," commented Joel Adams to Jason, as the wagons halted on the ridge. "I don't call that a prutty sight."

"That river's a mean one," added Seth, Joel's older brother, standing close by. "Her bottom's a bed of quicksand. D'ye see anything with horns movin' around?"

"Not a one," answered Joel. "Lor', how I ache to get goin'!"

Someone else had joined them . . . Ezra Fields. In the

bright light he seemed even thinner than usual and more gaunt. His dark eyes, shadowed with sorrow, also searched the plains, but Jason and the men standing near him knew he was not looking for buffaloes. There was a silence as Ezra gazed over the countryside and then turned back to his wagon.

Seth Adams drew a deep breath and spat a mouthful of tobacco at some weeds. "Lor', what a world! Here we go talkin' 'bout havin' a little fun shootin' buffaloes and there's that man cryin' his heart out! I've got so I can't go by the Fields' wagon. Mis' Fields sets there huggin' the new baby, an' always starin' up an' down the trail. She's got the girls' horehound candy tucked away in a drawer . . . savin' it for 'em. Lor', here's hopin' the old scout gets back with some news soon! If he don't, those folks'll turn back east an' they ain't in any shape to travel alone."

"They promised Aunt Liddy they'd go a piece farther," replied Jason. "She keeps talkin' to them an' they listen to her. The Morgans set a heap of faith in Bill Brewster an' Bill sent word for them to keep goin'. He may come in any day now."

"Can't come too soon to please me." Joel was again searching the hills, shading his eyes with one hand. "He'll be more welcome than the buffaloes. I say, Jason, you've not been sayin' much. How 'bout it? You plannin' to do a little huntin'?"

"I'd like to," Jason hesitated a bit, "but I guess I'm out of the runnin' parties. You see, I don't own a horse. Besides, I'm the only one drivin' Mis' Strong's outfit. If I should get lamed up, there's nobody to take over."

"You're jest right," agreed Seth heartily. "You show

good sense. Of course Cap'n Morgan's got the truth on't, runnin' is dangerous business an' we're all of us, Joel and myself included, actin' like kids . . . waitin' to bust out an' have a change. Wonder how long he can hold us in, though. This crowd is awful bean-weary!"

Buffaloes! Buffaloes! Always the talk of buffaloes! There were two ways of hunting the animals: the running method and the approach method. To run a buffalo herd, the hunter followed at the rear and sides of the galloping animals, shooting his rifle from the saddle and risking the chance of attack from an infuriated bull or cow. The approach method was safer, the huntsman remaining concealed and firing at his game as the buffalo plodded its way to a wallowing hole or down some hard-beaten path to the river. Captain Morgan shook his head dubiously over the running method.

"Men, we're greenhorns, everyone of us! Most of us have families and we're on our way west to make new homes. We didn't come out here to hunt buffaloes. Our horses are not trained and most of us can't hit a barn door. You're takin' chances to try the runnin' method. Just be patient a few days after we reach the river. They say there are plenty of buffaloes 'round Plum Creek and they can be had with the approach method. If Bill Brewster were here to lead you, I'd have less to say. He knows the ropes. But Bill's away. Play safe! Play safe! The Indians don't want us mixin' in with their hunts, either . . . remember that!"

Out of respect for their captain, the men formed no running parties after reaching the Platte River. But the excitement of the chase still possessed them.

To relieve pent-up emotions, contests in shooting took place. One man bet his rooster against another man's grindstone that he would bring down the first buffalo. A wall-eyed mule was wagered against a stiff-legged cow, bags of flour offered against sides of bacon. The train became an arguing, hilarious group of men, hungry for excitement as well as a change in their diet. The finest prize of all came from Elisha Jefferson, who promised one of his small pigs to the person who killed a buffalo in one shot.

"And the critter's to be hit in the small bare spot jest under the shoulder at the edge of the heavy hair!" roared Elisha. "Jest one shot, mind you!"

Elisha Jefferson's pigs were not to be ignored. They were a fine litter and, with the exception of the one which had been lost on the night of the first big storm, they had lived and prospered, each one named and petted by Mrs. Jefferson.

"Lots of folks would like to own one of those pigs," Joel remarked upon hearing the news. "If you could get it as far as the fort, you could trade it in for a blanket or a gun. 'Course, get the pig to Oregon, start breedin', an' you'd have a penfull in no time. No, I wouldn't mind ownin' one of those pigs!"

Rivalry, boasting, and betting continued and still no buffaloes were seen! Men became restless, the women anxious and nervous. To the wives of the train, buffaloes had now assumed the proportions of elephants. Tales of their stampeding, mowing down everything before them, caused more than one woman to shudder and tremble.

Jason, listening to both sides, felt his own blood rise with the excitement. The choice parts of a cow or calf, the hump, the tongue, the tenderloin and the marrow bone were delicious eating. With the meat dried in strips, known as jerky, food could be preserved indefinitely for the journey ahead. And the hide! It could be used as a warm robe at night or a rug for the new home in Oregon! The two horns would always be cherished as souvenirs. On the farm in Illinois he had talked and dreamed with others of killing a buffalo. He had practiced with his father's old rifle, shooting at a chalked star on a board at a distance of one hundred yards and hitting the star three times out of four. And here he was now, in the land of the buffalo, and he could not go. Elizabeth Strong's wagon had but one driver, Jason Coit. There were no two ways of looking at the matter. If only Sammy were there to help!

Meanwhile, Aaron had not escaped the contagion which swept the encampment. Gathering his courage one morning at breakfast, he announced to his father and aunt that he would like to join a running party as soon as one formed.

"Why, I never heard anything so ridiculous!" gasped Aunt Liddy. "In the first place, you're too fat. In the second, you'd get in the way. In the third, you ain't old enough. It's a man's work. In the fourth place, I need some shelves in the wagon to hold all these kettles . . ."

"I don't want to hear another word," added the Captain with finality. "It's settled, Aaron. You're not going. As captain of the train, I may have to . . . and one hunter in a family is enough. Who said there was a party going anyway? I haven't heard about it. And I notice Jason Coit is using his head. He isn't talking about any wild-goose chase into the desert!"

"He would if he could," argued Aaron, "but he hasn't got

a horse. An' we've got two! An' Aunt Liddy," here Aaron set his coffee mug down with a bang, "I'm *not* fat! I've pulled in my belt three holes since we left home."

"You don't tell me! I hadn't noticed," replied Aunt Liddy.

With this insult added to injury, Aaron rose from his seat and glared belligerently at his elders. He then took his departure, muttering something which concerned babies, long dresses and rattles and, in passing, aimed swift kicks at the kettles which were strewn on the floor. However, an hour later he was put to work building a shelf to hold the family pots and pans. He was in the midst of his labors when the hunting fever reached the bursting point. A running party formed and, after assurance from its members that there would be no unnecessary killing and wanton waste, Captain Morgan consented to take the lead.

There were thirty horsemen in the party which left for the western hills on the fifth day while following the Platte River. There were calls of good luck from those remaining in camp and the hunters disappeared in a cloud of dust, the women resignedly returning to their duties in their wagons. Jason stifled a long sigh as he watched them out of sight and then resumed currying the oxen.

The morning hours dragged. After sharpening his knives on a neighbor's grindstone, airing his bed and blankets, Jason determined to splice a new trail rope for Blossom from some strips of bull hide. The rope completed, he went in search of the cow and found her nibbling half-heartedly at some coarse grass within the circle formed by the wagons. With concern Jason noticed for the first time that she looked poorly. Her hip bones seemed a trifle sharp and her dark eyes unusually large as she looked up at him.

BUFFALOES!

Why not take her, as well as the six oxen, with rope halters to the near-by island in the river? The grass there was said to be fresh and tender and the water between the mainland and island only knee-deep. He would take Asa's gun in case he saw some game and be back at the encampment by sundown. Surely no harm could come of a little outing . . . With extra trail rope at his waist, shouldering his loaded gun, and with whip in hand, Jason spoke to Sally Adams of his plan. Sally approved of the island grass for Blossom. Whatever benefited the cow benefited her baby and she was quick to see it. A little lonely, but determined to make the best of a long hot afternoon, Jason went his way.

From the sharp metallic sounds inside the Morgan wagon, it was evident that Aunt Liddy's kitchenware was not receiving the gentlest of treatment from Aaron. Also the muffled blows of the hammer came few and far between. Having heard Aaron's tale of woe, Jason decided not to interfere and turned the oxen and Blossom down one of the paths made by buffalo towards the water.

Remembering the many stories of quicksands told around camp, Jason tested the pebbly bottom of the river before crossing. There seemed to be no difficulty and the passage to the shore of the island was made safely. Tired and sore feet sank into the depths of luxuriant grass, a welcome change from the hot sand they had traveled. Jason threw himself down to rest when Blossom and the oxen finally stopped to graze. His loneliness was gone and for the first time he realized that he was very tired. A pale yellow butterfly lighted on a blue flower close by his head and he tried to watch as it balanced, with wings quivering . . . and then the steady pull of grass and munching sounds as the animals fed, the blackbirds crying overhead and the ripple of the Platte's shallow water became fainter . . . fainter. . . .

An hour slipped by. When Jason wakened, Blossom and the oxen were halfway down the island, moving nearer the cottonwood stumps. Satisfied they were safe, he dozed again and dreamed that he and Aaron had found the little Fields girls at last! Anna and Jessica were running towards them on the trail, their arms outstretched, their faces shining with eagerness; but somewhere in the distance could be heard the shrill, angry cries of the old squaw. . . .

With a start, Jason sat upright. The dream and the little girls were gone but the shrill cries continued . . . a wild, weird chorus which rose and fell, stopped, and began again. A wave of numbness swept over the boy as he struggled to his feet, and his hands were ice-cold as he clutched his rifle. Indians! Unmistakably the noise came from the west which was now ablaze with sunset. As he listened more closely, he was conscious of a second sound accompanying the cries . . . a deep, roaring undertone. What could it all mean?

Shielding his eyes against the blinding sun, Jason tried to look straight ahead. As far as he could see, nothing moved along the sides of the barren hills. And then a yellow cloud appeared, mounting upward like a vapor, just beyond the farthermost ridge. Was it smoke? Were the Pawnees burning grass to catch rabbits? But fire at that distance would not make the deep roaring sound which seemed to be growing louder. Buffaloes . . . could the Indians be running buffaloes, and was the yellow haze dust from the desert?

BUFFALOES!

The cloud rose higher. It partially screened the setting sun, but Jason could still distinguish the distant row of sanded hills some four miles away. Where were Captain Morgan and his men? Were they aware of what was happening? Some strange new danger lay beyond those hills. . . . Should he run to warn the encampment or should he stay with Blossom and the oxen? Before Jason could make his decision, an impossible thing seemed to take place. One of the farthermost hills began to turn black! It was as though a wave of dark liquid were poured down its sloping sides, spilling over the entire surface and rolling towards him . . . a dark wave of living bodies . . . buffaloes! Buffaloes in stampede! Driven by Pawnees, hundreds of buffaloes, a maddened mass of clattering horns and thundering hoofs, would soon be crossing the island where he now stood!

11

ONE SHOT!

Terrified, stunned at the sight of the advancing buffaloes, Jason stood still a moment, his feet helplessly locked together, his whole body numb. Then reason returned, bringing with it a reminder of his responsibility for the stock, foremost and habitually in his thoughts these past few weeks. The oxen must be saved from joining the herd. Had he not heard the tales at camp of oxen following buffaloes? And had not Elizabeth Strong entrusted her oxen into his safekeeping?

After a quick glance about him, he knew there was only one way of escape left to him now. He must run . . . run with all his might towards the tree stumps, willows and tall grass at the extreme northern end of the island, driving Blossom and the oxen before him, giving the buffaloes all space possible for their crossing. Even there, the stock might not be safe from being drawn into the outer edges of this mad stream, but there was no other choice. Before and behind him and to the south lay instant death. He must act and act now! The animals moving slowly about and

ONE SHOT!

enjoying their leisure were two hundred yards distant; the tree stumps and willows at the end of the island were a quarter of a mile away. He must run two hundred yards towards the north even before he could snap his whip and stir the sleepy oxen into action! If only his feet were not so heavy . . .

The tall grass laced with vines caught him at every step as he began to run. An old log tripped him and he fell full length, the breath knocked from his body. Once he sank to his knees in a muddy pool. Startled birds flew upward, screaming, and snakes slithered silently away almost beneath his very feet. But still he clung to his rifle and whip. How far away were the buffaloes now? There was no time to stop and look over his left shoulder. If the buffaloes stayed straight on their course, the encampment a mile below on the river might be spared. The oxen . . . he would have to lash them, beat them, in order to start them moving. Was there enough trail rope to hobble them when they reached the end of the island? How else could he prevent them from joining the stampede? Blossom, small and gentle, would be trampled down but the oxen, big and stolid, would keep their feet and gallop on out of sight. If only he were on the mainland now, where the ground was hard and packed down . . . And then a hideous new fear gripped him, slowing his feet for an instant. Had he gauged his distance correctly or should he have remained where he was? How could he be sure he was not running into the very heart of the stampede?

A quick glance to the west now showed only clouds of dust blotting the distant slopes. There were no buffaloes in sight, though the pounding of their hoofs was growing louder. Soon the black masses of bodies would be swarming down over the nearer slopes. There was nothing left, Jason decided, but to abide by his first decision: reach the oxen and drive them to the end of the island. Already they had stopped grazing and appeared to be watching him as he came lunging at them through the grass.

"Sun! Tom! G'wan! Gee! Haw!" How small and faint his own voice sounded as he gasped for breath . . . how feeble the crack of the whip!

The ground was firmer here and he was making better time. Blossom was the first to turn about and move forward in a slow trot, mooing plaintively, as if a little frightened. Ah, Ben and King had also turned. But Sun had begun to paw the earth excitedly, his head lowered. There was going to be trouble with Sun. Tom, Joe and Zebe stood like brown rocks, listening as if their ears had caught some strange and yet familiar noise in the distance. . . .

Now he had reached them. The long two hundred yards were finished. Mercilessly he struck with the whip, putting all his strength into his arms. Would they never move? Anything to save them, to turn them about! The lash snapped and cracked like gunfire as it cut the air. Jason spared them nothing. Unaccustomed to such treatment, Joe reared, bellowed and swung sideways. Tom and Zebe cringed, hesitated, but Sun remained adamant, his head still lowered, bellowing. All were manageable but Sun. Again and again Jason lashed out at Sun, cruelly, steadily. His arms were without feeling, and he was drenched with sweat when Sun finally turned, unable to face the beating which descended upon him.

"G'wan! G'wan! Get over there! Gee! Sun! Gee!"

ONE SHOT!

They were all moving now, Sun reluctantly with sides heaving and eyes rolling. With the whip's length around Sun's neck, Jason pulled the oxen even faster as he shouted, his voice thick and hoarse. Blossom was now ahead in the tall grass and would soon be among the tree stumps. A second glance to the west showed clouds of dust much nearer, mounting higher, and in direct line with the island. The herd had not changed its course, he had not miscalculated his distances, and Jason gave a great trembling sigh of relief. If he and the oxen hurried now, they still might escape the full brunt of the charge. It was their only chance. . . .

"G'wan! G'wan!"

The sharp sting of the lash was doing its work at last! The foremost oxen were breaking into a trot. Welts were rising on Sun's broad back and despite his frenzied haste Jason found himself gazing at them curiously. He had never beaten an animal before. But he knew he must continue to beat this poor ox which had been the first to feel some primitive urge within, whose ears had recognized, in the ever loudening roar, calls of his distant kind. Hobbled, Sun would not be able to run far. If possible, Jason decided, he would hobble all of the oxen in pairs, lashing one animal's left foreleg to the second animal's right. Perhaps their neck-ropes might be tied in a center knot . . . then let them pull and strain as they chose!

Meanwhile, would there be any strength left in his arms when he reached his goal? His wet homespun trousers were caked with mud and seemed intolerably heavy. The air was filled with confused sounds, the shrill voices of the Indians, the bellows of the buffaloes, and even the sharp clatter of

their horns. They could not be far away. Just a little farther
to the tree stumps . . . Jason began to unwind the long
trail rope from his waist with his left hand as he grasped
his rifle and whip in his right. With his knife, he would
slash the trail rope in thirds. If only he could hobble the
oxen before the first buffalo crossed the island!

Forced to the edge of the shore among the thick willows,
the oxen came to a stop. Still subservient to the whip, they
followed Jason's commands dully. His fingers, however,
were slippery with mud and perspiration and he fumbled
at the knots. Sun and Ben, Joe and Zebe, Tom and King.
Sun shook as though he had the ague and Joe bellowed
on a high strange note. All six neck ropes were bound together, reinforced by the whip's lash; at last the six oxen
stood hobbled and tied in one body behind a screen of
willows. Blossom, mooing and trembling, was fastened to a
tree stump.

"There, there, Blossom."

Satisfied he could do no more, Jason turned to look back.
Dust billowed high behind the first row of hills. There had
been no time to spare! In another moment the first of the
buffaloes would come over the slope and through the water
trails he had passed only a few short hours before. Nothing
would stop those pounding feet! Exhausted, still gasping
for breath, Jason crouched behind a tall clump of grass, the
rifle in his hands. Behind him the oxen crashed among the
willows, pulling in different directions, but his knots still
held. In a little while, he would know. . . . If the flow of
buffaloes widened, it would be the end.

Waiting was torture. If he did not reach Oregon, how
would they let his mother know? Sammy would hear the

ONE SHOT!

news at Fort Laramie, provided he had continued on to the west. And it would be Sammy who would build the new home and care for their mother and Tacy. Sammy, his mother and little Tacy, how close they seemed to him in that moment, despite the great distances between! And how very dear . . . God bless them. Ah, this was no way to die. . . .

The first of the huge black beasts came pouring through the water trails that their own hoofs had made, as if following their old routes as a matter of habit. And then, like the first overflow Jason had witnessed in the distance, the animals flooded the hills, half-running, half-tumbling down the sandy slopes, their great shaggy heads and massive humped backs seeming to overbalance the rest of their bodies, their own weight propelling them forward. Water splashed . . . they had reached the Platte! An instant later, the foremost buffalo plunged over the very spot where Jason had rested in the grass.

On they came, a strange wild horde of another world with horns knocking and clashing, their bellows deep cries of pain and anger. The flow widened . . . A cow and a calf, their tongues hanging, galloped along the edge of the maelstrom only fifty yards away. Last year's fur still clung to the mother cow like tattered rags. Other buffaloes followed. An enormous bull with broken horns passed by, lumbering like a machine, his tongue also hanging, and cows . . . cows with calves struggling to keep pace. The Indians were directly behind, their yells growing louder. The main body of the herd was passing in a straight line, which meant that the encampment was safe. Jason gave a long sigh of relief. Aunt Liddy, Aaron, Sally Adams and her baby, the Fieldses . . . they were now all part of his life. What a mad, unbelievable scene it was, with the dust sifting down over the island, the grass flattened like a floor beneath the trampling hoofs! How much longer could it last?

. . . Fewer buffaloes now seemed to be passing. Perhaps the main body of the herd had crossed. If so, he and the cattle were safe . . . safe by the barest chance! Filled with new hope, Jason shielded his eyes from the increasing dust and looked back at the stock. Blossom stood like a statue, tied to her tree. Though the oxen still struggled among the willows, they were not yet loose. Dust made it difficult for him to see. . . . However, he suddenly realized that this same dust would serve as a protective covering, a safe-guard from the Indians. The keenest redskin would have difficulty in discovering either himself or the animals in this yellow fog.

Fear, which had tightened every nerve and muscle in Jason's body, gradually left him. He was safe . . . the oxen and Blossom were safe. To his own surprise, he found himself coolly measuring the distance from where he crouched to the nearest buffalo. If a buffalo should come as close to him again as fifty yards, would he shoot? The tall tufts of grass would act as a screen to the fallen body, and in the noise his shot might not be heard. Would he take the risk? This was what the men at the encampment had talked about, dreamed about, and almost fought about, the past seven days. Buffaloes! Could he remain behind a clump of grass with rifle in hand and merely watch? There was need of meat and hide, necessities for the long journey ahead. If only he could bring down one buffalo!

ONE SHOT!

But he must not fool himself with a sense of false safety. The danger now did not come from the buffaloes but from the Indians, jealous of their hunt, resentful of the white man's intrusion. Dare he risk one shot?

"One shot on the small bare spot just under the shoulder at the edge of the heavy hair . . . one shot, mind you!" He could still hear Elisha Jefferson's challenging voice. That was the place to hit, the small bare spot. One shot was all he would allow himself. Hidden by the tall grass, Jason rose to one knee, the rifle cocked and ready. The buffaloes were thinning and the Indians coming closer. If he were to fire, he must fire soon. Three dark bodies lumbered by in the dust. He must remember to aim a little ahead of the moving creature . . . Cows were the best eating, he reminded himself, and the best hides. If only he could see more clearly through the blinding dust . . . Another group was coming, out-shouldered to one side by the main current. They were pounding closer, closer . . . a large bull and three cows. He would take the nearest cow. "The small bare spot just under the shoulder" . . . He could not see the spot, he would have to guess. . . .

There was a sharp dry crack. The rifle kicked against his shoulder and blue-white smoke spurted from the barrel. His finger had squeezed the trigger automatically, as though the hand belonged to someone else. Leaning forward through the grass, he watched, tense, scarcely breathing, still clutching his gun. The cow had not stopped running! But she was turning, wheeling to the left into the high grass, as if off balance, her shaggy head low. Had he hit her? Now she had stopped. More buffaloes raced by and she remained there, motionless. Then slowly, irrevocably, her forelegs folded and she tipped heavily forward. There was a convulsive shudder and, a moment later, her big body turned over on its side.

For a little while Jason lay with his head lowered in his arms. He was limp from exhaustion, spent with excitement. He had killed his first buffalo! With his returning strength there came a fierce exultant urge to run forward and examine his prize, but caution made him keep his head down. The slightest movement might catch the attention of a passing Pawnee and there was no telling how far the sound of his shot had carried. Unexpectedly he coughed, choked, then buried his head still deeper in his arms. Oh, for a breath of clear cold air!

A quicker beat of hoofs, a distant neigh, told him the Pawnees were passing. They were not yelling but rode swiftly, silently. Lifting his head, Jason could just see their

ONE SHOT!

outlines, the small mustangs running with tense riders bent forward. The air was clearing. But he must wait . . . wait until he was sure that all had crossed the water on the other side of the island and gained the northern bank of the Platte.

The yellow dust had partially settled before Jason felt it safe to move. Even then he did not stand, but crawled on his stomach through the grass. Upon reaching the dark bulky carcass in the grass, he rose to his feet and stood staring down. This, then, was a buffalo! There was something repulsive about this strange heavy beast, its huge head, short horns and coarse tangled mane caked with mud from standing in some filthy wallow hole. The eyes were small and already glazed, the long tongue bloody. Kneeling, Jason felt of its hide, its flanks, and marveled at the solid hump of flesh upon the creature's back. But where had the bullet struck? At last his fingers found the bare spot of

skin just beneath the shoulder. There was no mark of any bullet and it was clear of blood. The discovery was a keen disappointment, but he really knew he had no cause to complain. He had come through a harrowing experience and with a buffalo to boot. Now rose the problem of skinning the creature. . . .

The sound of galloping feet finally roused Jason. Startled, he looked up to see a group of horsemen riding swiftly towards him and, for a moment, he stood motionless in sudden fear. Had the Indians returned? But these horses were larger than the little mustangs which the Pawnees rode. These were white men's horses and the rider who led the way was none other than Captain Morgan!

"Jason!" called the captain.

"Yes, sir. I'm over here!"

How good it was to see these hardy, sun-burned, dirt-streaked men and to hear Mark Morgan's voice! Jason ran forward and then stood still in surprise at his own unsteadiness. His knees were trembling and there was a lump in his throat.

"You all right, Jason?" Mark Morgan had slipped from his saddle and had come towards him, his gray eyes anxious in his perspiring face. "Sally Adams said you were over here. We came as fast as we could. Yes, everyone at the camp is safe," he added, seeming to read the question in Jason's eyes. "Of course they were scared. Some of the buffaloes came pretty close."

A few of the other men had dismounted . . . Elisha Jefferson, Seth and Joel Adams.

"Glad you're safe, boy," called out Seth. "Did you save your cattle?"

ONE SHOT!

"They're over there," replied Jason, pointing in the direction of the willows. The words came haltingly and it seemed difficult to speak. At that particular moment the tug-of-war in the willows had reached its crucial point. With loud bellows the whole group of oxen came crashing into the open, pulled by Sun and Ben, whose straining hindquarters and hobbled legs presented a ludicrous sight to the staring men.

"Why, he's got 'em all snarled up in a bunch!" and Elisha Jefferson gave a loud guffaw. "Some of you younger men go over before they get to hurtin' each other."

"Good work, son," and Captain Morgan's warm tone of praise sent a glow through Jason. "You used your head . . . and hands, too. How near did the buffaloes come to you? We saw them cross the island from the hills beyond the camp."

" 'Bout fifty yards."

"Prutty nigh," growled Elisha Jefferson, mopping his forehead with his sleeve.

"Too nigh for real comfort." Seth grinned. "Though I kinder wish I'd been here. The Injuns didn't see you?" he asked.

"I hid in the grass." Jason motioned behind him.

"Why, what's that?" The captain's searching eyes were now looking over Jason's shoulder. He had spied the dark form of the buffalo almost concealed by the high rank grass.

However, Joel had also seen it at the same time and was the first to reach it, shouting as he ran in long strides, "It's a buffalo, Cap'n, the kid's got a buffalo!"

"Well, I'll be slam-buzzled!" and Seth followed his

brother, after colliding with Cal Collins, who stood in his way. By this time all the men had dismounted and were hurrying to the spot, forming a circle about the buffalo as they looked over one another's shoulders.

"It's a cow, an' a fine one," announced Joel excitedly as he bent over the body. "He's a great one, that kid, never lettin' on it was here!"

"How many shots?" asked Cal Collins anxiously of Jason, standing on the edge of the crowd.

"One."

"One? Where? Where'd you hit her, boy? Where'd you hit her?" called out Elisha Jefferson, whose keen ears had heard the question.

"I don't know. I looked, but . . ."

"He doesn't know!" roared Elisha. "Look 'er over, boys. Find the hole!"

"Jason," called Captain Morgan from the other side of the circle, "didn't the Indians hear your shot? How did you manage?"

"There was a lot of noise . . . I didn't shoot till the cow came close to the grass, so she'd be hid." Jason's words were coming more easily to him now. He was happy in the other's excitement. It was a fine cow and everyone seemed to be glad he had shot it . . . everyone excepting Cal Collins. Cal at that moment was running about like a curious chipmunk to get different views of the body. Why, all the men were acting as though they had never seen a buffalo before. Kit, left alone, now came and stood beside the boy, nosing his arm. Dear old Kit! And then Jason heard Elisha shout, "Turn the critter over, boys, turn 'er over! If he hit the bare spot, he wins the pig!"

ONE SHOT!

The pig! So far no one had won the pig! Could this be the first buffalo down? Was this why Cal Collins had been so anxious, so curious? How stupid he was not to realize the buffalo had two bare spots, one on either side. The cow had wheeled just before she fell. Of course the bullet would have entered her other side! And now Jason left Kit and tried to squeeze himself into the crowded circle in order to see. There was a possibility, the faintest possibility . . .

"I don't s'pose I'll get any peace from Aaron now," the captain was groaning as he helped turn the carcass over. But it was Captain Morgan who leaned forward to search for the bullet hole. It was his hand which parted the fur at the shoulder and was then held up for all to see . . . with blood upon the fingers.

"The boy's won, men," announced the captain quietly. "It's the first buffalo down and he won fair and proper. He's beaten the whole lot of us. Jason, where are you? That cow must have turned after you fired . . ."

"I'm here, sir. She did turn. I sort of forgot she had two sides . . ." Jason's voice was tremulous with excitement. His was the only buffalo shot that day! All the terror and hardship he had suffered that afternoon were swept away by an almost overwhelming joy. All eyes were upon him, kindly, smiling eyes which understood. Not a man but liked this quiet, dark-haired boy and there was real affection in their bronzed weathered faces. Even Cal Collins smiled.

"Well, Jeff, you've lost your pig!" called someone.

"That's right," agreed Elisha heartily, "an' I'm proud to give it to 'im. Any boy that can take care of his stock the way he done an' bring down the first buffalo too can have the pick of my litter. I had a boy like you once, son. He'd a-done the same. . . ."

"Want to sell your prize, Jason?" asked Joel, half seriously. "You know, I wanted to win that pig. Or are you plannin' to trade it at the fort?"

"I'm keepin' it. I want it to start my farm."

"Now there's the true homesteadin' spirit for you," shouted Elisha Jefferson, greatly pleased. "Blamed if I don't like to see it in the young 'uns. If I could spare 'em, I'd give you the whole litter, boy. But I guess the most we can do for you now is to skin this beast and lug the meat back to camp. It's almost dark now. You willin' we should help, boy?" Already Elisha Jefferson had drawn a knife from his belt.

"Yes, sir. I'll share the meat . . . only I'd like to keep the hide an' horns. I'll help, soon's I see to Blossom and the oxen."

"Just a minute, Jason, before you go." A hand on Jason's shoulder detained him and he turned to look up into Captain Morgan's face. "There's something I've been wanting to say . . ." and there was a twinkle in the captain's gray eyes as he looked at the men about him. "You remember, way back, maybe, there was a little dispute over the hunting methods . . ."

Seth, anticipating what the captain was about to say, began to laugh.

"And I hope," continued the captain, smiling broadly himself, "that you won't take it amiss if I speak my mind right now. Having run all day long over the prairie like a pack of fools and come home empty-handed, I want to know, just for my own personal satisfaction, if anyone here

ONE SHOT!

says the approach method isn't good enough. This boy used it . . ."

There was a slight pause. Then an audible chuckle came from the group as thirty dust-stained faces smiled their acknowledgment.

"You win, Cap'n," called someone at the back of the crowd, "you an' the boy."

One big campfire boiled a huge kettle of rice and roasted the buffalo meat at the rear of Captain Morgan's wagon that night. What a gala time it was for the meat-hungry emigrants! Each person carried his own plate, cup, knife, fork and spoon to the gathering.

Voices rose higher and louder as women and men alike attempted to describe their impressions of the buffalo stampede. For the first time it was possible to count the Collins children, twelve of them, marshalled in a row by their mother, with lively anticipation written on their young, hawklike faces.

"Twelve of 'em," counted Jason, half whispering to Aaron, who followed him about like a worshiping shadow, one of his thumbs fatly bandaged with strips of calico. "I thought there might be more."

"Don't forget the baby," Aunt Liddy grimly reminded him, overhearing. "It's been left in the wagon. Thirteen in all! Well, Cal has an eye to business . . . he'll have plenty of help to work his land. . . . Looks to me, though, as if the fourth one from the end might be bustin' out with measles," she added suspiciously. "Now, wouldn't that be nice . . . to have the whole lot of us come down with measles!"

But even the possibility of this calamity failed to dampen the joy of all present. An expectant audience in faded calico and rough homespun watched the cooking with careful eyes. The sound of the fat sizzling on the meat, as it turned fragrantly on iron spits, was a welcome one to all ears, young and old. Despite his florid face, the measles-suspect in the Collins' row appeared to be the liveliest and the hungriest of the whole lot. Upon closer scrutiny, Aunt Liddy decided he was the victim of hives and the few who had overheard her earlier comments felt a certain relief.

The meat browned, dripped and sizzled into pans placed below to catch the fat. The first slices and the choicest portions were cut for Mary Fields, still invalided in her wagon, and Ezra bore them to her on a hot plate with rice and gravy. At last all were about to taste of buffalo meat! Before it was served, however, a small white pig was presented to Jason in the midst of much clapping of hands and cheering.

"I've named him Porky," Mrs. Jefferson told him confidentially, after the noise subsided. "You see, it's lonesome with just Elisha an' myself, an' I've taken to pettin' the pigs. Porky's right smart . . . sort of cheerful, an' has nice habits. 'T ain't like he'd ever lived in a pen. Our pigs are like dogs. I declare, I never thought I could get so fond of the little critters."

"I'll take good care of him," promised Jason, his dark eyes shining with pleasure as he held the small squirming animal in his arms. "There's a box in my wagon where he can sleep nights."

"That's fine." Mrs. Jefferson regarded him intently. "You know . . ." but she never finished her sentence. From out of the darkness into the firelight ambled a small gold-colored mustang bearing a tall slender figure dressed in buckskin. The horse stopped of its own accord and there was silence as all turned to regard the newcomer in surprise.

"Bill! Bill Brewster . . . it's you!" and Captain Morgan, the first to recognize the old scout, hurried forward. "Well, if I'm not glad to see you! Get down. We're just starting to eat!"

"Here I be!" announced the old scout, swinging a leg over the mustang's back and standing before them. "An' I'm glad to get here. I could smell that meat 'way down the river. But before I set down, whar's Ezra Fields?" and Bill Brewster peered about him among the shadows.

"He's in his wagon. Aaron, run and call him."

"An' you, boy," added the newcomer, his bright eyes catching sight of Jason, "I've got news for you, too."

"You've seen Sammy? My brother, Sammy Coit?" and Jason, still holding the small pig in his arms, stood before Bill Brewster, eager, tense.

"Well, no, boy, I ain't 'zactly seen him but I found signs of someone 'bout his size. Ever see cloth like this before?" and Bill held out to Jason a ragged piece of brown homespun. "It's woven finer than most."

"Yes, yes, it's stuff my mother weaves!" Jason examined the small piece nearer the fire for a better light. "She made all of our britches out of this cloth. See, it's just the same," and he held it with one hand against the knee of his own trousers.

"Where did you find it? Where is Sammy?"

"Jest a minute, son, an' I'll be tellin' the whole tale.

Here comes Ezra, an' I reckon his wife is with him . . ."

There was a hush as the crowd gave way and Jason knew he would never forget the sight of Ezra and Mary Fields as they came hurrying forward into the light. In the crook of one arm the tall man carried the new baby, Bluette, while his wife, frail and uncertain, clung to his other arm. Sorrow and suffering had left their marks on both faces, but now new hope shone in their eyes. Gathering strength at the sight of the old scout, the woman ran forward, her hands outstretched, her shawl flowing behind her.

"You have news? My little girls . . ."

"Good news, Ma'am." A flash of pity crossed Bill Brewster's face and he put his arm about her. "They're alive an' well, both of 'em, Ma'am. I've come 'way crost the river to tell you, so you won't turn back. You must go forward, Ma'am, you an' yer husband."

"Go forward?" repeated Ezra Fields. "You mean go on to the fort? An' they're well an' safe? How do you know?"

"If I can read signs," answered Bill, ". . . an' I've spent most of my life doin' jest that . . . the ol' squaw an' the two young 'uns are followin' the trail on t'other side of the Platte. An' I'm thinkin' Henri Jules an' this boy's brother are with 'em. They're travelin' like one party, though how they come together is more'n I can figger out. Don't cry, Ma'am."

Mary Fields was sobbing openly while tears streamed down Ezra's cheeks.

"You're sure? You're sure?" Ezra questioned as though afraid to believe.

"Sartin as the sun rises in the east," replied the old

ONE SHOT!

scout. "The leetle one . . . does she toe in a bit . . . jest a bit?"

"Yes, yes!" came from both parents.

"She's a lively piece an' the older girl keeps clos't by. They're ridin' a small hoss. The boy fetches water an' wood. The signs were four days ol' in the camp. We oughter reach Fort Laramie the same time they do, if we hurry."

"What makes you so sure of their continuing to the fort, Bill?" asked Mark Morgan.

"I ain't sure, I'm guessin'. But chances be the ol' woman is tryin' to get back to her people. She's a Crow an' will prob'ly go as fur as the Red Buttes. Remember, I'm guessin'. Also I'm guessin' when I say thar might be some dragoons at Fort Laramie. If so, they'd help us hunt. Folks is searchin' fer Henri Jules an' Henri'll take mountain trails that only trappers like hisself know of. . . . He'll be like a flea on a coyote's back in them woods. But we can try to run 'im out. Can't do no more'n try. . . . A few extra miles a day an' I'm thinkin' we'll strike the fort 'bout the same time."

"Are you all willing to add the extra miles a day?" asked Mark Morgan of the listening people.

"Yes, of course," came from every throat.

"Anyone not willin' to hustle a bit can stay behind," tersely announced Aunt Liddy as she led Mary Fields to a seat by the fire.

"It's Fort Laramie or bust!" called someone and loud cheers followed.

"An' while I'm speakin' to you, I might as well say the whole of it," continued Bill Brewster. "White folks ain't treatin' the Injuns square these days. . . . Now, trade

KEEP THE WAGONS MOVING!

fair's you can. Some folks ahead have slaughtered a heap of buffaloes an' left 'em rottin' on the ground. Them buffaloes are food an' clothes to the Injun. So play fair as you go along. Don't kill fer fun. I've promised to get you all safe through this here country, but I ain't toleratin' things like that. You'll be hearin' more of it later, but I thought I'd tell you now," and the old scout sat down abruptly.

"Thanks, Bill," replied Captain Morgan, "for being on the job. I don't think you'll have cause for any complaints with this train. As far as I know, every man and woman has treated the Indians well. We've shared our food," and for the eighth of a second the captain's gray eyes met those of his sister's, who unblushingly returned his gaze and began to serve large portions of rice on each plate, "and we'll tolerate no trickery. All we ask is safety while we go through this land to the west. All right, it's time to eat, folks!"

12

LIFE WITH A TRAPPER AND A SQUAW

Unfortunately for Sammy, Ol' Squaw, who was expert with a needle, seemed to take no interest in his welfare. Sammy was Henri's property, the black eyes seemed to say, and all her affections were wrapped up in the two little girls stolen from the palefaces. But she was not unkind and now and then gave a grunt of approval when Sammy helped her with some arduous task.

Meanwhile Henri, indolent and amused by his small captive's plight, always showed considerable interest in the torn trousers. Rarely did he miss an opportunity to remind Sammy that as soon as possible he intended to kill a fine young buffalo calf, whose hide, peeled from the hind legs, would furnish excellent trousers with no extra tailoring required. Moreover, Henri advised, with a mighty roar of pleasure and sweeping descriptive gestures, it might be well to let the tail remain where it grew, attached to the hide. Not only would it serve as an excellent trimming for the trousers, but it might bring good luck to its wearer.

"You tend to your own clothes," Sammy would shout back at him, "an' I'll tend to mine. When I get to the fort, I'll buy my own pants an' they won't be the hind legs off'n a jackass, either!"

"But de fort . . . we do not go near de fort, Lil' Firebran'," Henri told him almost affectionately. "Eet is not safe for Henri at de fort. We go to de woods in de north some other ways. De dragoons hunt for Henri, for you, an' your leetle squaws."

"They ain't my little squaws!" Sammy shouted so loudly and glared so ferociously that the two little girls, who were listening, cowered and drew close together.

"Ho! Ho!" roared Henri, delighted to have found something new with which to fret his prisoner. He sobered just in time to escape a stone thrown at him by the new owner of "the leetle squaws." Jessica and Anna continued to gaze large-eyed and frightened at this new show of courage on Sammy's part and Ol' Squaw, smoking her pipe as usual beneath her big umbrella, pretended neither to see nor hear.

The news that Henri did not intend to stop at Fort Laramie was a bitter disappointment to Sammy and Jessica. Also, Henri's admission that the dragoons were searching for him confirmed their suspicions of Henri as an outlaw and that something of great value must be hidden in the saddlebags. Only a few days prior, Jessica had moved the bags in order to sit closer to the fire and had received a thunderous rebuke from the French trapper.

"Nevaire," he roared at her, "must you touch dem bags. Nevaire!"

Her curiosity aroused, Jessica had eyed the saddlebags

with awe. Later that night she questioned Sammy closely as to what he knew.

"I don't know nothin'," Sammy replied in a hoarse angry whisper, "an' I wish you'd let me alone."

"But didn't you see *anything*, Sammy?" persisted Jessica. "You said once you met Henri at night and he hid somethin' in the bags when he heard you comin'. What color was it? How big was it? Was it jewelry? Was it gold?"

"Might be . . . I dunno. I never saw any gold. There was a bundle of some kind. Now stop yer jawin' an' let me sleep."

"Well, if Henri isn't going to the fort, we've just got to run away soon," Jessica announced with decision.

"I'm watchin' an' waitin'. It ain't time yet. I need a knife, a gun, a horse, food an' a blanket," and Sammy pulled shiveringly at the one corner of the blanket which covered him. "We can't start out on nothin'."

Each and every night was now proving to be a nightmare for Samuel Coit. With a single buffalo hide between them and the cold earth, the three children were obliged to share one blanket and a chilly night's sleep amounted to little less than a tug-of-war between Jessica and Sammy. To the great surprise of all, however, one noon Henri dug deep into his pack and with an important air held up a heavy wool blanket for them to admire. Sammy stared unbelievingly. Even Ol' Squaw showed her amazement and grunted with appreciation at its rich red color.

"*Voilà!* Is eet not mag-neef-i-cent?" Henri asked, holding the blanket high so all could see. "My leetle squaw will dance for joy an' cook me man-ee tings for this. *Voilà!* I must keep eet safe," he added quickly, as he noted Sammy's eager eyes and clutching hands. And then the blanket was folded and carefully returned to the pack.

But Henri had not reckoned with Ol' Squaw, who apparently believed that anything good enough for the young was good enough for the old. . . . While the big trapper and Sammy were away gathering buffalo chips as fuel for the evening meal, Ol' Squaw deliberately unfastened Henri's pack, spread the new blanket on the sand and with her knife proceeded to hack and slice the wool into strange ragged pieces. She was butchering the last quarter when Henri, accompanied by Sammy carrying the sack of chips, returned. The trapper's rage was nothing short of an explosion.

"Sacré bleu! Sacré bleu!" he managed to shout at last, after he had hopped up and down in silent frenzy, his eyes bulging and face purple. Then followed a stream of queer language poured upon the head of Ol' Squaw, who did not even stop to look up from her work while Sammy, miserable with disappointment, stood and gazed at the red havoc on the sand. All that day he had schemed and dreamed of possessing the blanket and here it was, strewn on the ground in crimson tatters. Henri, at last spent with his ravings and sensing Sammy's disappointment, turned to him for some sign of consolation.

"Eeet is de *diable!*" he cried with actual tears in his eyes. "De *diable!*"

Sammy, on the verge of tears himself, turned away and then noticed that a piece of red wool had caught on his boot and wound itself enticingly about his ankle. He stooped and freed his foot. Then, with a quick movement of his hand, he thrust the wool under his shirt. No one had noticed; and now, safe and warm against his stomach, was the most wonderful patch in the world for his torn and sagging trousers.

Curiously enough, no matter how much Ol' Squaw infuriated him, and although they argued long and vehemently together at times, Henri never lifted his hand to punish the old woman. She demanded and received a certain respect from the trapper, who explained to Sammy in mixed and devious words that he was Ol' Squaw's son-in-law and a son-in-law among the Crows never ill-treated his mother-in-law. So this was why Henri tolerated the old woman's presence! However, the loss of the blanket was a bitter blow to Henri, who ate no supper that night and brooded and sulked like an overgrown child.

During the following evening, both Henri and Sammy learned exactly why the blanket had been stolen and hacked into queer shapes. Peering nearsightedly at her stitches, with her small shrunken frame bent low, Ol' Squaw commenced sewing with all her might and main. One by one, the odd pieces were assembled together and gradually assumed the shapes of two sleeveless jackets and two very short skirts. With open mouths Henri and Sammy stared while the two little girls had their first fitting, Henri as usual exclaiming his *"Sacré bleu!"* between growls and groans. So the two little squaws were to have warm clothes while his own squaw went without. . . . Why, the two little squaws were not worth their weight in salt! *Sacré bleu!* If he had had Indian blood in him, he would have scalped them both in his fury and soused Ol' Squaw in the river until she ceased for once to smell of skunk's oil. . . .

Later Sammy, watching from beneath the battered brim

of his hat, sensed that Ol' Squaw was disturbed. Something had gone wrong with her sewing. A sleeve to one of the jackets appeared to be missing, and although she turned her own pack inside out, disclosing many treasures salvaged from the trail and hitherto hidden from Henri's eyes, there was no sign of the needed sleeve. Over and over she examined her treasures: the frame of a hoop skirt, an ostrich plume, bits of lace, silver-rimmed spectacles. . . . Where was the missing sleeve? The search was fruitless and Henri made no effort to conceal his pleasure at this turn of events. And because Ol' Squaw glanced inquiringly his way several times, Sammy moved away from the fire. As yet he had had no opportunity to install the red patch, and there was a perceptible bulge beneath his shirt as if he had eaten a hearty supper. Had Ol' Squaw mended the tear for him, there would have been no need of stealing a sleeve. Meanwhile, let the old woman hunt. . . .

The two girls appeared in their new clothes on the first cold evening, one sleeve of Anna's jacket made of brown elkskin. They were grotesque little suits and Anna cried at first because she did not like the feel of wool against her skin. The skirts came only halfway to the girls' knees and, with their brightly flaming hair, the sisters reminded Sammy of two misshapen red birds hopping about on skinny legs, one with a withered wing of brown. He would have liked to give way to his feelings by saying so, but suddenly remembered the red wool resting against his stomach. Any reference now to the missing sleeve would be foolhardy.

Up to this point, Henri had not paid much attention to Jessica and Anna except to call them French names beneath his breath. He tolerated them in much the same manner Ol' Squaw tolerated Sammy. But this barrier gave way on the evening the two girls appeared in their red suits and raised shrill piping voices, accompanying Sammy in song as he blew upon his jew's-harp.

> *"As I was goin' down the road,*
> *A tired team an' a heavy load,"*

                              they sang in perfect unison.

Henri stared and put down his pipe. The little squaws could sing! Now there would be more music, more cheer.

> *"I cracked my whip an' the leader sprung*
> *An' says day-day to the wagon tongue,"*

                              they sang mechanically.

The song finished, Henri whacked his knee, stood on his feet and burst into a roar of approval.

"Eet is mag-neef-i-cent!" he bellowed, looking down at the red-haired songsters with marked admiration. The little girls beamed. For the first time the big French trapper actually took notice of them; he even forgave them for having suits made of his blanket . . . yes, he was smiling! From then on, Jessica and Anna were given the nightly task of singing and they did not object. Somehow, the familiar strains brought home a little closer. Sometimes they sang with tears on their cheeks, Anna crying because Jessica cried.

Following a footpath inland along the Platte River was not entirely monotonous for the three children. Behind rolling hills of sand there were many interests. Besides coarse grass, nettles, ice-plant and yellow-flowered cactuses, there were occasional meadows starred with white poppies and sunflowers. Prairie dogs, strange little brown creatures slightly larger than squirrels, with heads resembling bull-dogs, sat in the doorways of their holes and barked shrilly. And there were antelope, who gazed at them from a distance with shy, friendly eyes, leaping swiftly away when frightened, carrying their tails like white powder puffs behind them. Each day brought forth some new delightful discovery in the strange world about them.

Although buffaloes passed within gunfire, Henri resisted the temptation to shoot, for fear of attracting emigrants on the trail, and contented himself with snaring rabbits instead. There was always plenty to eat, for both Henri and Ol' Squaw were supplied with berry pemmican—pulverized buffalo meat sweetened with wild cherries. When it was not possible for Henri to locate a water hole, prairie peas were gathered, crushed and eaten to quench thirst.

Of the three small captives, Anna bloomed the most of all, Ol' Squaw humoring her in every way and allowing Whitey, the pony, to become her special pet. Already the younger girl was repeating Indian words. She grunted instead of saying "yes," practiced with the bow and arrow and spent hours of play with a whirling toy made from an ox's toe bone painted red and attached to two sinews. The bond between the old woman and herself grew daily and the only tie to past conventions was the combing of her hair, which Ol' Squaw religiously performed. But the little girl was never washed. Stagnant water in the pools lay white-rimmed with burning alkali and the river was too far away. Bribed by a few pieces of horehound from Jessica's pocket,

Anna repeated her prayers at night but ceased altogether when there was no more candy.

"Anna begins to look like an Indian already," moaned Jessica to Sammy. "She doesn't ask for Mama and Papa any more. When I speak of them she just half listens, grunts and then runs off to pet Whitey or pick peas with that ol' woman. Yesterday she wore feathers in her hair. She always did toe in a little and now she's toeing a lot with both feet, copying Ol' Squaw. Tomorrow Ol' Squaw's going to sew elks' teeth on her jacket so she'll look like the rest of the Indian children. And she's dirty, awful dirty, and she doesn't seem to mind it at all!"

Neither had the lack of water for bathing purposes proved any special hardship for Sammy. He was conscious of acquiring a brown coat on his skin and comfortably laid it to sun-tanning. The use of the tin basin, yellow soap and the pump in his mother's kitchen, back in Illinois, was a routine he could easily forego without a qualm of homesickness. But the itching caused by insects known as "graybacks," which thrived on human flesh and lived in the seams of clothing, was the children's greatest discomfort. Only Ol' Squaw seemed to escape their torture. Even insects took exception to her favorite remedy—skunk's oil.

It was when little Anna burst into tears, vexed by frequent bites, that Ol' Squaw went into action. The little girls were disrobed in the small tepee and their clothing placed upon a large patch of earth six inches high and alive with ants scurrying to and fro. In no time at all the ants swarmed over the clothing and grappled and feasted upon the graybacks, leaving the clothing free of them. A short distance away, behind a rock, Sammy went through the same mode of purification. Before making his final appearance, however, he took time to insert the new patch into the seat of his trousers, darkening its crimson hue by dipping it into a muddy rain pool. And with great satisfaction he counted his money, nine dollars, and returned it to his secret inner pocket.

Henri was now intent upon crossing the Platte River. A safe sailing craft of some kind was necessary, as the flat winding river seethed with deep and unexpected currents and there was always danger of sinking sand. Returning one morning from a night of reconnoitering, Henri announced that he had found a mag-neef-i-cent boat and the crossing would be made that very evening. Because Sammy made no objections and accepted the news quietly, Jessica burst into tears of anger and disappointment.

"When we cross the river, we'll be leaving the wagons," she sobbed. "We'll be going farther and farther away from our folks on this side. There won't be any wagons on the other side. We ought to run away tonight. It's our only chance. I think you're afraid to run away, Sammy Coit!"

The words stung and left their mark. A flush mounted slowly from Sammy's neck into the roots of his yellow hair.

"I ain't afraid," he barked. "I ain't scared of nothin', an' you know it. We're goin' towards the fort an' all the wagons will be crossin' in a few days. You ain't got the brains of a gray-back."

But Jessica continued to cry, her body convulsed with sobs. "You don't do anything . . . you just sit around and watch. Anna will be an ugly, toeing-in squaw and you'll be an old, old man before we even start. I've waited and waited for you to do something and from now on I'm making my own plans . . . my very own plans," she emphasized. "You wait and see," she threatened, hiding her anguished face in her short skirt.

The boat was unusually large, round like a tub, and made of tough buffalo hide stretched over a framework of willows; truly a welcome find for Henri, who now appeared frantically eager to reach the opposite shore. Though the strange craft leaked, it was considered safe enough to use and with all five crowded within, it was launched into the river in the dusk of the evening.

Everything went smoothly until the current, strong and deep in places, seized and dashed their boat about in dizzying circles despite the best efforts of Henri, who pushed with a pole and hummed French boat songs beneath his onioned breath. Ol' Squaw, undisturbed, clung to Anna, who insisted upon trailing her hand in the water while Jessica, stiffly defiant, sat in a world apart, making secret plans of her own. Sammy, struggling to hold the ropes of Marie and Whitey, swimming behind, glanced anxiously at her from time to time. Since their quarrel, Jessica had remained ominously silent. She had changed, she was different . . . and her new manner foreboded trouble. . . . Gradually the shore faded into the fast-gathering twilight.

13

JESSICA ATTEMPTS ESCAPE

The country on the north shore of the Platte stretched for two hundred miles, level and timberless but for a single cottonwood tree. There were no wagon trains, no trading posts and the few people who traveled that side of the river were friendly Indians or occasional half-breed trappers. Although Ol' Squaw and Henri always spoke to these strangers, they never lingered to visit or shared their camp at night but kept exclusively to themselves, Henri watching his saddlebags and Ol' Squaw guarding her two red-haired girls.

As time went on, it was evident to Sammy that the son-in-law and mother-in-law had become congenial through necessity, each protecting the other's interests for his own sake. It would be difficult for Ol' Squaw to deny she was not aware of something precious in Henri's saddlebags, and Henri's acceptance of the two Fields children now made him guilty of the crime of kidnaping. Moreover, Henri seemed to be genuinely fond of the young squaw waiting for him somewhere in the mountains beyond. He had married into a large Crow family, no one of whom would tolerate insult or cruelty to one of their members.

Unburdening himself to Sammy one day, Henri made marks in the sand with a stick, showing how many people there were in his wife's family. Then, pointing at Ol' Squaw, Henri made another mark which counted forty-seven in all. Awed himself by the array of marks, the trapper muttered *"Sacré bleu!"* and remained a bit subdued the rest of the day.

At the first sight of the blue-black mountains in the west, Ol' Squaw and Henri slowed their pace and began to enjoy themselves, the trapper singing his French songs, the Indian woman showing the children where the strawberries grew thickest in the meadow.

Evenings were filled with music, Henri dancing by the light of the fire, graceful and agile despite his ponderous weight. However, beneath all this gaiety, Jessica had not forgotten her grievances. True to her promise, she discussed her plans with no one, but maintained a silence towards Sammy which perplexed and worried him more than he cared to admit.

Occasionally he would watch her as she sat silent, thoughtful, upon Whitey's back, following the trail, clutching Anna close to her; Anna dressed in her red jacket now trimmed with elks' teeth. . . . What was Jessica planning? There was no more horehound candy in her pocket with which to bribe Anna. How could she persuade the younger child to leave Ol' Squaw? To Jessica's credit, Sammy knew she would never desert Anna, who was rapidly becoming a small grubby Indian despite her glow of flaming hair. White blood was too strong in Jessica. To break her silence,

Sammy did everything he could to anger her: snatched the blanket from her as she slept, placed a small green snake in her shoe, and pinched Anna until she cried. But Jessica's mouth was sealed concerning her plans, though she fought back like a young tigress for her rights.

The tide turned one day and thereafter Sammy became a bit more wary of Jessica. Following a skirmish which again involved the one and only blanket, Jessica turned on Sammy, her face flushed, her blue eyes angry and an indignant forefinger trembling with rage.

"Maybe you think no one knows who stole Anna's sleeve, Sammy Coit! Well, I've known ever since we crossed the river! And I've seen you sitting and soaking your patch in every mud puddle ever since! Yesterday I saw you smear axle grease on it from that old wheel beside the road. You're a thief and a bad, bad boy, Sammy Coit . . . not a bit like your brother Jason! I think Ol' Squaw knows, too. I saw her looking. . . . I don't want Anna to have the sleeve now, it's too dirty. And I think it's loose. Yesterday I saw your skin." Later in the day, aware now of the wicked power she wielded, she reminded him again of the patch.

"It's almost loose, Sammy, and it's turning red again."

If Henri had observed the red sleeve, he gave no sign or indication of caring. As Jessica had said, the scarlet cloth was extremely dirty, although at times the grime gave way and the original color shone through. Meanwhile Sammy himself was often tempted to escape alone without the girls. He longed to be free of Jessica's taunts and Henri's demands, which were increasing daily. But the knife, the blanket, the gun and food were necessary to make any escape successful. His only asset was a small supply of matches, which he had stolen from Henri. However, each day's travel was bringing them all closer to Fort Laramie. There, camped outside the fort's walls, would be white people.

At the sight of two Indians and a white man crossing a field on horseback, Ol' Squaw and Henri very hurriedly chose a new path to the north. In a few days the party was lost in the gloom of high cliffs and deep ravines. Here the wolves howled nightly and frequently; the scream of the spotted panther was heard. These sounds did not seem to distress the Indian woman and trapper. At home in the wild fortress of rock towering above them, Henri aimed like a homing pigeon towards camping spots familiar to Ol' Squaw and himself.

It was while they camped beside a small brook some distance from the mountain road that two strangers unexpectedly joined them one afternoon. With their dark lean faces wreathed in smiles, daggers at their belts, ears pierced with gold loops and their heads bound in gay handkerchiefs, two French trappers riding small shaggy ponies descended upon Ol' Squaw and Henri with whoops of joy. Mountain men of the wildest kind! One could hardly hope for rescue from this gypsy-like pair, and Jessica and Sammy stared at the strangers in bitter disappointment. If only the trappers had been English and had spoken their own tongue!

Henri was noticeably quiet, not too cordial, and kept his eyes on his saddlebags. The taller of the two strangers was named Bateese. Minus a thumb on his right hand, he did most of his talking gesturing with his four remaining fingers. Little notice was taken of the children. The trappers were headed for Fort Laramie. Laramie! Both Sammy and Jessica caught the word, poured forth in a stream of French, Jessica with her eyes shining and lips parted in excitement. But before Jessica could listen further, Ol' Squaw sent her after Anna, who had wandered too far picking berries. Jessica left reluctantly, looking back over her shoulder, envious of Sammy, who could remain and hear more.

Bateese and his friend had been following the small brook southward. The tall trapper spoke frequently of the "rivière" and used the word "difficile" many times, pointing again with his four fingers at the heavy packs which a third pony bore. "Rivière" . . . did the word mean river? Undoubtedly "difficile" meant difficult. Was there something difficult about a river? Jessica, out of breath from hurrying, soon returned with Anna and the trappers took their leave almost immediately, following the small brook southward. Jessica still showed her excitement, and Sammy watched her warily. She had missed much of the trappers' conversation and knew only that Fort Laramie was close by.

Henri relaxed with unconscious relief as the two strangers left, his farewells obviously heartier than his welcome. When certain his visitors were actually upon their way, he seized the pack saddles and began to climb a narrow dirt path which ran crisscross up the side of the cliff. Sammy followed, leaving Ol' Squaw and the two girls below. He was now anxious to learn of the country about them and Henri did not object to his company. Both were breathing hard when at last the top was reached. To their great disappointment, the country below was shrouded in white mist, the ragged end of the crags emerging above in strange dark shapes. Even the last glow of the departing sun was screened by a milky haze. Henri, nervous and worried, stared towards the south in search of his departed friends and then, with a sigh, dropped his saddlebags and mopped his forehead on his sleeve. Sammy faced south, trying to see some sign of the fort. "Rivière" . . . surely the word meant river?

"Where's the river?" he asked Henri. "I'd like to see the river."

"Voilà!" and Henri waved a hairy hand to the south. "You cannot see. *Mes amis* say de reever is high. Mebbe dey cannot cross to de for'."

Sammy continued to look in the direction towards which Henri pointed. Somewhere below, beyond the blank wall of mist, lay Fort Laramie! Perhaps Jason was already there, waiting for him, eager to see him. In the wagon with Jason would be a warm bed and food such as he was accustomed to in Illinois. If only he could talk with Jason about home, their mother and Tacy, and of their plans for the future. But there was not the remotest chance of being with Jason now. . . . A wall of mist, white as a cotton sheet, cut off his view of all the land to the south. Without waiting for Henri, Sammy crept down the narrow path, a large lump in his throat. It was time now to tell Jessica that a river, deep and swift, lay between them and Fort Laramie. Would she listen? Would she believe him?

No one stirred in the camp below. Supper was finished and, weary after the day's travel, both girls were asleep beneath their blanket, Jessica's arm thrown protectively about Anna, the two red heads close together. Ol' Squaw snored in her tepee. There was rabbit stew, still warm in the kettle, and Sammy fished out pieces of meat with his fingers, watching Jessica as he ate. If only he could talk

with her and tell her of the deep river and warn her not
to do anything foolish now. Was she actually asleep? Both
girls were breathing regularly, gently, but once he thought
he saw Jessica's eyes open slightly, as though she were
watching him, too.

"Jessica," he whispered softly.

There was no sign from her and again he repeated her
name. At this point Henri arrived, puffing and blowing
from his scramble down the cliff, his saddlebags over one
arm. The only sounds now were Ol' Squaw's snores and the
noise Henri made as he ate gustily of the stew. A little
later Sammy crawled beneath his scanty end of the blanket.
He was certain Jessica was not asleep. Perhaps a little later
he would waken her . . . and then Sammy knew no more.

In the midst of a strange dream of leaping from crag to
crag above clouds of white mist to find Jason, Sammy awakened towards morning. Anna was not beside him and he
was in sole possession of the coveted blanket. Both girls
were gone! Sammy rose to his feet and stared about him in
the gray light. Only a few embers of the fire still glowed.
Marie and Whitey were securely staked. Ol' Squaw had not
moved since he saw her last, and Henri was giving out little
blasts of snores which regularly sent his whiskers upward
as he lay sprawled in his blanket, one arm protecting his saddlebags. Where had the two girls gone? Perhaps they were
not far away, the little donkeys . . . the little fools. . . .

Angry with himself for not awakening Jessica, and angry
with her for her stubbornness, Sammy cautiously felt his
way along the path by the brook. The trappers had followed
the brook, which undoubtedly led to the river. Jessica had
seen them depart. She would follow that same path, prob-

ably dragging Anna after her by one hand. . . . But how had she persuaded Anna to leave? There was no more horehound candy and, as far as he knew, Jessica had no other hold upon the younger child.

A bright flash of lightning, a loud clap of thunder reverberated among the rocky cliffs, and Sammy came to a sudden stop. A thunderstorm! This above all would terrify Jessica, and for the first time Sammy felt his anger soften a little. Jessica, who always covered her head and turned and twisted in desperation to shut out the light and sound, was now out in the storm. What would she do? Where would she go? And suddenly Sammy found himself running to overtake her. At any moment, as the lightning flashed, he might catch a glimpse of red, the crimson suits worn by the little girls. Then he would hurry them back to camp before all three of them were missed.

"Jess-i-ca! Jess-i-ca!" he called between rolls of thunder. If Jessica was frightened, it served her right. Jessica, with all her smug and secret ways . . .

"Jess-i-ca!" he continued to call.

A near-by tree crashed to the ground and an owl screeched overhead. For a moment Sammy crouched and hid his face in his hands, unable to bear the glare of the lightning. He then rose to his feet. Surely Henri and Ol' Squaw would be awake now. Would they follow in the storm or wait until it was over? Of course, he, Samuel Coit, would be blamed for the whole affair. Henri would laugh heartily upon their return and then force new duties upon him as punishment. Again Sammy's anger seethed to the boiling point as he continued to run beside the brook, the wet bushes whipping and stinging his legs.

The high cliffs were gradually disappearing. Now and then he glimpsed, through deluges of rain, open meadows in the distance. Perhaps he would find Jessica and Anna with the two trappers, camped on the shore of the river, unable to cross. The trappers would force all three children to return to Henri. . . . Perhaps Jessica, by now, had made the trappers understand that there was something mysterious in Henri's saddlebags. Jessica could be clever at times. . . . Then there would be a terrific fight between the trappers and Henri. . . . Henri had not trusted the trappers. . . . Perhaps by this time Anna and Jessica had been drowned, trying to cross the river alone. . . . Their bodies would drift past the fort and their parents see them. Sammy's imagination was now running riot and his fears, mounting every moment, were suddenly climaxed by the awful realization that he was not alone. Someone else was with him out there in the storm. A bear, a panther . . . Henri . . . the two trappers? Although he stopped and looked back, he could distinguish nothing in the gray light. And he had not even a knife with which to defend himself.

A beaver dam forced him to circle away from the brook and weave his own path through tall willows. Though he could neither see nor hear, he was certain he was not alone. Whoever or whatever was following him could be heard bending the willows down. . . . Every flash of lightning found Sammy looking back instead of forward and he stumbled frequently. When he had reached the brook once more, he felt happier. The brook now began to flow through a meadow. As soon as he dared he would look back again and see this *thing* which was following him. Ahead was a large rock with a slanting side, almost in the center of the meadow. If he could climb to the top of the rock he would be safer there. And then he thought he saw a flash of red at the foot of the boulder as lightning streaked the sky in the east.

"Jess-i-ca!" he shouted.

Holding his hand over his eyes to shut out the light, Sammy began to run through the deep meadow grass. Surely it was the girls he had seen close to the rock! No one could ever mistake the red color of their suits. . . . Again came the lightning and again he saw the same flash of color at the base of the boulder. The girls were there; he had found them at last!

"Jess-i-ca!" he shouted, spurting in leaps towards them. He did not look now to see if he were being followed. It was easier not to know. . . . In another moment his feet slid and seated him with a rush between two crouched figures who were struggling to find shelter beneath the slanting side of the rock. Yelling with fear and surprise, the rain-sodden little creatures turned and then pounced upon him, almost strangling him in their joy, their faces and hands smeared a startling red from the dye of their wet blanket-suits.

"Sammy! Oh, Sammy! I'm so glad you've come . . . this awful storm! How did you know we were here? I tried to follow the trappers. Oh, Sammy!" and Jessica's silence was broken at last. "There's a big river over there. I couldn't find a boat. Anna wouldn't walk any farther. Oh, Sammy!" and as another rocket of lightning tore the sky, Jessica began to dig with both hands in the earth, like a small rabbit burrowing into its hole.

With Anna's arms about his neck and himself still out

of breath, Sammy was now conscious of feet walking through wet grass behind him. Before he could turn his head, he knew the *thing* had joined them. One swift look . . . it was Ol' Squaw, who crawled beneath the slanted rock where she crouched motionless, with her usual manner of neither seeing nor hearing. Little Anna, with a shrill cry, crawled to her and hid her face in the old woman's wet shawl. And then there was silence but for the dull rumble of far-away thunder and the slash of rain against the stone.

Moving in single file in the dark and cloudy dawn, the three children and Ol' Squaw retraced their steps towards the mountains in the north. From the first rise of land, Sammy turned and looked back. There was a clearing below, far away. He could see the faint outlines of high whitewashed walls with tepees outside. Yes, it was Fort Laramie and probably Jason was there, waiting for him. No doubt the two trappers were there also, trading their hides, forgetting they had seen three white children traveling a mountain road. All hope of escape was now gone. In the days to come there would be no other opportunity. Jessica had spoiled it all.

To Sammy the only balm for his whole night's suffering was the look in Jessica's red-streaked face. Her blue eyes were pleading and she appeared utterly forlorn with her hair plastered to her cheeks in wet strands. Jessica was sorry, but she could not bring herself to say so. Anna, murmuring sleepily of "buyin' horehoun' at the fort," had to be helped over the rough places along the brook and was finally borne into camp on the old Indian woman's back.

14

TRIALS OF THE TRAIL

With one accord, Captain Mark Morgan's train traveled its extra mileage daily towards Fort Laramie, in every heart high hopes of rescuing the stolen children. Buffaloes were plentiful near Plum Creek and by the time the wagons reached the forks of the North and South Platte, every family was provisioned with meat, much of it being dried into jerky. Even Aaron was now satisfied, having brought down two fine cows for the Morgan family. All hunting was done by the approach method, as there was scarcely time for a running hunt.

"There's no need of killing more buffaloes now," the captain told Jason as they stood watching a group of men butchering. "It would be useless slaughter, for there's meat in every wagon. And none of our necks broken, thank goodness! Our next big business is the Lower California Crossing, not far from here. Bill Brewster says that you can manage Kit better than anyone else and so he wants you to lead the other horses and oxen across. He says he'll see that someone takes your wagon over for you."

"Of course," and Jason's dark eyes lighted at the idea. "I'll be glad to do it. But sometimes I think that Cal and young Bill don't like my managing their horse . . ."

"It don't matter what they think," replied a familiar reedy voice, and both turned to see the old scout standing just behind them, his long gray hair blowing in the wind. "Everybody in this train knows now that the hoss won't move a step fer either of 'em. It's your job, Jason."

From the moment the wagons rumbled out of Independence, Missouri, the ford on the South Platte, called the Lower California Crossing, had presented to all a menace and a liability. There were neither ferries nor bridges, and shallows obstructed the floating of rafts or boats. Conflicting rumors as to the river's height and width had perplexed more than one emigrant traveling westward.

"You can't tell anything 'bout her," grumbled Bill Brewster, besieged on all sides with questions. "Wait till you get thar. She's apt ter change overnight. The Snake's just like her, cantankerous an' unobleegin'. But whether she's high or low, folks must raise their beddin' on blocks an' watch out fer quicksand. The currents can dig holes in a level stretch quick'n you can say Zack Taylor. It don't pay to speak much about it, though. It gets some folks panicky an' we got two days of livin' an' travelin' with 'em yet." As he finished, the old scout twisted his thin weathered face into a grimace.

The water at the Lower California Crossing appeared harmless enough two days later, its gray-brown current flowing smoothly in the distance. All wagon beds were caulked the night before and water casks emptied and fastened to the sides. After a hasty breakfast the next morning,

Bill Brewster, mounted on Mustard, marked out the route with stakes for all to follow. An hour later, Jason prepared to take off on Kit, the last words of Mark Morgan ringing in his ears: "Keep the wagons moving!" Elisha Jefferson's deeper voice echoed the cry.

Kit, his chestnut coat gleaming with gold lights from the morning sun, his white forefeet lifted daintily and his whole body quivering with excitement, took his first steps towards the water reluctantly. A quick slide . . . and he suddenly dropped, with a snort, to a depth of four feet, rearing back a bit from the cold plunge. However, with Jason's hand on his neck, the horse went forward with little resistance, seeming to know what was expected of him. There was neither whip nor spur to urge Kit on, only the gentle monotone of Jason's voice.

Elisha Jefferson, watching and listening, turned to Mark Morgan with something like tears in his eyes. "It beats me how that hoss an' boy love each other. . . . I guess they'd go anywhere, long's they're together." Then, with a break in his voice, the big man added softly, "It was the same way with my boy Luke an' a big roan I owned. . . . That's why we're goin' West, Mary an' me . . . tryin' to forget our boy. . . ."

It was the first time Elisha Jefferson had spoken of his son, although his wife had talked freely among the womenfolk.

"I understand," and Captain Morgan nodded sympathetically.

Thirty feet from the shore, Kit came to a sand bar where the water was surprisingly shallow. A moment later the horse was shoulder deep once more. The muddy current

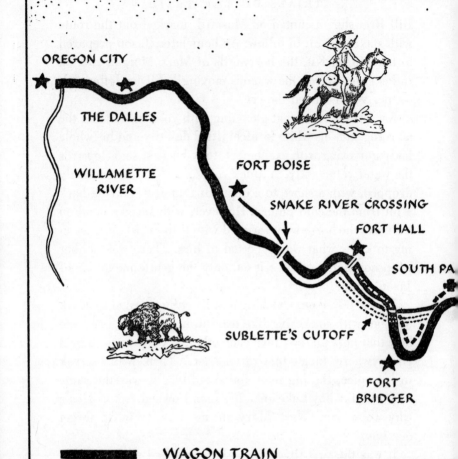

OREGON CITY

THE DALLES

WILLAMETTE
RIVER

FORT BOISE

SNAKE RIVER CROSSING

FORT HALL

SOUTH PA

SUBLETTE'S CUTOFF

FORT
BRIDGER

━━━━━ WAGON TRAIN

━ ━ ━ ━ HENRI JULES AND SAMMY

━━━━━ JASON'S TRIP ON KIT

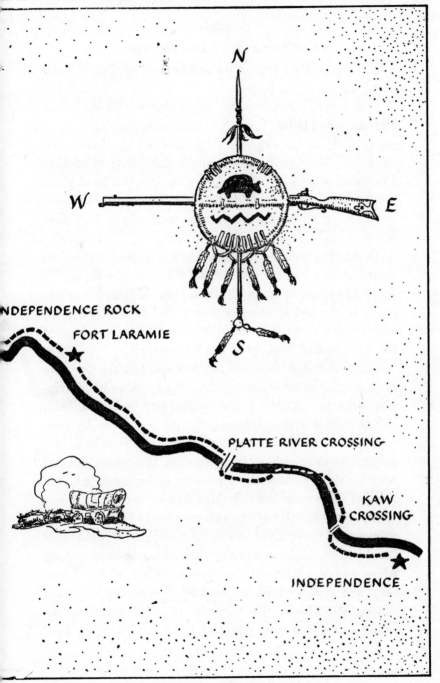

N

W   E

S

INDEPENDENCE ROCK

FORT LARAMIE

PLATTE RIVER CROSSING

KAW CROSSING

INDEPENDENCE

DOUGLAS DUER

boiled and seethed against the saddle as he picked his way along the uncertain bottom.

"Easy, boy," Jason would say whenever Kit sank into an unexpected hole. "Easy, Kit. Remember they're countin' on us to lead the way. We're showin' all the horses an' cattle back there that it can be done. Easy, boy, swim now. I'm right beside you. . . ." And with merely a hand guiding the horse, Jason would slip from his saddle and swim beside Kit until the horse's feet reached solid ground once more.

Those were the moments which both Kit and Jason loved. Together they had crossed the Big Blue and the Kaw. The horse was tuned to the boy's voice, controlled by his touch, ready to respond to every demand. And Jason, both awed and thrilled by his responsibility, was deeply conscious of the trust he had inspired in the big chestnut.

When at last Kit's white forefeet climbed the opposite bank and Jason stood beside him, both horse and boy dripping with the muddy Platte water, they waited quietly, happy in their accomplishment of a job well done. By now, every watching animal had gained courage from their example. Already two wagons were on their way, buoyed over the deeper places by the empty casks fastened to the sides of the wagon beds. A third wagon was tilting downward, almost upright at one end, as it dipped from the land to meet the river. Even at that distance Jason could hear the shouts of the drivers urging their oxen, the snap of long whips and the faint calls of women riding within. Later came the grating noise of sand-filled water as it rushed against the wheels, the whimper of small children, the splash of oxen as they struggled to hold the sagging line, and the hoarse encouraging cries of horsemen riding alongside.

"Gee, Tom! Gee! Steady, Star! Haw!"

All this for land in Oregon!

Upon the arrival of the Collins family on the north shore, Jason led Kit to their wagon. Bill, sullen, with his mouth pulled down at the corners, silently assisted him in drying off the horse's wet coat. Cal hovered close whenever possible, now and then offering advice. Cal, however, was constantly recalled to the wagon by Mrs. Collins, who was full of complaints and demands. Several of the children, vividly afflicted with a rash, were crying because of damp beds, while the baby, balanced on Mrs. Collins' right hip as she strode about, pierced the air with deafening howls.

"You, Cal, never mind that good-fer-nothin' hoss an' tend to yer kids," screamed Mrs. Collins above the uproar. "Come here an' haul out them blankets! Bill, you didn't finish yer job! All you two think of is that hoss! The fust chanc't I get, I'll trade it fer oxen! B-I-L-L, you hear me?"

This was no new story to Jason. He finished drying Kit, spoke to him softly, smoothing the arched neck, and then turned towards the river again, looking back once when the horse whinnied after him. For some reason Mrs. Collins' words rang in his ears more forcefully than usual. If the woman should carry out her threat and trade the horse for oxen at one of the forts, Cal and Bill would be powerless to stop her. Mrs. Collins was daily becoming more aggressive due to Cal's shiftlessness and Bill's incompetence. If only he might buy Kit for his own . . .

Seated upon a knoll in the sun in an attempt to dry his

wet shirt and trousers, Jason dreamed and figured as he waited for his own wagon to cross. With seventy dollars, his nest egg of two-years' saving, he could hardly hope to buy Kit and commence a new life in Oregon, too. Only a miracle would ever make the horse his own. Moreover, Sammy, too young to work steadily, might be dependent upon him for the next two years.

Thinking of Sammy, Jason's eyes searched the opposite shore in the vain hope of seeing a small red-shirted figure. Had Sammy already crossed at some other ford? Was he even now waiting for him at Fort Laramie? Despite the worry and trouble Sammy had caused him, Jason knew he would be glad to have his young brother with him. But what would be the effect upon Sammy of living with a man like Henri Jules these past few weeks? Had he been disciplined or was he more untamed than ever?

Bill Brewster himself drove Jason's wagon across the South Platte, every ox under control, with Blossom swimming patiently behind and Porky seated on the front seat. Jason, watching, smiled at the sight. The old scout, wiry and straight-backed, appeared to be enjoying himself and greeted Jason with a wave of his whip as the oxen drew the wagon up the steep bank.

"You folks are plumb lucky," called Bill as he stopped to enable Jason to climb up beside him. "The water ain't nigh as high as when I cross't last time. When we get to the top of Californy Hill I'll show you where we lost two wagons up the river a bit. The framework of the tops is still there, stickin' out of the water. One man was drownded, but his wife went on. They say she got some nice land in the Umpqua Valley. T'other folks lost everything an' turned back. All they had left was the wet clothes on their backs. The oxen went outer sight inch by inch in some quicksand. Thar ain't no meaner river than the Platte 'cept the Snake, mebbe," and unexpectedly the old scout leaped agilely to the ground and walked beside the oxen as they began the steep ascent ahead.

"That pig o' yourn," Bill complained as he strode along, "got outer the box somehow an' wanted to sit in my lap. I'd think that pig was a dog of some sort if I didn't know different! Did the hoss go back ter Cal?"

"Yes. Mis' Collins scolded a lot . . ."

"She's always scoldin'. What's the trouble this time?"

"She didn't want Cal and Bill to leave their work to dry off Kit. I don't blame her, in a way, but she really seems to hate Kit. She's threatenin' to trade him at one of the forts for oxen." There was a note of anxiety and yearning in Jason's voice which made Bill Brewster glance at him quickly.

"She did, did she? Oh, well now, women like ter yap. Don't pay too much 'tention to that screecher. Hear 'em sing!" and Bill put one hand to his ear as the sound of voices came from the other side of the hill. "Women are always like that . . . singin' hymns when they're sad or glad. It don't matter which. What's the name of that one now?" he asked curiously.

"*Rock of Ages*," replied Jason. "My mother sings it, too. . . . I hope the river will be low when she crosses next year."

Bill Brewster gave him another quick glance and then looked back at Blossom, who was mooing plaintively.

"What'd I tell you!" The old scout chuckled. "The fe-

males all have ter sing before or after danger. Yer cow's
doin' it now. Get inside the wagon, boy, yer teeth are
knockin'. Put on some dry britches while I keep the oxen
movin'. Aaron's ridin' Mustard fer me . . . I'm in no
hurry. You an' Kit did a fine job crossin' the river. I meant
to tell you when I fust seed you. An' who knows but what
I'll be right here helpin' when your ma crosses next year.
Get over on yer own side, ye pesky little hog!" and Bill
Brewster climbed up on the front seat once more as the big
Conestoga creaked forward in the deep ruts of California
Hill.

From the top of the slope, the country between North and
South Platte River was a wind-blown, barren sweep, gashed
with deep canyons . . . a great contrast to the plains, with
their rolling hills and monotonous skylines. With the dread
of the Lower California Crossing behind them, the names
of Windlass Hill, Ash Hollow and Fort Laramie were on
every tongue. All were eager to forge ahead. However, the
chasms beside the trail made more than one person's head
reel as he gazed below. Moreover, many were lessening the
weight of their loads, noting with concern their oxen, whose
pace was slowing. Reluctantly, grim-faced men and sorrowing women stopped their wagons in the long line and later
rolled on, leaving a treasured stove, a table, a chest of
drawers or spinet beside the trail.

" 'T won't seem home without that chair," Jason heard
one woman mourn, as she left a straight-backed rocker
swaying emptily upon a windswept bluff. "My grandfather
made it and my mother rocked me to sleep sittin' on it. An'

to think of me leavin' it here! The next folks who come along may use it for firewood!"

"I'll make you another," comforted a big man as he helped her mount to the front seat. "I feel the same way you do, though I ain't sayin' much. But we must save the plow; everything'll have to go but the plow. It's better to eat in Oregon than sit an' rock on an empty stomach. Mebbe someone follerin' will bring it along," he added hopefully, looking up at his wife.

" 'T ain't likely," and the woman brushed away her tears. "No one's takin' on anything extry in these parts 'cept the Indians. I expect I'm bein' silly, Joe. . . . Just so we don't have to leave the baby's cradle. . . ." But for a long time the woman's eyes remained upon the chair swaying on the desolate bluff. Finally the trail swung to the left and she could no longer keep it in sight.

There was a trunk belonging to Asa Strong within Jason's wagon. It contained sheets, pillow cases, toweling and Asa's best suit of black broadcloth, its vest trimmed with silver buttons. Although Mrs. Strong had requested that Asa be buried in it, no one had been able to locate it at the time and Mrs. Strong herself had been too ill to search or advise the people who had assisted. Was this not the time and place to lighten the load? Jason asked himself. All of the oxen were slowing down and King needed constant urging to go ahead. Mrs. Strong had told him to use his own judgment in all things. Bed linen, toweling and a dead man's suit were not as important as preserving an ox, almost worth its weight in gold, in this strange new country. With Seth Adams helping him, it did not take Jason long to remove the trunk.

"Sally oughter leave some stuff behind but Joel's too chicken-hearted to make her," commented Seth. "I s'pose you've heard the talk 'bout Windlass Hill. With no trees to drag as brakes, it'll be quite a drop. Only two of our wagons have brakes an' they don't count for much."

"What if the ropes don't hold?" asked Jason.

"Heaven help us if they don't," replied Seth fervently.

Although Jason had heard conflicting tales of Windlass Hill, he found himself startled as he looked with others over the treeless and almost vertical drop of a barren hill. The wheels of the former descending wagons had worn deep grooves in the sandy earth and the entire slope was rough and torn, the scene of many struggles. At the very bottom of the hill and off to one side lay the remains of a wagon now weathered and rusty.

"That fool thought he could do it alone," Bill Brewster explained. "Had some kind of a contraption he thought was a brake. You see what happened. Yes, he lived, but he footed it to Fort Laramie to pick up another wagon. The oxen? Three killed. He was a good tradin' Yankee, though, 'cause they say he sold the meat to folks on the next train. The valley down thar is Ash Holler. A little cabin is sort of a postoffice. Folks leave messages inside fer folks fol- lerin'. Well, have you picked a good stiddy wagon fer the windlass?"

"Elisha Jefferson has offered his," replied Mark Morgan, "and Lief Curtis says he'll go first. He's single and hasn't a family . . ."

"Lief's wagon is too light," interrupted the old scout with finality. "The heaviest wagon must go first while the rope's good. I've been lookin' 'em over and Jason here has the heftiest one in the whole train. Want to go fust, Jason?"

"He's nothin' but a kid," objected a voice. "Let a man go first."

"Age ain't got nuthin' to do with it," objected Bill Brewster, a little angry. "Jason's got the heftiest wagon, an' his oxen are sure. I've been drivin' 'em . . . I know. He ain't white-livered, either. Want someone else to drive yer wagon, Jason?"

"I'd just as soon do my own drivin'," replied Jason, a little taken aback at being chosen first. "What do I do? Unyoke most of my oxen?"

"All but two to hold up the tongue. Zebe and Joe would be the best, I'm thinkin'. Pack your stuff forward, solid. We'll treble the ropes if we can. Start movin'!"

An hour later, the big Conestoga wagon belonging to Elizabeth Strong slowly made its descent down Windlass Hill with Jason on the front seat, his feet braced hard to keep himself from falling out. Zebe and Joe, supporting the wagon tongue, walked slowly, carefully, seeming to stand on their heads as they inched along. Back from the edge of the slope was Elisha Jefferson's wagon, staked to the ground, with only two wheels free to turn, doling out rope which was wound about its axle. The other end of the rope was fastened to the descending wagon.

"Sit tight, young feller, you're halfway down! You're doin' fine! Swing a mite to the left an' keep in the ruts. Now swing to the right!"

Above the creak of the windlass came calls of advice and encouragement from the men on the top of the hill. Now and then a murmur arose when either of the oxen appeared to slip.

"Steady, Zebe, good ol' Zebe. Easy, Joe, haw! Steady, it's almost over now," Jason kept repeating, his voice shaky in spite of his effort to keep calm. The heaviest wagon in the train! Oh, why had Asa Strong bought such a wagon! Would the ropes hold? Should he jump if he heard them give? If only he had not consented to be the first to go down. . . . And even when the wagon had reached the bottom of the hill, he was still repeating Zebe's and Joe's names, his hand gripping the whip, his body wet with perspiration. A little cheer went up from the watching men as he got down from his seat and loosened the rope from his axle. It was over. He had come down Windlass Hill! With no weight behind them, the oxen and Blossom would follow easily enough.

All day long could be heard the creak of the windlass as it eased each wagon down. Once the rope gave way, despite its trebled thickness, but fortunately men walking beside the wagon held it back until the rope was retied. Sally Adams, hugging her baby to her, was strapped to the front seat for safety and Aunt Liddy, clutching her Rebecca-at-the-well teapot, descended in the same manner.

Red-faced and shaken by her experience, Aunt Liddy was half laughing and half crying as the Morgan wagon wheeled into its place in Ash Hollow late that afternoon.

"Well, I've called myself an awful fool for leavin' home before now. But I called myself worse'n that when we got halfway down that terrible slope an' I saw the bottom yawnin' up at me. Why, I nearly cracked my teapot, squeezin' it so hard. And you, Jason, you may stay at the end of the line for a spell. I don't like folks experimentin' on you, sendin' you 'cross the rivers first an' rollin' you down the hills to see how much a rope can take. Mark Morgan's goin' to get a piece of my mind this very night for such actions. An' that withered ol' possum, Bill Brewster, is goin' to hear what I think, too." And still scolding, Aunt Liddy climbed up the steps of the Morgan wagon to pack away her favorite teapot once more.

It was evening before Jason, accompanied by Aaron, was free to visit the little cabin called the postoffice. Each and every emigrant, whether he expected a message or not, scanned the larger advertisements posted outside beneath a lantern and read the more personal missives within by the light of flickering matches. Notices of straying cattle, horses, mules and dogs adorned the walls, and there was a pathetic notice from a young girl in a preceding train who had lost her pet cat, Lily.

"Look-a-here," beamed one elderly woman, holding up a piece of paper. "My son's makin' it fine in Oregon. His neighbor, goin' east, left this letter here for me."

At the same time, an elderly couple stumbled through the small door blinded with tears, stunned with the news of their daughter's death in California.

"I don't expect to hear from Sammy, but I want to look just the same," Jason told Aaron as the crowd lessened and they gazed about at the log walls. "I s'pose he's miles away on the other side of the river and yet . . ."

"Same as us," added Ezra Fields, standing nearby with his wife just behind him. "Jessica can write a little an' mebbe . . ." Ezra's voice faded into silence as he stared about him.

"There's nothing, Ezra, an' we shouldn't have looked," spoke Mary Fields gently. "We're making good time to-

wards the fort and that's all that matters now," she added
as if to comfort her husband.

"I know . . . I know," groaned Ezra, still looking about
him halfheartedly. "I guess you're right. I don't see nothin',
Mary. . . ."

Once more following the south shore of the North Platte
River, Captain Morgan's train struggled to retain its sched-
uled speed and reach Fort Laramie as soon as possible.
Again every emigrant was conscious of the weight of his
load, and more trunks and furniture were left behind; for
the oxen, due to constant travel and drinking of the river
water, were beginning to limp and lose flesh. Late at night,
a dozen or more of the suffering beasts were turned upon
their backs and tied to a rough framework while their sore
and split hoofs were filled with hot tar. Among Jason's
oxen, only King and Tom required this treatment. To counteract the effects of the river water upon the emigrants
themselves, buckets of the Platte water were drawn during
the evening and cornmeal sprinkled over the top. By morning the cornmeal had absorbed the greater part of the alkali and the water was fit for making coffee.

The first evidence of the Sioux Indians came after the
wagon train left Ash Hollow. A small village of tepees three
miles away in the west marked the horizon and a day later
several tall, slim braves visited the camp. Unlike the Pawnees, they were quiet, dignified and unobtrusive. Even Aunt
Liddy had no complaints of their behavior and admired the
women who accompanied their men later in the day. The
squaws offered to make beaded moccasins for the children
in exchange for mirrors and trinkets.

"They ain't always so friendly," Bill Brewster warned Aunt Liddy, Jason and Aaron, who were watching the Indian women sew. "If folks ahead hadn't been decent, they'd have taken their mad out on us. An' don't forget to call them Dakotas; they don't like to be called Sioux. Well, I swan!" and the old scout stopped short as his eyes lighted upon a group of young braves filing by. "What's he got on? That fust one in the bird cage?"

"Hoop skirt," answered Aunt Liddy, leaning forward to see. "Just look at them pink ruffles on the bottom? It's Mis' Jefferson's and I think she left it behind in a trunk before we came down Windlass Hill. Why, look at that second one! Am I seein' straight?"

Aunt Liddy's forefinger indicated something unusual and accordingly all four heads turned a bit further in that direction. A brave in a plumed bonnet with chin ribbons was hastening after his hoop-skirted companion.

"That's Mis' Jacobs' bonnet; she left it the other side of Windlass Hill, too. My, my!" and Aunt Liddy rocked in sudden mirth. "There must be a tea party goin' on somewhere!"

"Jason, look, look!" The last came from Aaron, who strove to keep his voice lowered in his surprise and amusement at the sight of a stout middle-aged Indian who had acquired some black broadcloth trousers. Finding them too confining, the new possessor had removed the entire seat but had continued to wear his customary flaps fore and aft. A vest fastened with silver buttons down the back completed his costume.

"Them buttons look sort of familiar," murmured Aunt Liddy vaguely. "I've seen them at camp meetin', somewhere." Catching sight of a strained expression on Jason's face, she stopped short. "It can't be . . . it couldn't be . . ." she stammered and then stopped entirely, her mouth open. "Shades of the dyin' an' the dead," she gasped finally, "if it ain't Asa Strong come to life again!"

Because of the train's eagerness to reach Fort Laramie, no extra time was given to sightseeing. Courthouse Rock, twelve miles away, was a pinkish blur of old sandstone, viewed by the emigrants in wondering curiosity. Other strange formations appeared in the distance. Chimney Rock, a shaft of marl and limestone, pierced the sky for some five hundred feet, and twenty miles beyond was Scott's Bluff, a high steep bank with the North Platte waters at its very base.

"Poor devil," exclaimed the old scout as they looked up the steep sides of the bluff, "that's his monument."

"Whose monument?" asked Aaron. "Scott's? Did you know Scott?"

"Lor', no, the poor cuss died a long time ago, 'fore my time 'roun' here. He was a trapper for the American Fur Company. Took sick on his way home from the mountains and his friends, if you wanter call 'em that, deserted 'im. Scott crawled on his belly for sixty miles an' died up thar by a spring. Wolves et his body. 'T ain't a purty story. Well, we're gettin' on into the west now. You'll be seein' changes. Tomorrer thar'll be dust, a valley of it. Soon you'll be seein' Laramie Peak. The fort is fifty miles from the spot we're standin' on."

Bill Brewster's prophecies always seemed to come about. On the following day, as the wagons crossed a sandy loam valley, columns of dust rose high, blinding animals and people alike. Children rode with their faces buried in their mothers' laps, while drivers with cracked and bleeding lips peered through the haze with straining eyes as each tried to follow the wagon ahead. Entering the darkened depths of a canyon, the train passed through and circled back to the North Platte once more, camping at Horse Creek where green grass, birds and flowers made amends for the long day's hardships. It was here, while gathering sunflowers and lavender daisies, that the children first discovered small bushes with silvery leaves . . . the beginning of the endless miles of sage which marked the Oregon trail westward. And looming darkly from a ridge farther on, beckoning the emigrants forward, was the high, lonely outline of Laramie Peak.

15

FORT LARAMIE

Built of sun-dried bricks and lime, Fort Laramie, established by the American Fur Company, appeared starkly white against the Black Hills in the distance. After a brief stop at a small trading post, Captain Morgan's train crossed the swift waters of Laramie Creek and encamped upon a plain a quarter of a mile distant from the fort. Six hundred and sixty miles from Independence, Missouri, in forty days of toil and travel! To arrive this far into the unknown West was a triumph in itself, and enthusiasm among the emigrants ran high. If the three children should not be found within the fort, the best hope was to secure aid from the United States dragoons said to be stationed near by. As yet, however, there had been no signs of the blue-coated soldiers. Instead, hundreds of buffalo-skin Indian lodges dotted the plains to the east.

Perplexed at the sight of this unusual number of lodges, Bill Brewster rode ahead to investigate and confer with Monsieur Papin, in charge of the fort. But the thin wiry figure of the old scout was nowhere to be seen as, later in the afternoon, Captain Morgan, Ezra Fields, Aaron and Jason hastened up the hill towards the fort.

"I don't see Bill an' I don't see soldiers 'round here," Ezra kept repeating nervously as they walked along. "Just lodges, hundreds of lodges. D'ye s'pose Bill has found my girls an' they're inside talkin'?"

"Steady, Ezra," and Captain Morgan laid a hand on the man's trembling arm. "If we don't find the little girls here, we'll find them farther on. Not so fast, Jason. You know we can't get inside that gate till Papin gives the word."

Jason, almost running in his excitement, brought himself to a sudden stop. He must be patient for a few moments longer, he told himself, and then, perhaps, he would be seeing Sammy. Sammy, freckle-faced, tow-headed . . . Would Sammy swagger a little as of old, or had the French trapper and the hard life on the trail tempered him a bit? It would be disturbing to find Sammy too changed. . . .

Walking more slowly, Jason looked up at the clay walls of the fort, some fifteen feet high. Surmounting the walls was a palisade where a sentinel, shading his eyes against the lowering sun, gazed out across the plains as he walked up and down, a gun upon one shoulder. Over the main gate loomed a blockhouse, the front of it adorned with a painting in vivid red of a horse running at full speed. At either side swung two brass swivel guns.

From the tapering lodges which littered the grounds just outside the walls there now poured forth Indians of all ages, singly and in little groups, stumbling over dogs and children as they hurried forward to stare at the newcomers. And suddenly from one of the more impressive lodges came Bill Brewster, wiping his mouth on his buckskin sleeve, undisguised pleasure on his thin face at seeing his friends.

"All right, Cap'n," he yelled. "Over here!" pointing back at the lodge from which he had come. "Met an ol' friend of mine an' he has news!"

Before Bill could enter the lodge once more, a tall Indian wearing a white buffalo robe stood imposingly in the doorway. Two squaws, their cheeks painted with vermilion, their ears hung with long pendants of shells, peered out from behind him, while a group of fat puppies wrangled playfully at their feet. A strong odor of cooking meat filled the air.

"This here's Two Horns," introduced the old scout, pointing to the dignified Indian. "A good Dakota, if ever I seed one. He knows everybody this side of the Rockies an' t'other side, too."

"How!" and Mark Morgan walked forward and put out his hand, motioning to the others to do the same.

"How!" replied the Indian, reaching out his hand awkwardly.

"Bill, Bill . . . are they here? Where are they?" Ezra Fields, in his anxiety, scarcely knew that he shook the Dakota's hand.

"I ain't seed 'em, but he has," answered the scout, nodding at the Indian. "Tell 'em, Two Horns, what you told me. The children belong to this man an' this young feller," and Bill Brewster pointed to Ezra and Jason in turn. "You understand?"

Two Horn's coal-black and expressionless eyes stared at the four strangers before him without blinking. Then there was an almost imperceptible movement to his straight lips as he gave a single grunt.

"You tell white men, Two Horns, or shall I talk?" persisted the old scout.

"Beel talk."

"All right. Two Horns says he an' his women was travelin' the Platte on the north side 'bout four days ago. They passed Henri Jules, his mother-in-law, an' three white kids. Two girls an' a boy. They had hosses. The girls had hair the color of the settin' sun. Two Horns wanted to stop an' ask Henri some questions 'bout roads, but Henri was in a hurry, like he was skeered of somethin'. Two Horns didn't make nothin' of it till I told him folks from New Mexico was searchin' for Henri. He useter see Henri at the rendezvous, years back."

"Four days ago," Ezra whispered hoarsely. "Where are they now? Where did they go?"

"Two Horns says they didn't cross the river but kept goin' on the north side. Prob'ly headin' for the Crow country, 'cause he says the ol' woman has Crow blood in 'er an' is skeered of Dakotas. All these Dakotas you see here have come to talk war on the Shoshones an' Crows."

"But the dragoons," faltered Ezra. "Ain't they goin' to help?"

"There ain't no dragoons . . . that was hearsay, I'm fearin'. If they're comin' to the fort, they ain't got here yet."

"How can I be sure it was my brother, Bill?" asked Jason. "Can Two Horns tell what the boy looked like?"

"What boy look like, Two Horns?" asked the scout of the Indian.

"Boy small. Beeg . . ." and Two Horns pointed to Captain Morgan's hat.

"Hat," supplemented Bill Brewster. "Did your brother wear a big hat?"

"Yes," replied Jason. "Some trapper gave it to him when they were on the boat."

"Were the children well?" asked Mark Morgan.

Another grunt from Two Horns implied that they were.

"Injuns are good to children," offered Bill Brewster, "an' the children like them so much that after a while they forget they're white. Two Horns says that later that night he heerd the kids singin'. An' the ol' woman had an umbrelly . . ."

"That's the one, that's the one!" interrupted Ezra Fields, his voice rising high with excitement. "Let's get goin', Bill. I'll pay for the hosses an' your time. Let's ketch 'em quick!"

" 'T wouldn't do no good, Ezra," soothed the old scout gently. "By now Henri's lost in the hills. An' onc't he suspects anybody's on his trail, he an' the ol' woman would go deep into the mountings like wild critters. You'd never see them girls again, mark my words. No, lissen to ol' Bill Brewster. The woman is part Crow an' sort of a leader 'mongst 'em. She's always travelin', independent-like, an' no one seems to cross 'er. They'll aim for Independence Rock, a hundred an' seventy miles from here, 'cause Henri is friendly wi' some of the Cheyennes. Then they'll go to Red Buttes whar the ol' woman'll feel safe. We'll prob'ly cross the river near Iron Creek an' then be on their side of the river . . . not before. Papin's away, so I talked with Bordeaux in charge here. He knows Henri an' says I'm guessin' right."

"Well, I reckon it's best then," and Ezra began to twist his hands. "I wish't I didn't have to go back to the wagon to Mary wi' that news, though. She's waitin' . . . watchin' for me to come down the hill wi' the girls. Oh, God . . .''

"I know, Ezra," and Mark Morgan put an arm across the tall man's stooped shoulders. "We were all hoping. It's hard on Jason, too. Now go back to your wife and tell her the children are well. Two Horns said they were even singing. . . . Aaron, you walk back with Ezra."

"No, no, let the boy stay," replied Ezra brokenly, trying to smile. "I'm all right an' I'll get holt of myself before I see Mary. Aaron wants to see the fort. Any young feller would. I don't mean to be so spleeny. It's just 'cause I hoped to see my girls. . . . Well, I'll be goin' back to the wagons now," and with no further words, Ezra turned and walked slowly away.

"Poor fellow," said Mark Morgan under his breath, "he's taking it very hard. He's always felt it wouldn't have happened if he hadn't threatened the old squaw during the big storm we had in Kansas. How are you, Jason? Your courage good?"

Jason, watching Ezra descend the hill, turned slowly, his thoughts far away. The cool evening wind blowing over the desolate plains chilled him through and through. But his throat felt hot and thick.

"I know how he feels," Jason said at last, his eyes following Ezra's departing figure. "I was hopin' to see Sammy tonight. I've been steelin' myself all day in case he wasn't here, but somehow it's not easy. . . . I'm glad he's all right . . . an' the girls, too. If they're singin', they can't be so bad off," and there was a little catch in Jason's voice. "Sammy always carried a jew's-harp . . . maybe he's got it with him now."

"I say we start in the mornin', Cap'n. Thar ain't much use of our hangin' 'round here. Things is high-priced. Too many Injuns. Bordeaux says they're fussin' a lot 'cause the white men are killin' off the buffalo. The sooner we get goin', the better. What say, Cap'n?" and Bill Brewster turned to Mark Morgan.

"I'm willing," replied the captain.

"I'll sound out the rest an' I'm guessin' they'll want to start. By the way," the old scout went on after they had said good-bye to Two Horns and were approaching the big gate, "you didn't come soon enough."

"What do you mean, Bill?" asked Mark Morgan solicitously, as he observed the scout rubbing his stomach with a mournful expression on his face. "Don't you feel well?"

"Not too good. Did ja see them pups rantin' 'round outside Two Horns' lodge?"

"Yes," replied Aaron eagerly. "They were pretty good-looking for Indian dogs. I was wondering what I could trade for one. I'd like a dog . . ."

"Well, I've got one right inside me I wish't you had," said Bill, continuing to massage his stomach. "Sure I've et it before, but somehow dog meat don't set too well. I can't seem to get used to it. An' if you don't eat yer bowlful, the Dakotas feel awful hurt. Well, here we go . . . they're openin' the gate for us. The short dark feller inside is Bordeaux. He always takes over when Papin's away."

Monsieur Bordeaux, harassed and weary from his many duties, nodded briefly at Bill Brewster and his party as they entered. The old scout led the way towards the Fur Company's storerooms. The odor of drying skins and cooking meat rose in suffocating fumes from small separate compartments which lined the three walls of the court and were occupied by the squaw wives of the clerks of the company. Barking dogs and crying children tumbled underfoot. At the storerooms Bill and his party were joined by Elisha Jefferson and other men from the train. They, too, it was apparent, had learned from Monsieur Bordeaux that the missing children had not turned up at the fort.

"I'm sorry, boy," and Elisha Jefferson pressed Jason's arm, "but keep up yer spirits. Most of the folks want to go on tomorrer from what I hear. Goin' to buy anything tonight?"

"I don't need much." Jason's sober face smiled a bit wanly at the big man. "I guess things are kind of high. . . . I'm glad if we're leavin' tomorrow."

"Sure, sure," and Elisha patted his arm again, opened his mouth as if to say something more and then disappeared into the crowd.

"Don't you buy *nothin'*," whispered Bill Brewster in Jason's ear. The boy nodded and then gazed about him. In the misty part of his mind was a picture of Myron Slade's store in Brownsville, Illinois. There had always been a strange mixture of odors in Mr. Slade's store. But dried apples, vinegar, spices, molasses, kerosene, dye from bolts of cloth and escaping fumes of liniments were nothing in comparison to the stench of hides piled high to the ceiling in the storeroom of the American Fur Company. Shelves of merchandise . . . rings, beads, vermilion, calico, shirts and trousers, knives and firearms . . . lined the wall at one end.

"Coffee, sugar, tobacco, one dollar a pound," droned a clerk. "Flour? Fifty cents a pound."

"Whew!" Aaron stared at his father and then at Jason. "Bill said it was high. Wonder what Aunt Liddy would think . . ."

"I know what your aunt would think," replied Mark Morgan grimly. "Don't buy."

"Too high for me," boomed a voice, which Jason recognized as Elisha Jefferson's. In another moment Elisha had started towards the door with others following, when a stranger suddenly entered, blocking the way.

"I beg pardon, sir." Although his face was weather-beaten, the stranger had a cultured voice and his bearing was dignified despite the rough fringed frock of deerskin which he wore. "Do the prices seem high?" he asked courteously.

"Too durn high for us," Elisha exploded. "It's just plain robbery."

"We can do better farther on, I'm thinkin'," added someone.

"I've just come from Fort Hall," replied the stranger easily, his keen blue eyes glancing from face to face. "Prices are about the same there, maybe a little less. The next stop in California . . ."

"Well, it happens we ain't goin' to Californy." Elisha's voice rose louder. "We're bound for Oregon, thirty wagons strong. This is our cap'n. Cap'n Morgan," announced Elisha as Mark Morgan advanced.

"How do you do, sir," and the stranger bowed. "I trust you have been making good time on the road."

"We've done average," replied Mark Morgan. "You say you've come from Fort Hall. Did you, by chance, meet or see a French trapper, an old squaw and three white children on your way?"

"Why, no, I'm sorry." The stranger rubbed his chin thoughtfully. "I saw no party of that description. . . . Do the children belong to your train?"

"Yes. We hoped to find them here. If possible, we mean to overtake them along the road."

"I am returning to Fort Hall immediately. If we can help you there, we will."

"Thank you. Did I understand you to say the prices are a little less at Fort Hall than here?"

"Slightly less. However, there is not as much needed to take one to California. The roads are better, the climate warmer. Most of the wagons are turning that way, especially if the oxen are tired. A wise man doesn't go to Oregon these days . . . if he does, he leaves his wagon behind him eventually."

"Roads pretty rough?" asked a man from the back of the room.

"Impassable in places. Already there is snow on the Blue Mountains and last week a man was drowned crossing the Snake."

"Well! An' what of the Injuns?" queried the same man in the back of the room.

"They're growing more and more unfriendly."

"Any worse'n usual?" asked Elisha Jefferson.

"I would not say that conditions are improving," answered the stranger smoothly.

"Let's see . . . Fort Hall is controlled by the British, isn't it?" asked Mark Morgan as smoothly as the stranger himself.

"Yes, it is," and there was a pointed silence during which all eyes stared at the stranger.

"We're Americans, most of us." Captain Morgan spoke slowly, distinctly. "We're homesteaders. There's land waiting for us in Oregon and that's where we plan to settle. Marcus Whitman and others got their wagons through and that's good enough for us."

"As you please." The stranger bowed graciously. "I'm only telling what you will hear again many times on the trail. I admire your courage, sirs, more than I can say. Five pounds of sugar, please," and in another moment the man left with a bag of sugar under his arm.

"Well, folks, that's your first run-in," announced Bill Brewster to the silent emigrants after a moment or so. "You'll get more of it later on, like that man says. 'T won't do no good to argue, just go ahead. There's Britishers all along the line ready to turn you back, or tell you to head for Californy . . . anything to keep you out of Oregon. They want that land themselves. Sure there's snow on Blue Mountains. Sure the Injuns are peppery. But what of it? You want to get to Oregon, don't you? Then stick to your oxen an' keep travelin'."

"He's a well-spoken man," commented Mark Morgan. "Have you seen him before?"

"Have I seed him before?" and the old scout spat a stream of dark tobacco juice on the floor. " 'Course I've seed 'im. He's one of Cap'n Grant's right hand men at Fort Hall. Name's Benson. He's told that same story so many times that he can't help tellin' it here, though the Britishers generally wait till you get along further west. A word here an' a word thar does the trick wi' the skeery ones, an' by the time they reach Fort Hall, they believe them stories. An empty stomach an' lame oxen try any man's nerve. No use fightin' back, though. Just tend to your own knittin'. Like the Cap'n here says, they never stopped Whitman, did they?"

After purchasing a small quantity of gunpowder, Mark Morgan and the two boys, piloted by Bill Brewster, wandered about the fort. French Canadian trappers, their squaws and families, traders, emigrants in brown homespun and visiting Dakotas in white buffalo robes, made up a strange company, speaking a strange jargon of languages. Upon hearing a bell ring for supper, Bill Brewster led his small party up some narrow steps to the palisade where they could see, in the dim light, the vast barren plains that spread in all directions.

"You'll get better food in your own wagons," Bill remarked as he saw Aaron look longingly down at the people filing into one of the rooms below for supper. "They've got corned beef here, but heaven help the feller wi' poor teeth. Now you see that?" and with his long forefinger he pointed towards the west where some platforms, built high, could still be seen.

"Yes. What are they?" asked Aaron.

"Injun cemetery. The bodies of Dakota chiefs. The Dakotas think the Crows'll leave their chiefs alone if they're left near the fort. Ha! Here they come. I've been waitin' for 'em."

"Who . . . the chiefs?" asked Captain Morgan, smiling a little.

"No, the hosses . . . back from feedin' in the meaders.

The guards are drivin' 'em in. The critturs are half wild an' belong to the fort."

From out of the twilight, a stream of fifty or sixty horses could now be seen as they crossed the plain, entered the narrow gate of the fort and continued on into a corral. Like a turbulent rush of water they flowed through, manes and hoofs flying, eyes rolling. The guards with lashing whips followed but it was some moments before the animals quieted, their cries of mingled rage and pain as they bit and kicked one another gradually subsiding.

For one panic-stricken moment, Jason, leaning over the rail, believed he saw Kit among the horses, and then he realized that his fears were groundless.

"Mis' Collins wouldn't trade Kit here at the fort, would she?" he asked. The thought of Kit loosed among these untamed creatures made him feel weak and ill.

"Oh, no, I shouldn't think so," answered Captain Morgan comfortingly. "My guess is that she'll trade farther on where horses are scarce and prices higher."

Jason, however, was unable to shake the depression which had descended upon him and he turned away from the strange lonely scene before him, suddenly wishing he were home. Home . . . with the familiar walls of the old farmhouse about him; his mother, Tacy and Sammy close by. Oregon seemed very far away at that moment. He was tired . . . tired in every bone of his body. Disappointment at not finding Sammy, the Englishman's insidious warnings of hardships ahead, the barbaric scaffolds outlined on the silent plains, the worry of losing Kit, made him realize, more than ever, the great task he had undertaken. In all this strangeness about him, he felt lost and longed for something familiar, something to reassure himself that he was still Jason Coit. Even the wagon where he slept alone and the friendly little Porky were better than this. . . .

"I guess I'll go back." With that, Jason turned towards the steps.

"I reckon we'd all better go," replied Bill Brewster quickly. "That mongrel stew ain't settin' too well yet." It was obvious the old scout sensed the boy's low spirits, and Jason thanked him with a faint smile.

"I say, Bill," said Aaron, pulling at the scout's sleeve, "what's dog stew taste like, anyway? Does it taste like our beef?"

"I'll cook you up some, one of these days," promised Bill, "an' then you can see for yourself. No, it ain't like beef, it's more like mutton . . . mutton stew thickened with hairs. . . . If I take to barkin' an' growlin' all of a suddint, don't go gettin' skeered. Anyway, it's a lot easier on my ol' legs than the cricket cakes the Fishin' Falls In-juns feed you."

"What did the cricket cakes do to you, Bill?" asked Mark Morgan, evidently enjoying the old scout's recital.

"Why, they just wore me out," complained the old man mournfully. "They had me hoppin' an' chirpin' over the sandhills all night long. No, give me mongrel stew any time, even wi' the tail thrown in," and Bill Brewster continued to rub his stomach tenderly as he followed the others down the narrow steps to the floor below.

16

IN AN OLD CEMETERY

Henri had no words of reproach for the three wet and cold children upon their return to camp. For once he was industrious, humming beneath his breath as he reheated the rabbit stew. The rain had stopped. Sammy, huddled close to the fire, drank thirstily of the hot broth and gazed uneasily at the trapper when the latter was not looking. What was Henri planning to do? Mete out new forms of punishment farther along the trail? Or had he already recognized Jessica as the real culprit? Perplexed, but too weary to keep awake, Sammy rolled himself into an extra flannel shirt of the trapper's and slept.

The remainder of the day continued sunny and was spent quietly. While their clothes dried on a rack of sticks before the fire, Jessica and Anna draped themselves in gaudy shawls which came from the depths of Ol' Squaw's packs. Anna was delighted and forgot her disappointment at not obtaining horehound candy at the fort but Jessica was silent, revolted by the disagreeable odor of skunk which pervaded all of the old woman's clothing. Meanwhile Henri, carrying the saddlebags, climbed frequently to a high perch on the cliffs above. It was evident that he feared the return of the trappers. Travel was resumed at nightfall, and in the early dawn camp was made in a remote meadow where the half-starved ponies could graze.

For the next three nights they pushed westward. With Henri worried and irritable, all conversation was made in whispers and there was no music. Then travel was resumed by daylight and living returned to normal. By now Ol' Squaw had discovered that her missing sleeve had been used as a patch in Sammy's trousers. She squinted at it frequently and called Anna's attention to it, as if to excite the child to claim her rights. Henri, amused, listened but took no part in the byplay. He was hurrying to reach Independence Rock and thought of nothing else.

One evening Henri explained to Sammy the reason for his haste. All his life, he said, he had wanted to see his own name added to the names already there upon the rock . . . Sublette, Bonneville, Serre, Henry Clay, Fremont, Carson. And then with childish eagerness he produced a little copper can with a wire handle. The can contained some black paint which Ol' Squaw had concocted. Some people, continued Henri, spent hours chiseling their names in granite but he, Henri Jules, was willing to have his name lettered in paint. It cost nothing, he added, to write one's name on the rock . . . that is, if one knew how to write. . . . And here the trapper paused significantly and gazed at Sammy with eyes which reminded the boy of a big Saint Bernard dog he had once seen in Brownsville.

"Huh, you can't write an' you want me ter climb up there an' do it," said Sammy bluntly. So this was the reason

Henri had remained so sweet-tempered after Jessica's attempt to escape!

"Yass, yass. It will be mag-neef-i-cent! Henri Jules in beeg black lettaires. Dere I shall leeve in de sun an' rain alway . . ." and the trapper's big hairy hands waved ecstatically.

"But ain't the trappers goin' ter see it?' questioned Sammy. "Them trappers you're runnin' away from?"

Henri hesitated a moment, a short flash of doubt and fear in his eyes, and then shrugged. "Mebbe. But Henri Jules, he takes hees chance!"

Henri had considered all angles. Sammy knew there was no use denying he could write, for he had been caught several times printing his own name in the sand. His hope had been that Jason was close behind on the trail and would see it. But Henri's large flat feet had stamped out the name and all hope each time. The single letter H in the name Henri was the only letter that was familiar to the trapper.

"What'll you gimme ter do it?" asked Sammy, always ready for a trade. He wanted a knife badly but concentrated his gaze upon Henri's belt. The belt was a finely braided affair, the length of his mother's trunk strap at home and especially prized by the trapper.

"I was not an-gree wit you an' your leetle squaws when you runned away," said Henri, as one hand caressed the belt protectively.

"You know I had nothin' ter do wi' that," retorted Sammy. A long pause followed and Sammy continued to stare at the belt. " 'Course, if you don't wanter trade the belt," he finally compromised, "gimme a knife."

"No, no," and Henri shook his head decidedly.

"The ol' one you whittle with . . ."

"No, no."

"I ain't goin' ter climb that rock fer nothin'. . . . An' the more I think 'bout it, I guess I don't want the job." Sammy turned away as though the matter was closed.

"*Sacré bleu!* Nevaire have I seen a rascal like you! You weesh my belt, you weesh my knife . . ."

"The ol' woman's got a knife," and Sammy faced him again. "It's worse'n yours. The blade's worn off. But I might do the printin' for it . . . an' the patch, too," he added as a happy afterthought. "The ol' woman keeps lookin' at it."

"But she like de knive." Henri seemed to be in pain because he was making so little progress. "De patch, she belong to mese'f," and Henri peered down hopefully to see if the patch was still in Sammy's trousers. "I will geeve you de patch if you climb de rock."

"I want the knife too. The patch an' the ol' woman's knife. You can fix the trade if you wanter."

"Yass," agreed Henri wearily. "But you won't get de knive til' dat print she is finished. Already you have de patch. *Sacré bleu!*"

Henri made his bargain with Ol' Squaw. Long ago he had found a moustache cup of heavy china among furnishings discarded by the emigrants. Ol' Squaw had coveted it for some time. With an alacrity which astonished Henri, she traded the knife and all rights to the patch for the moustache cup, which now became one of her choicest possessions.

Days passed slowly. Long days of sandy plains and

KEEP THE WAGONS MOVING!

alkali marshes. . . . Gradually hills began to take shape in the distance. When at last two high bluffs of reddish color were passed across the river, both Henri and Ol' Squaw gave way to rejoicing and exclamations of satisfaction. In some way these bluffs were of peculiar significance. Henri's party was now traveling parallel to the main Oregon trail and the children could see once more, far below the mountain paths they followed, the familiar cloth-topped wagons, grayer now, stained with rains and dust. Jessica could hardly contain her excitement. Willing now to rely upon Sammy's judgment, she helped him hide a small supply of berry pemmican under Whitey's blanket-saddle. Their greatest problem, they both agreed, was extracting Anna from Ol' Squaw's clutches. The horehound candy ruse had failed and Anna was as wary of promises as a young fox.

From across Sweetwater River, the first glimpse of Independence Rock sent a dubious thrill down Sammy's backbone. It resembled a huge animal ready to spring. Were any knife and patch worth the climb up this rock? For a moment Sammy felt unusually short and small. But the names of Sublette, Bonneville, Serre, Henry Clay, Fremont and Carson challenged him. If others had climbed that high, he, Samuel Coit, could do the same. . . .

In a thick blanket of mist at daybreak the following morning, Sammy and Henri set out to do their job. As he walked along, carrying the copper can of black paint and a brush made by binding a jack rabbit's tail to the end of a stick, Sammy's eyes searched constantly for Jason's name on the rock high above. Had Jason come and gone without adding his name or was it hidden by the low screen of mist?

IN AN OLD CEMETERY

The rock appeared less of a monster close at hand. Crevices lined the smooth sides, making it possible for one to mount safely if he used care. Henri was not backward about choosing a difficult spot upon which to have his name emblazoned.

"Way up high, over dere," he demanded, pointing energetically.

"You got the knife ready to gimme when I get down?" Sammy asked for the tenth time.

"Yass, yass," groaned Henri, holding up the old knife with the thin curved blade. "Now you believe?"

"Yup. An' when I come down, throw it up on that ledge there. If you don't, I'll climb back an' mess up the printin'," Sammy threatened.

"Yass, yass," groaned Henri again.

Shrouded in mist, Sammy started his climb. The crimson mainstay of his trousers was the last which Henri saw of the young painter. Very soon, however, little stones came rolling down, which showed he was still on the climb. When the stones ceased to roll and the noise of scuffling boots against the rocks was silent, Henri knew Sammy had reached the chosen spot even though he could not see him through the mist which hung over his head like a white canopy.

"You are dere?" called Henri softly after a time. "You print de name?"

"What d'ye think I'm doin'?"

"Do not leave out one lettaire, an' make heem beeg," directed Henri as he nervously paced below with the saddle-bags over his arm. A little later there were sounds of further climbing.

"You are dere?" called Henri again.

There was no answer and Henri continued to walk back and forth. Suddenly the empty copper can clattered down the sides of the rock wall and barely missed Henri's head. A moment later Sammy appeared, a vague figure feeling his way along a lower ledge.

"Where's my knife? Gimme my knife or I'll go back . . ."

"Here is de knive," and Henri tossed it deftly to the ledge above. "But I cannot see my name in de mist," he complained.

"Look out! I'm comin'!" Sammy yelled and made an unexpected landslide, riding on the red patch the last fifteen feet of the journey. None the worse for his slip, he picked himself up and walked away.

"You can see it from here," he called to Henri. "Ten letters with a big H. Nice, ain't it?"

Henri joined him and stared upward. The wet paint gleamed and the large H stood out handsomely. Henri's lips and heavy black beard moved ten times and then came a grunt of approval. "It is mag-neef-i-cent! It is mag-neef-i-cent!"

Henri tore himself away from Independence Rock with an effort. And though he gazed at other names now clear of the mist, his eyes turned again and again to his own as he walked towards the camp in the hollow. Sammy swaggered after him, his hat perched jauntily on the back of his head. It was a beautiful morning. . . . Now he owned a knife; it was old, the blade was thin, but it was a knife and he had earned it honestly. He also owned the patch in the seat of his trousers. For the first time in his life he was glad his mother had made him go to school. He could read, write and count, and he realized that knowledge was power. Henri's name, painted upon the rock, looked very well indeed, but his own . . . SAMUEL COIT . . . painted higher up, looked even better . . . and Jason might see it. . . .

In June, life along the Sweetwater was pleasant. The river itself was a delight after days of arid plains with only stagnant pools of poison. There were prairie dogs to watch, and antelope; blue skies overhead and tremendous snow-capped mountains to the right of the trail. The nights were cold. The girls were obliged to sleep with Ol' Squaw in the tepee. Sammy slept snuggled against the trapper's back and turned with automatic precision whenever Henri turned. There were no further signs of the cloth-topped wagons, though both Sammy and Jessica scanned the road below at every opportunity.

On the third morning after leaving Independence Rock, Henri appeared with a large piece of ice wrapped in one of Ol' Squaw's shawls which he slung over one arm; he had the saddlebags over the other. He would make little explanation concerning the ice, merely saying it came from the ground and that he had to dig down under the grass to reach it.

Icy Slough! They were close to Icy Slough! How many times Sammy had heard Jason speak of this spot, where ice was to be found deep beneath the swamp grass. Emigrants often stopped here to make iced drinks with lemon extract. It was one of the pleasant stopover places along the trail. Jason had marked it with a red cross on the map above the kitchen table at home. Beyond to the west, stretched the Wind River Mountains and South Pass, which Jason called "the backbone of the continent." Even with his eyes closed, Sammy could see the map with its black line of the Oregon Trail winding across the country. Ah, they had come a long way. . . . If only he and Jessica and Anna could make their escape that night and join some wagon train at Icy Slough! But Henri was too wise and wary to let them out of his sight. . . .

Of late the trapper had not slept well. He had turned and twisted the night before and so, of course, had Sammy. However, there had been a moment, his first opportunity to investigate, when Sammy had poked and prodded the saddlebags just above his head. There was undoubtedly an object within, hard, irregular, shaped like a dog's bone and swathed in something soft. Sammy had withdrawn his hand just in time as Henri, with a powerful lurch, suddenly turned, reached for the saddlebags and drew them closer to him. A narrow escape! It was a few moments before Sammy could go to sleep again. Was Henri fearing the return of the wild-looking trappers or the dragoons? Towards dawn, the trapper roused the entire encampment out of a sound sleep and moved them to another spot. Ol' Squaw, suffering acutely with rheumatism, protested vigorously but Henri was adamant.

One evening, the last stop on Sweetwater River, Henri appeared out of the gloom, with a plank which he had ripped from the floor of some deserted wagon on the main trail and a bucket with a bit of black tar in the bottom. He was beaming with pleasure and had apparently come to an important decision.

"My head," and Henri pointed to his shaggy mane, "she have great ideas."

"Huh?" asked Sammy doubtfully.

"Yass. I weesh to see de name Henri Jules on dis board. Should I die," and Henri looked soulfully at the stars, "you shall put de name on de grave."

"Ain't you feelin' all right?" Sammy gazed at the trapper with round eyes. It had never occurred to him that either Henri or Ol' Squaw might sicken and die. This was a new side to Henri. The discovery came with no rush of regret.

"Ah," and Henri gazed skyward again, "to-day I am well, but to-morrow . . . who knows? Wit de name on de board, I am ready."

This time Sammy did not wait to trade. He immediately heated the tar over the coals and made a fresh brush from Henri's supply of rabbit tails. It was rather a pleasure to print Henri's name in such a good cause, and he made several fancy swirls above and below the lettering, which pleased the trapper immensely. There was nothing dismal about the proceeding, for Henri was appreciative and graves along the road had been a common sight. A pile of rocks to keep the wolves away, a marked cross, a wagon wheel or the bleached skull of a buffalo often designated the burial place of an emigrant. That Henri wished to advertise his dying was quite in keeping with his way of living. The trapper had lived with a flourish and he would end with a flourish. Moreover, with Henri at rest beneath the headboard and Ol' Squaw crippled with rheumatism, escape would not be so difficult. . . .

Sadly enough to Sammy's watching eyes, Henri continued

to remain surprisingly healthy. His cheeks lost none of their ruddy hue and he ate heartily of all foods. Moreover, this new interest in death appeared to put new life into his step and former worries seemed to drop away. The mystery deepened as Henri, carrying his cherished headboard under one arm, marched along softly humming a French martial air. Sometimes it was difficult to keep up with him. Was he planning to lie down upon some special spot ahead and die? Jessica was interested now. Henri's decease meant liberty.

"Marchons! Marchons!" hummed and sang Henri.

Mountains rose high on all sides. They were climbing constantly, Henri swinging north to a bridle path which ran fairly close to the base of snow-topped crags. This was familiar territory to the trapper and Ol' Squaw, and on the second afternoon after leaving Sweetwater River, camp was made near a small burial plot close by a large dead tree.

Henri seemed to be in the best of spirits and health as he retired for the night as usual. Towards morning, Sammy was conscious of being alone under the blanket but, too weary and drugged with sleep to care, he continued to sleep. Awakened by the trapper's return and the heavy snores which followed, Sammy for the second time dared to reach out a hand and feel of the saddlebags above his head. The hard object which had once been inside was gone. . . .

On his way to catch and saddle Whitey after the morning meal, Sammy caught a glimpse of a new grave in the cemetery. He approached cautiously and with some awe. Freshly-dug earth and a pile of stones told of a very recent burial. His eyes then lighted upon a headboard fastened securely among the rocks. The letters painted in tar read HENRI JULES, and there were fancy swirls above and below the name. Astounded and hardly able to believe what he saw, Sammy turned back to camp to make certain it-was actually Henri himself who was stamping out the breakfast fire, preparing for the day's travel. Yes, it was Henri, robust and vibrant with health, singing with the sheer joy of living. And at one side, tossed carelessly upon the ground, were the empty saddlebags.

Late in the afternoon of the same day, Ol' Squaw and Henri suddenly came upon a band of Crows, moving east in single file along the narrow path. Ol' Squaw recognized them as old friends and appeared delighted. Startled at the sight of the noisy, dark-skinned people, all three children shrank timidly behind Henri but soon lost their fear. The Indians proved a friendly lot. Almost fifty in number, they were of short, squat stature, their ponies carrying back-breaking loads of blankets, puppies and children. Some of the larger dogs were pulling travois. Old and young paid homage to Ol' Squaw, and all stared at the three white children. Several young squaws, tattooed and dressed in mantles of birds' skins, ran their hands through Jessica's and Anna's bright hair, expressing their amazement by covering their mouths with one hand. Henri, no longer burdened with the saddlebags, mingled among them, laughing and talking and appeared to be well acquainted with the leader of the band, an elderly Crow dressed in panther skins.

Camp was made in a meadow. Three wizened old squaws set up tepees, using very long lodge poles. With Sammy to do her work, Ol' Squaw clutched her umbrella tightly as though she did not exactly trust all these dear friends and walked about the encampment, visiting with the different families. Anna, who usually shadowed her, did not follow but remained behind, lost in admiration of a papoose swinging in its carrier from the doorway of a tepee.

"Look at Anna over there," whispered Jessica, who was helping Sammy put up Ol' Squaw's tepee. "She thinks that baby is a doll. You know she lost her doll the day we were stolen from our wagon. She's wanted one ever since. Do you think we will live with these people now? They seem to be very kind. . . . I guess we'd have enough to eat. But I don't want to be an Indian. I want to go home. Oh, Sammy, it's going to be awfully hard to get away from all these people!"

Tears were streaming down Jessica's face as she bent to pull the edges of the buffalo hide over stakes which she and Sammy had just pounded down. At that moment it was no disgrace to cry and Sammy, watching, almost envied her. From the hour that the band of Crows hove in sight, his courage had remained low, having dropped like a piece of lead into the soles of his boots. To escape so many people would be impossible. . . . How close they had been to Icy Slough and yet he, Samuel Coit, had made no attempt to reach the wagons which generally stopped there. His one hope now was that perhaps the Crows would continue east and Ol' Squaw and Henri go their way to the west. This he voiced to Jessica, who nodded her head disconsolately and burst into fresh tears. A little angry at this turn of events and to cheer himself somewhat, Sammy made up Ol' Squaw's bed doubly short, in apple-pie fashion, telling himself he was tired of doing old women's work. Also he was tired of sniveling girls, mountains, trails, and the west. . . . He wished he could have some of his mother's newly-baked bread, spread thick with freshly churned butter, and feel her hand as she sometimes used to touch the top of his head.

The moon had risen by the time the Crows had finished their supper of sausage-like meat, wild rice and dried berries, and had gathered about a huge fire of brightly burning sagebrush. Jessica, clutching Anna by the hand, followed Sammy about and finally settled near him, just beyond Ol' Squaw and Henri who were the center of attraction. But they were not to remain quiet for long, as Henri, spying them, suddenly decided there should be music. It was not the moment to refuse. Fifty pairs of coal-black eyes watched in anticipation and fifty pairs of ears waited to hear. A little later the girls' high clear voices rang out in the cold night air. Anna, sleepy and not interested, dragged and flatted but sang nevertheless, *The Monkey's Wedding* being her favorite:

> *"The monkey married the baboon's sister,*
> *He gave her a ring and then he kiss'd 'er,*
> *He kiss'd so hard he rais'd a blister—*
> *She set up a yell."*

Other songs followed: *From Greenland's Icy Mountains, Sam the Slick Pedlar,* and *Home, Sweet Home,* Jessica's voice faltering as she looked out over the rolling hills to the south and then up at the snow-capped mountains above gleaming frostily in the moonlight. Her voice had almost stopped when suddenly the elderly leader in panther skins rose to his feet and stood listening, his face turned towards the east. The music ceased and others rose, while all waited to catch some sound. Gradually there came the beat of a horse's hoofs.

Sammy, now straining to see, caught the dim outlines of a single horseman coming towards them. It was an Indian. Crouched low in his saddle, he half fell from his horse and stood swaying as he delivered a message in broken sentences to the leader. A pause followed and then pandemonium let loose. The messenger was taken within a tepee, men saddled their horses and called for firearms. Women hurried to obey, screaming as they ran. Dogs barked and children got underfoot. Even Henri, mounted on Marie, soon dashed out of sight. Seated once more by the fire, women beat their breasts, pulled their hair and chanted in sing-song voices. At last, after a frantic search, Sammy and Jessica found Anna crouched beside Ol' Squaw who, like the rest of the women, had covered her head with a shawl. Anna was also crying. Seizing her by both hands, Sammy and Jessica dragged her with them to the quiet of Ol' Squaw's tepee, where they paused breathlessly.

"A white man's killed the chief's son . . . Henri told me," announced Sammy.

"Ol' Squaw's cryin'," sobbed Anna. "She wouldn't speak to me."

Jessica, silent, watched with startled eyes as Sammy proceeded to roll up two of Ol' Squaw's blankets.

"Are we going now, Sammy? Are we really leaving?" she asked timidly.

"Go get Whitey an' don't talk," ordered Sammy. "Hang on to Anna while I hook a bag of that dried meat. I'll meet you. Quick, now. Don't stand there like an idjit."

At last Samuel Coit had sprung into action. The long-

IN AN OLD CEMETERY

awaited moment had come. Jessica, grasping Anna by the wrist, dragged her forcibly through the small doorway. The younger child's cries could not be heard above the chanting around the fire and Ol' Squaw, singing with her own people once more and sunk with them in their grief, neither saw nor heard. The wind blew cold against them as Sammy, leading Whitey, with Jessica riding and holding the rebellious Anna close to her, disappeared into the night.

17

ATTACK

As Fort Laramie had little to offer by way of supplies, it was not difficult to persuade the entire train of emigrants to continue their journey westward on the following day. Arrangements were made with Monsieur Bordeaux before their departure, however, that if the missing children should appear at the fort they were to be cared for and sent on to Oregon with reputable people in a later train.

For Jason, the fort had offered nothing but disappointment and he was glad to see the whitewashed walls grow dim with distance. The knowledge that Sammy was ahead, still following the trail, and the hope of overtaking him near Independence Rock, acted as a spur, constantly urging him to travel faster. Distance and time challenged him and threw him into feverish activity, even when the wagons were at rest.

"Your wagon don't need greasin', boy," admonished the old scout, as he watched Jason remove a wheel to examine the axle, long after the others had gone to bed. "Lor', it don't squeak like most. Better get your sleep. I see Cal still has his hoss. His woman ain't sold it yet."

Jason, crouched beside the wheel, looked up, the light from the flaring lantern exaggerating the shadows in his white face.

"I brushed him off this mornin'," said Jason, his expression brightening at the remembrance. "There were too many horses at Fort Laramie . . . but she may try tradin' at Fort Bridger," and the brightness faded.

"She might . . . an' she might not," replied Bill Brewster after a long pause. "We'll see. Now go to bed, boy. Got ter keep rugged an' spry if we're goin' ter ketch up wi' that brother o' yourn. Rough road tomorrer."

Black Hills, low, bristling with rough stunted cedar, warned all wayfarers of difficult miles ahead. Heeding the advice of the old scout once more, the emigrants left furniture and even farm implements beside the trail in an effort to lighten the loads of the oxen. It was not unusual to see a cherished mahogany four-poster, a walnut whatnot, or a maple cradle chopped and split and later burned as fuel to warm some evening meal. On they traveled, past Warm Springs, Bitter Cottonwood Creek, Horseshoe Creek, Big Timber Creek, with tall solitary Laramie peak keeping guard on the left. Most of the oxen, now lamed by sharp stones, walked slowly with heads lowered, their hoofs encased in small bags of buffalo hide.

"We're over the worst of the Black Hills now," encour. aged the old scout, "an' most folks has stood it well 'ceptin' the Collins family. They look to me like they had repeatin' measles. Sometimes I've wondered if Cal warn't playin' possum . . . But I seed him this mornin' an' he looked right peaked."

The Collins' wagon had become strangely silent. Almost

every bed was filled with feverish patients. Mrs. Collins and the baby appeared to be the only members of the family to have escaped the tortures of a flaming rash which itched to the point of distraction, and all the chores fell heavily upon the poor woman. However, she was not lacking in courage. Dressed in Cal's trousers, wearing his hat over her short-cut hair, she met her tasks manfully. Despite her rough ways and talk, she slowly began to gain the good will of men and women alike, all offering assistance when they could. Within the Morgan wagon, Aunt Liddy often cared for the tiny Collins infant. It was Jason's duty to look after Kit, staking the horse each night, brushing the chestnut coat until it shone and riding him over the swollen creeks.

"Sometimes I don't know whether I'm speakin' to a man or woman," Aunt Liddy frequently told Jason. "But I like Mis' Collins' spirit, I do. She's worth three of Cal. Some of the women act a bit shocked by her wearin' Cal's trousers, but far's that goes, she's always worn 'em. She's the head an' he's the tail . . . a worn-out mangy tail, if I ever see one."

Small bands of Indians were now passing the train, rarely stopping and traveling some distance from the regular trail. Their sullen and unresponsive attitude caused the old scout considerable anxiety. According to Monsieur Bordeaux at Fort Laramie, a man named Mills had left the fort two days prior to the train's arrival, journeying west with six others in two wagons, in search of adventure rather than land and homes.

"Bordeaux didn't like 'em," Bill Brewster told Mark Morgan. "They had a mean way with 'em. You can tell a man by his tradin'. Mills cheated two Dakotas right thar at the fort. I dunno. I'm fearin' he'll make mischief ahead. An Injun don't think very fast. All white men look alike to him. One man's skelp's good as another. . . . Soon we'll be passin' Red Buttes an' meetin' Crows. They're friendly, though like as not they'll steal the eyelashes off'n yer if you're asleep. But this Mills . . . I dunno . . . I dunno."

Under Bill Brewster's guidance the entire train passed safely over the cold snow-laden waters of the North Platte near Deer Creek and arrived rejoicing on the opposite shore. The Collins family, riding in their wagon upon a roughly constructed raft, waved from various openings and cheered feebly when the trip was done. Other trains, however, had not been so successful. The bodies of two horses and three oxen lay strewn along the bank and a wrecked wagon lay piled upon some rocks.

"That's some of Mills' outfit," pronounced the old scout grimly. "See that box over thar with his name painted on it? He don't know how ter travel, the fool! I'm hopin' now we'll ketch up with him. It's safer traveling with him than after him. Now we've crost the river, we're on the same side with yer brother," he told Jason later. "Before we reach the big rock, I'm plannin' to sign up some men fer a searchin' party. Of course it's all guesswork, son. But if Henri does like I think he will, he'll stay put a while near the rock. That's his favorite hangout. If he ain't thar, he'll be further down the line. It's any man's guess."

The country on the north shore of the North Platte afforded more wood and food for the animals and the train rested half a day before starting for Independence Rock. From then on, however, the trail became more and more sandy, trees disappeared and the great struggle for drinking water commenced. Pools of brown stagnant water, rimmed with biting alkali, tempted the hot and thirsty cattle, but every driver, warned of the danger, strove to keep his animals and wagon in line. One ox, escaping a lax driver, drank of the poisoned water; and while the entire train waited, bacon on a stick was pushed down the animal's throat to counteract the alkali. A little later, Porky decided to take a jaunt of his own and disappeared into the clouds of billowing dust created by the rumbling wagon wheels. Jason, tormented with the fear that the small pig might drink the poisoned water, could not leave his oxen to give chase. When the train halted beyond Poison Spider Creek near fresh clear pools, Jason, exasperated and concerned, walked the length of the line asking for Porky.

"No pig 'round here," came the reply on all sides.

Returning to his wagon, wondering if he should walk back in search of Porky, he was unexpectedly greeted by a little pig who came running out joyfully from under his own wagon wheels. The animal's entire body was colored a grimy buff. With alkali coating his pink snout and his tail wilted, Porky was hardly recognizable.

"I see you've still got yer farm with you," chuckled Elisha Jefferson, as he watched Jason wash the small runaway in clear water. "His feet all right?"

"They seem to be. My, but was I glad to see him! I didn't know I was so fond of the little critter. . . . 'Pears he was runnin' beneath the wagon all the time . . . I don't s'pose I'll ever know. That soda's powerful stuff; it ate half the sole off Seth Adams' shoe. Do you think I should give him some bacon?" and Jason nodded his head in Porky's direction.

"Don't seem necessary. He looks happy 'nough. What you feedin' Porky now? He ain't thin an' he ain't fat. Just right."

"Someone shot an old buffalo last week. The meat was too tough for reg'lar eatin' so I made jerky for Porky. I soften it in warm water . . ."

"Boy," and Elisha Jefferson's eyes twinkled in his weathered face, "you're goin' to make a good farmer, 'cause you take care of your stock better'n most. Any ideas where you're stakin' your land? I'd be glad to have you for a neighbor."

"I'm much obliged," and Jason's dark eyes showed he was pleased. "I don't know just where I'm locatin'. I'd like to be near you an' Mis' Jefferson, though. . . . I've got to find Sammy first. Are we making good time, Mister Jefferson?"

"Little better than reg'lar, they say. Willow Springs tomorrow night and Independence Rock the next day. You may be meetin' your brother on the trail any day now. If I can help wi' the searchin' party, let me know."

At the edge of Sweetwater River, emigrants and their stock paused to drink of the pure water. With thirst quenched, the wagons corralled, it was not long before a few energetic members of the train were climbing the steep sides of Independence Rock to add their names to those of Clay, Fremont, Carson, and others. Even Jason, his mind filled with plans for a scouting party which was to search for Sammy and the girls the next day, wondered if he should not leave his name for his mother and Tacy to see as they passed that way the following spring. Gazing at the names already there in large print and small, chiseled and painted, he was roused by a shout from Aaron, who came towards him carrying his father's spyglass with him.

"Jason, come down this way. Someone's written Martin Van Buren's name . . . looks like it was done last year. You don't think he came here himself an' did it, do you?"

"Why, I don't know," Jason replied, walking in Aaron's direction. "Maybe someone wrote it for him."

"You take the glasses and look. It's just above that fresh black paint up there. Here, stand where I am now and look up. See it?"

It took Jason a moment to adjust the glasses to his eyes. "Yes, I see it . . . Martin Van Buren. It was done last year, all right. It's faded some compared to that fresh paint beneath. Why, Aaron!"

Aaron, gazing in another direction, whirled quickly at the tone of Jason's voice. Jason was staring through the glass at the new lettering beneath Martin Van Buren's name, and his jaw dropped in astonishment as he struggled to read what he saw.

"S-A-M-U-E-L C-O-I-T! Aaron, I can't believe it! Look! Up there under Martin Van Buren's name! It's Samuel Coit . . . and I'm positive it's Sammy's printing! He's always made his S that way, ever since he was a little kid. Samuel Coit! Why, I'd know that printing anywhere. . . . Here, take the glasses an' see if I'm crazy or what," and Jason, trembling with excitement, passed the telescope to Aaron. "Am I wrong? Am I seein' things, Aaron?"

Almost as excited as Jason, his friend peered through the

glass and read the freshly painted name slowly. "SAMUEL
COIT . . . why, Jason, you're right! Well, I'll be dog-
goned. It's funny I didn't see it before . . . I looked just
above. Samuel Coit . . . that's what it is. Your brother's
been here. Just a minute . . . let me look some more,"
and breathless with excitement, Aaron moved the glass
about and finally stopped with a visible start of surprise.

"Holy smoke! Take the glass and look, Jason! Over to
the right . . . lower down. It's Henri Jules! He's got his
name up there, too. See it? Holy smoke, let's go find Pa!"

In another moment, still shouting in surprise as they ran,
Jason and Aaron started towards the wagons with their
astounding news.

There was much to be done in the two days' sojourn at
Independence Rock on Sweetwater River. Women washed
clothes and baked, while some of the men mended broken
axle trees and tongues of their wagons and others removed
from wheels tires shrunken loose by heated sand. Thinly
shaved hoops of wood were tacked to the rims and the tires
reheated and replaced to make the wheels substantial once
more . . . tasks which demanded patience and time. But
those who were able joined Bill Brewster and scoured the
countryside for the missing children.

Within her wagon, Mary Fields waited and stood silently
staring up at the fresh black name beneath Martin Van
Buren's. Hope and fear were written in her face as she
clasped the small Bluette tightly in her arms.

At last prints of the little girls' shoes were discovered in
a hollow north of the big rock.

"Accordin' to prints an' the paint on the rock, they're still 'bout four days ahead," was the old scout's verdict. "Aimin' fer the Pass, I reckon. We'll move on tomorrer. They may have met up wi' some friendly Crows by now. . . . That fool Mills is worrying me more'n the young'uns. I know his type, ridin' free an' easy, cheatin' the Injuns as he goes along. You can't blame the Injuns for skelpin' some folks."

Following a sandy inland road, the wagons moved up Sweetwater Valley the next day. And it was while they were encircling a gorge that the fears and predictions of Bill Brewster became a reality. Half concealed by the silvery-gray leaves of sagebrush was the short stocky body of a young Crow, lying face downward beside the trail . . . dead.

"Shot through the back! Mills again! Well, it's like I said," repeated the old scout, his thin face drawn in tense lines as he turned the Indian over in an effort to establish his identity. "You can't blame Injuns fer skelpin' some folks. . . ."

Within the hour, and under Bill Brewster's leadership, there was a tightening of discipline in Mark Morgan's train of thirty wagons. Whenever the trail permitted, and especially near nightfall, the schooners traveled in four columns with guards riding ahead, behind, and at either side. At the sound of the bugle and the cry "Corral! Corral!" the outer columns pushed ahead, drew in, and the inner columns angled out, leaving a space for the loose stock to be driven through by the herders. With all ends closed, the thirty wagons looked like an oblong fortress, with every gun loaded and in readiness. This maneuvering required

ATTACK

some practice but all set to work with a will. The Crows, when roused, were not an easy enemy to reckon with, the old scout warned the emigrants.

"An' that dead Injun warn't no common redskin," he emphasized. "His moccasins had finer beads than most an' his arrer heads were 'specially carved. He warn't on foot, neither. Most likely Mills is ridin' his hoss. Thar'll be no picnicking at Icy Slough," he announced firmly. "This ain't no time fer diggin' ice an' foolin' 'round with lemody water."

Nothing short of an Indian attack could have prevented the emigrants from picnicking at Icy Slough. For days Aaron had talked of nothing else and even Jason had found himself anticipating the unusual experience of digging for ice in the depths of a spring-fed swamp. Dreams of ice-chilled drinks flavored with extracts haunted every thirst-ridden emigrant. But with possible danger so close at hand, every member of the train forgot Icy Slough in the work before him. Guards were doubled in the night watches and every ear and eye were alert through the day for the least unfamiliar sound or sight.

The first serious warning of trouble came just before sunset on the third day, when Joel Adams, head scout, was seen galloping back through clouds of dust, calling the words, "Corral! Corral!" The bugle sounded and almost immediately the four columns of wagons formed their fortress. While the loose stock was being herded inside, the other scouts returned from all directions. Then Joel Adams, with lips bleeding and parched from the hot sun, told his story, one arm about his young wife as if to protect her from what he was about to say.

"I was ridin' 'bout a half mile ahead when I smelt smoke," Joel told his listeners. "I left my hoss in some willers an' crept on my belly over a rise so I could see. There warn't a sound. It was the Mills party, all right . . . every one of 'em dead. Skelped. The wagon was upside down, burnin', the hosses gone, the oxen's throats slit. There was feathers all over the place, on everythin' . . . someone had ripped open a feather bed. It was awful. . . ." And Joel's honest bronzed face showed his abhorrence, as his arm drew Sally Adams nearer to him.

"No sign of Injuns?" asked Bill Brewster. "No one hangin' 'roun'?"

"Not a sign."

"They're most likely circlin' to the left." The old scout peered out over the plains now tinged red by a glowing sun. "Or they might be slippin' down the riverbanks under the willers. They may come before dark. . . . Cap'n, keep your cattle inside tonight. Stake all the stock. No grass, no water. Go easy on your own drinkin' water, 'cause we might have to stay here a few days if they surround us. If it's a long siege, we'll dig trenches an' crawl in. Gol durn that man Mills and everyone like 'im!" and in sudden rage Bill Brewster pounded a fist into the palm of his other hand. "It's folks like him that turns the plains into a livin' nightmare. We was peaceful till his breed come along."

Supper was early and a hasty affair . . . a piece of bread and cold meat. The men worked fast. Barricades were formed of trunks, ox yokes, barrels, bales of hides, and blankets to protect the women and children. Men took their places on the ground behind the wheels of wagons, resting guns upon the spokes. With Jason's wagon next in line to the Morgans', it was possible for Aaron and Jason to be together. Occasionally Aunt Liddy, forgetting to whisper, could be heard as she gave directions to the women for making bandages. She was calm, cheerful, efficient as always, her tread even and heavy on the floor overhead as she moved about. Once she called down to the two boys below to ask if they could use as ammunition some old hard biscuits she had saved.

"Did you ever know anyone like Aunt Liddy?" Aaron asked Jason in a low whisper.

"I never did," and Jason shook his head decidedly.

"Well, she's sure different from most women. Just before supper, when we were overhaulin' the guns, she said she hoped the Indians would come, seein' we were makin' all this trouble to receive 'em. An' then she said it would be such a pity if I didn't have a good story to tell my great-grandchildren some day of how I crossed the plains an' fought the redskins. Even Pa, worried as he is, had to laugh. Something tells me he knows about the sour beans, though. . . . Now she's havin' all the skeery women make bandages as if they were gettin' ready for a party. She's got an old blunderbuss up there . . . say's she's goin' to use it. I hope Sammy's not mixed up in this," Aaron added, suddenly aware that Jason was only half listening.

"I hope not . . . the Crows might turn on white children if they get mad enough. Maybe Sammy an' the girls are at Fort Bridger by now. . . . I'm wonderin' all the time what Sammy's doin', what he has to eat, an' if he's warm enough. . . . I keep lookin' at that old bowie knife of his . . . Sammy's got a lot of sass an' spunk for his age . . . almost too much . . . but I hate to think of some greasy trapper or redskin beatin' it out of him." There was a long silence and then Jason heaved a deep sigh. "This country is almost too big, Aaron. It's like huntin' for a needle in a haystack to find one person. Don't you feel it?"

"I know what you mean. I've felt it ever since we left Fort Laramie."

Another pause. A pale half moon came out from behind banked clouds. It was still twilight and quiet, as if a thick blanket of silence had fallen over the plains. Only the shrill chorus of crickets, which rose and fell with the regular rhythm of a drumbeat, broke the silence.

"Where's Kit?" Aaron asked.

"Cal's out of bed now. He hitched him to the side of his wagon."

"It's gettin' darker. Bill Brewster says Indians don't attack at night, as a rule. They've got some superstition 'bout it. But it isn't quite night yet. . . . I wish I had a nice cold drink with ice from Icy Slough in it. They say at Soda Springs . . ."

A sharp piercing whistle suddenly interrupted Aaron, who half rose to his knees. One of Jason's hands reached out and pulled him down again.

"Down, Aaron, they've come! That was an eagle-bone whistle . . . I've heard them before."

"Fill in the wheels!" called Mark Morgan. "Don't fire until I tell you. Don't waste your powder. Stand by your guns!"

The pounding of horses' hoofs and weird high yells now came from the direction of the river. A galloping line of Indians, barely visible in the distance, became clearer as they began to circle the wagons.

"They're spreadin' out," called Bill Brewster's voice. "Thirty of 'em! Get ready!"

A sudden shower of arrows thudded into the drill covering of the wagons and a few, curving high, dropped inside. An ox moaned and pulled at his iron chain. The Indians had now encircled the wagons. There were no riders to be seen but Jason knew that each Indian hung on the furthermost side of his pony, ready to shoot his arrows from beneath or above the animal's body. Dust rose in stifling clouds and there was the sound of lashing whips.

"All right, boys, give it to them!" ordered Mark Morgan.

A blast of rifle fire rang out and there were muffled cries of surprise and pain. Jason, staring out from between spokes of wheels, saw gaps in the ranks of the Indians. Several ponies were down, struggling on the ground. Dark figures were running, leaping upon the backs of horses ahead. The gaps closed and evened. Another shower of arrows! Horses within the enclosure of wagons whinnied and reared and several cattle plunged to one side. A woman screamed and there was the sound of running feet as the third onslaught of arrows cut the darkness.

"Stand by your guns, every man of you!" shouted Captain Morgan.

From then on, the rifle fire continued relentlessly. There was powder smoke everywhere with its hot salty smell. From above, Aunt Liddy's blunderbuss gave forth a dull roar. Yelling derisively, the Crows rode even closer but, seeing more ponies fall, moved farther away, widening the spaces. Still yelling, they finally disappeared over the sandhills to the left. The attack, sharp, brief, and fierce, was over. No one spoke until a child's wail broke the silence.

"You boys all right?" asked Captain Morgan suddenly from behind.

Jason turned quickly but Aaron remained motionless, standing on his feet and staring out into the night.

"We're both all right," replied Jason. "It didn't last long, did it?"

"What is it, son? What are you looking at? You aren't hurt?" asked Mark Morgan again, his voice anxious as he came closer.

"I'm all right, Pa. . . . It's that thing out there . . . I killed him, Pa. I saw him throw up his hands when I fired."

Mark Morgan flashed his lantern in front of him and Jason and the captain leaned forward. Just beyond lay the form of an Indian . . . a small, elderly man dressed in panther skins.

"His horse ran off with the others," Aaron continued in a strangely subdued voice. "Pa, I killed him an' now I wish I hadn't. . . ."

"Might not have been your bullet, Aaron," comforted his father. "Besides, even if it was, you were doing a man's work."

"But I've killed a man, Pa . . ."

"I know how you feel, son. I know."

There was a silence. Aaron was suffering, awed, and shocked.

"It could have been my bullet, Cap'n Morgan," offered Jason. But there was no conviction in his voice and Mark Morgan turned towards him and nodded understandingly.

"It doesn't matter, boys, whose bullet shot him. We were all trying to protect our women and children. There's another man out there and I daresay no one knows who shot him. Forget it, Aaron. You aren't a boy any longer now. . . . Everyone in here is safe except Cal Collins."

"Cal?" asked Jason quickly.

Mark Morgan bowed his head. He now had an arm across his son's shoulders as the boy continued to stare into the darkness.

"Cal heard a horse get loose. He thought it was Kit. He left his gun and ran out from beneath his wagon. An arrow got him between the ribs. He's dead . . . he shouldn't have left his post."

There were two more attacks at dawn. With faces painted black, and chanting as they rode, the Crows swooped down upon the wagons from the rear in an attempt to carry off their dead. It was Bill Brewster's advice to let them succeed.

"Let 'em have their dead," he urged. "They're 'feared we'll skelp the ol' man in panther skins an' then he can't go to the happy huntin' grounds. Let them have 'im. I reckon he's their leader. Now mebbe they'll quit, seein' we're on guard. We'll leave the ol' man here an' bury Cal as we go along."

Like all the other emigrants who died on the way, Cal Collins was buried with his head to the west, in a small grassy plot beside the Sweetwater. Cal's love for his horse had been his undoing and no one knew this better than his widow. Now, with a colony of hungry mouths at her heels and with only slow-witted Bill to help, Mrs. Collins was doubly anxious to be rid of the horse. It became generally known that Kit would be traded for oxen at the next trading post, Fort Bridger.

"That is, if it's a good trade," added Mrs. Collins sagely.

On, up through the valley of the Sweetwater went the wagon train, steadily climbing the gentle ascent while scouts rode ahead and guards protected the sides and rear of the wagons. There was little sleep for women who knew their men to be on night duty. However, there were no more attacks from the Crows as the snow-crowned Wind Mountains loomed nearer. Tension eased and courage strengthened.

"Not much chance of their attackin' here," Bill Brewster announced. "The land's too open. But don't get lax. This is Injun country an' we're trespassin'. I only hope they ain't layin' fer the next wagon train down below. Keep yer eyes open!"

Mountains and sky! Cold nights when sagebrush, used as fuel, failed to boil water quickly or to warm shivering, blue-lipped homesteaders. Yet it must be used; for sagebrush was hot and quick and left no glowing embers. Then there was mountain fever. Aaron, quiet and thoughtful since the killing of the Indian, was among the sufferers. He tossed feverishly at night but refused to remain inside the wagon during the day.

The train continued to pull upward and finally arrived on a flat summit, a broad valley twenty miles wide. The South Pass at last!

"Seems strange," commented Aunt Liddy to Jason, walking beside the Morgan wagon as it lumbered along the broad open road. "Folks back home think of the Pass as narrer, full of Injuns, sharp rocks an' sarpents. But look at us! Green mountings on the left an' snow up there on the right. An' look at the clouds. Seems like I could reach my hand up an' touch 'em, they're so near. I guess this is as near as some folks will ever get t' Heaven," she added thoughtfully.

"We'll be seein' Oregon soon . . . just think of it!" replied Jason enthusiastically. "Bill says we'll see it goin' down the west slope."

"Yes, we'll be seein' Oregon, but there's still a thousand miles to travel before we can settle. . . . Dear me, I do hope there ain't any sagebrush in Heaven," continued Aunt Liddy, still busy with her thoughts. "I'm dreadful tired of lookin' at it. What's Aaron doin'?"

"He's drivin' for me. I got him to sit up on the front seat."

"He oughter be in bed with that face, red as a peony! But I can't do nothin' with him," Aunt Liddy complained. "An' he dreams all night of shootin' that Injun. Queer it should stir him up so. I tell him I kilt that Injun with my blunderbuss, but he don't believe me. Now 'twouldn't have bothered me a bit if I had," and Aunt Liddy's gray eyes glared belligerently from the depths of her faded sunbonnet. "But Aaron's always been soft-hearted 'bout hurtin' animals an' things. Mark says we're all different an' I guess it's so. He'll get over it . . . but I don't like that fever burnin' 'im up."

Mountains and sky . . . mountains and sky . . .

"It's about here," Bill Brewster announced a little later. "This is the halfway point. From now on you'll be seein' the water run west. You'd better say good-bye to the East, 'cause you won't see it no more once we start goin' down. An' if I ain't mistook, thar's a storm brewin'.'"

"Keep 'em movin'! Get 'em over the top! Keep the wagons movin'!"

There was neither time nor opportunity to say good-bye to the East. Those who had been yearning to return to their former homes were given no last lingering look, no moment in which to shed nostalgic tears. For rain and hail descended with such force that the drill covering above their heads was slashed and torn. Women clutched their children to them. Others climbed forward to take their places on the front seats of wagons. Fathers, brothers, sons and husbands were bent double as they walked against the wind, frantically urging the sore-footed oxen forward.

"Nearer My God to Thee," sang a high soprano voice between rolls of thunder. Others, taking courage, joined in. Jason, walking beside King and shielding his face from the stinging hail, added his voice. In the storm, cruel in its ferocity, the wagon train moved slowly, as though barely alive and in great pain.

Three hours later, thirty torn, ice-coated prairie

schooners emerged from dense clouds into sudden sunlight. They had reached Pacific Springs. Though his clothes were frozen stiff with sleet and his face cut and bleeding, Jason was no longer conscious of discomfort. From the western slope of the Great South Pass, Oregon lay before him. Oregon! Oregon, with its uncharted wilderness, its endless rivers, forests, mountains. . . . Somewhere in its untamed immensity was land . . . his land . . . acres to be fenced, ploughed and planted, a home to be built. A sudden exultation seized him and his voice held a clear ring which made Mark Morgan, walking ahead, turn and stare.

"Cap'n Morgan! Cap'n Morgan! It's Oregon! It's O-R-E-G-O-N!" East had become West for Jason Coit.

18

FROM FORT BRIDGER
TO FORT HALL

Fort Bridger, one hundred and thirty-three miles from Pacific Springs, was the first trading post established for emigrants in the wilderness west of the Missouri River. At the sight of the small and mud-chinked log houses at the foot of the snow-topped Uinta Mountains, a cheer rose from the foremost wagons of Captain Morgan's train. Fort Bridger was no longer a penciled cross on a piece of paper. Here was refuge, as well as welcome from Jim Bridger, well-known scout, trader, trapper and friend of Bill Brewster's. And here might be found some word or trace of the three missing children.

Hope and fear tore at the hearts of Ezra Fields and Jason Coit as the heavy gate of timber swung open. To the surprise of all, Jim Bridger himself stood before them, a tall man dressed in a loose coat of deerskin, with a broad-brimmed hat over his long gray hair. From afar he had recognized Bill Brewster and now showed his satisfaction in a wide tobacco-stained smile.

"How, pardner!" he called.

"How!" Bill swung an arm in greeting. Still seated upon his mustang, the old scout then introduced Mark Morgan, who had walked forward with Ezra Fields and Jason.

"This here is Cap'n Morgan, squar' as they make 'em," and Bill swung his arm again.

"How!" acknowledged Jim Bridger, his eyes meanwhile roving the length of the wagons in an appraising stare. "Green River high?" he asked after a slight pause.

"Much too high," replied Mark Morgan.

"We tripled wagons at the ford," added Bill Brewster significantly.

"Yer oxen look beat."

"That desert don't help man or beast. But before we unload, we wanter find out somethin'," pursued the old scout.

"Spit 'er out," encouraged Jim Bridger.

"See any young'uns go by?"

"Young'uns?"

"Boy an' two girls. Party here is wantin' to know."

"Naw," and Jim Bridger's eyes had returned to the anxious faces before him. "I ain't seed any young'uns. But one of my squaws was berryin' on a hill north o' here. She seed three young'uns an' a hoss on the ol' cut-off, travelin' west. Boy had a red shirt on an' a big hat. She was too fur away to speak. Looked like two gals an' a boy."

"God be praised!" exclaimed Ezra Fields hoarsely.

"How long ago?" asked Jason, conscious that his voice trembled.

"Let's see . . ." Jim Bridger lifted his hat and scratched his head thoughtfully. " 'Bout two-three days back, I reckon. Kin o' yourn?"

"My brother. The girls belong to him," replied Jason, nodding at Ezra. "But were they alone? Wasn't there a man an' an Indian woman with them?" The suspense was almost unbearable as Jim Bridger deliberated.

"Well, now, my squaw said jest three young'uns an' a hoss. She spoke 'bout it two-three times, wonderin' 'bout 'em. She thought they took the wrong road . . . some folks do. The boy was walkin' an' t'others ridin'."

"Must be they're rid of the ol' woman an' Henri Jules!" exclaimed Ezra excitedly.

"You say Henri Jules?" asked Jim Bridger.

"Henri Jules," affirmed Bill Brewster. "You heerd 'bout Henri?"

"Sure," nodded Jim Bridger. "He's wanted fer stealin' a nugget belonging to the San Roy mines in New Mexico. Party through here t'other day says Governor Abernethy's holding a big reward fer the nugget at Oregon City. A thousand dollars!"

"Whew!" whistled Bill Brewster softly. "That's a good sum."

"Well, it's a good nugget. If I didn't have my hands full here, I'd go a-gunnin' fer Henri. Like as not he's in the mountains now, though. Where'd they see 'im last?"

"Didn't see 'im. But he left his name on Independence Rock."

"Lor', he's got a nerve, with half the country huntin' fer 'im! Well, if the kids are free of 'im, they oughter be halfway to Fort Hall by now. The cut-off jines the trail near Big Muddy. An' the Injuns are friendly. They like white kids." Once more Jim Bridger was studying the weary oxen and ragged cloth-topped wagons. "You best spread out in the meaders," he advised, "an' feed yer oxen. Unhitch an' unload," and with this welcome and a casual nod, Jim Bridger turned on his heel and silently departed.

"Two-three days back" . . . . The children were not far away! To Jason came great relief and something else . . . pride in Sammy. Sammy, the irresponsible, the stubborn, the unaccountable, was seeing his job through. He had not deserted the two little girls and in some way, between them, all three had managed to escape, unharmed by the trapper and old squaw. Three children and one pony! How had they managed to cross the long stretch of Green River Desert and then Green River itself, a roaring flood of ice-cold water? If only Jim Bridger's squaw had been near enough to call and bring the children to the warmth and comfort of the fort. . . . However, in a few days the British agent, Captain Grant, would be listening to their story. Possibly the Englishman named Benson might be present and remember the conversation at Fort Laramie concerning the three missing children. And the Indians were friendly . . . Surely there was much to be thankful for!

Mary Fields had joined her husband and now both were openly crying from relief and disappointment. Jason, close to tears himself, turned away. A sudden glimpse of Kit standing patiently at the rear of the Collins' wagon only added to his torture. This was the place on the trail where Kit would leave the train, to become the property of a stranger. . . .

In another moment Captain Morgan had given the signal and the train started once more. The circle was formed in a meadow and soon wisps of smoke from campfires rose as women prepared the evening meal.

Jason, unable to eat, stared blankly across the meadow at the low outlines of Fort Bridger's walls. Later the men would go to the fort to buy, trade and visit. Dressed in her late husband's trousers and accompanied by Bill, Mrs. Collins would go to the fort, leading Kit. It was generally known that Jim Bridger had oxen on hand to sell or trade. Ah, yes, greedy eyes would stare at Kit; strange, rough hands would pass over his chestnut coat. The horse would be nervous, frightened, and he, Jason, would be forced to stand by helplessly and watch the transaction.

"I guess I'll go to bed early," he told Aaron a little later. The latter, propped up on his bed, had been Aunt Liddy's patient for the past few days. A cold unexpected plunge in the waters of Green River had not improved Aaron's fever and he was now running a temperature which alarmed even his father.

"You're not goin' to the fort?" asked Aaron in surprise, as his thin hands moved restlessly over the blanket. "Why, I s'posed everybody, 'ceptin' the women, of course, would go. Pa an' Bill Brewster are there now."

"Blossom isn't acting right tonight. Walkin' across the desert left her sort of ailin'."

"But Pa said . . ."

"Jason's tired, can't you see, Aaron?" asked Aunt Liddy a little sharply. "He's sensible . . . he knows when it's time to stop an' rest. Besides, he's just told you Blossom's ailin'." Aunt Liddy, darning beneath the light of the kerosene lantern, was plainly tired herself. There was a little stoop to her generally erect shoulders, and worry over Aaron had robbed her cheeks of their color.

"You got flour enough, Jason?" she continued. "Bill

Brewster says Jim Bridger'll give us fair prices 'cause they're ol' friends. Now, Jason," and Aunt Liddy looked up sharply from her work, "if you're short of money, Mark would help you out."

"Oh, no, Aunt Liddy. I've enough flour. Thanks."

"Two days of good grass an' Blossom'll pick up. That little hog all right?"

"Porky's fine."

"Well, there's no need of worryin' over Sammy. If he's crossed that desert an' the Green wi' the two girls an' got this fur, he'll reach Fort Hall," and again Aunt Liddy gave Jason a quick look.

Something was troubling Jason, Aunt Liddy told herself after the boy had gone. Blossom was thin, but not so sick that Jason needed to remain away from the fort and look after her. There were dark shadows under Jason's eyes; worry shadows, Aunt Liddy called them. Jason was fretting, grieving over something. It wasn't money, nor Blossom, Porky, or that imp of a Sammy. Something else . . . something else . . . Suddenly Aunt Liddy put down her darning, reached for her shawl and wrapped it about her.

"Aaron, I'm goin' to the fort for a few minutes."

"Aunt Liddy!"

Aaron sat up straight in his bed and stared at his aunt with amazement. A fort swarming with Indians, trappers, traders and rough men ready to fight over bargaining was the last place anyone would expect to find a lady at night. What would Bill Brewster and his father say when they saw her enter? Why didn't she remain at home in her wagon like other women? A second glance told Aaron that Aunt Liddy was determined.

"Then I'm goin' with you!" and one of Aaron's bare feet appeared from beneath the blanket.

"No, you're not! You stay in that bed!"

A second bare foot followed the first and then Aunt Liddy's voice rose higher. "Aaron Morgan, do you hear me? If I ketch you followin' me I'll whale you, sick or well! I've got business there nobody else can 'tend to," and now there were two bright red spots on Aunt Liddy's cheeks. "You get back into that bed!" and before Aaron could reach for his trousers hanging on a near-by peg, she seized them and wrapped them snugly in the ends of her shawl. Then, spying his boots, she added them to the bundle.

"Aunt Liddy!"

"Now you can't come, 'cept in a nightshirt," she stormed, edging towards the door.

"But, Aunt Liddy, I need a drink of water. There's lots of things I'll be needin' . . ."

"You've just had a drink an' I won't be gone more'n an hour. I'll ask Sally to stop by soon's she finished her dishes." And with that Aunt Liddy was gone.

Aaron slowly pulled his feet in under the blanket once more and lay staring at the ceiling of the wagon. There were more trousers and boots in a chest near by, but Aunt Liddy always carried the key in her petticoat pocket. Someway or other, she always seemed to get her own way. Despite the hot glow of fever which mounted and surged over him, Aaron turned over on his side, smiling a little. Aunt Liddy at Fort Bridger! Aunt Liddy, who hated the raw strange smells of primitive living and who could not be persuaded to step inside the gate at Fort Laramie, had chosen of her own accord to go to Fort Bridger alone. Alone!

But *why* had Aunt Liddy gone to Fort Bridger?

Early the next morning, Jason dressed himself slowly, thoughtfully. It had been his custom for many mornings to single out Kit, speak to him and pet him while others slept. The horse always seemed to expect him, to watch for him. But where was Kit now? Probably at the fort among the horses belonging to Jim Bridger, in a large yard enclosed by a picket fence . . . or was he already gone with a trapper, traveling some strange mountain path?

The uncertainty of not knowing the whereabouts of Kit was more unbearable than witnessing the actual trade transaction. Jason had sunk into a deep sleep the first part of the night, only to waken before dawn, condemning himself, thoroughly miserable. As a friend, he had failed Kit. Selfish in his own grief, he had stayed away from the fort not wishing to see Kit sold. Had he been less cowardly, he would have been present and found a way to talk with the new owner. There were many things to tell the new owner about Kit: that gentle talking instead of whip lashing would persuade the horse to ford any river, how the notes of the whistle-call would bring him running, and the way Kit liked his coat brushed. . . . But he had made no effort to say any of this and now perhaps the horse was gone forever. This last realization threw him into a final panic of dressing. His belt twisted, the buckle broke, and he stumbled twice over Porky, who insisted upon walking between his feet.

In a few moments Jason was out of the wagon, hurrying

in the direction of the fort. In another moment he was passing a low flat meadow where the horses and oxen belonging to the train were staked for the night. There was not the remotest chance of Kit's being there among them, yet something slowed his feet, made him stop. Two guards from Connecticut, a father and son, were just leaving, their night duty finished.

"Lookin' fer someone?" called the father, a tall grizzly man in his early sixties. The son, tall and lanky, seemed to be only half awake as he yawned and rubbed his eyes. They were a friendly pair, with guns over their shoulders. A coffee pot dangled on a thong from one of the barrels.

"I'm on my way to the fort. Did Mis' Collins trade her horse last night . . . were you there?" The words came out painfully and the seconds seemed hours before the father answered.

"Sure, I was there," he drawled, "an' so was Pete," pointing a thumb in the direction of his son. "They had quite a session, they did. For some reason Bill Brewster didn't want Jim Bridger to take the hoss. I saw him make all kinds of signs behind Mis' Collins' back, but Bridger kept on; he liked the hoss awful well. He was willin' to trade a big Durham fer 'im."

"Did they trade?" asked Jason breathlessly.

"No. Things were gettin' purty hot when in come Elisha Jefferson all out of breath like he'd been runnin'. Elisha had gone home to bed an' someone hauled 'im out again. Elisha offered money, jest like that!" the man snapped his fingers, "An' the deal was closed. Now Mis' Collins can buy the Durham an' have a bit left over. There's somethin' queer about it all. Some say there was a woman in a shawl outside, eggin' 'em on. Well, Jefferson owns the hoss now. . . . Fer gosh sake, look at that boy leg it!"

Already Jason was out of hearing. Kit was not far away. His head was up, his chestnut coat red-brown against the frost-tipped grass and he was watching, nickering softly, calling. . . . Kit was still with the train.

The next two days were spent restoring wagons and jaded oxen. If Jim Bridger had any ill feeling over the loss of Kit, he gave no evidence of it. Possibly Bill Brewster had soothed his ire. Meanwhile, Kit was staked with Elisha Jefferson's two horses and Mrs. Collins added a large Durham ox to her dwindling supply of stock. There were questions as to who had notified Elisha Jefferson. The woman in the shawl, who was said to have managed the whole affair, remained unknown. More than one person, Bill Brewster among them, congratulated Mrs. Collins upon her good fortune.

"You done right well," the old scout told her. "Funny thing, Elisha's been eyein' that hoss all the way over the trail an' jest waked up ter the fact you was sellin' last night. He hopped outer bed an' nearly broke his neck tryin' to reach the fort in time. Now wi' that nice Durham an' money in yer jeans," here Bill Brewster stopped short and stammered a bit as he looked down at Cal's trousers, "you'll have somethin' in Oregon ter give you a start. You done right well."

Because of Aaron's ill health, Mark Morgan was as eager to continue on the trail westward as the Fieldses and Jason. It was claimed by many at Fort Bridger that mountain-fever temperature would drop as soon as the patient

reached a lower altitude, and concern for Aaron was beginning to be felt by all. Meanwhile Jim Bridger emphasized
how important it was for the people to continue on to
Oregon.

"Don't let them leetle Johnny Bulls at Fort Hall skeer
you," he warned them over and over again. "Them Britishers don't want folks settlin' in Oregon 'cause it's their huntin' grounds. They'll tell you all sorts of tales, part of 'em
true, to steer you down Californy way. Sometime there'll
be a vote, an' if thar's more American heads than English
that land'll be our'n. Don't argue with Cap'n Grant but
go your own way. He's a good enough man, 'cept it's his
business ter keep Americans away. The Injuns ain't any
worse'n they have been, an' the rivers ain't high. It's time
England an' us came to terms purty soon. All this argufyin'
keeps us het up," he complained.

The first day after leaving the fort, camp was made on
the south shore of the Little Muddy River.

"Jason, come here a minute."

Aunt Liddy's sunbonnet was thrust out between the curtains of the Morgan wagon and a hand beckoned as Jason
passed by leading Blossom towards some green grass. The
boy came closer and looked up at Aunt Liddy. There were
tired lines in her face and he knew there had been little
sleep for her the night before because of Aaron's sickness.

"Your cow better?" she inquired listlessly.

"She's fine now," replied Jason. "You needin' somethin',
Aunt Liddy?"

"Yes." Aunt Liddy came carefully down the small steps
at the rear of the wagon. "After you leave Blossom in the
grass, will you come an' set with Aaron a bit? I need to

wash some things in the river. He's asleep an' you mustn't mind if he talks a little queer. Seems like he's always hearin' voices. Jason," and she looked searchingly at him as she struggled for words, "is Aaron goin' to die? Are they tryin' to keep it from me? He's awful sick . . . he don't know me most of the time. If only he'd speak, call me like he useter . . ." and here Aunt Liddy choked, stumbled and sat down unexpectedly on the bottom stair, with both hands over her face, her shoulders shaking.

"Aunt Liddy, don't . . . don't cry. No, they're not sayin' that . . . honest," and Jason, distressed at Aunt Liddy's tears and sick with fear himself at hearing her words, leaned over and awkwardly patted her arm. Aunt Liddy crying! Aunt Liddy, who was always so brave and selfreliant!

"Oh, no," he continued, gaining strength at hearing his own words. "Jim Bridger says that just as soon as we reach Bear River Valley, where the land is low, all fevers drop. An' he knows . . . he's been through it himself. You're tired, Aunt Liddy. . . . Here, I'll stake Blossom an' come back, an' you go out somewhere. Don't, don't, Aunt Liddy," as the woman's sobs continued.

"I know . . . I know I shouldn't cry, but oh, Jason, if anything happens to Aaron, it'll kill Mark an' me. I've taken keer of him ever since he was a week old. I useter complain 'cause he was too fat, an' now . . . now he's skin an' bone. I wish we'd never left Missouri . . ."

"Aunt Liddy!"

Startled, Aunt Liddy jerked her head back and looked up at Jason through tear-filled eyes. The voice was Aaron's, weak and quavering, but nevertheless Aaron's! In another moment both Aunt Liddy and Jason were up the stairs and into the wagon, leaning over a blanketed figure in a short-legged bed.

"I heard you, Aunt Liddy." Aaron's eyes were wide open, unusually large in his thin, flushed face. "I couldn't help hearin'. I'm not goin' to die. Jason, tell her I'm not goin' to die."

"I did tell her, Aaron, an' she believes it now. She's just tired an' worried."

"I know. . . . Aunt Liddy," and Aaron turned his head restlessly, finally looking up at the peg on the wall where his clothing had hung, "I want my trousers an' boots. You took 'em away the night you went to Fort Bridger an' you never put 'em back. If I could see 'em round, near me, like I was goin' to get up an' put 'em on, I'd feel better."

For a moment his aunt stared, uncomprehending, and then she nodded. "Of course, Aaron boy," and with trembling hands she lifted the top of the chest, hung the trousers upon the peg and then lifted up the boots for Aaron to see. "There . . . I'll put 'em back just like before. See, there's mud on the heels, just as there was when you last wore 'em. I put 'em in the chest 'cause I kept stumblin' over 'em."

"I'll wear 'em tomorrer. Don't take them away again, Aunt Liddy . . . don't go to the fort tonight . . ." Aaron's mind was rambling again as he lay there with one of the boots clutched in his hand. "Jason, don't let Aunt Liddy go to the fort tonight."

"She won't go, Aaron. She'll stay here."

Aaron's eyes closed and his words became muffled and indistinct as he quieted.

"I ain't leavin' you, I promise," comforted Aunt Liddy,

soothing his hot forehead. "Don't worry over anythin', son."
There was a pause and Aaron's breathing became regular,
slower. Aunt Liddy turned her head and looked at Jason,
tears of joy streaming down her cheeks. "He's better,
Jason! Oh, praise the Lord, he's better! He knew me an'
he knew you. Go find Mark an' tell him Aaron's better.
Mark's worried sick."

"I'll find him," and Jason turned away quickly. Aaron
was going to get well! Burdened with his own troubles, he
had not realized just how sick Aaron had been the past few
days. As always, Aunt Liddy had kept her troubles to herself. He had reached the top step when the word "fort"
filtered through his mind. "Fort" . . . "fort" . . . what
had Aaron said about Aunt Liddy's going to Fort Bridger?
What had she been doing at Fort Bridger in the evening, of
all times? She, who always avoided Indians and traders.
The woman in the shawl who managed the sale of Kit . . .
had she been Aunt Liddy?

Jason turned and looked back at Aunt Liddy as she dried
her eyes on the hem of her checked apron. "Aunt Liddy,
what was Aaron talkin' 'bout? He said somethin' 'bout you
goin' to Fort Bridger. I never knew you went to the fort for
anything."

"Now, Jason, you hurry outer here. Don't you realize
Aaron is sick, jest mumblin' words? He's apt to say anythin' that pops into his head. Now go find Mark."

"Yes, I'm goin' . . . but Aunt Liddy, was it you who
went to the fort the night Mis' Collins sold Kit? Folks have
been sayin' some woman in a shawl got Elisha Jefferson
out of bed to go to the fort. Bill Brewster was tryin' to stop
Jim Bridger from buyin' Kit but he couldn't make him

understand. Anyway Jim Bridger was crazy 'bout the hoss an' wanted him. It was almost settled when Elisha Jefferson came in with a big offer and bought Kit. Mis' Collins took the money. But someone got word to Elisha. It was you, Aunt Liddy, it was! I can tell by your face."

"You get outer here, Jason Coit!" Aunt Liddy had fully recovered her fighting spirit and now she fairly bristled. "I ain't the only woman in this train that owns a shawl! An' what if I did go to the fort that night? I had some of my own business to 'tend to. . . . An' if ever I hear a peep outer your mouth to Mark Morgan, I'll never speak to you again, Jason Coit. Why, Mark'd shoot me dead if he heerd of such doin's. Me, Liddy Morgan, mixed up in a hoss deal! Sure, I waked Elisha. He was dead set on that hoss, same's you, an' didn't know the tradin' was goin' on that night. I talked to him a little, only a little, an' he did the rest. Elisha's well fixed. He lost his boy 'bout your age. . . . Now you forget 'bout it. The hoss is still with us, ain't he? He's got a good home. That's all that counts. Elisha'll let you ride him an' take keer of him. What you fussin' 'bout anyway? Go find Mark, but remember, no talkin' 'bout my goin' to the fort. Mark's awful set on some things. Here now, stop it. Don't be silly," and Aunt Liddy made a futile attempt to avoid Jason as he suddenly dove beneath the brim of her sunbonnet and kissed her cheek.

There was a clatter of boots across the wooden floor and he was gone, taking the steps in one leap.

"Lor' save us," gasped Aunt Liddy, looking after him as one hand felt of her face, "I ain't been kissed since Jed Parson took me to a huskin' bee. Then it was a red ear of corn . . . an' now it's a hoss. No use talkin', men are fools," she muttered, and then impulsively leaned over the sleeping Aaron and laid her cheek against his.

Bear River Valley brought health and a lift of morale to all. Three days of lower altitude reduced Aaron's temperature to normal and it was now Aunt Liddy's task to appease his appetite. But food was plentiful. The meat of bear, elk, mountain sheep and antelope, flavored with wild onion, simmered in every family kettle. Also the rich meadow grass, mixed with bluejoint, barley and wild oats, restored the stock, while their owners watched over them with jealous eyes, rejoicing at every pound of added weight. Roving bands of Shoshone Indians along the banks of the river proved friendly but stared blankly when questioned as to the whereabouts of three white children traveling alone.

"Can't tell a thing by 'em," stoutly encouraged the old scout, undismayed by the blank expressions. "The Injuns that were here last week are prob'ly south of here this week. I'd like to see Peg Leg. He'd tell us a thing or two."

"Who's Peg Leg?" asked Aaron and Jason simultaneously.

"Peg Leg? Ain't you heerd of Peg Leg Smith?" and Bill Brewster gave the back of his neck a vigorous swat, eliminating several large mosquitoes. "Why, I s'posed everyone livin' had heerd of Peg Leg Smith. He's white, got a wooden leg, an' has lived wi' the Shoshones round here fer twenty-five years. Sort of a king to 'em. No Injun sells a hoss without Peg Leg's say-so. He rules the roost . . . everything but these plaguy mosquitoes" and the scout whacked again at his neck. "When Peg Leg's powder gets low an' he's in a fightin' mood, he takes off his hick'ry leg, hops on one foot an' cleans up the crowd. Queer cuss. He's mild enough in some ways, though, an' he'd be good to the young'uns if he met 'em on the trail."

"Maybe we'll see him yet." Aaron looked hopeful.

" 'Tain't likely." The old scout shook his head. "He don't mix much with folks. Well, I'm movin'. Can't stand these bugs any more," and Bill Brewster strode away, slapping at the back of his neck and waving his arms in an attempt to free himself of the mosquitoes which swarmed over the encampment. Except for the pestilence of these humming, biting insects, life along Bear River would have been ideal.

"If only we could follow this river to The Dalles," sighed more than one emigrant.

"With no mosquitoes," others never failed to add.

It was not uncommon to see eyes swollen tight with puffy lids, hands twice their natural size, or people so wrapped in shawls and scarfs as to be disguised beyond recognition. Horses, oxen and mules suffered as well and the scent of smudge fires clung to the clothing of every man, woman and child.

Soda Spring, Beer Spring and the warm bubbling waters of Steamboat Spring. . . . Armed with jugs, young and old filled them with the strange, brown, metallic-tasting water. Many women made bread, finding that the medicinal properties of the springs acted as yeast. However, the wagons made no stopovers for the enjoyment of the novelty, but continued at their regular pace towards their goal, Fort Hall.

Six miles beyond Steamboat Spring, friendly, sluggish Bear River turned sharply to the south around some mountains. Four days later the wagons stopped before the log stockade of Fort Hall, situated upon a slight elevation a mile distant from the banks of the Snake River.

Fort Hall, possessed and controlled by the British, flew a red flag with the lettering H. B. C. . . . Hudson's Bay Company . . . above its whitewashed walls of adobe. Unlike the experience at Fort Bridger, there was no spontaneous welcome at the big gate as the emigrants arrived. An austere silence surrounded the place and even the Shoshone and Bannock Indians, sitting in the doorways of their dirty lodges outside the stockade, remained stoically indifferent, scarcely looking up to gaze at the newcomers. After some waiting, a guard slowly opened the gate and Mark Morgan, Bill Brewster, Ezra Fields, Aaron and Jason entered.

"Cap'n Grant's been here twenty-five years as factor," whispered the old scout, as they crossed a courtyard. "He don't like me too well 'cause I'm a free trapper. He'll be awful perlite but before he's through he'll have his say 'bout Californy. Remember what Jim Bridger said . . . let 'im talk but don't take no stock in it."

Ezra Fields was not listening. His eyes were searching for his two daughters, his ears striving to catch the sound of two high-pitched young voices. Jason, watching him, torn with hope and doubt himself, entered with hands clenched, the nails of his fingers biting into the palms of his hands. If Sammy were here, would he not be running to meet him by now? How much farther would Mary and Ezra Fields go if they failed to find their children here? Would they turn back? And what would he do? Go on, of course. There could be no turning back with another's oxen and wagon.

He was not free to choose. The oxen and wagon must be delivered to Elizabeth Strong's cousin at The Dalles.

They went across the inner court, where there was a fountain of water playing in the center, up some steps, and then were in the presence of Captain Richard Grant, elderly, gray-haired, ruddy-faced, and over six feet in height. The captain, who wore his well-fitted deerskins with a worldly air, received them courteously, speaking crisply and with a strong British accent.

"You have had a successful journey, I trust." Captain Grant raised his heavy gray eyebrows as he regarded each person before him.

"Tolerable," answered the old scout, acting as spokesman. " 'Course we've had our ups an' downs like most," and then, without preliminaries, Bill Brewster told of the missing children, of Henri Jules and the old squaw who accompanied them, and of the hopes of the entire train that the youngsters would be found at Fort Hall.

At the close of the story, Captain Grant, now seated at his desk, shook his head. "We've seen no white children, gentlemen. Mr. Benson, upon his return from Fort Laramie, told me of your distress and we have been watching. I'm sorry."

Ezra Fields sank to a bench where he remained half crouched, his face white, his hands shaking. Jason continued to stand but his legs felt as if they bore a great weight.

The factor continued, kindly enough and in well-chosen words, "However, gentlemen, you spoke of Henri Jules. I might be able to help you in that respect. Johnson," and he turned to a clerk who stood at attention in the doorway, "bring Henri Jules here to me . . . Henri Jules, the trapper. There are some questions I would like to ask him. . . . Be seated, gentlemen. Johnson will bring him in directly. Rest while you are able, for you must be weary after your long journey."

19

TWO BROTHERS

Nights were cold along Bear River. And, as matches were scarce, sometimes there were no fires at night to warm three shivering children. If one found the right berries and roots, or caught a fish from the river, well and good. However, pemmican mixed with buffalo hairs was not an appetizing dish, although Anna ate her share with the relish of a plainsman and asked for more. Nothing bothered Anna. Although mosquitoes surrounded Jessica and Sammy, the insects did not bother her. With a bedraggled feather in her hair, glass beads about her neck, and smelling of skunk's oil on damp days, Anna was content with living. The fact that she no longer kicked and fought to get back to Ol' Squaw after the first days of escape was comforting and seemed a good sign to Jessica and Sammy.

"Watch 'er," warned Sammy, "or she'll be like one of them antelope gallopin' back to Ol' Squaw if she gets loose. She don't talk much, but she does a lot of thinkin'."

Whereupon Anna was frequently fastened to a stump or tree by a long rawhide leash. Here she remained sullenly silent, pouting as she fingered the beads about her neck.

"If only I could get a doll for her," sighed Jessica, ". . . a doll with a china head like the one she owned before we were stolen. It is the only thing she ever asks for."

The Shoshone Indians had been kind, almost too kind. Sometimes it had been difficult for the children to take their leave of them, for again the red hair of the two girls and Sammy's jew's-harp proved a mighty attraction. Even the white man called Peg Leg Smith, who was idolized by the short, crook-legged Shoshones, and who had assisted the children in crossing Green River, offered to take them to his home in the south.

It was not difficult to hide away the jew's-harp in Sammy's back pocket, but who could hide two heads of long red hair? In a moment of discouragement Jessica declared both she and Anna would be wise to cut off their hair and wear it short to prevent trouble. Whereupon Sammy volunteered his services. He still possessed the knife earned by painting Henri's name upon Independence Rock and carried it in a buckskin sheath which he had made himself. The blade, though worn and dull, would cut. Upon two occasions when they had made ready for the operation, Jessica had hedged and invented at least a dozen excuses for keeping her hair a few days longer. Each excuse was introduced by the word "perhaps." Perhaps she would be cold that night without the heavy hair over her shoulders. Why not wait for a warmer day? Perhaps they might not meet any more Indians on the road to Fort Hall. Why not wait and see? Perhaps, if they could find a better knife, a sharper knife, Sammy could do a better job. . . .

From the time he followed the cut-off and missed the road to Fort Bridger, Sammy had lost caste with Jessica. No longer did she consider his word law. Her tart remarks and evident lack of faith in his leadership added considerably to his own mortification. He felt that once Jessica's hair had been cut, and as close to the scalp as possible, his own feelings would be appeased, whether the trio ever saw another Indian or not.

It was a week since their meeting with Peg Leg Smith, the white man who boasted of amputating his own leg and whittling his wooden one from a hickory tree . . . Peg Leg, who had kind eyes . . .

"Maybe we should have gone with him," complained Jessica one noon, as all three sat in some tall grass a little distance from the trail, while Whitey grazed. "Perhaps he would have taken us to Fort Hall later. . . . I just know we aren't on the right road. I wonder if we'll ever see the fort. We never did reach Fort Bridger . . ." and there was so much doubt in Jessica's voice that Sammy's ears burned and his cheeks flushed.

Only that morning he had told Jessica, solemnly and with dignity, that Fort Hall was now within easy distance, just around the other side of the huge mountain which had suddenly appeared at their left. This statement, though guesswork on his part, buoyed his own courage. Her last taunt, however, added to the rest of the week's total, plunged him into action. It was time *now* to show Jessica that he, Samuel Coit, was still boss. With a quick movement he reached for the knife at his belt and then felt for the broken whetstone he carried in his pocket. With slow precision he began to sharpen the blade and it pleased him to see Jessica watch him intently, a little fear in her eyes.

"What are you going to do, Sammy?"

"Cut your hair."

"But I don't want my hair cut today. It might be very cold tonight and . . . and perhaps I might sneeze and keep you awake . . ."

"I'm goin' to cut your hair an' Anna's before we meet any more Injuns. It ain't safe goin' along this way. Next thing we know, we'll be livin' with Injuns again. I've got to get to Oregon, an' them red mops an' all them 'perhapses' ain't goin' to stop me. Well, who's gonna be cut first?" and Sammy turned towards Anna, who sat placidly eating blueberries from some low bushes which edged a near-by rock.

"I . . . I will. Don't touch Anna, she wouldn't understand. If she sees me get mine cut, she'll want to try it, too. . . . If the fort is really 'round that mountain, I won't need to cut my hair. By tomorrow we'd know. If it's not there, you can do it. I promise."

"Sure the fort's 'roun' the mountain. I told you this mornin'! But we're liable to meet Injuns 'fore we get there . . . any minute, mebbe ten feet from here. After I cut it, I'll bury the stuff. It's a turrible color, ain't it? Where'll I start, back or front? Wish I had my bowie knife an' then I'd make quick work of it!"

"You know, Sammy, I've been thinking. We're so close to the fort now . . . and when Papa and Mama see us, they'll feel bad. We'll look just like you do. I don't know any girls at home who wear their hair cut short. Perhaps . . ."

"Your papa an' your mama may never see you again if

we run into Injuns this afternoon. Come on . . . sit down on this rock. Where do I start?"

"The back, I guess . . . where Anna can see it. Look, Anna, Sammy's cutting my hair off. Then there won't be any more snarls. Won't that be nice? Perhaps you can have yours done, too."

Anna gave her customary grunt and moved to where the berries were larger and sweeter. For once she was unleashed and enjoying her freedom. With no more ready excuses, Jessica seated herself hesitatingly upon the rock, as though primed to jump and run at any moment. A glimpse of Sammy's face, as he advanced with the sharpened knife, convinced her she now had no choice.

"It wouldn't hurt to cut your own," she said scathingly, looking up under Sammy's hat as he stood over her. "Your hair always makes me think of the pumpkins and squashes in Papa's garden. Maybe that is why you always wear that hat," and a hysterical giggle escaped Jessica. The giggle was followed immediately by loud yells of protest as Sammy took an unnecessarily firm grip of the hair which flowed down Jessica's back.

"Now don't you pull, Sammy Coit, or I'll yell! I'll yell just as loud as I can!"

"You're a crybaby," he shouted at her, forgetting to keep his own voice lowered, and a bit nervous at this new undertaking. "What if I do pull? If you ever get skelped, it'll hurt a lot more. Come to think on't, we won't bury your hair. Whitey's tail is gettin' thin. Mebbe I can tie some of this on. It'll keep flies away." The knife descended and began to saw the hair close to Jessica's scalp.

"Ow! Ow! Ouch! You hurt! Stop it, Sammy Coit! Stop

it! Please . . . please . . . your knife's no good!"
screamed Jessica, as she struggled to pull clear of him, trying with both hands to protect her head. At this moment,
Anna, for no reason whatsoever, began to scream also. In
the midst of the uproar Sammy seized a second handful of
hair in the region of Jessica's right ear. In savage joy, he
had sawed halfway through this thickness when a voice behind him made him stop and whirl about. Someone, a man,
seated on a large chestnut horse, was coming rapidly towards them through the tall grass.

"Sammy! Sammy!" The voice was his brother Jason's!

Unable to answer or move, Sammy stared, a long tress
of red hair in one hand, the knife in the other. Anna was
the first to recover from surprise. Like a small wild creature, she scuttled for some brush, only to run into the
arms of a tall, thin white man who appeared from another
direction, leading a gold-colored mustang. And now Jessica
had come to life. She ran stumbling through the grass
towards the man on the chestnut horse.

"It's Jason! It's Jason!" she shouted.

Still unable to speak, Sammy took a few steps forward
and then suddenly sat down. His legs refused to carry him
any farther. He tried to loosen his fingers about the knife
and the lock of hair, but both hands were clenched like a
vise. Jason had dismounted and was now coming closer,
Jessica running by his side.

"Sammy! Sammy! What's the matter, Sammy?" called
Jason. "Are you hurt?"

"Naw, I ain't hurt." Strength had returned to Sammy's
legs. He stood up. Jason and Jessica had reached him and
the thin stranger, dragging Anna by one arm, was close

behind. Tears were streaming down Sammy's grimy cheeks but no one seemed to notice.

"Sure you're all right?" and Jason, the best brother in the world, was beside him, his arm about him, hugging him tight. To Sammy's surprise, Jason seemed to be crying, too.

"Golly, Sammy, I began to think I'd never see you again!" And then Jason took a deep breath and stood off and looked at him. "I wish Ma was here, right this minute, an' Tacy, too."

"Well, well!" The tall thin stranger holding Anna couldn't seem to think of anything else to say. Finally his bright blue eyes spied the red hair in one of Sammy's hands and the knife in the other. Then they traveled to Jessica and noted the shorn appearance of one side of her head.

"So that's what you was doin'! Skelpin' the girls! You turned Injun?"

"Naw." Sammy was now able to relinquish his hold on the hair and he cast it from him into the grass. Slowly he slipped the knife into its sheath. "She wanted me ter cut it. The Injuns bothered her. I didn't pull a bit, either."

"No? Well, it's a wonder them howls didn't bring a whole tribe runnin'," and the tall man winked at Jason. "This 'un," he straightened the feather in the top of Anna's hair, "looks like she might have turned. Lor', but she's a spry 'un. Jest ketched 'er in time."

"This is Bill Brewster, Sammy," explained Jason. "He's scout for our train. We left Fort Hall this mornin', tryin' to find you . . . and then we heard all that yellin'."

"Fort Hall? This mornin'? Are we that near?" Sammy's eyes grew wide with excitement.

"Within a stun's throw," replied the old scout. "Over the bluffs, down the river a piece, an' you'd a bumped plumb into it."

"Huh," and Sammy glared triumphantly at Jessica. "I knowed we was 'most there." Then he gave Jason a crooked little smile as he asked the old and familiar question, "Think I've growed any, Jason?" and drew himself to his full height. There was expectancy and hope in the gray-green eyes beneath the sagging hat.

"A good inch, anyway." Jason's voice was husky but he was smiling. "An' you've done a big man's work to get this far alone, Sammy. Been tough goin'?"

"In spots," answered Sammy, eyeing the big chestnut horse. Could this be the one he had seen on the day Jessica and Anna had been stolen? Someone, probably Jason, had been drying off a big chestnut horse.

"Nice hoss, ain't he?" commented Sammy. "Yourn?"

"Prettiest I ever saw. No, he's not mine. I just take keer of 'im."

"What's his name?"

"Kit . . . named after Kit Carson."

"Huh. Got anything to eat? I'm kinder tired of berries an' things," and Sammy gazed hopefully at the saddlebags.

"Some sowbelly. We'll eat as we go along. The sooner we get back to the fort now, the better." Jason turned towards Jessica. "Your pa an' ma are there, an' you've got a new little baby sister."

"A baby sister!" Amazement and joy shone in Jessica's blue eyes. "Anna! Anna!" turning to the younger child and shaking her vigorously by the shoulders, "Mama's got a new baby! A papoose . . . a real live doll. Now you can play with *her*. We're going home to Papa and Mama!"

Slowly a smile grew on Anna's solemn face. "A real doll?"

"A real live doll."

"An' some horehoun' canny, too?" she asked after a thoughtful pause.

"Oh, I'm sure Mama has saved some candy for us. Oh, Anna, we're going back to Papa and Mama!"

With no remonstrance, Anna allowed Bill Brewster to lift her to his saddle and lead the way back to the wagon trail. With Jessica riding behind Jason on Kit and Sammy following on Whitey, the small procession wound its way down a short steep bluff to Fort Hall.

20

SAMUEL COIT TELLS
HIS STORY

It was Elisha Jefferson, high on a ladder mending the torn sailcloth of his wagon, who announced the approach of Bill Brewster and Jason with the missing children. In a few moments the entire encampment poured forth to meet them. Running swiftly with outstretched arms, Mary Fields was among the first.

Dogs howled, women wept, men shouted and threw their hats in the air. Two mules became loose and tore off across the meadows but no one chased them, no one cared. After a search of a thousand miles, the lost children had been found. An almost impossible achievement! Din and confusion continued as the two little girls were swallowed up in the welcoming arms of young and old. Sammy, watching from the edge of the crowd, remained quietly by Jason until some over-zealous matrons came swooping towards him. At this crucial moment, Elisha Jefferson appeared and swung him high onto his shoulder where Sammy was content to perch, frankly relieved to have escaped his admirers below. And then a second wave of excitement swept over the people as someone brought forward the small Bluette and Jessica and Anna took turns holding her.

"Ain't that a sight for sore eyes!" and "Bless the little darlin's!" could be heard on all sides.

Meanwhile, Aunt Liddy, after drying her eyes, approached Sammy as he sat upon Elisha's shoulder, and surveyed him from all angles. With no audible comments, she marched back to her wagon, stirred up a fire, put on kettles of water and warmed some stew. From the depths of a chest she produced a large cake of yellow soap and then bustled back to the gathering once more.

"Jason," she whispered loudly in the latter's ear, "bring him to me when you're done. There's work to do. I've put over some water to heat but I'll need more. He must have food an' a good soak. Lor' me, go roun' back an' look at the patch on his seat. 'Nother step an' he'd a lost it. An' that hat! Who in tarnation put that hat on him! I must go an' find some clothes. Mis' Woods," and Aunt Liddy hailed a woman whose sunbonnet completely hid her face, "you saved any of Willie's clothes? I want 'em for Sammy here, Jason's brother. I gave all of Aaron's to Mis' Collins."

"I've got a jacket," returned Mrs. Woods, "but everything else is wore out."

"I might have some trousers," offered another woman standing near by. "I'll go to my wagon an' look. They may be patched but they're clean."

"That's the main thing," agreed Aunt Liddy vigorously. "It don't matter how they look, long's they're clean," and she emphasized the word "clean" loudly. "Mis' Fields' girls are all set 'cause their mother saved their dresses. But she'll have to burn the ones they're wearin', I reckon. My, my! Jessica ain't got any hair on one side. Looks like someone tried to skelp her an' she cut loose 'fore they finished. Mercy me, ain't this a happy day for us all!"

Jason noticed that Sammy was a little slow in descending from Elisha Jefferson's shoulder. It had been impossible not to overhear Aunt Liddy's comments. Undoubtedly the word "soak" more than offset the word "food," and the younger boy seemed to have lost some of his self-assurance as he followed Jason to the Morgans' wagon. No one molested him on the way, for the majority of the emigrants were still surrounding the little girls. It was quiet inside the wagon and a little later, over the hot fumes of a prairie-hen stew, Sammy gave Aunt Liddy a shy smile.

"Tastes like Ma's cookin', don't it, Sammy?" asked Jason, watching his brother eat with keen enjoyment. He received an emphatic nod in reply. "There's so much I want to ask you that I don't know where to begin," continued Jason. "But you look kinder peaked an' I know I ought to let you eat your fill first . . ."

"He'll be fine after he eats an' I give him a scrub with my yellow soap," enthused Aunt Liddy. " 'Pears like he's crusted over. I sent Aaron for more water. There's no tellin' what kind of bugs them Injuns carry."

"I can do my own scrubbin'," interrupted Sammy with sudden spirit. "I don't want no woman hangin' 'roun' my tub."

"I'll help," offered Jason hastily. "You'll feel a lot better when you're cleaned up," he assured Sammy.

"How'd you know there was a tub?" asked Aunt Liddy, regarding Sammy curiously. " 'Tain't in sight."

"Huh. I heerd the noise when you set it down back of them curtains. I ain't deef. A brook's all right for me . . . I don't like tubs. I've got a nice swimmin' hole at home . . ."

" 'Tain't what you like, young man," reprimanded Aunt Liddy severely, with fire in her eyes, "seein' we've got to live with you from now on. They say Henri Jules' shirt was so dirty that it stood up straight when he peeled it off."

"Who . . . who'd she say?" and as he hesitated between mouthfuls Sammy fixed inquiring eyes on Jason.

"Henri Jules. Henri's at the fort here."

The conflict with soap, water, energetic women and tubs was suddenly of no importance. Sammy's spoon fell back into his soup bowl with a clatter as he straightened up and stared at his brother. There was a quick flash of fear in the round gray-green eyes, as though the boy had forgotten he was now free and not under the trapper's control.

"How'd he get here? I don't wanter see 'im!"

"You don't have to see him," and Jason leaned forward protectively. "Henri's locked up in the fort. He's wanted for stealin' hosses an' gold. Two of Cap'n Grant's men found him north of here."

"Locked up?" The fear gradually died out of Sammy's face. "An' did you say he had some gold?"

"Well, he didn't have it with 'im. But they're holdin' 'im 'cause they think he's hidden it somewhere. I'm hopin' you can tell us a lot about it. I've been waitin' for you to finish eatin' so I could ask you. It's a nugget . . . weighs about twenty pounds . . . an' there's a big reward."

"A reward? Money? How much?" Sammy had lost none of his shrewdness and there was the old familiar greedy note in his voice.

"One thousand dollars for the return of the nugget. Governor Abernethy at Oregon City is holdin' the money. It seems that a Comanche Indian stole it first, an' Henri Jules robbed the Comanche. Soldiers traced Henri for a while but lost 'im on some mountain trails."

Aunt Liddy, who had been listening intently, now broke in, her voice rising with excitement. "If you know where that gold is, young feller, be keerful who you tell. Like as not, forty Injuns an' trappers'll jump hosses an' tear off for it. An' don't you tell Cap'n Grant, either. Now, *do* you know where that gold is?" and Aunt Liddy gazed keenly at the ragged, dirty boy before her. "Somethin' tells me you do," she added with finality.

"If you know," warned Jason earnestly, "tell Cap'n Morgan, Bill Brewster, or Elisha Jefferson. They're friends of ours, yours an' mine. But don't tell anyone else. It might be you can win that reward, Sammy . . . that is, if you really know somethin'."

Sammy took another mouthful of stew before he answered, his eyes studying Aunt Liddy the while. Then he turned his head and looked directly at Jason. "I've got a few notions, Jason. I think I know where that gold is . . . that is, if Henri ain't dug it up since he buried it."

"Buried it? Very far away? You can tell us, Sammy."

"South Pass. In a cemetery near a big ol' tree. There's a board with Henri's name on't an' the gold's in the grave."

"The wicked creature!" exploded Aunt Liddy. "Takin' 'vantage of the dead. The Lord'll punish 'im fer such actions!"

"The South Pass! Way back there! Could you find this place again, Sammy?"

SAMUEL COIT TELLS HIS STORY

"Guess so. There's five graves with piles of stones on 'em to keep the wolves off. An' the sign's a good sign. I painted it myself. I've done quite a lot of good paintin' since I left home," added Sammy modestly.

"Yes, I know. We saw the names on the big rock. But we can talk about that later. Now, Sammy, did you actually see Henri bury that gold?" insisted Jason. "An' are you sure it was the gold?"

"Naw, I ain't sure of nothin'," replied Sammy. "I'm jus' tellin' you what happened. Henri had somethin' he was awful choice of in his saddlebags. I felt of it twice . . . it was hard an' heavy. We met two trappers near Laramie an' Henri seemed awful skeered of 'em. After he dug the grave one night an' put his name up, he warn't so keerful of the bags. Kicked 'em 'roun' any ol' way, 'cause the bags was empty. Mebbe he was skeered of the dragoons. I dunno."

"Did anyone else know Henri buried the gold that night?"

"Naw. Ol' Squaw had rheumatiz an' she was nursin' her leg. Right after that we met some Injun friends an' then we run away. I didn't tell Jessica much, 'cause she blabs when she gets mad. I kept it to myself."

"You sure the squaw wouldn't go back an' dig it up for Henri?"

Sammy shook his head decidedly. "They was all excited 'bout meetin' their ol' friends, some Crows. That night the chief heerd how his son was killed an' all the men ran off. Henri went with 'em. We took Whitey an' went 'nother way."

"A son was killed? Sammy, what did the chief look like?" asked Jason suddenly.

"I dunno, 'cept he was kinder ol' an' wore panther skins."

" 'Kinder ol', panther skins'?" repeated Aunt Liddy quickly, a startled look on her face. "Why, Jason, was that the one?" and she stopped. A significant exchange of glances passed between them as Aaron entered, lugging a pail of water and breathing fast as though he had been running.

"This ought to be enough, Aunt Liddy," and there was a note of protest in Aaron's voice. "The tub's almost full now. Besides, Pa, Mister Jefferson an' Bill Brewster are comin'. They want to talk with Sammy."

"Oh, Lor'," exclaimed Aunt Liddy, "now he'll never get his soak! The water'll just stand an' chill. Aaron, drag that bench out. I'll lissen from here," and Aunt Liddy seated herself in a rocker and pulled out her knitting from a drawer. "Mebbe we can get a scrub in later," she added hopefully.

Sammy never did partake of the bath prepared for him. For the next hour he was catechized by all three men and, to Jason's surprise, answered their questions unhesitatingly and in detail. The descriptions of the mountain trails, the visit of the two trappers, and the burying of the gold near the bridle path were told clearly and without contradiction. Aaron, sent out frequently to reconnoiter, reported no eavesdroppers, but all voices were kept low.

"An' what did this Bateese look like?" questioned Bill Brewster.

"Kinder fierce. No thumb on one hand."

"That's Bateese. I've seen 'im. Chances be, he didn't

know 'bout Henri's stealin' the gold, but heerd it later when he reached Fort Laramie. 'Course he'd turn back an' try to ketch Henri. They warn't sech great friends but what Bateese would trade Henri in fer one thousand dollars. But that Henri's a sly one . . . You can tell from the way he schemed that grave business. Most trappers can't read, an' if they could they wouldn't dig up a grave . . . they're too superstitious. You never did see what was in them saddlebags, then?"

"It was too dark the mornin' I met Henri near Independence Rock. But Henri thought I saw the gold, I guess. That's why he made me go with 'im. Then he kinder liked my jew's-harp. An' when I was aroun' he didn't have to keep the fires burnin'."

Jason gazed wonderingly at his younger brother. This was not the Samuel Coit with whom he had lived under the same roof in Terryville, Illinois. This Sammy had lived in another world . . . where food was scarce, soap unknown, and life a gamble of wits. Aaron was frankly fascinated, absorbed in Sammy's story, Bill Brewster impressed, and Captain Morgan and Elisha Jefferson not a little amused at the apparition of freckles and dirt before them. Aunt Liddy, rocking back and forth with nervous energy, had completely forgotten her knitting.

"Henri never spoke of any reward offered for him, did he?" asked Captain Morgan.

"I never heerd 'im. He talked 'bout the dragoons. Sometimes he talked big an' sometimes like he was awful skeered."

"Kinder surprises me he had his name printed on Independence Rock," observed Elisha Jefferson.

"He said he'd take his chances. He wanted it up there awful bad."

"How about your name, Sammy? Did Henri know you printed yours up there, too?" asked Mark Morgan.

"Naw," and Sammy grinned. "Henri can't read."

"Elisha Jefferson, ain't you got a hat you could spare Sammy?" asked Aunt Liddy, still intent upon Sammy's wardrobe.

"Mebbe."

"I ain't needin' another hat," objected Sammy instantly. "I'm wearin' this one clear to Oregon. I promised myself," and there was a determined thrust to Sammy's jaw.

"Sure, let him wear it," agreed Elisha. "A feller's got the right to wear what he pleases, long's he can see out from under. . . . You know that ol' bridle path, Bill? Ever been on't?"

"Yes, I know that ol' bridle path. Runs two an' a half miles north of the reg'lar trail an' was thar before the wagons come through. The kid knows what he's talkin' 'bout. I remember the cemetery, too. You turn left by an ol' dead tree 'bout six miles up the trail. Sammy," continued the old scout, "strange you didn't meet Peg Leg Smith somewhere along the way."

"We did meet 'im," replied Sammy. "He helped us cross the Green."

"The ol' varmint! Now ain't that jest like Peg Leg!"

"Jessica was sick . . . ate too many bullberries. He helped us make camp."

"You didn't tell Peg Leg 'bout the gold, did ye?" asked the scout quickly.

"Naw." Sammy's eyes were beginning to blink heavily.

The bowl of stew was finished and there was a sleepy satisfaction on his face.

"I've been wonderin'," and Elisha Jefferson tilted his hat back from his forehead. "You say, Bill, you know that ol' trail. Where does it start goin' eastward?"

"It swings left below Pacific Creek. Fremont follered it four years back."

"You turn below Smith's Fork for the Sublette's Cutoff, don't yer?" pursued Elisha.

"That's right. What's on yer mind?" and the old scout stared at Elisha keenly. "You thinkin' of goin' back?"

"I've been wonderin' who's best fitted to take that trip back there," continued Elisha slowly. "I've got a fine hoss for someone to ride," and for a quick moment his eyes met Aunt Liddy's. That lady stared back innocently. "One thousand dollars is a neat sum. Seems like someone oughter try an' get it. How many miles in all, Bill?"

"I cal'late it's 'bout four hundred odd, comin' an' goin'."

"How long should it take?"

"I don't wanter say. Depends on hoss, weather an' circumstances. Less'n a month."

"Seems like someone oughter try it," repeated Elisha Jefferson, turning and facing Jason. "How 'bout you, boy? Your brother's located the gold, done his part. Now couldn't you take Kit an' go back an' fetch it? Then the two of you could split the reward."

"Why, yes, I could do it," answered Jason, startled at Elisha's directness. In some way the man had divined his own thoughts and desires. One thousand dollars! Between them, he and Sammy would get a fine start together in Oregon! And to ride Kit . . . he'd make good time with a horse like Kit beneath him. . . . But what of Elizabeth Strong's stock and wagon? Jason was now conscious that all eyes were upon him. Even Sammy was wide-awake and sitting up straight.

"I'd like to do it," and here Jason's eyes turned to his brother, "if Sammy'd go on wi' the wagon. I promised Mis' Strong one of us would get it through to Oregon. But Sammy's pretty young to try it alone . . ."

"Ever drive oxen, Sammy?" asked Elisha.

"Sure," nodded Sammy. "But mebbe I'd better go along with Jason, 'cause I know jus' the spot . . ."

"You'll do nothin' of the kind, you young whippersnapper," declared Aunt Liddy. "You'll stay wi' the wagon."

"I can't go if you don't stay," Jason appealed to the younger boy.

" 'Course he'll stay," put in the old scout, "an' I'll help 'im . . . that is, if you really wanter go, Jason."

"Thanks, Bill. I'd like to go. . . . You think it's all right, Cap'n Morgan?" and Jason turned eagerly towards the captain, who had remained silent throughout the conversation. "You were there when we talked at Mis' Strong's. If Sammy could manage, with Bill helpin', would it be all right for me to leave?"

"Don't see why not," replied Mark Morgan slowly. "I remember the day we talked with Elizabeth Strong, just before she left for home. She had confidence in both of you boys. There's no great danger, is there, Bill?"

"Not if he finds the bridle path, which ain't too plain, keeps his mouth shut and digs up the grave without bein' caught," replied the old scout. "Them trappers don't want their graves tampered with. I can draw a map which'll help, an' the rest'll be up to him. He may have to hunt some fer the path . . ."

"I can hunt," promised Jason. "I'll just hunt till I find it. I'd like to go, Cap'n Morgan. We need the money . . ."

"I understand, Jason. And, if you decide to go, don't say a word outside but leave quietly. If folks ask where you've gone, we'll say you've gone on business. If you find the nugget, bring it back to us. Don't stop at Fort Hall or confide in anyone there or anywhere, for that matter. Ride through in the night. You'll find us along the Snake somewhere and it would be quicker and better to deal with the American law in Oregon. I know someone who knows the Governor very well. His name is Joseph Meek . . ."

"Do you see, Sammy," interrupted Jason eagerly, "what it would mean? We'd earn a lot of money an' half of it would be yours," he went on persuasively. "An' I wouldn't be gone long 'cause I'd make good time on Kit, thanks to Mister Jefferson. What d'you say, Sammy? If you give me your word, I know you'll mean it. You're a Coit, an' a Coit keeps his promise. You like to earn money . . . how much have you got now?"

"I've got nine dollars, same's when I left home," and Sammy patted his pants' pocket affectionately. "Be kinder nice to have five hundred an' nine," he added, nodding his head. "All my own, Jason?"

"Every dollar."

"Huh."

"Will you stay with the wagon, Sammy?"

"I reckon so . . . sure," and at Sammy's final answer, Jason heaved a deep sigh of relief.

"Pa, what about my goin' with Jason?" asked Aaron, who had been hanging on every word. "I might help in some way, be comp'ny for 'im." But all further conversation was squelched by a frosty look from Aunt Liddy, and Captain Morgan shook his head.

"I can't spare you now, Aaron . . . and remember, you're just getting well."

"One man an' hoss can go faster alone," said Elisha, smiling sympathetically at Aaron.

"Well, now," piped up Aunt Liddy, unable to remain quiet any longer, "if Jason comes back wi' the gold an' wins some money, mebbe he can buy Kit for hisself," and she looked meaningly at Elisha Jefferson.

Elisha gave a sudden chuckle and then put his hand up to his mouth, as if to muffle the sound. "I guess we could fix up a deal," he remarked after a pause. "Funny how some folks have a leanin' towards hoss-tradin'. An' when a woman gets that way, there's no stoppin' 'er. . . . For the land sakes, the little feller's gone to sleep!"

"I ain't either," protested Sammy feebly.

"Roll 'im up in some blankets," advised Bill Brewster. "The kid's all tuckered out an' needs to rest. He's done a good job, that boy. Paints his own name on Independence Rock, travels with a man the hull United States is searchin' fer, locates a nugget an' half skelps a girl 'fore he finishes. . . . Yes, he's done quite a job. Jason, let's go to your wagon an' talk this thing over. You've got a good hoss to ride, now what about supplies? I'll draw ye a map an' tell ye a bit more 'bout that path. An' remember, folks, no whisperin' 'bout this business with anyone," he warned the others. And then to Jason in a lower tone as they descended the step, "Thar ain't any time to waste, boy. Someone might start diggin'. Gold means more'n superstition sometimes."

21

JASON TRAVELS EAST

It was still dark the next morning when Jason rose and looked outside. A moon, three quarters full, hung low in the sky, but dawn had not yet begun to streak the east. Near the door, his saddlebags lay packed, and tacked to the wall were a list of daily chores and a note for Sammy. Though he had been eager to leave only a few hours earlier, now Jason hesitated. If only there was someone to speak to, someone to wish him Godspeed before he launched out into the darkness upon his strange errand. Sammy had slept the night in the Morgans' wagon. There was no real need to waken him and say good-bye, yet Jason lingered. . . . As a parting gift and surprise for Sammy, he had left the old bowie knife with the twisted elk-horn handle where it could easily be seen, in the center of the table. Had he forgotten anything? The map, a small pick and shovel, two blankets, a skillet, gum-sack, jerky, flour, coffee, fish lines and fish hooks, bullets and powder, all had been stored in the saddlebags under Bill Brewster's direction. Somewhere beyond Fort Hall he planned to eat breakfast. It would be best to leave soon before the people at the fort awakened, as they might stop him and ask questions. . . . Yes, he must go at once . . . Kit was staked only a short distance away. . . .

As he waited, still hesitating, someone whistled softly outside. Startled, Jason moved swiftly to the door. Elisha Jefferson stood at the foot of the steps and the large dark figure of Kit loomed beside him.

"Thought I'd have 'im ready," whispered Elisha as Jason joined him. "Less explainin' to the guards. All packed?"

"I'm just leavin'."

Kit nickered softly and Jason touched his cheek with one hand and then felt for the saddle. Something was different . . . it was not the old saddle to which he was accustomed. This was of smooth leather, firmly built, with a tall Spanish horn.

"Why, Mister Jefferson, you've put on your good saddle!"

"Of course, boy. You'll want to ride comfortable."

"It's . . . it's mighty fine of you, Mister Jefferson," Jason stammered. The big man's presence in the early dawn, his thoughtfulness at this particular time, were almost overwhelming.

"You got your map?"

"Yes, in my saddlebags. . . . I've never thanked you for lettin' me take Kit, Mister Jefferson. I'll be careful of him."

"I'm not worryin'. Come back wi' that nugget an' you'll be able to buy him. Cheap, too. I guess Liddy Morgan'll make me sell him whether I want to or not," and Elisha gave one of his deep chuckles. "How's yer courage this mornin', son? Bill give you plenty of directions?"

"Told me all he knows. I'll have to hunt to find the bridle

path, I guess. But my courage is fine . . . even better since you came. It's kind of nice to speak with someone before I leave. Sammy's asleep and I didn't want to wake 'im. He's worn out. Will you keep an eye on 'im for me, Mister Jefferson? Sammy's all right if he's not bossed too much."

"Sure I'll keep an eye on 'im. He's a nice little feller, jest full of spirits like a colt. He'll stiddy down an' be sober as an ox in a year or two."

"An' if I don't come back with the nugget, I'll be owing you something for taking Kit. You'll be trusting me, I hope . . ."

"I'll trust you anywhere, anytime, Jason Coit. If you live near me in Oregon, just be neighborly . . . an' what I do for you, I do for Oregon. We'll be needin' your kind in the new country . . . boys who take keer of their mothers. My boy Luke," and here Elisha's voice faltered, "if he was alive, he'd be one of your friends . . . mebbe goin' along with you. Mary an' I want you to live close so we can see you now an' then. Come back safe, boy," and he laid a hand on Jason's shoulder, "or I'll never forgive myself for urgin' this trip."

"I'll be back. . . . Quiet, Kit."

The saddle and saddlebags were adjusted and Jason mounted, his rifle resting in front of him.

"It's easier to leave with you here, Mister Jefferson. Thanks for coming."

"We'll see you along the Snake. Come back safe, boy."

According to Bill Brewster's map, Sublette's Cutoff led eastward from Bear River, over mountains, across Green River and a desert of some fifty miles, and then rejoined the Oregon Trail between Dry Sandy and Little Sandy Rivers, close to South Pass. Because of the rough roads, wagons as a rule traveled to the south by way of Fort Bridger. A man on horseback, however, could make good time and save many miles by crossing due east along the cutoff, provided he was not delayed by rain or a snowstorm.

"Like as not, the desert'll be hot as fury," the old scout had told Jason. "Grass is skeerce, even in the ravines, so fill a bag fer your hoss right after you leave Green River, and yer gum-sack with water. Folks comin' west generally travel through the night. You'll have to use yer own jedgment. Your biggest trouble will be meetin' up with folks who'll ask questions. Folks get lonely on the trail an' wanter talk. Switch 'em off by askin' questions, too. Say you're travelin' on business an' keep by yerself. It's lonesome, but it's safer."

Bridle paths, overgrown with brush and seldom used, were difficult to locate in the wilderness. Even Bill Brewster admitted this as he pounded his right fist into his left palm for emphasis.

"Be sartin," Bill pounded, "you ride north three mile after you turn left below Pacific Creek. Watch yer mileage best you can an' keep yer mind right on't. Before we finish talkin', I'll tell you 'bout circlin' back . . . goin' over the same ground twice. It's a hard job, but don't give up huntin'. Injuns an' trappers know that path. No use worryin' folks here 'bout it too much, but I'm tellin' you straight, so you'll know what you're up against. Once you spot it, your eye'll follow it good enough, but you might cross it a dozen times an' not see it. But be sartin," and Bill again pounded out the words, "you ride three mile north. Mebbe more. It'll be up to you, boy."

"An' there's an ol' dead tree close by the cemetery?"

"You can't miss it. An' do yer diggin' at night. Thar'll be a full moon by then. If the nugget ain't thar, well, swaller yer disappointment an' start west again. But if you do find it, sleep at night with it in the saddlebags under yer head, the way Henri done. Don't let it out of your sight. An', like the cap'n says, don't stop at Fort Hall on the way back, but pass by it in the night. You'll find us along the Snake somewhar. Thar won't be no trouble from Injuns, but look out fer them trapper friends of Henri's. Injuns and trappers have strange notions 'bout their dead. . . . If you meet 'em, use yer wits an' get away as fast as you can. I don't have to tell you how to take keer of the hoss. You know 'im better'n I do. More I think 'bout it, I wish I was goin', too," and Bill Brewster ended his long talk with a deep sigh.

Danger, illness, sacrifice and tragedy along the trail had planted deep roots of friendship among the members of Mark Morgan's train. Rifts and bickerings had occurred among them, as in any other train, but the wagons continued to roll along together. The captain's tact, his sense of justice and quiet reasoning had met all emergencies and Bill Brewster's guidance had proved unerring. Jason, now turning away from their protection, felt a sense of loss as he rode into the waning night. His was a lonely journey, and none save a few loyal friends would know he had left until the train was on its way following the Snake River. The old scout would see to that.

He must not fail. . . . So much depended upon the success of his journey! Home . . . perhaps in the Willamette

Valley if the new roads opened up. And in the home, little extra comforts for his mother and Tacy. . . . And neighbors, congenial neighbors in the wilderness meant almost life itself! It pleased him that Elisha Jefferson wished him near. Unconsciously Jason's hand patted Kit and felt of the smooth leather of the saddle. Ah, yes, faithful friends and kindly, still sleeping in the wagons below. But he must leave them now, and find them later along the winding Snake.

"An' you, Kit," he half whispered a moment later, as the horse's white feet clipped along the trail which led to the east, "you will belong to me . . . if I can find the path an' if the gold is there."

"If the gold is there" . . . Like a song, the words seemed to beat in time to the rhythm of Kit's hoofs. "If the gold is there . . . if the gold is there . . ."

Facing a cool morning wind, Jason watched the new day unfold. After a quick breakfast of coffee and cold sowbelly, he was again in the saddle, bent upon his strange quest . . . a nugget of gold buried in a grave on South Pass.

It was not difficult to recognize the places where Captain Morgan's train had camped the week before. Jason, noting the charred wood and wheel ruts where the wagons had formed their circle at night, could see again each schooner in its place and hear once more the familiar voices.

The Narrows, a stony road between high cliffs on which young hawks and eagles nested, led directly to Smiths Fork. Two miles farther on Jason swung to his left, and the journey across Sublette's Cutoff had begun. The trail was now unfamiliar and he was forced to make his own selection of camping spots and use his own discretion as to how many miles Kit should travel a day. In the midst of thunderstorms, he forged his way over mountainous country and rested at Hams Fork, weary but content with his progress. It was here that some Shoshone Indians visited his camp, offering him roots of thistles that were the size of carrots and sweet to taste, serviceberries, and the black sticky roots of pond lilies, steamed and pounded. And it was along a level stretch marked Fontenelle Creek upon his map that Jason encountered his first train of emigrants, six white-topped wagons drawn by mules and four horsemen riding single file in advance. It was impossible to avoid them and Jason braced himself to meet the questions which he knew would be hurled at him.

"Howdy!" called the foremost horseman. "What's the news ahead?"

"Howdy. . . . No special news," replied Jason.

"Where you from?" called the second horseman.

"Fort Hall."

"Crossin' the Green?" asked the first man. The four horsemen had now stopped and were gathered about him. They were men in their fifties, with parched and weathered faces.

"Why, you're a young feller!" exclaimed the first man. "My name's Stevens. We're all from the east. Goin' to Californy, if we can get there. Who might you be?"

"Oh, I'm from Illinois . . . name's Coit. How's the road ahead?" If possible, he meant to ask question for question, as the old scout had advised.

"It's no road for wagons," Stevens told Jason wearily. "We hoped to save ourselves travelin' south to Fort Bridger by takin' this here shortcut, but I guess we'd a done a sight better to have gone aroun'. You'll make it all right on a hoss, but with a wagon it's slow work. You crossin' the desert?"

"I reckon so, if I can ford the Green. Is she high?"

"Lost three mules yesterday. One fell in a hole an' dragged the others down. Watch for the stone marker . . . it's a big slab of rock an' it's the best fordin' place on the Green, we're thinkin'. The storms have been awful. Snow and rain all of a suddint."

The six wagons had stopped and several women with children running beside them approached and stared at Jason curiously. Their faces were tired, worn, old before their time. A tall lank woman, the first to reach him, passed him a tin dipper.

"Here, boy, drink some buttermilk. I made butter this mornin'."

Jason thanked her, drank the milk and returned the dipper, wishing he could say something to hearten the flagging spirits of these people.

"You'll find Hams Fork a good place," he encouraged. "Plenty of grass. The mountains are steep but there are some good roads goin' round. I'm sorry you've had such trouble."

"We've had more'n our share," returned the man Stevens. "You all alone?"

"Yes. How'd you manage for grass on the desert?"

"We loaded up before we started. Filled our barrels an' kegs with water at Big Sandy. They say it's fifty-two miles from water to water. Why you goin' east alone?"

"Business. Guess I'll have to be on my way."

"Well, you'll make good time on that there hoss," and

Stevens' eyes held a wistful expression as he gazed at Kit. "I useter own a hoss like him back home. I wish I owned him now. It's a wonder you got by them thievin' Pawnees comin' west. When'd you leave the east?"

"Last May. Good-bye . . ."

"How long you been on the road from Fort Hall?"

"Three-four days. Good-bye."

"Good luck to you, young feller. You wouldn't be goin' as far as Laramie, would you?"

"Oh, no, I'll probably catch up with you along the Bear somewhere. Good-bye," and with a nod at the woman who had brought him the buttermilk, Jason was off, with Kit traveling at a swift trot. Would all passing strangers prove so curious?

For the first time since leaving Fort Hall, Jason was aware of the risk he ran in riding a horse like Kit. One could scarcely ignore such an animal. Lean but delicately covered, with muscles flexing in perfect rhythm whenever he walked or trotted, his chestnut coat flashing with burnished lights in the sun, Kit might well cause envy and longing in the heart of any horse lover. Jason determined to keep closer guard in the future. No longer would he let Kit stray about a meadow or wander off to graze by himself.

"From now on, you're staying right with me, Kit," Jason told him. "I don't like the look in some folks' eyes when they watch you."

Kit, on the whole, seemed to be enjoying his adventure. His four white-stockinged feet appeared tireless, always ready to move forward at the slightest sign from Jason.

"It's time to quit now," Jason would say, even before the horse showed weariness. "You've done over twenty miles

today. Whoa, boy, we're stoppin' right here for the night,"
and he would pull Kit up beside some covered spot hidden
from the trail. Later he would say, as he sat beside a small
fire with the horse feeding close by, "If I were sure of the
path an' the gold bein' there, this would be a lark . . . a
real lark. If I were only sure . . ."

Green River, ice-cold, with a green-shaled bottom, ran
deep and powerful, and a slab of stone marked the ford.
Swimming beside Kit, Jason made the opposite shore safely.
There was no sign of the three dead mules belonging to the
man Stevens, nothing to show of the struggle save fresh
wheel ruts on both banks of the river. How fortunate Captain Morgan had been in his selection of Bill Brewster as
scout! Not an ox, horse or cow had been lost in all their
river crossings.

With the gum-sack filled with water, and extra grass for
Kit in the saddlebags, Jason began the long, tortuous ride
across Green River Desert in the early dawn. There was
nothing to break the monotony of the arid miles; not even
a badger appeared from the many holes which dotted the
sand. All the remainder of his life Jason knew he would
remember this ride, its silence and its pall. . . .

In the afternoon, a few snowflakes fell and a cold wind
whipped in from the north. That night Jason camped once
more by the side of Oregon Trail, in a sheltered gap between Little Sandy and Dry Sandy Rivers. Morning would
bring him below Pacific Creek, and then would begin the
search for the bridle path which led to the old dead tree
and the trappers' cemetery.

22

THE SEARCH FOR GOLD

The land below Pacific Creek lay wild and broken, a rolling sagebrush country mounting gradually to the east. With snow-covered peaks gleaming like polished silver, the Wind River Mountains formed a high, formidable wall in the north. A desolate land, a jumble of earth and sky fit for neither man nor beast. Little wonder, mused Jason, that Bill Brewster had showed concern over his finding the brush-grown trail.

"Kit, it looks as if we'd have tough goin'!"

As if in answer, the big horse whinnied and stopped of his own accord. Jason dismounted and stared about him. It was almost impossible to associate Bill Brewster's map with the scene before him. Somewhere in the wilderness ahead lay a path leading to a cemetery that was guarded by a tall dead tree . . . the only tree for miles around.

"You'll look fer tracks from the time you start, of course," Bill Brewster had directed. "When you've gone west two mile, you better go afoot an' go slow. Look ev'ry-whar . . . up an' down fer ev'ry sign. Remember it ain't a reg'lar trail an' it ain't used much. When you've gone three mile an' ain't found nothin', turn east an' circle back to yer own tracks. Go ahead north some more an' if thar's still no signs, make a bigger circle back. Keep lookin' all the time at ev'rything."

The traveling was rough, even more difficult than it ap-peared from a distance. Before Jason had gone a short way, he found himself at the edge of a gulch so steep that he was forced to dismount and lead Kit across at a further end. Keeping in direct line with one of the taller peaks of the mountains ahead, he again forged his way north, finding before him a misery of rocks. Steep little gullies and un-scalable cliffs meant circling about, with time slipping away. . . .

Once Kit stumbled and fell, a sharp rock grazing his side. Apparently there were no serious effects from the fall. Nevertheless, thereafter Jason walked, remembering the skeletons of horses he had seen along the trail . . . horses which had been shot because of some injury. Wolves had left little to tell the story. . . .

"Easy, boy, easy, boy," Jason kept repeating beneath his breath. He sighed with relief when they passed the gullies and reached a stretch of sandy waste that stretched for about a mile. Covered with thorny plants, straggling vines, sagebrush and greasewood, the sand lay level as a table top, with no marks of travel. The third mile was a gradual climb northward, and as Jason and Kit ascended, the air grew increasingly cold. At times they were forced to slide across glazed surfaces of snow. Now and then they climbed a green slope aglow with yellow flowers watered from the top by melting ice. A little way beyond, the rolling plains began again, the sagebrush and the greasewood . . . a strange, unaccountable land. . . .

"We must be three miles north by now."

It was time to circle, to make sure he had not missed the path. Swinging to the east, Jason hurried in a semicircle back to his own prints in the sand. He was glad to see them, finding in them a sense of companionship. . . . Again he struck north. Surely he would locate the path within the hour by some small token: the prints of a boot, a horse's hoof, the ashes of a campfire . . .

When about to travel his second semicircle back, his eyes suddenly caught sight of long wavering lines in the sand, as though poles had been dragged beneath heavy weights. The first marks of any kind! With a shout Jason ran forward and fell upon his knees beside them. There, in the earth, were also the faint outlines of a pony's hoofs. Indians! Indians had passed that way, their ponies and dogs pulling travois. The traces were several days old and as he crawled on his hands and knees beside them, he found the ground pressed hard, packed down. Examining it closely, he saw that it was an indistinct path extending east and west. The trail . . . he had found the trail at last! The joy, the relief of locating it, sent him running back to Kit.

"It's all right, Kit! We've found it! We've found it! Just a few miles and we'll be there! We'll see a big dead tree first, Kit . . . Bill Brewster says we can't miss it!"

The dead tree appeared sooner than Jason expected. Its lightning-blasted trunk and two naked branches made a grim silhouette against a twilight sky. Not far away were five graves piled high with rocks. Four of the graves were marked with crosses and the headboard of the last bore the name, HENRI JULES.

Sammy had done his work well. The H in Henri was elaborate and the J in Jules swung with a long tail. Above and below were funny childish scrolls but Jason, with a lump in his throat, had no desire to laugh. Poor little Sammy in the big hat . . . he could see him plainly, bending over his work while Henri towered above, watchful, demanding. . . .

Silence hung over the cemetery. Not a breath of wind stirred. Far away to the south could be heard the faint "yip-yip-yuea-h" of coyotes. . . . Jason was alone in the quiet company of the dead.

Remembering the old scout's warning, "Trappers don't want their graves tampered with!" Jason searched the narrow trail carefully while it was still light. There were no fresh tracks of passersby. It was midnight by the time both he and Kit had been fed and rested and he felt it safe to open the grave of Henri Jules. With his rifle primed and close at hand, Jason approached the grave with a shovel. Beneath the moon's white light the headboard had a realistic dignity and despite the fact that he knew Henri Jules to be alive and well at Fort Hall, Jason felt he was being almost sacrilegious as he removed the rocks which lay piled upon the grave.

The night was bitterly cold. Water had frozen in small pools by the edge of the path. A fox barked further down the trail and an owl hooted from a branch of the dead tree. Jason shuddered and then laughed at himself. He had heard the same sounds back in Illinois on many a night . . . why should they distress him now? His task became easier as he began to think about the gold within the grave. . . . However, as he pulled away the heavy stones, the thought flashed through his mind that perhaps Henri, wily and crafty as an animal, might purposely have dug this grave to mislead Sammy. Perhaps he had placed the nugget in one of the other graves! The prospect of digging into all five of them was appalling, and Jason began to lift the rocks a little faster. Was any sum of money worth the strain and labor the last twenty-four hours had caused him, he asked himself? Yes, in Oregon . . . where dollars were scarce and life was hard. His mother must have a stout warm cabin, Tacy and Sammy must go to school, and then . . . there was Kit. . . .

When he had pulled away the last stone, his fingers ached so from the cold that he was tempted to build a fire. But even a small blaze might attract a wayfarer to the place, and what possible explanation could he give of his seeming desecration of a grave? What a strange dream it was . . . He, Jason Coit, digging into a trapper's grave at night in search of gold . . . Alone, hundreds of miles from home. . . .

Kit was feeling the cold and pawed impatiently.

"Quiet, Kit, I'm right here," Jason called softly.

There was light enough. The moon seemed very near, very white, just over his shoulder, but it did not seem friendly like the yellow moon in Illinois. Every object was distinct: the clumps of sagebrush by the path, the gaunt lines of the dead tree, his own hands on the handle of the shovel. In the thin white light, what would the gold nugget look like?

Now and then his shovel struck a stone and the sharp metallic sound made his heart beat faster. Would the nugget be wrapped in skins or packed in a wooden box? Kit whinnied and pawed the ground.

A little later, the shovel scraped on a floor of rock and Jason knew he had finally come to the bottom of the grave. He dug feverishly to remove the soft earth but soon found a large round rock blocking his way. It had not been there long, for bits of moss still clung to its sides. The rock removed, he dug still further, standing within the grave itself, his whole body wet with cold perspiration, his breath rasping in his throat. Rocks and more rocks. Had Henri Jules placed them there to give shape to the grave? Two flat slabs of slate next appeared, carefully braced together. It took but an instant to pry them apart. A roll of leather, tied with thongs, lay between. He lifted it. The roll was heavy, heavier than rock of its size. . . . In another moment he had slashed the thongs with his knife and torn aside the leather wrappings. The object within was smooth and heavy but his eyes were blurred and he could not see. With his breath now coming in hard gasps, he struck a match and looked down. Beneath the flickering light he caught the glint of yellow, warm sparkling yellow . . . gold!

The narrow path was not difficult to follow on the return trip west, and with the nugget safe in a saddlebag, Jason reached the gap between Dry Sandy and Little Sandy late in the afternoon. On the bank of a brook he built a fire and made coffee while Kit, still saddled, nibbled at the green tips of willows. Now that he had reached the familiar trail again, Jason felt safe, happy. . . . From there on, there would be no trappers like Bateese to be feared, merely the ordinary emigrant following the open road. Soon he would be on his way over Sublette's Cutoff after he had gathered a little grass for Kit and filled the gum-sack with water.

He had hardly finished his coffee when he heard voices. Rising to his feet, he stooped, picked up the coffee pot and his rifle and then stood very still, every nerve taut. The voices were growing louder. . . . A few moments later, two men on small shaggy horses with a pack animal following came splashing up the brook. The voices suddenly ceased as the men caught sight of Jason.

The newcomers were typical mountain trappers, bearded to the eyes and dressed in buckskin frocks and fur caps. Could one of them be Bateese? If only he had not stopped by the brook but pushed on into the desert! According to Sammy, Bateese was without a thumb . . . Perhaps the two men would stop only a few moments and then move on . . . It would never do to let them see he was uneasy. . . .

"How!" Jason greeted them.

"How!" answered both trappers in deep voices, and walked their horses nearer, their dark eyes staring at him. Gold earrings dangled from their ears and there were knives and pistols in their belts. Typical mountain men! For the first time the tall leader caught sight of Kit and he made no attempt to conceal his admiration and covetousness. With his knee, he guided his own horse to the bank and muttered something to his short and stocky companion, who immediately followed his example. With deliberation both men tied their animals close together in the lee of a large rock. Seemingly they paid no attention to Jason, yet he sensed in a flash that he, the gold nugget and his beloved Kit were in danger. There was a quick hot beat in his throat as he turned and hurriedly put his foot in the stirrup. If ever he were to get away, he must leave now!

"Why you hurree? Beeg storm . . . she blow."

Jason looked over his shoulder. The tall man was smiling, but his hand was on his hip, very close to the butt of his pistol. Turning slowly away, Jason stared out over the desert. Dark clouds hung low in the west and a strong gust of wind was blowing. Before he could speak, a small sharp hailstone stung his cheek, and then he remembered that the man Stevens at Fontenelle Creek had spoken of these storms . . . sudden, terrible storms of rain and hail.

"I ought to be gettin' on," he replied, hoping that dismay did not make his voice quaver, "but I guess you're right." And with that he took his boot out of the stirrup. He had no choice but to remain.

Leading Kit to the sheltered side of the rock, Jason tied him to a willow as far from the Indian ponies as possible, and at the end nearest the desert, fully conscious that the tall trapper was eyeing Kit, the fine saddle and saddlebags. Pretending to loosen the girth, Jason quickly threw a blanket over the horse and fastened it carefully.

"Why you not unsaddle de hoss?" asked the tall trapper, coming a few steps nearer.

"He's all right . . . he's used to it," replied Jason, very conscious of the awkward pause that followed.

The tall trapper, muttering something, turned away and Jason followed. The short trapper had scooped a hole at the base of the rock and dumped into it a sack of dry leaves and brushwood. The tall trapper impatiently ordered his companion to hurry and spoke in a disgruntled voice as he called him Antoine. Upon hearing the name Jason breathed more freely. Possibly if he listened closely he would catch the tall trapper's name . . . and he hoped that it was not Bateese.

For covering, both trappers now wore long white capotes with the hoods pulled over their heads. In a few moments they motioned to Jason that he was to share their fire. With his second blanket about his shoulders and carrying his rifle, he joined them, choosing a position where he could watch both the trappers and Kit. It was impossible to see if the tall trapper was without a thumb, as both hands were concealed by his cape.

"You cross the san', mebbe?" asked the tall trapper.

"Yes, I'm crossin' . . . soon's the storm's over."

Antoine was evidently the cook of the party. From one of his many packs he produced wood and a dozen large trout wrapped in leaves. The fish were soon frying over the fire on a thin sheet of iron while a black brew of questionable aroma simmered close by. This was finally poured into buffalo horns and served as coffee. Jason was glad of the food, and the coffee, though bitter, warmed him. Whenever he could, he watched the tall trapper, who appeared to use only his left hand while eating. It was when he wished more fish and was forced to reach some distance that he used his right hand. A jagged scar ran across the back and then . . . Jason saw there was no thumb. The tall trapper was Bateese!

Startled in spite of himself, Jason, in the act of swallowing a mouthful of coffee, choked and coughed. Tears ran down his cheeks as he struggled for breath, but only Antoine looked up.

"*Voilà!* My *café* . . . she strong!" he commented, and both trappers continued with their supper, unconcerned.

Every moment spent with Antoine and Bateese spelled danger. Undoubtedly Bateese was guarding the entrance to Sublette's Cutoff, still determined to capture Henri Jules and the nugget of gold. Yes, Bateese was still searching for Henri, little dreaming that the gold nugget was almost within reach in the saddlebag upon Kit's back. What a precious haul for the two trappers . . . the gold nugget and Kit as well!

There was no mistaking the admiration and ugly greed in Bateese's face whenever he looked at Kit. Storm or no storm, Jason knew he must leave. The rain and hail might act as a shield. Kit was rested . . . and the trappers' ponies would not be able to keep up with him once he had a good start. A good start . . . how would he go about it? If only he might reach Big Sandy and hide in the thick willows which lined its bank. No one could find either the horse or himself there. . . .

The cold was increasing. Already the side of the big rock gleamed with ice. Needles of ice showed in the rain-filled hollows. The brim of Jason's hat was crusted and poor Kit was miserable, snorting occasionally and pulling at his rope, resentful of the presence of the bickering ponies. Once Bateese pretended to quiet them, but for the most part he centered his attention upon Kit.

With their supper finished, both trappers conversed in a strange language and smoked their pipes. Bateese appeared eager, talked rapidly and sometimes gestured with his thumbless hand. But Antoine, stolidly indifferent, sometimes shaking his head doubtfully, sat staring into the fire. That they were talking of him Jason was certain. And as he drew his wet blanket closer about him, he wondered what Bill Brewster would do under the circumstances. In some way the wily old scout would outmaneuver his opponents at the point of a gun barrel or knife. With one hand grasping the hilt of his knife beneath the blanket and with his gun close beside him, Jason crouched against the rock, his eyes closed as he pretended to doze. He must think and think fast. Every moment counted. . . .

Gradually a plan pieced itself together. It involved a terrible risk, but any risk was better than idly waiting for the end of things. The plan might work . . . Everything depended upon Kit and his own coolness and grit.

For the last half hour Kit had been standing quietly, his head lowered. Was the horse asleep? It was a great relief to Jason when a pony squealed and roused Kit into an answering neigh. With every effort to act naturally, Jason rose slowly and, carrying his gun close to his side, walked towards the horses.

Both trappers sat upright, suddenly alert. Bateese was the first to spring to his feet.

"Where you go?" he called.

"I want to look after my horse," replied Jason without stopping. If he kept in the direct line of the horses, the trappers would not fire for fear of injuring their own animals. It took all his courage to keep walking and when he finally looked around, he found both trappers behind him.

"You take off de saddle now, mebbe?" Bateese spoke smoothly enough but there was an unmistakable leer in his manner as his left hand sought his pistol. Antoine, half asleep, was smiling as though amused.

Jason did not reply, but with his left hand straightened Kit's blanket. And then with a suddenness which surprised

The butt of his gun caught Bateese beneath the chin

both trappers, he whirled about, bringing his right arm up. With a crashing blow, the heavy butt of his gun caught Bateese beneath the chin. The trapper staggered back, dazed, his pistol falling to the ground.

"Don't move! I'll shoot if you move! Throw down that pistol, Antoine!"

Antoine, his mouth half open, stared stupidly into the barrel of the gun pointed at him. Slowly he reached for his pistol and then dropped it. It fell with a dull thud at Jason's feet. At the sight of it on the ground, Bateese spat out a mouthful of blood and then turned on Antoine, letting out a stream of ugly names.

"Shut up, Bateese! Now, both of you, hands up! Move back against that rock!"

Both trappers raised their hands slowly, reluctantly. Jason's voice was hoarse, demanding, unfamiliar in his own ears. The two pistols at his feet gave him courage. If only he could keep the two men at a safe distance . . .

"You, there, BACK, I say!"

Antoine had stepped back but Bateese stood motionless, blood trickling from one corner of his mouth. As Jason advanced a step, Bateese slowly retreated. The tall trapper was quiet now, but in the light of the fire his eyes shone and glowered like a wild beast's. His silence brooded no good.

"Now, then, turn around. Face the rock. FACE THE ROCK . . . QUICK!"

Both trappers stared at him, refusing to move. Jason now lifted his rifle higher as if to take better aim. Together, Antoine and Bateese turned and faced the rock.

"Keep your hands up. I'll shoot the first one who moves!"

With his gun still aimed, his eyes scarcely leaving the

backs of his prisoners, Jason advanced, stooped down and picked up the pistols one at a time. The first, a Colt of recent make, he thrust into his belt, the second into a back pocket. Meanwhile, so gradually that it was hardly noticeable, Bateese was lowering his hands.

"Keep 'em up, Bateese!" Slowly Bateese raised his hands again.

"Easy, boy . . . easy, Kit," Jason soothed the horse, who had become excited and was pulling at his rope.

There was one more thing to accomplish before Jason felt free to leave. The Indian ponies must be loosed and driven off so that there would be no pursuit. Bateese and Antoine were still facing the rock, their hands held high. With his rifle within reach, Jason cut a long willow switch. A few moments later, the three ponies, their legs stinging, were galloping wildly into the desert.

"Don't move! Keep those hands up!"

Bateese and Antoine, almost beside themselves at the loss of their ponies, had half turned. Once more they were forced to obey.

And now the blanket was removed from Kit's back, the halter cut. In one leap Jason was in the saddle, his rifle before him.

"Go it, Kit, go it!" he shouted, leaning close over Kit's neck.

He was not a second too soon. Even as Kit plunged forward into the stormy darkness, a knife spun through the air, grazing Jason's right shoulder. On, on into the night shot the big chestnut, like an arrow loosed from its bow.

23

SAMUEL COIT FOLLOWS THE TRAIL

Two families in Captain Morgan's train turned their wagons left at Raft River and headed for California. Persuaded by the British that negotiations for a treaty between England and the States would not be settled for some time, that snows would block their way across the Blue Mountains and the Indians prove unfriendly along the Snake River, the two families firmly believed California to be their promised land. Rumors floating about Fort Hall had done their work. But the other twenty-eight wagons held valiantly to their course. The trail along the edge of the Snake was back-breaking, blistering, endless. Oxen lagged and miles dragged.

"Where's Jason? Has Jason gone ahead? Has he gone back east? Kit's not with us. . . . Why, Jason hasn't gone to California, has he, the blitherin' softy?" Many were the comments upon Jason's absence from the train but Captain Morgan offered no explanation other than that Jason would join them farther ahead on the trail.

Samuel Coit, in the big hat which flapped more dismally than ever about his ears, and wearing his patched shirt and hand-me-down trousers, drove his oxen faithfully, in tight-lipped silence. The old bowie knife left as a parting gift from Jason had been a pleasant surprise, and his first week alone had not seemed especially arduous. Perched upon the big front seat of the wagon, playing his jew's-harp, Sammy was in a particularly happy state as mentally he spent his five hundred and nine dollars in reckless abandon for horses, guns and knives. As these amusements waned, however, he stared back over the trail in search of Jason. Already he had heard how Jason killed the first buffalo and had been given Porky as the reward, and the fact that Jason had also won the affections of the train was not lost upon Sammy. Pride in his older brother mounted daily and likewise a growing concern at his absence.

"You sure you made that map awful plain for Jason?" Sammy would ask the old scout at least ten times a day. "There warn't no beginnin' nor endin' to that bridle path. How's he goin' to find it? Hadn't he oughter be here by now?"

"Well, I made the map best I could," Bill Brewster would answer patiently. "But give 'im time. Thar's lots to consider. They call this a dry year, but in some parts the water comes down in buckets. Been a lot o' black sky banked in the south. An' thar ain't no use lookin' fer 'im yet, son. Why, he ain't been gone six days yet . . ."

"Seven," replied Sammy, pointing at a row of pencilled crosses on the wall of the wagon. "It's seven days. I'm keepin' count."

Sammy's relations with Aunt Liddy had scarcely improved. When finally driven to take a bath, the boy searched diligently for a swimming hole like the one he had left in Illinois. Failing, he at last resorted to a brook where, not wholly by accident, he dropped Aunt Liddy's last and priceless cake of soap. It zigzagged down out of sight and was seen no more. Bubbles frothed over the rocks, and that was the end. Feeling ran high, and three days later, when Sammy announced in the presence of the Morgans that if Jason did not return soon he intended to go back on Whitey and find him, Aunt Liddy rose like a trout.

"You'll do no sech thing, you little soap-wastin' idjit!" she snapped. "An' if I hear any more talk like that, I'll tie you in your wagon." Poor Aunt Liddy, her hands and face swollen by mosquito bites as she spooned out the breakfast mush, was having trials of her own.

"Oh, shucks, Aunt Liddy. Sammy's just tryin' to tease," protested Aaron. "He's not leavin'."

"Of course not," added Mark Morgan. "Sammy's given his word to Jason to stay with the wagon. Give that brother of yours a full chance, Sammy. You can't do Jason's work and he can't do yours just now." There was a slight note of rebuke in Captain Morgan's voice and Sammy felt his face flushing.

Snake River, rushing through a great valley, twisted itself deeper and deeper into the earth. The wagons followed the brink of the canyon more closely than was really safe. There were times when they were forced to follow narrow roads almost overhanging the abyss. Grass was scarce and drinking water difficult to obtain. The more venturesome, armed with buckets, at first found fun in the perilous descent, but as the days passed, going down for water became

irksome. Because of mishaps, there was sometimes little enough water left in the buckets when the top was regained.

"All that water down there an' we burnin' with thirst!" was the cry. The stock suffered from thirst more than the emigrants, sometimes traveling two and three days before a path could be found for them to descend. The first casualty occurred one night when an ox belonging to Joel Adams slipped. It was dead when Joel reached the rocks below. Later its flesh was dried as jerky on top of the Adamses' wagon.

Courage was tested during those days. The beauty of the wide valley with snow-topped mountains north and south was scarcely noticed. There were days when the emigrants choked in their own dust and made but three miles. Beneath the scorching sun lips cracked, tongues were swollen, and yet the sound of cool water could always be heard. At night the icy wind from the mountain snows caused those who had thoughtlessly disposed of bedding during the torrid days along the Platte to shiver sleeplessly in their jersey coats.

More than one family, however, met every situation uncomplainingly, with prayers of thankfulness in their heart and on their lips. To Ezra and Mary Fields especially, an physical suffering along the trail was of minor consequen compared to their former agonies. Their children had turned. To be sure, Anna had grown wild as a young Cr and fought vigorously against soap and water, someti talking in an outlandish tongue. Bribery with the horeho candy so carefully preserved by Mary Fields still hel charm, although the supply of candy was fast dwind Jessica, less affected by their weeks of roving life, fell easily into the former ways of living. And small,

haired Bluette flourished, despite the shortage of cow's milk, while other infants showed ill effects from the scanty diet.

"Things'll be better further on," Bill Brewster promised the worried parents. "Thar'll be grass soon an' at Fishin' Falls, you'll get a change o' victuals. Fer a pair o' ol' pants or a fishhook, you'll get all the soup an' salmon you can lug. But look out fer them cakes I tol' you of. They're made o' crickets, lizards, an' the Lor' knows what kind o' bugs. Sometimes the Injuns give 'em away free. They've got a good flavor goin' down 'cause they're sweetened with honey, but afterwards they make a feller feel kinder funny."

Fishing Falls appeared little short of heaven to the hungry and exhausted homesteaders. Like birds' nests, wattle huts lined the open banks of the river. In them lived Shoshone Indians dressed in soiled and scanty rabbit skins. Cries of "Haggai, haggai!" filled the air as each Indian sought to trade a kettle of steaming fish soup or one of the salmon drying in red lines behind every hut. With eyes swollen and sore from staring into the bright water, the Indians presented a pitiable sight.

The fish soup, steaming hot and well seasoned, appealed to all, but nobody partook of the cakes except Sammy. In the hope of shocking Jessica, he swallowed five cakes offered him by generous Indians on the outskirts of the crowd. He was loud in his enthusiasm and this was too much for Anna, who stood near by. Always a glutton for sweets, she lost no time in eating all the cakes proffered her by admiring Indians, and she grunted her approval, Crow-fashion, as she ate. The orgy was ended by Jessica, who, horrified, ran screaming to her mother for help. Samuel Coit suddenly

found himself in great disfavor. And despite his bravado, the words of the old scout repeated themselves insistently in his ears: "They make a feller feel kinder funny." . . . In a few moments he unswallowed the five cakes, his face the color of a tallow dip as he disappeared in the direction of his wagon.

Anna maintained her poise and the sweetened cakes as well. None the less, she was given a large dose of rhubarb, and for a time Samuel Coit ceased to be any kind of a hero in the Fields family.

"He's Satan's own child!" declared Aunt Liddy as she came away from the wagon where Sammy lay. "An' if he didn't look so awful sick, I'd put 'im right over my knee!"

The ford on Snake River, twenty-seven miles below Fishing Falls, presented a problem to every train on its way to the west. Due to the height and fierceness of its current, many preferred not to cross but to continue following the southern shore of the river, which led through barren miles of rock and sand.

"Nobody'll cross that river fer a week, I'm thinkin'," announced Bill Brewster, as the wagons stopped and people gazed in dismay at the rushing torrent. "They've had a cloudburst up yonder somewhar. Gen'rally speakin', them two islands make it easier crossin', like steppin' stuns, but it ain't so now. With yer cattle weak an' pindlin' an' no good hoss like Kit ter lead, you'd best keep to the south shore."

"But how'll Jason find us?" asked Aaron and Sammy in the same breath.

"I s'pose he'll ford, 'less I get a message to 'im someway. Thar's an ol' Injun with a covey of squaws near here. Name is Singin' Frog. Mebbe Singin' Frog would watch fer Jason as he comes along. It's the best we can do. If Jason gets by 'im an' fords, he'll go on to Fort Boise an' we'll meet 'im thar. . . . I don't like follerin' the south shore. Grass is skeerce. But there's no use riskin' lives in that water."

So Singing Frog was notified and the train, heeding the advice of the old scout, continued along the south shore of the Snake instead of crossing. Sammy, visibly disappointed that Jason had not caught up with the train, remained by himself, saying little. And as the days passed, there were lines of worry on Elisha Jefferson's face. Once he secretly conferred with Bill Brewster and Captain Morgan.

"He ought to've ketched up with us some time ago," Elisha said, shaking his head slowly. "An' now I wish I hadn't put the idea of goin' back for that gold into his head. What makes him late, Bill? What's the worst that coulda happened?"

"A dozen things coulda happened," replied Bill Brewster. " 'Tain't no use tryin' to figger it out. I'm jest hopin' an' guessin' like the rest o' you. I dunno . . . I dunno. Chances be that dumb fool Singin' Frog didn't see 'im at the ford an' he crossed the Snake. If so, we'll meet 'im at the Fort ahead. Meanwhile we've got to keep the little feller Sammy quiet. He's restless as a water bug. Seems like he's grown to think a sight of his brother since they was separated. Watches the road all the time. He's quit chalkin' down the days, don't talk about his money, nor play his jew's-harp. Kinder homesick, I guess."

It was on a cold morning with a lemon sky ahead that Sammy appeared at Captain Morgan's wagon a trifle late for breakfast.

"More like snow than rain," Aunt Liddy was predicting for the twentieth time in an effort to keep up the conversation. Unconsciously Aunt Liddy often spoke of snow these days, although she never alluded to the Blue Mountains ahead. Of late there had been a pinched look about her mouth and nose, and her dress hung loosely from her shoulders. Worry over Jason, little sleep, and the constant nursing of others had thinned her down, but her shoulders were as squarely set as of old and the same fire blazed in her gray eyes. Mark Morgan, the old scout, Aaron and Sammy constituted her family for breakfast, and it was at this hour that Aunt Liddy held forth, dictating orders for the day. Although the group listened respectfully, each one did as he pleased a little later.

"Ain't you got somethin' more to put on?" she asked Sammy, noticing that he shivered and wore no jacket over his red shirt. "You're sittin' there shakin' like a leaf. Here, drink this hot milk. I warmed it a-purpose."

Without answering, Sammy drank the milk obediently, trying to keep the hand which held his tin cup steady. All eyes were turned upon him, for Sammy had been unusually quiet and there were shadows under his eyes. With a resigned sigh, Aunt Liddy sniffed the air from the northwest, murmured something about snow again and disappeared into the wagon. She emerged a moment later with a jacket which Aaron had outgrown.

"Where'd you go last night?" she asked as she gave Sammy the jacket. "I went down to your wagon to get yer shirt to mend, but you weren't in yer bed. Only that fat, dirty pig was a-lyin' there. Where'd you go?"

Sammy took his time before answering. Some of his old

arrogance had returned and he grinned saucily as he looked up at her.

"Huh. Must 'a' walked in my sleep."

Aaron laughed and then caught himself as his aunt gave him a scathing look.

"Walked in yer sleep! Well, if you don't want blisters, you'd better empty them boots. They're full of sand."

Sammy dutifully removed his boots and poured out a stream of sand upon the ground. It was now plain to all that he had been gone most of the night, retracing the sandy stretch of trail which the wagons had traveled the day before, hoping to meet Jason. . . .

No one spoke. Finally Mark Morgan broke the silence. "I reckon Jason's traveling right along with us on the other side of the river," he commented casually. "And we'll be seeing him soon at Fort Boise. I'm certain now that Singing Frog missed him at the ford."

"No harm done," supplemented the old scout. "Kit can swim the Snake all right an' after a while, when he don't overtake us, Jason'll know we came the south shore. He'll be visitin' with Payette at the fort soon. Payette's a Frenchy, a nice, friendly feller. You'd best get yer sleep nights, Sammy. Thar ain't no use prowlin' roun'. Say, how 'bout a little music tonight? Jessica says you, her an' Anna know a lot o' tunes. . . . Yes, Cap'n, 'nother swaller o' coffee. Got a day of sand ahead but we oughter be campin' near grass tonight. The grass'll make Blossom pick up a heap. She's been lookin' peaked."

But Sammy was not listening. There were so many conflicting doubts and worries over Jason in his mind that nowadays he scarcely heard the conversation around him.

The bridle path . . . could Jason possibly find a small winding path in a wilderness of sagebrush, rocks and hills? And even though his brother found the path which led to the trappers' cemetery, was the gold to be found within the grave? And what of Bateese and his friend? Had the two trappers discovered Jason digging among their dead and exacted some terrible penalty? Where was Jason now? Jason, Jason, Jason . . . his mind was always on Jason. Without Jason, all days were alike and the road to Oregon endless.

It was dark and Aunt Liddy stumbled over something as she climbed the steps to Sammy's wagon that night. Muttering to herself, she entered, lighted a lantern and then stared down at the boy who lay in the middle of the feather bed, his eyes closed and his hat hung on a near-by nail. With the hat removed, he appeared small and very young, but this did not deter Aunt Liddy, and her voice was grim when she spoke.

"Ain't you 'shamed, Sammy!"

Sammy's eyes slowly opened but he made no answer.

"To think you'd leave them poor li'l girls all alone singin', pipin' like two tree toads, while you skun off with your jew's-harp! What's the matter with you, Sammy? Why ain't you perlite to folks? Why, all the people in the train come a-purpose to hear you an' you left 'em there, scratchin' an' battin' at the mosquitoes, waitin' for you to come back. An' you runnin' off like a skeered polecat . . ." Short of breath, Aunt Liddy was forced to stop.

There was no answer from the feather bed.

"Your ma's goin' to be scandalized when she hears how

you've been actin'. . . . A li'l music would ha' done us all a heap of good. We could have ended with a few rousin' hymns an' gone back to the wagons cheered an' comforted."

There was a stir now among the feathers. Sammy's head moved and his chin appeared over the top of the patchwork quilt. The gray-green eyes watching Aunt Liddy had an angry glint in them and when Sammy spoke his voice was unusually high-pitched.

"I wish you'd go home an' stop botherin' me. I ain't ever done anything to you! I'm sick of singin', I'm sick of music. I don't want to hear any more, ever! My mother . . ." The rest of the sentence was lost and Aunt Liddy wondered if she caught the faint sound of a sob.

"I reckon your ma's a mighty fine woman," she said, after a pause. "Mebbe if she'd given you more whalin's . . ."

"If you think I'm so awful, why do you come roun' botherin' me?"

Suddenly Aunt Liddy chuckled. "I come here often but you don't know it. I told Jason I'd keep an eye on you, though Jason said you promised not to leave the wagon an' your word was good enough for him. He said a Coit never broke a promise. But I ain't so sure. You've got a rovin' spirit an' you ain't much like the Coits I know."

"What makes you think I've got a rovin' spirit?" asked Sammy indignantly, lifting his head higher. "An' you don't know the Coits."

"I know Jason. He's enough Coit for me. An' as to your rovin', I can't help but notice you left Illinois an' your ma without much of a good-bye an' you're 'way out here 'bout fourteen hundred miles from home. If that ain't rovin', I don' know what you call it! An' now you're plannin' to rove some more!"

Aunt Liddy's final words had a dynamic effect. As though pulled up by an unseen hand, Sammy sat up straight, showing himself to be fully dressed.

"How did you know I was leavin'?" he asked, forgetting his anger in his surprise.

"I kinder guessed," replied Aunt Liddy calmly. "You had Whitey tied to a wagon wheel. An' I 'most fell over your bundle on the steps. You've still got your boots on. Most times you take 'em off."

"Well, I ain't goin'. I decided I wasn't goin' just before I fell asleep. So don't think you changed my plans. I *was* goin', an' then I remembered how I promised Jason. Now, will you go away? I wanter be alone."

" 'Course. I'm gettin' ready to leave right now. I think," and Aunt Liddy paused as though searching for words, ". . . I think I like you the least of any young'un I know." She waited for this announcement to sink in before she continued. "But if you'll come over to my wagon in the mornin' an' not come stragglin' in late, I might make you some cakes with a bit of 'lasses on 'em. It's the last of my 'lasses. You comin'?"

Sammy shifted his feet suddenly. There was a general movement and muffled squeal from beneath the patchwork quilt.

"I might," he answered finally, directing his attention to his feet, "if I ain't too busy wi' the stock an' things."

Aunt Liddy left abruptly, after blowing out the light and stepping adroitly over the bundle as she went down the steps. As she approached the Morgan wagon a few moments later, she gave a deep sigh.

"I guess I'm fallin' for that li'l green-eyed scamp. He don't look bigger'n a pint of cider, in among them feathers. . . . Been tusslin' with his conscience an' won out hisself, thank the Lord! I guess he's worryin' over Jason more'n we knew. An' he's sick of drivin' them oxen. Don't know's I blame 'im. But that pig now . . . just as if I didn't know a pig's squeal when I heered one! Long's I live, I'll never get used to folks sleepin' with pigs. In my day, pigs was kept in pens on the lee side of the barn, outer sight, smell an' hearin'!"

Fort Boise was stationed slightly below the smaller mouth of the Boise River and was controlled by the Hudson's Bay Company, with a Frenchman named Payette in charge. Wagons following the south bank of the Snake crossed at the mouth and then stopped at the fort for supplies as well as to exchange horses and cattle for fresh stock. The fort, a small squat affair, was built of adobe, and while it reeked with the odor of stale fish and reverberated with the yells of noisy Indians, it would be a welcome change for Captain Morgan's train. At Fort Boise there would be salmon to eat and berry cakes made by the Bannock Indians. Payette was said to be a jovial man, stout and cordial. Moreover, Jason might be found waiting. . . .

Water at the ford was not as high as usual and the wagons had no special difficulty in crossing. With his eyes riveted on the fort ahead, Sammy sat tensely upon the front seat of his wagon with Bill Brewster, who was driving. All was proceeding as usual when the old scout, in the midst of a blood-curdling tale of his own making, was startled by his small companion, who suddenly stood up and waved both arms.

"It's him! It's him. It's Jason!"

No one failed to hear that piercing cry. Every eye strained ahead across the sunlit water towards the fort. And then a moment later, an answering cry rose from the throats of men, women and children alike.

"It's Jason Coit! He's comin' on Kit! Jason! Jason!"

On came a large chestnut horse, head high, white forefeet prancing, urged by a brown homespun figure in the saddle. Jason! Jason was back!

Sammy choked, unable to yell any more, and stood listening as cries sounded down the river, cries so loud that people came running from the fort to stand by the water's edge and stare. Above the splash of wheels through water, the bellow of oxen and bray of mules could be heard the voices of the advance riders as they rode forward to meet the single horseman.

"Hello, Jason Coit! Where you been? Are you all right? We've been expectin' you before this. . . . Glad to see you, Jason!"

And then above the din Sammy heard Jason's voice, clear and happy.

"I'm fine. Bad rains held me back. I crossed the Snake at the lower ford, but it doesn't matter, now I've found you all. . . . Where's Sammy, my brother Sammy? Where's Cap'n Morgan? My! It's like comin' home! Steady, Kit, steady. Sammy! Hello, Sammy!"

24

THE HOME VALLEY

Jason's report to Captain Morgan, made in the presence of Sammy, Bill Brewster and bystanders, was brief but sufficient.

"The job's done, Cap'n Morgan."

Lean, tanned, his clothes faded and worn, Jason showed the effects of long hours in the saddle. However, his dark eyes spoke eloquently of the success of his journey.

"Good work, son! We're all glad to see you!" Mark Morgan's voice showed his great relief and satisfaction. "Come and see me this evening after we get ashore. You look played out now, so get into your wagon and sleep. Bill will see that someone takes care of your horse."

Camp was finally made near Fort Boise. All that afternoon, despite the howling of the Indians selling their fish and berry cakes, Jason slept within his wagon on the feather bed, fully dressed, with the saddlebags beneath his head. Curious visitors who stopped by to call were made even more curious at the sight of a small militant figure in a red shirt and large hat who guarded the steps of the wagon with a gun across his knees. No one, according to Samuel Coit, was allowed to see Jason; no one could enter.

Later in the evening, after supper, Jason and Sammy walked to the Morgans' wagon, carrying the saddlebags. With the Jeffersons' dog Trot left outside as guard, Jason then told of his experiences on the long journey east. Mark Morgan, Elisha Jefferson, Bill Brewster, Aunt Liddy, Aaron and Sammy listened with scarcely an interruption. At the end of the tale, Captain Morgan opened the roll of leather Jason had brought and laid the nugget of gold on the table. One by one, each person examined it.

"It's shaped like a bone which has been left out in the weather," observed Mark Morgan. "See all the little hollows, darker than the surface parts. Must measure about nine inches and weighs . . . well, my guess is twenty pounds. It's really beautiful! See how it shines under this light! The whole train will be proud of you, Jason, when it knows the story!"

"I just can't believe it," Aunt Liddy whispered excitedly. "Me, Liddy Morgan, lookin' at a real piece of gold! Lor', ain't it pretty? Ain't it heavy! Guess I'll have to get out my ol' blunderbuss to-night. I'll have no Injuns or trappers hangin' roun' *this* wagon."

"Boy," Elisha Jefferson's blue eyes smiled at Jason over the lantern as he balanced the gold in one hand, "now I'm glad I talked you into goin'. I've been powerful worried these past days, though, when you didn't ketch up with us. Just to see you come down the trail skin-whole, without hoss, saddle or gold, would 'a' been all right with me. An' to think a little bit of yellar rock like this could make so much fuss!"

"When will Jason and Sammy get the reward money, Pa?" asked Aaron eagerly, as both he and Sammy took their turns. Aaron's joy at Jason's return was unmistakable. The only son of Mark Morgan had come to look upon the Coit boys as his two brothers and his pride in their success was unbounded.

"It's hard to say," replied Captain Morgan thoughtfully. "We still have a job to do: get the gold safely to Governor Abernethy in Oregon City. Meanwhile I shall try to reach Joseph Meek. He's a close friend of the Governor's and will arrange an early meeting, I'm certain. Also I'll ask Payette to send a sealed letter to Captain Walker at Fort Hall, telling him the nugget has been found and to keep a tight hold on Henri Jules."

"Wait till all the folks hear the news!" exulted Aaron. "I'd like to tell 'em now, to-night! An' I'll say this for Sammy, Jason. While you were gone he never peeped, not a word!"

"I couldn't have found the gold at all without Sammy," answered Jason. "An' I never realized it more than when I first saw that headboard with his printing on it."

"By the way, Sammy," interrupted Mark Morgan, "what did you finally decide to do with your five hundred and nine dollars? You had quite a few plans, last I heard."

"I dunno," replied Sammy, after a little hesitation. "Guess I'll have to talk with Jason."

His brother's long absence had evidently brought about a change in Samuel Coit. Loneliness and distance, the uncertainty of ever seeing Jason again, and the adult responsibilities heaped upon his small shoulders, had fostered within him a new respect and affection for his older brother.

"Them trappers now," Bill Brewster was speaking, his mind far away and pondering over Jason's story, ". . . which one threw the knife?"

"Bateese, I think. Kit was wonderful; he seemed to know we were in danger. He fairly flew over the ground."

"Golly, I wish I'd been there," sighed Aaron. "Did your shoulder hurt much?"

"It was just a scratch and healed fast."

"Well," and Aunt Liddy looked directly at Elisha Jefferson, "I guess Jason can buy that hoss pretty soon now. You promised to sell 'im cheap, Mister Jefferson. Awful cheap, if I recollect."

"No two ways 'bout it, Miss Liddy," agreed Elisha. "The hoss is Jason's now, if he's got a dollar. Any day he can pass me a silver dollar, he can own Kit, head, tail an' hide. It's a bargain, but I've got a little string tied to it."

"A dollar!" Jason drew in his breath sharply. "You can't mean *a* dollar, Mister Jefferson! Why, I can pay you a dollar tonight . . ."

"It's what I said," repeated Elisha. "A dollar with a string hangin'."

"A string? What kind of a string?" Jason's dark eyes gazed wonderingly at the older man.

"Well, let's call it a gentleman's agreement, mebbe," and Elisha winked knowingly at Bill Brewster. "It's this way, Jason. We've got to be neighbors in Oregon, so I can see if you treat my hoss well."

"Of course. I see . . . that wouldn't be hard. Only Sammy an' I haven't any plans yet."

"Mebbe the way to do is to travel together till we see the right land. You're leavin' Mis' Strong's wagon an' oxen at The Dalles, ain't you?"

"Yes."

"From The Dalles on, you can travel with Mary an' me. You've got a tent to sleep in an' only a pig for stock. Since you left for the east, Jason, we've brewed quite a few plans. A man at Fort Hall told us of a new road runnin' from The Dalles to Oregon City. We've heard rumors before, but this man talked facts. The road's been opened up by a man named Barlow. This means your ma an' sister won't have to foller you to the Willamette by boat."

"My, that's fine! That's awfully good news!" In his excitement Jason rose to his feet. "You say the road runs clear through to Oregon City?"

"Clear through. Makes it easy for you to see the governor, too."

"Why, it's right on the way! Then I *can* be your neighbor, Mister Jefferson, an' I'd like it mighty well! An' you're sellin' Kit to me for a dollar. May I pay you now, Mister Jefferson?"

"Whenever you can spare it, son," and Elisha grinned broadly as Jason reached deep into a pocket and passed him a round silver dollar. "An' I call it a good trade."

"You're really givin' me the hoss, Mister Jefferson, an' I can't tell you how much obliged I am. It's . . . why, I can't believe that I really own Kit! I'll try an' make it up to you. . . . An' to think that Kit belongs to me now. . . ."

"All yours. Sit down, boy, an' let me finish my story. It seems that a lot of us have decided to hang together.

We're kinder one big family now. I don't see how we can let go one 'nother, after comin' all this way from the east. So if the Morgans, Fields, Adamses, Jeffersons, an' the Coits," Elisha counted them off on his fingers, "can find a valley along the Willamette, say in Polk County, what could be better? Each man could mark off his six hundred acres of prairie land an' forty acres of timber, put up some buildin' within six months, accordin' to the land law, an' we'd kinder own that valley. Seth needs water for his gristmill, I'm needin' good soil for fruit trees, an' all of us need the right land for wheat. I reckon we can get together on likin' the same spot. Later we'll have our own church an' schoolhouse, an' not have to travel to some other valley."

"I was kinder hopin' we wouldn't settle too near a school," broke in Sammy cautiously. "I'll be too busy for much schoolin' from now on. There'll be fencin' an' plowin' . . ."

"Why, you good-fer-nothin' little mess of freckles!" exclaimed Aunt Liddy, unable to keep silent. "If you hadn't known how to read or write, you couldn't have left your name on Independence Rock or painted that wicked sign for Henri Jules! Of course you're goin' to school!"

"Aunt Liddy's right, Sammy. If you hadn't known how to print that headboard, I couldn't have found the grave," added Jason.

"That was good printin', warn't it?" asked Sammy, straightening up a little. "Kinder fancy, too."

"It was clear even in the moonlight. It's awfully important to know how to read an' write, Sammy. . . . Do you think I can raise enough wheat to pay my taxes the first few years, Mister Jefferson? The governor might be slow payin' out that reward money."

"Folks say it's a great wheat country in Polk County. Not much snow. We figger on plowin' after the fall rains. But I don't think you'll have to wait long for that reward money."

"There'll be good huntin' an' fishin', Jason," enthused Aaron. "We'll have plenty to eat."

"Someday I'll tell Singin' Frog 'zactly what I think of 'im, the blasted weasel," and Bill Brewster, still busy with his own thoughts, suddenly pounded the table with his fists. "If the durn fool had stayed by the ford, like he promised, Jason would have been with us long ago."

"Mebbe his squaws made 'im move," piped up Sammy.

"Mebbe, mebbe," and Bill Brewster, now understanding Sammy's dislike of the opposite sex, gave a short guffaw. "Lor', Sammy, you'll be gettin' over it. Why, in a few years you'll be courtin' Jessica an' settlin' your own land."

"Well, he'll have to treat 'er better'n he does now," muttered Aunt Liddy. "Can't go skelpin' yer wife in the new country 'cause she's got red hair. Folks won't stand for it. An' Jason, while I think on't, you ask Mis' Strong's cousin to sell you the wagon cover. There ain't much cloth in the new country an' I could make both you an' Sammy some good warm coats outer that top. Put on fur collars an' line 'em with wool an' you'd be set for winter. Don't forget."

"I won't. It would help a lot. Cap'n Morgan," and Jason turned to the captain, who had been silent for some time, "I heard another rumor on the way back."

"Something about the treaty?" asked Captain Morgan quickly.

"Yes. I met some folks from the east along Bear River. They were fine people an' sold me some supplies. The cap'n's name was Taylor. He said there was a lot of talk about the States settlin' with England on the forty-ninth parallel an' givin' Vancouver to England."

"That wouldn't be bad," replied Mark Morgan slowly. "Both countries would have an outlet to the Pacific. I call it pretty fair, though lots of folks will be disgruntled. If it's a rumor, it's a good rumor."

"News travels powerful slow, 'specially government news," sighed Elisha.

"Speakin' of rumors, did yer frien' Taylor say anything 'bout Henri?" asked the old scout.

"Yes, the cap'n spoke of him. Said the men in his train were interested in the reward. I didn't say much . . . only that Henri was caught an' was now at Fort Hall."

"I guess folks all over the country'll know 'bout this train . . . Mark Morgan's train wi' the two boys named Coit who got the best of Henri Jules," chuckled the old scout. "Makes 'nother good story to tell roun' the campfires at night. An' you hang on to yer hat, Sammy. Someday it'll be a relic. That's the hat Henri give you, warn't it, bullet holes an' all? Take keer of it. We're makin' hist'ry these days. Wear it to the Willamette, like you planned."

"I'm wearin' it," and Sammy's grimy hand caressed the drooping brim.

With Bill Brewster's new slant on the value of the hat, all eyes stared at Sammy's headgear. Worn and shapeless, streaked with grease and dirt and ventilated with bullet holes, it had at last taken on new importance. Even Aunt Liddy refrained from scoffing.

But Jason's eyes were upon the boy beneath the hat. "Seems as though you've grown some, Sammy!" he exclaimed after careful scrutiny. "I meant to speak before . . ."

"I was waitin' to see if you'd noticed," replied Sammy, his face breaking into a pleased smile. "My sleeves are short an' I don't think they've shrunk, either. I guess I'm startin' up now, Jason. Ma'll be surprised."

"You boys better write your mother a letter from here," advised Captain Morgan. "Someone going east will take it. Your mother will be glad to hear that you're together. I think after another day we'll roll along. Payette says the mountains are clear of snow. The sooner we start, the better."

"Suits me," agreed Aunt Liddy quickly. "Them Injuns is awful noisy an' just watchin' them salmon hop aroun' in the water makes my back ache. Now Jason, you an' Sammy get to bed. It's twelve o'clock an' time for all decent folks to be asleep."

Despite Aunt Liddy's peremptory orders for Jason and Sammy to go to bed immediately, there was another hour of visiting before either one could quiet down to sleep.

"From now on Porky's got to walk more," announced Sammy, as he pushed the pig, who was sleeping soundly in the middle of the featherbed, closer to the wall. "All he does is eat, sleep, grunt an' sit on the front seat of the wagon. This bed's gettin' narrer for three of us. Get over, Porky. Haw!"

"Porky's fillin' out," commented Jason. "An' Blossom looks good, too. The oxen seem lots better'n most. You did

a good job, Sammy, gettin' here. An' to think I own Kit
for a dollar! I can't get over it! I keep harkin' back to it
in my mind. Mister Jefferson's a mighty fine man. . . ."

" 'Bout that reward money," offered Sammy shyly.
"Long's we're partners, mebbe we'd best spend it together.
We'll need a lot of things on the farm."

Jason, surprised and touched by Sammy's generosity,
turned and looked at him thoughtfully. Intent upon removing his boots, Sammy did not look up.

"That'll be fine," replied Jason, after a moment's pause,
"Seems to me you're not only gettin' taller, Sammy, but
that you're growin' in other ways as well."

Long after Sammy closed his eyes, Jason lay awake
planning. Somewhere in the Willamette Valley there was
land to be claimed for the Coit family. In a few short years
the land would yield ample wheat. The Coits would possess
the finest home they had ever owned and he would have his
younger brother to thank for half of it. Yes, Samuel Coit
was growing up. . . . With the care which a mother might
have shown, Jason tucked the quilt snugly about his small
brother's shoulders and then blew out the light. It was one
of the happiest days he had ever known.

On, past the hot springs of the Malheur to Farewell Bend
where the wagons left Snake River. Here Bill Brewster took
his leave of the train, heading east again to be hired as
a scout for other trains traveling west in the spring.

"I'll be watchin' out fer yer ma," he promised Jason and
Sammy as he said good-bye, "an' that Mis' Strong you talk
about. I'll take good keer of 'em. See you in your own
valley some day!" Kind old Bill Brewster! It was hard to

have him go, his straight wiry figure disappearing into the distance through clouds of dust the same color as his horse Mustard. And so the wheels rumbled on without him, across Powder River and down into the beautiful Grande Ronde Valley with its fields of red top, ever nearer the Blue Mountains, the one barrier which lay between the emigrants and their journey's end.

And when at last the Blue Mountains were sighted and the summit found to be free of snow, there were laughter, shouts, tears and thanksgiving. Old Oregon lay below. Like two sentinels in white, snow-crowned Mount Hood and Mount Adams, the highest of the Cascades, were beckoning, offering fruits of the land and quiet firesides.

Abner Strong, one of the first settlers at The Dalles, greeted Jason and Sammy cordially, keeping up a running fire of conversation as he examined the wagon and stock.

"So Elizabeth and Emmy will be here next year! And maybe your mother! Well, that's fine. Sorry to hear about Asa. . . . These oxen are better than most. You may be sure I'll take good care of them. Glad to see four wheels on the wagon. Most of the wagons coming through have been made over into pushcarts.

"So you're headed for the Willamette on the new road. Pretty valleys down Polk County way, they say. My, I'd like to be going with you. . . . You want to buy the old wagon cover? Well, I guess you can have it. I wouldn't take any money for it. You've done Elizabeth a good turn and I know she'd be glad to give it to you. Any two young men who could bring her stock here looking as well as these oxen and cow, have earned six wagon covers, to my way of thinking."

There were houses in Oregon City, two-story houses of clapboards; and there was a steepled church, the first Jason had seen since leaving home. An unexpected wave of homesickness swept over him as he and Sammy, accompanied by Mark Morgan, Elisha Jefferson and Aaron, climbed the steps of the governor's home. Terryville, Illinois was now over two thousand miles away!

"Captain Morgan, you are welcome!" Governor George Abernethy, a smooth-faced man in his early forties, came forward with hand extended. "It is good to see you. Mr. Meek notified me you were coming. Of course I know what you are here for," and the Governor's face broke into a broad smile. "Which lads are claiming the reward?"

"These two brothers, Governor. Jason and Sammy Coit from Illinois." Mark Morgan motioned Jason and Sammy to come forward. "We have the nugget in this saddlebag."

An elderly gentleman named Hancock wearing steel-rimmed spectacles took the nugget to a table upon which stood some scales. The little group silently watched as he proceeded to weigh and compare the measurements of the nugget with a diagram which had been sent to the governor from the San Roy mines in New Mexico.

"This is undoubtedly the stolen nugget," Mr. Hancock commented once, looking up over his spectacles. "It weighs almost to the grain. However, I wish to go over it again. We want no question to come up later."

The delay which followed was unbearable for Samuel Coit. He shuffled his feet, dropped his hat and finally asked in a whisper which cut the silence like a buzz saw, "We gonna get the money, Jason?"

The governor chuckled. "The laddie loves his siller, I see."

"Sammy always did have an eye to the main chance," explained Jason.

At length Mr. Hancock solemnly announced that he had completed the identification of the nugget. There was positively no doubt, he said, of its being the one stolen. A little cheer rose from the bystanders, Sammy's high-pitched voice sounding above the others.

"In regard to the reward money," the governor soberly told Jason and Sammy a little later, "I have a bit of advice. Both of you have already proved capable of taking care of yourselves, but in these new settlements, another kind of danger lies ahead. The country is full of strangers good and bad, the latter, I am sorry to say, not above stealing. You will have widespread notoriety. I recommend that you leave the greater portion of the money here in Oregon City. It can be left in my custody until such time as you have claimed and settled your land and have actual need of it."

"You have given these boys some excellent advice, Governor Abernethy," warmly approved Captain Morgan. "Jason, you would do well . . ."

"I'll be glad to leave the money in your care, Governor Abernethy," agreed Jason unhesitatingly. "Both Sammy an' I are much obliged."

"But Jason, ain't we even goin' to see all that money?" came a muffled wail from Sammy.

"Sammy, you little shoat, keep still! This is the best way, the safest way . . ."

"This is undoubtedly the stolen nugget," Mr. Hancock
commented

"The only way," finished Elisha Jefferson.

"Oregon welcomes you, my lads," and in parting Governor Abernethy shook hands warmly with Jason and Sammy. "We want young folks like you in this country. Let me hear from you often, and goodspeed and success to you both!"

Late one November afternoon, four battered wagons creaked to a halt on the ridge above a valley. It was a valley primeval, wide with meadows, edged with timber.

Mark Morgan walked to a high knoll, shaded his eyes and scanned the green spaciousness below.

"That's fine . . . that's *fine*," he repeated, turning to the little group of men beside him. "There's a good stream running through; looks to have fall enough for your gristmill, Seth."

"Seems so. An' just look at the growth in them meaders," Seth answered.

"Pa, it sure is the best valley yet!" Aaron shouted from his perch in a near-by tree. "An' there ought to be some mighty fine huntin' in those woods."

"Seems as if there's everything we'll need," drawled Elisha Jefferson. "Those long slopes look absolutely right for apples. How 'bout it, Ezra? Ain't that what you're plannin' to raise?"

"Plums an' apples," replied Ezra Fields. Still stooped, and as gaunt as ever, Ezra had a new look of strength and hope about him. "Somehow I've a feelin' that I've been here before. Dreamt it, mebbe," he said softly. "Anyhow, it's the most beautiful valley ever I see!"

"How do you Coit boys feel about it?" asked Captain

Morgan. "Would your mother be happy living down there?"

Jason, standing close by with a hand on Sammy's shoulder, turned quickly, his eyes bright with enthusiasm. "Ma would love it." He shook his small brother gently. "Wouldn't she, Sammy? Wouldn't she like these mountains, and the stream, an' everything?"

"Sure. An' look at that swimmin' hole down there." Sammy pushed his hat back to see better. " 'Pears like a good 'un, an' it's twice as big as the one at home."

Elisha gave one of his deep chuckles.

"That makes it unanimous," declared Mark Morgan. "The women back there in the wagons are all agreed, too. Even Liddy's nodding and smiling. . . . I guess this is our valley, men. Shall we go down now, or camp here until morning? There's no road."

"I say: Sleep in our valley to-night; go down now." Elisha took a step forward, as if to start that very moment.

"Kit an' I could go ahead," offered Jason eagerly. "We could mark the road."

Captain Morgan took a deep breath and squared his shoulders. "All right, then. It's settled. Jason, you scout ahead. Aaron, you come down out of that tree." And with a buoyant step the captain walked towards the wagons.

"We are going down now, folks." Mark Morgan's voice rang out clearly, and all could hear the joy in it. "Journey's over. This is our valley. We are home at last! Jason is going ahead, *on the first road in!* Folks, get ready. Chain the wheels for the hill; hold back on the ropes, and—KEEP THE WAGONS MOVING!"